D1505384

MARY & JOSEPH

MARY & JOSEPH

A Novel

ROBERT MARCUM

Covenant Communications, Inc.

Cover images: Front: *Journey to Bethlehem* © Joseph Brickey and *Jerusalem* © Linda Curley Christensen.
Back: *Jerusalem* © Linda Curley Christensen

Cover design copyrighted 2006 by Covenant Communications, Inc.

Published by Covenant Communications, Inc.
American Fork, Utah

Printed in Canada
First Printing: November 2006

11 10 09 08 07 06   10 9 8 7 6 5 4 3 2 1

ISBN 978-1-59811-182-8

PREFACE

This book is a fictional portrayal of the lives of two of the greatest people to ever come to earth. Like Adam and Eve, Joseph and Mary were "foreordained before the foundation of the world" to carry out one of the most important missions given to man—the raising of the very Son of God.

This is not an attempt at pure history. Other than what we have in the scriptures, there is little reliable historical information about Mary and Joseph. What I have tried to do is illustrate the nature and type of people who were the earthly parents of our Lord, while staying as faithful to the scriptural-historical account as possible.

The absence of facts leaves a good deal of room for us to ask ourselves what might have happened. For example, who were the wise men? Why was all Jerusalem "troubled" at their coming? Why did Herod take their visit so seriously? And why don't we have a historical account of the slaughter of the infants in Bethlehem? What were the lives of Joseph, Mary, and Jesus like during the time they spent in Bethlehem? Why did they flee to Egypt instead of going back to Nazareth where they could hide with the support of their families? How could the shepherds make "known abroad" that Jesus had been born without giving away his identity and making it unsafe for him?

The questions are endless. This is simply an interesting way of looking at them. I hope you enjoy the effort while realizing that I give you only intriguing possibilities, *not* definitive answers.

Nevertheless, this book is my witness about the lives of two wonderfully intelligent, wise, and dedicated people. They loved God with all their hearts, and when He spoke to them, there was no wavering, even though they experienced fear, pain, and heartache. I have come to love them more deeply than I imagined I would.

I believe they loved one another deeply, nearly as deeply as they loved God. It is this undying love for Him and for each other that made them strong and gave their lives purpose and meaning. We who belong to His Church and are part of His covenant could learn a lesson from them about what it takes to really make a marriage work.

If you carefully read the scriptural account as you read this book, it will mean much more to you. To answer possible questions about the history, the culture, and even the doctrine, I have given a list of sources you can turn to, many of which can be found through GospeLink or your local LDS bookstore. You may not agree with my position, but I hope you will study it thoroughly before judging too harshly.

May God bless you, and I hope you have fun seeing these important people through the eyes of one writer who loves them dearly, both for their examples and for their sacrifices. But remember, it is mostly fiction.

PROLOGUE

It was almost dawn. Though the high walls surrounding the temple kept the priests from seeing the hundreds of people already entering the Court of the Gentiles for the morning sacrifice, Zacharias's years of experience told him that they were there and would be anxious to get on with the business of it.

"We will now draw the third lot," the officiating priest said.

Zacharias stood. Finally, it was time. Several priests bumped past him, but Zacharias hardly noticed, his eyes settling on the facade of the temple. The gold-leafed marble walls danced in the reflection of the firelight, but he could not see the doors of the Holy Place. They stood in the deep shadows behind the great pillars. It had never been his privilege to officiate at the altar of incense, the one duty all priests coveted because it placed them closest to the Holy of Holies and the very presence of God while the congregation of worshippers and priests prayed for all Israel's salvation.

"Perhaps today, Zacharias."

Zacharias turned to see his dearest friend standing a few feet away with a tall, lanky young man at his side. "Yes, maybe today," Zacharias said, forcing a smile. "It is good to see you."

"And you, my dear friend." Jeremiah said it with genuine admiration. Zacharias was the most respected priest in their course, both because of his experience and because he was known to be of the direct lineage of Aaron, as was his wife. No small thing among priests. But Jeremiah loved Zacharias because he was a truly good man. In a day when self-importance and politics seemed to play an ever-increasing role in the lives of the priestly clans—and genealogies were unclear and often forged—Jeremiah knew men like Zacharias were growing scarce. He glanced at his son. "Zacharias, this is my son Ebenezer."

"Ah," Zacharias said with a forced but pleasant grin. "Ebenezer, welcome, welcome! I did not recognize you, it has been so long!" Zacharias felt the ache pinch his heart. Having no son of his own no longer pained him—until moments like these. Then it seemed to stop his heart. For generations, his family had been represented among the priests of the temple, but that was no longer to be. He and Elisabeth, try as they might, had been unsuccessful in having children, and his sweet wife had long ago passed the time when such things were possible. Though Zacharias had mourned their barren condition and had prayed and offered sacrifice that God would open her womb even as He had the womb of Abraham's wife, such a blessing had not been theirs. He was reconciled to God's apparent will and had stopped burdening the Lord with further prayers on the subject, but the pain still burst through on occasions when others gloried in their sons taking a place alongside them.

They stepped into the large circle of priests standing around the officiating priest for the casting of the third lot. "Our number will be eighty-three," the priest said.

He stepped forward and removed the head cover of one of the priests nearly opposite Zacharias. Automatically, the priest raised two fingers. The priest next to him raised four, the one next to him five. Zacharias watched as fingers were randomly raised and the number grew from twenty to forty and on to fifty before it had made a complete circuit and began a second round. He held his breath as each priest once more raised his fingers with a number and was a bit shocked when it was his blessing to raise a single finger to make the number eighty-three.

"Zacharias, the blessing is yours," the officiating priest said with pleasure. The rest of the priests whispered words of agreement, and several spoke openly of their joy.

"A blessing to all Israel," said one.

"A righteous man, a righteous duty. Surely a blessing will come to Israel today," said another.

There was muffled agreement before the officiating priest raised a hand for silence and told Zacharias to choose two to assist him.

Zacharias had to mentally pinch himself to respond, his disbelief at this great blessing nearly causing paralysis. "Jeremiah and his son Ebenezer," he said.

"Very good. Begin then," the officiating priest said.

Zacharias, nervous sweat already gathering on his brow, forced himself to think of what he was to do. *How odd,* he thought. *For years I have waited for this moment, prepared for it, thought about every detail of what must be done, and now that it is here, I can't think of a thing!*

He felt a steady grip on his arm, and he turned to look into the face of his dearest friend. "Come, we must wash," Jeremiah said with a genuine smile.

Zacharias nodded, and the three of them went to the laver. As they washed, Zacharias cleared his head, prayed to remember, took a deep breath, and then began giving the instructions. "Jeremiah, you will fill the golden censer with incense."

Jeremiah nodded as Zacharias opened a nearby cupboard and removed a golden bowl. "Ebenezer, go to the altar and fill this with hot coals, then meet us at the Magrephah." The boy seemed frightened, and Zacharias put a calming hand on his shoulder. "You have been trained?"

Ebenezer nodded.

"Then go—everything will be fine."

Ebenezer nodded and started for the ramp. Zacharias watched him retrieve the coals, then he went to the Magrephah and picked up the padded bat. When the three of them stood together, ready to enter, Zacharias said a silent prayer and struck the Magrephah, a signal that all priests were to hasten from all parts of the temple complex for worship and that the Levites were to go to the place of song and prepare. As Zacharias was about to enter the Holy Place, he turned back and looked directly through the Nicanor Gate to see hundreds of men gathering in the Court of the Women. They would prostrate themselves in prayer and wait for his return. He took a deep breath, his flesh tingling with fear and anticipation, then entered.

Though Zacharias had assisted others chosen to light the incense, just as Jeremiah and Ebenezer were assisting him, the sight of the veil hanging from ceiling to floor directly opposite them still overwhelmed him.

Ebenezer stopped in his tracks, then went to his knees, his shoulders shaking. Zacharias remembered the feelings, the fear of being so close to the Holy of Holies, the fear that God would find him unworthy and strike him dead on the spot. He reached down and took Ebenezer by the arm and lifted him. "Are you worthy?" he asked.

Ebenezer stared at the veil, fear in his eyes, but after a moment's soul searching, finally nodded. "Then you have nothing to fear. You are God's priest—He will not harm you."

The three priests stood still for a moment, the light from the lamp stand, lit by those chosen in the second lot, reflecting off the figures of cherubim sewn with gold thread into the veil's massive folds.

"It . . . it is magnificent," said Ebenezer.

The others only nodded, then stepped toward the incense table. When directly in front of it, Zacharias told Ebenezer to spread the coals across the top while Jeremiah placed the incense at the edges. When they were finished, Jeremiah took Ebenezer's arm and both backed toward the door in a bowed, reverent posture. Seconds later, Zacharias was left alone in the Holy Place to await the signal to burn the incense.

As he waited, Zacharias tried to remember the prayer he must say, but the words eluded him, and he nearly panicked. He took a deep breath and calmed himself, forcing his mind to think of what was happening outside, where all priests would remove themselves from the Court of the Priests and prostrate themselves with everyone else in the Court of the Women. He had never heard such quiet! It was as if he were in a different world and the very presence of God surrounded him. He felt weak and though he tried to prevent it, he fell to his knees, the fear of failing his God leaping into his heart. "Dear God, give me strength," he said.

He felt a sudden flood of peace, the prayer to be said leaping into his mind as the sound of the shofar signaled to begin. Knowing all men outside would speak with one voice to emulate what they could only trust was being said by him, he was able to get to his feet and begin sprinkling the incense on the coals, sending the smoke heavenward, the symbol of Israel's prayer, which erupted with all gratitude from his lips.

"True it is that thou art Jehovah and our God . . ."

The words flowed from his heart and reverberated in the room as he reached the second stanza. "Be graciously pleased, Jehovah our God, with Thy people Israel, and with their prayer for the coming of their Savior and King . . ."

His eyes flashed open as he realized he was not alone. He stumbled back, then fell once more to his knees, shielding his eyes against the brightness of a personage that stood on the right side of the altar. Fear pulsed through him as he tried to think what he had done that might cause the wrath of God to be sent to drive him from His house.

"Fear not, Zacharias, for thy prayer is heard."

Zacharias felt the fear swept away as if by an unseen hand and lowered his arm as the light seemed to grow gentler except directly around the heavenly personage. Could it be? Was he dreaming? What had he prayed? It was for all Israel, for the coming of the Messiah, for peace and acceptance by God in spite of their sins. What did the angel mean? How was it to be . . .

"And thy wife, Elisabeth, shall bear thee a son, and thou shalt call his name John. And thou shalt have joy and gladness; and many shall rejoice at his birth. For he shall be great in the sight of the Lord, and shall drink neither wine nor strong drink; and he shall be filled with the Holy Ghost, even from his mother's womb. And many of the children of Israel shall he turn to the Lord their God. And he shall go before him in the spirit and power of Elias, to turn the hearts of the fathers to the children, and the disobedient to the wisdom of the just; to make ready a people prepared for the Lord."

Zacharias's mouth went dry, his heart thumping against his ribs as if trying to burst from its moorings. At last, all that he had known, felt, and studied his entire life—it was true! God was sending the Messiah! He would come! Israel's prayers were to be answered! Tears sprang to his eyes as a mixture of emotions rushed through him like fire. Gratitude—deep, humble gratitude, coupled with a witness that the promises to his fathers would be fulfilled and aided by his family—pushed his chin against his chest in humility. Then, just as suddenly, there was doubt, confusion. How could this be? Surely he must be dreaming. Elisabeth could bare no sons!

He gulped, his eyes returning to the kindly face of his visitor, the words of doubt cascading from his lips before he could stop them. "Whereby shall I know this? For I am an old man, and my wife well stricken in years."

Zacharias wished the words back the moment they echoed off the walls of the Holy Place. He instantly felt ashamed for his doubt, then leaned back with fear as the angel stepped closer.

"I am Gabriel," he said softly, "that stands in the presence of God, and am sent to speak unto thee and to show these glad tidings."

Even as the angel spoke, Zacharias realized that this alone should have been proof enough of the message. How could he doubt such a thing? He put his forehead to the floor in abject humility as the angel spoke again.

"Behold," he said firmly, "thou shalt be dumb and not able to speak, until the day that these things shall be performed, because thou believest not my words, which shall be fulfilled in their season."

Zacharias closed his eyes tightly against the pain that struck at his heart. When he opened them again, the light was gone and Gabriel had vanished. Zacharias closed his mouth and bowed his head in humble acceptance. He had asked for a sign; it had been given.

Suddenly aware of where he was and his purpose for being there, Zacharias forced himself to his feet and toward the door. The angel's message had taken time. Surely the congregation was anxious at his delay! He must hurry.

Opening the door, he saw the people but could hear nothing. Dumb . . . and deaf as well. Surely God was displeased with him!

The priest who trimmed the lamp stood in front of him, his lips moving, his eyes filled with confusion and a tinge of anger. Further disgruntled by Zacharias's silence, he pushed past to once more enter the Holy Place that he might fulfill the last part of his duties by kindling the two lamps still unlit.

Zacharias blinked at the light of day, then at the crowd that stared so hard in his direction. He sensed their anxiety, and it quickly stoked his own to near panicky proportions. There was still more of the service to do, more to say, but how? How was he to speak the final benediction and blessing on the congregation? He could not! He must get away!

Stumbling through the door and onto the porch, Zacharias tripped. Only the strong hands of Ebenezer and Jeremiah kept him from a bad fall down the steps. Getting his balance, he prayed for the strength to control his fear, his panic. Jeremiah gently pulled him back to the top step where they and the other priests who had actually entered the Holy Place must stand until the first sacrifice of the morning was offered—where Zacharias must utter the benediction.

Taking a deep breath, he watched the rest of the priests gather at the foot of the steps, their eyes darting from him to the altar where the first sacrifice was about to be made. Like everyone else, they were curious about his delay, and yet the service must go on, the sacrifice made. Zacharias continued to pray for calmness as the priest ascended the altar and was handed the pieces of the lamb. He scattered them about the edge of the altar where no flame could reach them, then he arranged them in the similitude of the animal.

Zacharias heard the words of the angel again, "Thy prayer is heard." The Lamb would come, his blood would be shed, and Israel and the world would be saved from their sins! If Zacharias could but shout it to them, tell them what he had seen and heard!

The priests at the foot of the steps faced him and joined their hands in the familiar grasp, waiting his benediction. He looked across the expectant crowd. They would follow his blessing with a response, a prayer of their own: "Blessed be the Lord God, the God of Israel, from everlasting to everlasting."

Though he could not hear, he could see. The crowd was quiet, waiting. Sweat broke out on his face. What could he do? The sacrifice was not complete without the benediction.

Jeremiah squeezed his arm as if to nudge him to do his duty. Zacharias opened his mouth, tried to speak, but nothing crossed his lips. He tried again, but then only shook his head in frustration and acceptance.

He could feel the crowd stirring, saw the questions, the turning to one another, the pointing at him, then the shouting he could not hear. Jeremiah nudged him again, harder, and Zacharias knew he must do something. He lifted his hands for quiet, then, using his finger he pointed to his mouth and ears, shaking his head as a sign of his inability to hear or speak. Then he pointed to heaven, his eyes lifted to the skies.

The crowd grew quiet, confused, unsure of what he meant. He repeated his signs, then watched one of the priests mouth the words in amazed disbelief. "He is deaf and cannot speak."

Then another, "He points to the heavens. God has done this thing. He . . . he has seen a vision."

Zacharias saw the excitement spreading like fire through the congregation. Though he could not hear it, he could see that quiet was quickly turning to a loud cacophony of jubilation mingled with curiosity. Jeremiah, realizing what might happen next, pulled Zacharias down the steps and toward the door to the Hall of Hewn Stone.

Suddenly, the congregation broke through the barrier of Levites at the gate and rushed to the balustrade that separated them from the Court of the Priests. Zacharias could read the questions cascading from their lips. "What did God tell you?" one shouted.

"Tell us! Tell us what has happened! What was your vision?" cried others.

Ebenezer blocked the first of the worshippers who jumped the balustrade to touch Zacharias, crying for answers. Zacharias felt a firm grip on the sleeve of his robe. Another grabbed at his cap, and Zacharias ducked, then darted farther from the balustrade, down the last of the steps and through the heavy oak door of the hall. Jeremiah and Ebenezer quickly closed it behind them and dropped the deadbolt in place.

Exhausted, Zacharias sat down on a bench used by members of the Sanhedrin.

Jeremiah, pale and sweaty, sat down next to him, collecting himself. Other priests had received visions at the temple, but nothing in this generation. He saw a writing tablet on a nearby table and quickly grabbed it and used the top board to press the words from the wax, then wrote Zacharias a message.

What has happened? What did you see?

Zacharias read the words and wrote a response. *An angel.* He hesitated. What more should he say, even to Jeremiah? Israel's prayers had been answered. The Messiah would come, and Zacharias's family, his son, would play an important part. Should he say it? Should he have Jeremiah deliver his words to the congregation, to the priests? What would such an announcement mean?

A sudden sense of foreboding sent a chill down his spine. Such a son could be perceived as a threat to the High Priest, to the Herods, and to the Romans. His very birth would, at the very least, signal the coming of the Messiah and thus the overthrow of governments and kingdoms and the replacement of wicked high priests and their greedy families. Some might even claim Zacharias's son to be that Messiah. His life would be over before it had begun. Zacharias must protect his revelation; he must protect his son.

He wrote, *Tell them I am ill, that is all,* then stood and walked a few paces away, leaving Jeremiah to read the words.

* * *

Jeremiah read Zacharias's words, then looked at his old friend. It was not like Zacharias to tell a lie, but that was exactly what he was doing. He thought for a moment to challenge him, but found it impossible to utter the words. He loved no man more than he loved Zacharias, and there were no others who deserved the kind of respect that he did. Jeremiah would honor his decision. In time, Zacharias would tell him more.

There was a loud pounding at the door, and Ebenezer hurriedly opened it to find the officiating priest outside. He quickly came in and walked toward Zacharias, but Jeremiah stood and blocked his way, then handed him the writing tablet. The priest read it, then searched Jeremiah's face.

"Ill? That is all?" he said disbelievingly.

Jeremiah only nodded. "He has lost his voice and his hearing."

"A punishment from God is more likely," said the priest, handing back the writing tablet. "What sin has he committed?"

Jeremiah bit his tongue, and the priest turned on his heel and walked to the door before turning back.

"I will tell the congregation. Take him to his house in the Ophel. His presence here will only stir up trouble."

"He will want to return to the temple tomorrow."

The priest thought a moment. "He must purify himself seven times, then he can return, but he cannot stand in the circle for casting of lots. He is to do nothing to draw attention to himself, is that understood?"

Jeremiah nodded, and the priest left.

"It is more than illness, isn't it, Father?" Ebenezer asked.

Jeremiah nodded but said nothing. He was already writing instructions for Zacharias, who read them and nodded before clearing the tablet and writing another message.

I need to send a messenger to Elisabeth. Will you make the arrangements?

Jeremiah nodded. "Of course. But . . ."

Zacharias patted him on the arm, but gave no indication of telling him more. Jeremiah could only sigh, then stand and follow Zacharias from the Hall of Hewn Stone. Something important had happened to his friend. Answers would come. He must be patient.

It would not be easy.

CHAPTER NOTES

1. Regarding the casting of lots, some scholars believe it was done in the following manner. "The priests stood in a circle around the president, who for a moment removed the headgear of one of their number to show that he would begin counting at him. Then all held up one, two, or more fingers—since it was not lawful in Israel to count persons—when the president named some number, say seventy, and began counting the fingers till he reached the number named, which marked that the lot had fallen on that priest. The first lot was for cleansing the altar and preparing it. The second for those who were to offer the sacrifice and those who were to cleanse the candlestick and the altar of incense in the Holy Place. The third lot was the most important. It determined who was to offer incense." (Alred Edersheim, *The Temple,* 150).

2. Zacharias was chosen by lot to burn incense inside the Holy Place. As Israel's representative, he prayed "for redemption, for deliverance from the Gentile yoke, for the coming of their Messiah, for freedom from sin. The prayers of the one who burned the incense were the prelude to the sacrificial offering itself, which was made to bring people in tune with the infinite, through the forgiveness of sins and the cleansing of their lives. 'And the whole multitude of the people were praying without at the time of incense'—all praying with one heart and one mind, the same things that were being expressed formally, and officially, by the one whose lot was to sprinkle the incense in the Holy Place. The scene was thus set for the miraculous event that was to be." (McConkie, *The Promised Messiah,* Vol. 1, 308). Zacharias may have also wished for a son, but that would not be his focus during this important responsibility.

3. Though the angel said Zacharias would only be struck dumb, in Luke 1:62 we read that "they made signs to his father, how he would have him called." This indicates that the priest was also deaf. As S. Kent Brown says, "The angel had abruptly taken away his ability to speak and, as we learn from a later scene, his ability to hear because he was unable to hear the question about the name of his new son" (*The Life and Teachings of Jesus Christ,* 1:95).

PART ONE
THE ANNUNCIATION

CHAPTER 1

Six Months Later

The sweat dripped off the tip of Joseph's lightly bearded, square jaw as he forced his thin but muscled frame farther up the shaky scaffolding for a better angle. The gold leaf had to cover every inch of the carved cornice or the military governor would not be pleased.

Joseph felt the sway of the scaffolding as he reached the top and planted himself on the hurriedly-built platform. Letting it settle, he held his breath and moved to the edge, leaning outward to peer around the top of the pillar. One spot left. The scaffolding slipped again, and he grabbed for the edge of the outside board as if doing so would somehow steady things; he waited with his heart in his throat. They had carved and leafed the cornice work on six pillars in the time they usually took to do three, using this rickety contraption. Was their foolishness about to catch up with him? At more than thirteen cubits above the marble floor, it would not be pretty if it did. The scaffolding settled, and Joseph started breathing again.

Forcing himself to forget about a fall, he concentrated on carefully moving his body the last few inches to view the unfinished spot—half a span of wood glaring at him through the gold leafing. How had he missed something so large? *Never mind,* he told himself, *just get it done before you end up a grease spot on the palace floor.*

Joseph pulled a thin sheet of prepared gold leaf and a mallet from the small satchel belted across his chest. As he extended both arms to accomplish the delicate task of covering the wood, the thin, smooth handle of the mallet slipped from his sweating grip. He fumbled to get it back, then gritted his teeth as it eluded his fingertips and plummeted earthward to where his friend Matthias and others steadied the scaffold.

The expected curse was instantaneous and made Joseph cringe. His friend and partner for this job was never shy about language— even among the rabbis. Joseph looked down and muttered, "Sorry." Even as he said it, he knew it wouldn't be enough, and he gripped the sides of the scaffold against what was coming.

Matthias was a tall, strong man of twenty-six years. At a height of more than four and a quarter cubits, he towered over most men, and his arms were thick with muscle, giving him the ability to pick up and move stones most men could hardly budge. And if his size were not formidable enough, God had blessed him with deep-set, dark eyes and a heavy beard that fell nearly to his belt, making him look like Jeremiah or Elias, sent from God to bring down the very wrath of heaven.

Anyone who knew Matthias, however, knew the exterior did not show the man. Although when angered he could crush a man's head with his bare hands, it would take monumental stupidity or grievous injustice to bring on such a show of his Samson-like strength. What most people did not see was that Matthias had a heart made of pure gold, soft and malleable. The very presence of women in the same room made him stutter and fumble, while little children could wrap him around their small fingers quicker than wool thread. His brusque and direct manner hid this part of Matthias like the hard earth of the desert hid the cool pools of water beneath it. If one took the time to look past the surface, they invariably found themselves rewarded.

The rickety contraption immediately began to shake. "Forgive me, Joseph! Lost my grip. *Sorry*," Matthias jovially called back. Joseph hung on tighter, weathering the storm. Sometimes Matthias had a warped sense of humor.

"Matthias! Enough!" Joseph finally yelled.

"On with it then, before I leave these poor boys to hold it together all by themselves. Heaven only knows what will happen then."

The boys they had hired for this day were truly just boys—day workers willing to work, though their strength had proven a bit lacking. Only Matthias's size, hardened muscles, and knowledge of such things would hold the tower of ropes and boards together, and both of them knew it. "If you ever hope to see my children, Matthias, you had better stay where you are!" Joseph yelled. He retrieved a second mallet from his bag, hanging onto it more carefully.

"Hurry it up then, before that thief comes for his inspection!" Matthias's voice sounded like thunder as it echoed off the marble walls around them. Few men could make such a sound, even in the cavernous great room in which they worked. The loudness of it concerned Joseph only because he knew that the "thief" Matthias spoke of was the governor's steward.

"All right, all right, Matthias. Keep your voice down!" Joseph said it with an irritated edge. Though they had never seen the governor's steward personally, his reputation preceded him. He was an angry, cheap little man, a Jew who had changed his name to make himself more agreeable to the Herods and the Romans, a man known for cheating the laborer to ingratiate himself with the powerful, a man who had his sights set on greater heights and felt no compassion for those he might have to use to get there. The governor's lackey held enough power to have their heads if he liked, and Joseph felt to keep his, not lay it out for the axe man by thundering his dislike through the halls of the governor's remodeled palace!

The new governor had only been assigned a few months earlier, his steward coming with him. The old one had been beheaded, his goods and land confiscated, his family made destitute. No one knew why until it was rumored that he had been involved in a plot to overthrow Herod, a plot that involved Herod's son Antipater.

Most in Galilee did not miss the governor but relished the rumor. Herod was hated here. His heavy taxation and brutality among Galileans had begun when he was military governor in this same city years earlier and had continued once he was made king by the Romans. Though he was supported by the rich Jews of Israel and by the corrupt priesthood at Jerusalem, all of whom benefited from the king's corruption and power, the commoners despised his heavy hand and thievery and considered him nothing but a brigand under a king's crown. Taxes had never been higher, nor had the incidence of confiscation of lands and imprisonment of owners. Between Herod and the endless agents, kin, and elite who served him, a man lost nearly half his freedom working for little or nothing. The new governor had already proven that he was no better than the last—most men working on his new palace worked for nothing but food at the end of the day. Fortunately, Joseph and Matthias were not among them, but if Matthias did not keep quiet, that could very easily change.

Carpenters were artisans, and as such they were paid wages according to their talent. Joseph and Matthias were highly regarded, and their skills were in great-enough demand that they were not among the very poor. They were not wealthy, but they had homes and small bits of land on which they could raise food and graze a few sheep and goats. Few others in Nazareth could make such a claim, most of them working as tenant farmers for the bounteous estates of the Bet Netofa Valley. The rest were either priests at the temple or struggling farmers working small tracts of land and praying that the Herods or their prosperous friends would not set their sights on what little they had. For them it was only a matter of time. Most land was now in the hands of the rich, with former owners working as angry slaves or joining the bands of thieves that preyed on landowners and caravans in order to survive. It was a condition that had nearly over-whelmed Galilee, making it a hotbed of anger and unrest. Joseph was sure it would soon explode into outright rebellion if things did not change, but there seemed little hope of such change. The new governor continued the heavy taxation of labor and property, and had confiscated half a dozen small pieces of land near the city to make his already opulent lifestyle even more so.

A sudden surge of anger made Joseph press too hard, and the tool slipped off the column and dug into the finger of his left hand. "Ahh!" he said under his breath. He sucked on the wound, then removed a small rag from his bag and wrapped the finger to keep the blood from staining the gold leaf while he finished his work.

He did not like working for such men, but there was little choice these days. A carpenter could not make much of a living in a village the size of Nazareth, and with Sepphoris, Herod's seat of power in Galilee, only a few hours' journey, the request for artisans and carpenters could not go unheeded. It was a year of drought in Galilee, and even the smallest coin would be needed to survive a winter in which little grain would be left after the Herods and Romans took most of it.

Plus, there was the bride gift.

Mary, the daughter of Joachim and Anna, had been at the center of his heart since his childhood, but her father was one of the few landowners who had kept free of the debtor's scourge. Though not considered a rich man, he was at least among God's highly favored simply because he still had his land when so many others had lost theirs. For this alone, his daughters would fetch a high price, but Joachim was also a direct descendant of David, and his wife's kin included priests at the temple. This added even greater value to Joachim's daughters, and even the wealthy had been clamoring for Mary's hand, making it almost unimaginable that a carpenter, even a skilled one of the house of David, would have a prayer of ever earning enough to be considered. After all, a rich son-in-law could protect Joachim's home, land, and family. Why should he think of marrying his daughter to anyone else?

But Joseph had not given up hope, putting away every extra coin he could, planning and building a new home, and dreaming of the day he could actually present a worthy bride gift to Joachim. Nonetheless, all his efforts seemed pointless the day he heard Joachim had been visited by an especially well-to-do estate owner in the Bet Netofa Valley.

It had been a dark day for Joseph. For days after the rich man's visit, Joseph had anguished over what he thought surely was the end of all hope, but on the fifteenth day, and much to the surprise of everyone, Joachim had turned down the rich landowner. He had done it gently, but he had turned him down just the same, setting the entire region upside down with gossip that caused a good deal of embarrassment to the rich man's family and forced him to vow that he would have Joachim's land as his own before another year passed.

It was no small threat from such a person, and one that most men could not ignore. Joseph feared Joachim might change his mind just to protect himself, but he did not. In fact, it had seemed to be a rather shrewd move. Seeing the high price the rich man had placed on Mary, others took notice, and the next few months crawled by as other suitors were seen at Mary's home, making their appeals, offering a good deal more than Joseph could even dream of raising. His hopes seemed dashed upon the rocks of Joachim's apparent greed as the prices went higher and higher.

Finally, Joseph had decided he must act. Surely he would be turned away, his gift laughed at, but he felt a driving need to try. He loved Mary more than he loved life. He could not just let her be taken by someone who wanted a prize and bragging rights. He traveled to Jerusalem at

Passover, offered sacrifice and pleaded for acceptance, then returned to Nazareth to ask for Mary. He simply could not live without her.

It had been so easy. He had met Joachim at the synagogue and presented his request. It had been granted without a single argument! Joachim had actually been waiting for him! It had been the greatest moment of Joseph's life—a moment that he did not fully understand. Why him? Joachim had never said, but Joseph was sure God had intervened in his behalf. What other explanation could there be?

But there had been another reason. He did not find out until after the initial contract had been signed, but it had boggled his mind. Mary had asked for him! The revelation had been overwhelming, and he had fled into the hills to both weep and rejoice. He would never forget that day, and he would never stop loving her for how it had made him feel.

Now he worked for enough to finish their house, buy a few inexpensive carpets for the floors, and put even more money into Joachim's hands to show his gratitude. Though he hated the Herods and the governor and all the elite for what they were and what they did to others, in good conscience he could not curse them. Without this work, he would never have been able to approach Joachim, never have been able to provide even a small portion of all that Mary deserved in the way of a home.

He stretched, forcing his body to move forward until his upper torso hung over the ends of the boards and rested on thin air. Wiping his sweating hand on his sleeve, he gripped the mallet once more, reached over the distance to the pillar with his other hand, and carefully placed the gold leaf against the wood surface. Gripping the side of the scaffold platform with a single leg, he then stretched out his mallet-laden hand and began tapping the gold lightly, forcing the thin sheet of precious metal to stick to the imported Lebanese wood. Moments later the task was finished, and he used what strength remained to pull himself back to the safety of the platform, where he lay for a moment to catch his breath.

"Well done, Joseph!" Matthias's words rang through the great hall. "Well done! Now come down from this miserable pile of wood and rope before it dumps you on top of us." Matthias's laughter echoed around him even as Joseph began the precarious descent. When he reached the floor, his friend was already giving instructions about the dismantling of the shaking monstrosity. "If Mary were to see what I made you climb," he shook his head with a groan as he patted Joseph on the back of his broad shoulders, "she would never forgive me. Never."

Joseph smiled at the thought. Though they had not had the final ceremony, he and Mary were betrothed. She was his, and though seldom alone, they had begun to speak of their future together, to learn of one another and their hopes and dreams. He'd thought he had loved Mary before her father agreed to their marriage, had been sure he could not love someone more deeply when he found out she loved him, but that love had sunk deep roots into his heart, and he was sure they would never let go.

"The grand project is finished! The governor now has his silly pillars sheathed in gold," Matthias said, his smile disappearing. "It makes one wonder how many people will starve tonight because of his need for such monstrosities!" He said it loudly enough, and with enough dislike in his tone, that Joseph flinched.

"Matthias, one day your quick tongue will get you into trouble." Joseph forced a smile.

Matthias's face remained hardened. "The governor is like the rest of the Herods, Joseph—cunning and evil. He, like the king and his entire family, is also deaf and blind. If you do not believe it, just go into the streets of this town and see how many beg food while we hammer gold to the pillars to please this . . . this glorified tax collector." He yanked on a piece of rope, breaking it free from its hold on a board tied to the scaffolding. The plank hit the floor with a bang.

Joseph said nothing. He could not argue the point, but he would be glad to be done with this place before Matthias did get them in trouble. Matthias was a direct and vocal man. Keeping quiet, even on matters that could get him thrown into prison for the rest of his days, just wasn't Matthias's way.

They quickly pulled the boards from the scaffold, their young helpers carrying the boards out of the building. "What you need is a good woman," Joseph said.

Matthias chuckled. "Yes, you're probably right. It surely has mellowed your nasty spirit!" He grinned.

Joseph knew little of his friend's past. It was a subject never broached in their time together, but Joseph knew something difficult had happened both before and after Matthias moved to Nazareth with his mother plus an aged man and his wife. Gossips had conjured up enough stories to fill a scroll the size of Isaiah's writings, but all that was known for sure was that Matthias had left the village a young man and did not return for nearly four years. Had he joined the bandits as some said? Had he been part of the rebels' bands that swore to rid Palestine of both Rome and the Herods? Possibly; many had. Matthias seemed to disappear from time to time, and there was the wound on his shoulder. He had returned to Nazareth with it, said it was from a fall, though the scars looked a lot like those worn by Roman soldiers when cut by the sword. Joseph did not know, but Matthias had disappeared less and less lately, seeming content to work and rebuild the house left to him in Nazareth.

But Matthias was a free man, and Joseph was not one to pry into another's past. He supposed that there might come a time when his friend would tell him more, but it would be when he felt to do so, not because Joseph demanded an explanation.

When the scaffolding was down and the hired boys had hauled the last of the boards from the hall, Matthias and Joseph walked carefully around the remaining pillars looking for flaws in their workmanship. Though this was their third check of their work, both were perfection-ists, and shoddy work simply wasn't tolerated. Their trained eye saw the beauty of their labors, and they started picking up their tools.

"This should give you enough for the marriage celebration, shouldn't it?" Matthias asked.

Joseph couldn't help grinning but kept working, answering with only a quiet, "Yes," and a nod of the head. A marriage celebration went on for a week, and the entire village must be invited, along with prominent guests from other villages and families. Though much of the food would be donated by villagers, good fruit of the vine was hard to come by in the spring. He intended to have the best. "It will be a celebration not soon forgotten in Nazareth," he said.

He glanced at the door, then the windows high above the floor. The amount and direction of the shadows indicated it was getting late. If they left soon, they could get back to Nazareth before the sun set. He still had furniture and doors to build for their home before he could arrange a date for the celebration, and he did not want to lose a single moment of work time.

He had just finished gathering the rest of his tools when he saw two men enter the hall dressed in fine linen and silk. Joseph knew immedi-ately that this must be the Jewish steward of the governor—he had come to do his inspection. Joseph felt his mouth go dry. Though he knew such an inspection must take place before they received payment, he did not like it. The man had a reputation for making others grovel, and groveling was not in his character. Worse, Matthias would walk away before bending to such a man, and that might mean the loss of their earnings. Joseph needed this money. He needed it badly.

As Joseph watched the steward come down the great hall, he could see that his fears were well founded. Pompous and loud, the steward wore his authority for all to see, and Joseph knew there would be a confrontation.

The steward had a scribe with him, a man who did most of the work while the steward took most of the credit. He seemed to be dictating something as they walked, the scribe writing fervently while nodding his absolute agreement. Joseph couldn't help but smile. When the governor entered this hall, this steward in tow, it would be the steward doing the furious writing and nodding, the kowtowing and obeisance.

"Well, well," Matthias said with distaste. "If it isn't Crispus Gallus."

"You know this man?" Joseph asked.

"Yes, I know him. A Jew, raised in the same city as I. I heard he had found position, but I am surprised he has risen this high. The man is a weasel; a dishonest one. Let me handle him."

"Now, Matthias, watch your tongue. Please, I need—"

"You will have your money, Joseph," Matthias said. "Crispus and I are old friends." He said it with an edge of extreme dislike in his voice, and Joseph had visions of being dragged from the hall and thrown into chains.

"I see you are done," Crispus said coldly. "You have removed all of your materials?" He said it as if the timbers might leave some sort of plague behind.

Joseph watched his eyes. They were empty of emotion, cold, calloused. Surely he had recognized Matthias.

"Removed," Matthias responded with a chill of his own.

Crispus seemed to stiffen, then waved his fingers effeminately over the dust and small pieces of debris still remaining. "And this? What do you intend to do about this?"

"Nothing. We are artisans. The governor's servants can sweep and mop."

Crispus knew this. It had always been such, but he meant to assert himself. And it would not be he who would bend.

Afraid that the confrontation was already escalating out of control, Joseph spoke. "Matthias, our boys can—"

"Leave it be, Joseph," Matthias said coldly. He forced a smile. "We are artisans, and Crispus knows we do not do the work of slaves."

Crispus's face turned red and the muscles in his neck tightened. "You will do it, or there will be no pay!"

Matthias's chin hardened into granite. "You will pay, and you will do it now." He stretched forth a hand to receive the money.

Crispus smirked. "Either clean up this mess or forfeit your wages. The governor will not have shoddy work done in his palace." He turned to leave.

Matthias took one step, grabbed Crispus under the arm, flipped him around, and with a single, powerful hand grabbed the steward by the throat and lifted him from the floor.

Joseph drew in his breath as he watched the influential advisor turn white and gasp for breath. The scribe and the workers had wide eyes, their chins dropping nearly to the floor. One didn't do this to the governor's steward, not if one wanted to live very long.

"Matthias! Put him down." Joseph hissed his words through clenched teeth.

"I told you once, Joseph. Stay out of it," his friend said in a calm voice. "Now, *Crispus,* tell this frightened little man next to you to count out the price agreed on. You owe us fifteen sesterces, five of which will go to the tax collector and ten for us. Pay it now, or I will squeeze until your eyes pop from your head." He squeezed a little harder, and Crispus, his feet dangling inches off the floor, felt panic and gave a rapid signal for the scribe to give Matthias his payment.

The scribe, shocked, nervous, and fearful, tried to open the bag, fumbled, then dropped it entirely. The coins scattered across the floor, and the fearful little man scrambled to gather them, finally getting hold of the last one just as Crispus seemed about to expire from lack of air. He placed the lot in Matthias's free hand, and Crispus was placed back on the floor.

Joseph felt both relief and fear. Surely he would call for soldiers. Surely they were doomed to chains!

Crispus coughed and grabbed his throat while Matthias calmly counted the coins. "Aw, an extra sestertius. You recognized the quality of our work and wish to thank us!" He gripped a still-struggling Crispus by the shoulders and kissed him on both cheeks. "It is a wise man who pays for quality when he sees it. We shall be proud to work for you anytime." He slapped Crispus on the back in mock gratitude, nearly knocking him on his face, and turned toward the door, signaling to Joseph and the others that they should follow.

Crispus finally found his voice and croaked after them. "You will regret this, Matthias ben Hanni. I promise you."

Matthias turned, and with cold eyes stared at his foe. "How is your family, Crispus? Well, I hope."

Crispus swallowed hard, his eyes glaring red hot at Matthias. "Do not suppose you can—"

"Your brother and your father, have they found physicians?"

"Matthias, so help me—"

"My friend and I will want to work in Sepphoris again. Should our reputation be smeared by your quivering lips, I will see you ruined," Matthias said. He forced a smile. "Do we have an understanding, Crispus?"

Joseph couldn't breathe. He watched fearfully as the steward measured his words, hate flashing from his eyes like the rays of the ark that must have destroyed the enemies of Israel at the time of Moses. Surely they were dead men!

Crispus straightened, collecting himself. "The day will come when the past will not protect you, Matthias." He glared at Matthias. "When that day comes, I will see you in chains."

Matthias smiled. "We shall see, but for now I ask you again. Do we understand each other?"

Crispus glared a moment more, then turned on his heel and stomped back the way he had come. Matthias and Joseph watched until he disappeared, then Matthias turned and walked away. Joseph forced his legs to move, and they quickly walked into the warm sun of day.

"If looks were swords, one would be sticking through your heart, Matthias. What do you know about Crispus that makes you such a fool?"

Matthias laughed as they stopped long enough to pay the workers and send them on their way before walking through the maze of

ROBERT MARCUM

people to a nearby fountain, where they set their tools aside and began washing themselves.

Matthias finished first and loaded his tools on the sturdy but short donkey they had tethered to a holding post near the fountain.

"I know that Crispus was involved in a plot to kill Archelaus, the son of Herod and probably the next king of Israel."

Joseph stopped dead in his tracks. "What?"

Matthias laughed at the look on his friend's face. "The white pallor of your skin is not very becoming, Joseph."

"But how could you . . . surely . . ." He shook his head in disbelief. "He will have you killed to be rid of such knowledge. You could have him crucified!"

"I am not the only one who knows, and . . ." His face turned somber. "Crispus is a fool, but he is not stupid. I am not easily killed, and if he tried and failed, he knows what I would do."

Joseph felt his mouth go dry. "How . . . how could you have such knowledge, Matthias?"

"Because I was the one who was supposed to send Archelaus to the grave."

"But Archelaus still lives," Joseph said.

"Only because Crispus failed in his part of the plot. But enough. I can tell you no more, and you would not wish to know it if I could. Suffice it to say that my past is just that. Let it go, Joseph. I can tell you no more."

Joseph felt the words filter down his spine and chill his flesh but said nothing further. The conversation was ended. Joseph felt a new urgency to be rid of the city. Quickly loading his own tools, he led the donkey along the main street going toward the east gate, Matthias falling in behind him.

"There is no need to panic, Joseph," Matthias said. "Crispus will do nothing."

The words did not comfort Joseph, and he kept up his pace. If Matthias had a weakness, it was in underestimating what men would do to protect themselves.

Sepphoris was built as a fortress, and the outer walls were twenty feet thick at the base and thirty feet high at their lowest spot. There were several inns along the main street and a marketplace just outside the main gate where goods from the surrounding valley were bought, sold, or traded. In leaving the inner city, they passed a dozen camels belonging to caravans carrying goods from one place to another, along with several cattle-drawn carts hauling grain.

"Where do you go?" hollered Matthias to one of the drivers.

"Tyre. The grain goes to Rome," the man answered.

"More of our crops, our food, being shipped off to foreigners," Matthias mumbled.

Joseph only nodded. The tax on grain was one-third, while on fruits it went up to one-half. The Romans required a quarter of that portion, the Herods the rest. With drought haunting the land, there would be hunger in Galilee this year.

They arrived at the gate, tied the donkey, and hurried into the taxing office to pay the five sesterces and receive a payment form in return. As they stepped back into the street and approached the gate, they waited while another caravan of camels passed. A moment later, they were free of the city's smell, and Joseph breathed deeply of fresher air.

He was no fanatic, but Joseph was always glad to be out of the cities. "We must find water for purification before we return to Nazareth," he said to Matthias.

"We will go to the usual spring," Matthias answered with a sigh of resigned frustration. "Sometimes you amaze me, Joseph. You are not a scribe and not a Pharisee, and yet you follow many of their traditions."

"Some of what they teach is helpful, Matthias."

"It is a ridiculous belief that walking through a gentile city, or touching a Gentile, or touching something a Gentile touched, makes one unclean. Sin is not a disease that can be spread from one person to another, and anyone who thinks it does must be a fool."

Joseph was about to speak, but Matthias raised his hand to prevent it and went on. "I understand God's wish to have a clean people, pure of heart and mind. I know He has given us commandments concerning that which is clean and unclean, but these endless traditions of the scribes concerning Gentiles are not among them, and God does not hold us responsible for them. Nor is there some blessing attached because we do them. They have nothing to do with God, and you can wash as long as you like, but it will change nothing."

Joseph did not answer immediately. Matthias was a passionate man who spoke his mind, and when he did, he was often deaf to the words of others. A few minutes and Joseph would explain. They were nearing the stream fed by fresh spring water when he decided

Matthias might be ready. "I do not wash to be clean of gentile taint, nor for the scribes. Not even for a blessing. I wash to remember."

"Remember? Remember what? The number of times you might have touched a Gentile? How many steps you may have walked on stones touched by gentile feet? You flee Sepphoris like it were hell itself."

"I admit that I dislike being in Sepphoris and near its temples to false gods, and I certainly would feel unclean had I been to such places, but I have not, and I do not need to wash to be clean from their stain. No, Matthias, I wash to remember the lamb, the dove, the red heifer. I think of their sacrifice, the shedding of their blood and what it means for me—for all of us." He paused, leading the donkey into a stand of trees along the stream. They were lucky today. No one else was using the spring, and they would have privacy. He tied the donkey to a tree, and they both removed their clothes and entered the water, Matthias immediately swimming to the other side.

"You speak in riddles," Matthias said.

Joseph immersed himself, then returned to the surface and swept his hair from his face before dipping his palm under the surface and scooping up a handful of the clear liquid. "Water is a symbol, Matthias. So is blood. They both stand for something more important." He swam toward the shore, leaving Matthias to ponder the words before following. Joseph stood in water to his waist, his eyes closed, his lips moving in prayer. He then submerged himself again, resurfaced, and repeated the process a second time before starting for shore. He dried himself off with a large, clean rag from his clothing bag, then wrapped himself in a clean loincloth before he pulled on a fresh linen outer garment and wrapped it with his linen sash.

"Another riddle," Matthias said stiffly. "Speak plainly or leave me be."

Joseph sighed. "Water and blood do not clean us of themselves but are to remind us that the Messiah will come and free us from all that is unclean. It is him I think of, him I pray for, because until he comes, we will never be free of the unclean, never be clean enough to live with God again."

They finished dressing in silence.

"Come, we must go," Joseph said. He untied the donkey and walked back to the road.

"Joseph?"

"Yes, Matthias?"

"You say that the lamb, the dove, all of our animal sacrifices are symbols of the Messiah. I have heard you say it before and I still don't understand it. How can this be? The animals give their lives. Surely our Messiah comes to save our lives, not to give up his own." He shook his head adamantly. "This is not what the rabbis teach."

Joseph put a hand on his shoulder. "And not what you want to believe, right, Matthias?"

Matthias looked his friend directly in the eye. "It is not what any man who loves freedom wants to believe. The prophets say he will be our King and rule and reign over us. How can he do this if he dies trying to save us?"

"And doesn't Isaiah also say, 'Surely he hath borne our griefs, and carried our sorrows: yet we did esteem him stricken, smitten of God, and afflicted. But he was wounded for our transgressions, he was bruised for our iniquities: the chastisement of our peace was upon him; and with his stripes we are healed. All we like sheep have gone astray; we have turned every one to his own way; and the Lord hath laid on him the iniquity of us all. He was oppressed, and he was afflicted, yet he opened not his mouth: he is brought as a lamb to the slaughter, and as a sheep before her shearers is dumb, so he openeth not his mouth. He was taken from prison and from judgment: and who shall declare his generation? for he was cut off out of the land of the living: for the transgression of my people was he stricken. And he made his grave with the wicked, and with the rich in his death; because he had done no violence, neither was any deceit in his mouth. Yet it pleased the Lord to bruise him; he hath put him to grief: when thou shalt make his soul an offering for sin,' and so on. What of these words, Matthias? Are they not to be fulfilled as well?" Joseph breathed deeply. "I do not question the teachings of the rabbis. Our Messiah will come to rule and reign, but he will come to die for us as well. He must, because if he does not purify Israel with his blood, our momentary freedom from Herod will be buried with us in the grave."

"But how can he do both?" Matthias asked with some frustration.

"I don't know *how* he will do it, Matthias, I only know that he *will* do it. My fear is that when he does, we will not be ready for him. We will be the ones to afflict him, not the Romans or the Herods. We will refuse him because he does not do it as we suppose he should, and because we refuse, many of us will have to be purged from the earth as well."

"Turn away from the Messiah? No, Joseph, you are wrong! We will surely know him. We will never turn away from our King! Never!"

Joseph only sighed, wondering if his friend had really heard anything he had said. "Never mind. I am sure you are right. We must hurry if we are to be in Nazareth by sundown." They picked up the pace, talking of things more mundane—the work that might be available in Capernaum, where they were repairing the synagogue and building new ships, the feast of Passover at Jerusalem. Yes, they would go this year. Hopefully Joseph would have Mary in their new home by then. But mostly they walked in silence, each in his own thoughts. Joseph planned the design of the new door for the house he would share with his bride. When that was finished, he would start carving the dishes for eating. Then he must purchase rugs and cushions for sitting; for those he would have to go to Capernaum where the best he could afford were woven. Altogether this journey would take a month. Then he would visit Mary's father and arrange the wedding. In six weeks' time, they would have the celebration, and she would come to his house, be his wife.

Six weeks.

It seemed like an eternity.

CHAPTER NOTE

1. The reader will note that there are some Hebrew names and some English names (derived from the Greek) in this story. (In the Hebrew, Jesus would be Yeshua, Joseph would be Yosef, Mary would be Miriam, Anna would Hannah, and James would be Yacob, etc.) The inconsistency was allowed in order to preserve a Hebrew feel to the story, since at the time the Hebrew names would have been used, but also to avoid confusion regarding the most commonly known names as taken from the Bible or other established traditions—Mary and Joseph, Jesus, etc. Thus, regarding characters with no known names according to scripture, it was decided that we would use standard Hebrew names of the day or names taken from other long-held traditions regarding the holy family. For instance, because there are no known names in the scriptures for Mary's parents, I use the traditional names mentioned in the Protoevangelium of James, an Apocryphal book of much later date. The tradition is well enough known that to use other names here would only cause confusion.

CHAPTER 2

Nazareth sat in the hollow of a hill just above and east of the Jezreel Valley and southeast of Sepphoris. Few outsiders visited the small village, and most of its inhabitants were content to have it so. Violence and hatred had roiled across the country for generations, and the Nazarenes were grateful they did not see as much of it. Though several priestly families lived in the village, and priests of the Course of Jedaiah gathered here to journey to Jerusalem to fulfill their temple duties, Nazareth had little else to bring it to the world's attention. Most of the men of the Jezreel Valley worked on estates of the rich, but Nazareth was the exception. Here, most families still owned land and raised sheep, goats, wheat, and olives, along with several different kinds of fruit. Others were carpenters, potters, and weavers who not only provided services for the village but worked or sold their wares in Sepphoris, Capernaum, and even Jerusalem to the south and Damascus to the north.

Joseph and Matthias traveled the road from Sepphoris, stopping to rest on the rim of the hollow that held Nazareth just as the sun was about to drop into the western sea. The village was already in shadow, and smoke lifted from several dozen cooking fires as women prepared the evening meal. Joseph saw boys leading their sheep or driving their goats around and above the village or down to the well for water. From there, the animals would be taken to holding pens at houses around Nazareth. Joseph loved Nazareth, especially at this time of day when families came together, their work nearly done.

The synagogue sat on the western side of the central square and was the focus of most village activity. Even now, men stood around its entrance after the call to evening prayers. After completing the prayers, some men would remain, sitting on benches placed against the front wall facing the square and discussing matters of religion, politics, or economics before hurrying home for their evening meal. Later, they and others would return for instruction and prayer or further discussions of what had transpired that day at places as far away as Jerusalem.

Joseph's eyes settled on a house that sat on the southern perimeter of the village near the top—Mary's house. It was far enough away that he could not see it well in the growing shadows; he squinted as if doing so would somehow reveal his espoused to him.

"So this is what love does to a man." Matthias mocked Joseph by squinting ridiculously hard himself. "It blinds him." Matthias chuckled.

"Very funny," Joseph replied. He picked up the rope tied to the donkey's halter, and they began descending to the village. "You should be so blind."

"Marriage is not an institution I look forward to as you do, my friend," Matthias responded. "It ties one down too much, makes him old before his time. How can I see the world with home and family lashing me down?"

"You will find no place in the world as good as this, Matthias."

"And you are an expert? A lad in his nineteenth year who has never been farther away than . . . than Jerusalem? There is Rome and Alexandria, Damascus and Ephesus, Joseph! They say that Athens alone can make a man forget his sorrows!"

"Athens will only make you a fool, Matthias. It is a sinful place, as are all those cities you so zealously covet. They will turn your heart to stone."

"Then I will find a woman to make it flesh again. A woman with golden hair and skin as soft as the down of geese. I—"

"Enough!" Joseph said. "Why do you speak this way, Matthias? Do you do it to tempt me? If so, you serve the devil, and both of you will be sorely disappointed!"

Matthias laughed loudly, then slapped a hand onto Joseph's shoulder. "To goad you, my friend, to see if you are normal. Just once, I would like to see that you have entertained the same thoughts as other men. Just once!"

"Other men don't entertain these thoughts, Matthias. At least most don't."

Matthias squeezed Joseph's shoulder with affection. "I will see you at synagogue." Releasing his grip on his friend's shoulder, Matthias removed his tools from the donkey's back and turned into the gate of the second courtyard along the road. Inside the courtyard was a single house with a barn and workshop to its right and left.

"Do not be late, Matthias. Remember your promise. This night you are to read from the scrolls. Shalom," Joseph said.

"Joseph, I—"

"You promised," Joseph stated without looking back.

Matthias sighed, then closed the gate behind him.

CHAPTER NOTE

1. Joseph's age at the time of his marriage to Mary is debated. S. Kent Brown states, "Later Christian tradition portrays Joseph as an older man and the father of several children when he marries Mary. However, no early source, including the New Testament, presents this view. Customarily, the groom was a few years older than his bride, as we can observe in the Near East today. Because a young woman could become betrothed between twelve and twelve and one-half years of age, followed by marriage about a year later, [normally] the prospective groom was to be at least thirteen and no older than eighteen. Hence we can reasonably believe that Joseph was in his mid or late teens when Mary was betrothed to him." (*The Life and Teachings of Jesus Christ*, 102–3). I have taken the liberty to use the highest number because of the spiritual, emotional, and physical maturity Joseph needed to carry forward his responsibilities.

CHAPTER 3

From her roof, Mary watched the two men until they disappeared inside the walls and courtyards of their homes. She was relieved. She did not like Joseph being away so long, even though the wages were good and hastened the time when they would be together.

Excitement filled her dark brown eyes as she sat on the thin wool carpet and resumed grinding wheat with the use of her hand stone. Though a full year had not passed since their espousal, she hoped it would not be long before Joseph presented himself to her father to conclude their marriage. Though both excited and frightened by the responsibility of her own household, she longed to begin her life with Joseph.

From the time she was old enough for her mother to discuss marriage with her—and for her father to begin discussing it with everyone else—fathers had come to their house in pursuit of Mary as a wife for their sons. Her father listened and considered, but gently turned them away, frustrating Mary's mother to no end.

"If you keep turning them down," her mother said, "Mary will grow old unwed, then what? Then who will take care of her?"

"Mary will have a good husband," Joachim replied.

"A good husband? Would not Abel ben Zabanoth have been a good husband? His father is the richest man in the valley and he comes to you, a lowly farmer, to ask for your daughter! She could live in a mansion, have many children, be comfortable all her life, and we would always be safe from debt, and you say no! Sometimes I think I married a fool."

"She will have more than money," her father said softly.

With that, Anna had walked out of the house, mumbling something about someone being out of his mind, leaving Mary to ask her father the obvious question.

"Who is it you wait for, Father?"

He smiled, then sat down on a chair near the loom where she worked. "You are nearly thirteen, Mary, and beyond the age when many are betrothed, but as yet . . . well, God has not seen fit to show me the one you are to marry. Possibly you can help."

"Me? But Father, what do I know of such things? I—"

He touched her on the shoulder. "You know what you feel inside, Mary. Your heart will show us the way." He paused. "You know the young men in the village. You see them at work, at synagogue, around their families, with their herds. If you could pick one to marry, who would it be?" Soft dimples appeared in his cheeks just above his heavy beard.

She thought for a long time. There were at least a half dozen young men of marriageable age in Nazareth, and many more in the valley, some of whom she had thought about as possible husbands, especially those whose fathers had come to the house. She had never told him this—it was not her place—but some of those visits had given her sleepless nights. She had seen one of these suitors beat his goats unmercifully on Wednesday, verbally abuse and mock his sister on Friday, and attend synagogue with the apparent piety of an angel on Saturday. She could not abide such hypocrisy, nor could she think kindly of the rich man's son who had so much and gave so little. Abel ben Zabanoth went nowhere without his slaves to wait upon him and held his nose so far in the air that she was sure he would drown in the next rainstorm. She could not live with such a man; she was sure of it.

There was really only one man in the village who had impressed her—Joseph. He was not wealthy or particularly handsome, but there was a quiet majesty about him that had mothers *and* daughters secretly watching him when he walked past the well. Among the men, his knowledge of the Torah was well known, though he seldom spoke or gave commentary at synagogue. He was intelligent, his words well thought-out, his education beyond the norm because of his own personal dedication. Even her father had deep respect for Joseph's understanding of the law. Yes, it was Joseph whom she wanted to wed, and if her father were sincere in giving her a choice, she would pick no other.

She had answered her father's question, and he had nodded lightly, a smile on his face. "Ah, yes. I should have seen it. And I think he cares for you as well."

They had not spoken about Joseph again. Over the next two years, other suitors had come and been turned away. Then, on a fall evening just a week before the family would travel to Jerusalem for the Feast of Tabernacles, her father had come home and handed her a beautifully carved wooden box filled with a rolled-up document and two dozen silver coins.

She immediately feared it was a rich man's dowry, for no other could possibly raise a year's wages. The thought of Abel ben Zabanoth as her husband nearly stopped her heart from beating! The fear must have shown in her face, because her father immediately spoke gentle words.

"Look inside." He pointed at the box. "The marriage contract." His eyes smiled at her as with shaking hands she opened the contract to find Joseph's name. Tears of joy erupted from the corners of her eyes, and her father knelt beside her.

"This is Joseph's price for Mary?" Her mother had asked in disbelief while staring at the coins.

Her father nodded. "Yes, it is Joseph's. As you can see, it is much more than the value of what Mary could possibly take with her."

Anna sat down and took the box in her hands, staring at the contents. A man or his family gave a price for a bride. Part went directly to her and part to her family to replace what she would take from her father's household in the way of clothing and other goods. It was intended to replace that which was lost so that the bride's family would not suffer and so that funds would be available for the marriage of her brothers and sisters without taking on dangerous debt. Joseph had paid much more than was expected of a village carpenter, even a very talented one like him, thus giving Mary's family opportunity to make good marriages for the other children while still having enough for the taxes for several years.

"Well, it is not as much as Abel ben Zabanoth, but it is impressive." Her mother sighed. "Maybe you are right," she added softly. "If he cares for Mary enough to make such a sacrifice, to work so hard, he will be a good husband."

At that point, the whole village had shown up to celebrate Mary becoming Joseph's wife. It had been an unforgettable evening. But in Galilee, religious laws were very strict about any contact between the

new couple until the final marriage ceremony. Though Joseph came
to the house occasionally, it was with the entire family present for a
meal, light conversation, or discussion of the Torah with her father.
Though she and Joseph were together, they were never alone; when
they spoke, it was in generalities, never in intimate sentiments;
though Mary longed to hold Joseph, she could do no more than show
her love with a glance or by washing from his feet the dust of his long
walk from Sepphoris. She longed for the moment when they would
speak their final promises and begin their lives together in earnest,
when she could know his heart, feel his touch, and truly love him.

But there were advantages to the requirement that time must pass
before a final wedding. A new family required a new household,
much of which must be created after betrothal. Such things took
time, but everything was progressing nicely. She, her mother, and her
female kin had woven blankets, dyed linens, and sewn clothing for
them and a first child, whether boy or girl.

Joseph, a good, careful carpenter, had started on their house
months before the betrothal, but there had been much to do to finish
it. There was still the furniture. He had made an eating table, chairs,
and a loom, but there were still dishes, shutters for the windows, and
a real door to be finished. An intricately carved door! She sighed. It
was all very nice, but it was taking far too long for Mary. She wanted
to tell him that she would be willing to live in a hovel, with no rugs
and no furniture, and certainly no rich man's door, if he would just
initiate the final ceremonies of marriage!

But she could not. It was Joseph's nature to do his very best,
which strengthened her love for him even more. She did not want to
change his nature. She must have faith that it would not be much
longer, even if the feelings of her heart made it hard to hold her
tongue . . . very hard.

She brushed aside her dark hair. At fifteen, she was five years
younger than Joseph, but such age differences were common. Her
friend Rachel had been fourteen when she was betrothed and had
three children before she was twenty.

Children! Mary wanted so many! Even more than Rachel. As
Solomon the Wise said, "As arrows are in the hand of a mighty man; so
are the children of thy youth. Happy is the man that hath his quiver full
of them." She intended to give Joseph a dozen, if God so blessed her.

The shadows deepened, the sun well past the crest of the hollow in which Nazareth sat. It was less than an hour from disappearing altogether, and men were returning from the fields, their small children running up the road and into waiting arms. Laughter and greetings floated to Mary's ears like music. Such happiness would be hers soon.

"Back to work, Mary. The flour is needed for tonight's meal, and you still have not mixed it."

Mary turned to find her mother at the top of the steps that led from the main level of the house to the roof. Short and squat, but with the firmness of a woman who had worked hard all her life, Mary's mother was already rolling up the sleeves of her gown to mix the flour to make bread. Mary had never seen a woman with more energy. One grew weary just watching her work. Even her father rolled his eyes at his wife's constant movement.

"You daydream too much these days, daughter," she said. "Where is Dinah?"

Mary looked over the edge of the roof and down to the small shelter for animals at the back of the house. Her younger sister was still asleep on the hay. With a glance, Mary saw that her mother wasn't watching, and she pulled from her pocket a pebble used to scare birds away. She tossed it at her sister and saw the rock hit her on the leg. Dinah did not move. Mary tossed two more pebbles, the last hitting her sister in the chest and awaking her with a start. Mary signaled that she should get to work, and Dinah jumped from the hay, picked up the wooden bowl of grain, and disappeared inside the shelter. The excited cluck of chickens satisfied Mary that her sister was doing her duty.

"You cannot protect her forever. She is ten and should not have to be told so often," her mother said.

Mary sat down and quickly began turning the small grinder over the wheat but made no response. She had finished the task, sifted the grain, and was mixing the dough when her mother spoke again.

"Your father and brother will be coming soon. You should go after water. The cistern is nearly empty, and the water should be fresh. You will need to go to the well."

"But you need my help. The bread—"

Anna smiled at her daughter. "Joseph has returned, hasn't he? He will come for dinner, and you must have fresh water for him as well as your father and brother. Besides, with your daydreaming, you are useless here.

Now, away with you, and please do not dawdle. Tonight, there is a meeting at synagogue for the men, and they will want to leave early. Go!" She waved her hand in dismissal and settled back to mixing the flour.

Mary had been daydreaming! How could she forget Joseph would come? She leaped down the stairs two at a time, grabbed the large clay jar from near the front door, and hefted it to her shoulder. As she hurried through the door in the outer wall, she was careful to shut it behind her so that the animals could not wander out of the courtyard and into the fields.

Wrapping her headscarf across the lower portion of her face, Mary greeted several neighbors on her way to the central square. As she approached the well, a young girl looked her way and immediately grinned, jumped to her feet, and ran in Mary's direction. "Mary!"

Mary put the jar down and stooped to hug her youngest sister, Ruth, as several of her friends joined them, encircling Mary like leaves of a tree.

She gave hugs where appropriate, calling them by name and briefly talking with each. The last to reach her was Lebbaeus, a boy with a limp from a broken leg that hadn't healed properly.

"Hello, Lebbaeus," Mary said with a smile. He held a piece of wood that he was carving, and Mary extended her fingers to take it from him. "May I?"

Lebbaeus nodded and handed her the carving. The largest part of the piece of olivewood was untouched by Lebbaeus's knife, but a rough design of several Hebrew letters was beginning to blossom from a corner of its surface. He had wanted to carve a sheep, but God's law concerning graven images prevented it.

"Well done, Lebbaeus," she said. "You are a very quick student."

"Joseph is a good teacher," Lebbaeus said.

Mary nodded. When Lebbaeus's leg had healed poorly, the other boys had left him behind, then laughed at him for being around the girls all the time. Joseph had seen it and invited Lebbaeus to join him in his woodshop, where he taught him some of the skills of a carpenter. Lebbaeus was particularly fond of carving and now was seldom seen without a piece of work in his hands. Mary knew that Lebbaeus looked forward to Joseph's sparse presence in the village nearly as much as she did.

"Has Joseph made arrangements for the wedding yet?" Lebbaeus asked it as quietly as he could, but the other children heard and several of the girls giggled, making Lebbaeus's face turn red.

Mary gave them a hard look, and they quickly fell silent as she put an arm around Lebbaeus. "No, little one, he hasn't, but it will be soon. Then we will have all of you come to eat a meal and see our new house." She picked up her jar and started for the well, the children tagging along. Mary recognized several older boys watering their animals in a trough a few feet from the mouth of the well. "Hello, Nathaniel, Azariah, Benjamin. Your sheep are looking very fat."

They smiled at Mary, but she could see they were eyeing Lebbaeus and about to make some snide remark.

"How are your studies Nathaniel? Let's here you recite."

Nathaniel, the eldest and tallest of the boys, turned sheepish, his eyes dropping to the ground. A hardworking boy whose mother had died more than a year ago, Nathaniel had lost interest in his schooling until Mary had talked with him. He was ten, she told him, and it might only be another seven or eight years before he would choose a wife. If he wanted a woman's father to look at him as a serious candidate, his mind must be as strong as his back. Nathaniel had nodded agreement if only to make the subject disappear, but Mary kept after him, and this moment would be no exception.

"He doesn't know anything," said Azariah. "How can he recite when he hardly ever goes to my father's school?" Azariah was the son of the rabbi and would probably follow in his father's footsteps, but his pride brought a hard look from Mary.

"I *do* go, and I *have* learned," Nathaniel declared anxiously. He wiped his sweating hands on his robe, obviously thinking hard about what he could quote.

"But, behold, . . . Zion . . . Zion hath said . . . the Lord hath forsaken me, and . . . and my Lord hath forgotten me . . . but . . . but he will show that he hath not—"

"That is Isaiah, not the law," said Azariah. "You must learn the law first, then—"

Mary sensed that Nathaniel was about to smack the younger boy and quickly spoke. "Isaiah is Israel's greatest prophet, Azariah. His words give us hope. It is a good choice. Go on, Nathaniel."

At the correction, Azariah's face blushed red.

Nathaniel's look softened as he struggled and finally gave up. "I . . . I can't remember."

Mary put a hand on his shoulder. "Let me help you. 'For can a woman forget her sucking child, that she should not have compassion on the son of her womb? yea . . .'" she waited for Nathaniel to continue.

"Yea, they may forget, yet will I . . . not forget thee. Behold, I have graven thee upon the palms of my hands; thy walls are continually before me."

"That was very good," said Mary. "You *are* doing very well."

Lebbaeus tugged on Mary's sleeve. "If Joseph doesn't hurry and marry you, I will repay the bride gift and marry you myself." He looked at the ground as the other children giggled at him.

She shushed them with a wave of her hand as Lebbaeus broke free and ran up a street, quickly disappearing through the door of his father's house, the other children giggling again.

"He is a fool," muttered Azariah.

"Then you do not think I am worthy of such a compliment?" Mary asked.

The boy turned red, his head going down. "No, no, I mean . . ."

"Do not make fun of him, Azariah. It is always nice to know others care for you. There is too little kindness today, don't you think?"

Azariah nodded reluctantly as Mary stood and picked up her jar, then ruffled his hair. "You are a good boy, but children like Lebbaeus need you to be even better. You are God's voice to him," Mary said. "Be kind to him, all right?"

Azariah, the other boys, and even Ruth and her friends nodded compliance.

"Good, now I must go. Father will be home soon, and Joseph is coming to dinner. There is much to do." She turned to her sister. "Ruth, Mother needs your help. Time to run home."

Ruth said good-bye and dashed up the street while the others returned to their play or remembered their own chores and started for home. Benjamin and Azariah had finished watering their sheep and started to lead them home. Only Nathaniel remained. He picked up one of the two leather buckets he had filled from the well and poured it into the trough.

"Mary . . ." he started hesitantly.

The mouth of the well was wide to allow for spring runoff, but the well was now less than half full. The path spiraled down the outside of the hole until it reached the water's level. Mary had already begun walking down it when Nathaniel spoke. She turned to face him. "Yes, what is it, Nathaniel?"

"The scripture. The one I recited," he said, blushing. "Do . . . do you think God really does remember us?"

Her headscarf dropped slightly and revealed a pleasant smile. "Yes, Nathaniel, I am sure of it." She wanted to reassure him further, but several women were crossing the courtyard toward the well and Nathaniel turned away, concentrating on his sheep. Mary could see that any more attention on her part would only make him more uncomfortable.

She was about to turn and go deeper into the well when she saw the women speaking in whispers, their eyes darting between themselves and Nathaniel, their gossip obvious. Realizing that they were talking about him, the boy picked up his staff and called his sheep from the well, hurrying them off toward his home.

Disgusted at the conduct of the women, Mary turned down the path to retrieve her water. She had never liked gossip. It was a waste of time and energy, usually at the expense of another's reputation. Though Nathaniel was shy and his family the poorest in the village, they did not deserve to have their names pummeled about by prattling women trying their best to outgossip one another.

The cool air in the bottom of the well relieved Mary's anger a bit as she stooped to fill her jar with fresh spring water. When it was full, she set it aside and scooped up a handful to sip, then splash on the warm flesh of her face. Drying off with her headscarf then wrapping it around her neck, she hefted the jar onto her shoulder to return to the warmer air of the village square, humming as she climbed.

It wasn't that she did not enjoy hearing the news of the village— who was traveling where, what son was thinking of marriage, or what family had been blessed with the news of a child to be born—but too often news was set aside for rumor. Even now, she could hear the three young women talking nonsense about Nathaniel's family. She tried to ignore it, but this time it was difficult.

"But if the rabbi has put them out of the synagogue, what *are* we to think?" asked one. "There must be good reason or—"

"The eldest son is to be married," interrupted another. "What kind of bride can he get now? I certainly wouldn't want to marry him."

"The boy's father questioned the words of Rabbi Yacov. It is blasphemy. He got what he deserved."

Mary felt her mouth go dry. Nathaniel's father had been put out of the synagogue? It could not be! He was a fine man, one of sound knowledge and dedication to God, a dear friend of her father! It was only gossip. As usual, the women did not know what they were talking about, spreading rumors, droning on to hear the sound of their voices. It angered Mary, and she pushed herself up the path to confront them, arriving at the level of the square at the same moment a half dozen horsemen entered it. Soldiers!

Realizing her face and head were still uncovered, she frantically put aside her pot and hurried to put the scarf in place. When she looked up, she found herself alone with six Roman soldiers. Mary bowed slightly, keeping her face down, her eyes averted, then as calmly but as quickly as she could, she turned away and hurried for the street that led to her home.

"You!" yelled one of the soldiers.

Mary's legs weakened. She could not move, could not speak. The Romans frightened her, had always frightened her. Stories of their cruelty, their punishment of those who even remotely challenged them, and their treatment of women made her blood run cold. It was one reason she loved Nazareth—soldiers seldom came here. She prayed for strength, prayed that her legs would move.

"Our horses need water. Bring it now." They were already dismounted, and Mary felt footsteps close behind her.

"I am talking to you!" shouted a gruff voice so close behind her that she felt faint. Knowing he was about to grab her, she quickly turned to face him, backing away as she did.

He was a foot taller than she was, wide as a donkey clear to the ground, and the hand that reached for her was as thick as her father's upper arm. His helmet and breastplate made him look fierce as death. Her eyes widened as the man groped for her, forcing her to dart backward to prevent it.

The dark eyes showed evil intent mingled with humor at her discomfort. "Come here, you little wench . . . I'll—"

"Leave her be," commanded another voice. "Draw your own water." The soldier stiffened at the reprimand, obviously struggling with whether to obey and be humiliated in front of his friends or disobey and answer to the man who had moved his horse to within a few feet of them. He finally grinned, laughed lightly, and turned back to the watering trough to do as he was told.

With her face tightly covered, Mary bowed a thank you in the direction of the still-mounted soldier before turning and hurrying away. When she was out of sight, she leaned against a building, her entire body shaking with fear and relief. Thanking God for deliverance, she took several deep breaths before remembering that she had left her water jar behind. The thought of returning for it appalled her, and yet she needed the water, and the pot would take time to replace. Surely she must return and retrieve it, and yet if they used it, it would be declared unclean by the village elders, unfit for use anyway, and then there was the danger . . .

She heard footsteps behind and quickly turned to see the soldier who had helped her. He was standing only a few feet away, a curious tilt to his head as she backed away again.

He had removed his helmet and carried her filled jar effortlessly in one hand. He lifted it as he spoke. "You left this behind."

She stared at her feet as she nodded gratitude again even while fear grasped her stomach. What was this Gentile doing? Did he not understand their people? For a woman to speak to a man, any man old enough to marry, tainted her as a woman of loose morals.

"Alexander has no manners," the soldier said. He hesitated as if waiting for a response. She gave none. She should run, leave the water jar and him behind, but her feet seemed to be nailed to the ground.

* * *

"Thank you."

Relief filled Mary as she quickly turned around to see Joseph standing a few feet behind her, one hand on the knife at his waist. "My wife and I are grateful." He gave Mary a glance of comfort as he walked past her, placing himself between her and the soldier. "My name is Joseph, son of Jacob. My wife is Mary." Joseph could see that this one wore the uniform of a Roman soldier.

"I am Marcus Vitellius. We are on our way to Jerusalem from Damascus to serve Herod but needed water, food, and a place to stay the night. We came upon your village and—"

"Roman soldiers do not come here often," Joseph replied with a forced smile.

"I alone am Roman. The others are Gauls. I have been hired to train some of Herod's soldiers, and they will serve in his army. Thus my authority over them. Possibly you know of where we might make a camp for the night."

"There is a small hollow just over the hill there." Joseph pointed south. "It sits in a stand of ancient cypress trees and is well protected."

The Roman nodded his thanks. "We have little food. We will pay."

"That won't be necessary. I will bring you something as soon as I can," Joseph indicated.

"Thank you." The Roman bowed and extended the jar to Joseph. To Mary's surprise Joseph accepted it.

The soldier walked back the way he had come. Joseph joined Mary. "Are you all right?" he asked.

"How did you know to come?" she asked softly.

"Nathaniel saw them and hurried to the house. Did they harm you?" He stepped toward her, taking her arm and gently turning her toward home. When he let go, separating from Mary a respectable distance, she reacted.

"Do not leave me," she begged.

He only nodded. He did not want to leave any more than she wanted him to. She was his wife, and regardless of what others might think, what their rabbi might say, he would see her home safely.

"The jar is defiled," Mary pointed out.

"No, it is not. The touch of a Gentile, even one who worships idols, does not defile. Only when we worship with them or honor their false gods are we unclean."

"But my father . . . the elders of the synagogue . . ."

"Take a different view, I know, but it is not the view of Torah, or of God. His law separates us to protect us from becoming idolaters, not because we can catch impurity from them like we catch a cold."

They continued on in silence a few paces. "I . . . I hope you won't think me too bold, but I have missed you these last few days," he said quietly.

Mary turned a bit red. "If I am missed so much, why is that you do not come for me? Is the house not finished? Do you prefer to admire me from a distance? Are you afraid I will not be suitable? Have you changed your mind?"

Joseph was caught off guard and stammered. "No . . . I mean, yes, it is finished, and no, I do not wish to admire you from a distance. I mean . . . I am not afraid you will not . . . I do not wish to change . . ." He took a deep breath. "I . . . I am just beginning the furniture, and I must still go to Capernaum and purchase the carpets. Only another few weeks—"

"Joseph," Mary said firmly, cutting him off in frustration. "It is too long, and if you do not come for me soon, I . . . I will make you wish you had by . . . by burning your food, refusing to mend your clothes, and never giving birth to a single child, do you understand?"

He stopped in his tracks, a shocked look on his face. She turned to him, frustration in the rise of her brow. "I will live in a stable and sit on a . . . a bare floor rather than wait! It is time, Joseph. You must talk to my father about the ceremony, and very soon." With that, she turned away and walked adamantly toward her father's house.

Joseph was stunned and hesitated before coming to his senses and quickly catching up. "You are right. I must talk to him soon, but not tonight. I must purchase carpets, and the shutters, and dishes—"

Mary turned to face him, her hands on her hips. "When, Joseph? Just tell me when." She took the jug from him.

"Next . . . next week. Ten days, no more. I will go to Capernaum tonight and—"

"Ten days, then. If you take one hour longer . . ."

"No, no, ten days. I promise."

She turned and walked away. Joseph hurried to catch up. "You are right. It is past time. I will go to Capernaum and purchase the carpets after supper. The dishes, the shutters, even the new door can wait."

She gave him a rewarding smile. "Why wait until after supper, then?" She started walking again. "I will see you in ten days, Joseph."

He watched her for a moment, a slight smile turning up the corners of his mouth. *Yes, why wait?* He turned and started for his home at a fast walk. He must get the food for the Romans and take it to their camp on his way. Excitement welled inside as his thoughts turned to what must be done in so short a time, and before he realized it, he was at home, packed, and leading his donkey from its small stable, a bag of food for the Romans in his hand.

The sun had disappeared, but there was still light enough that he could see the road. When he reached the top of the hill, he caught his breath while looking down at the village. Cooking fires lit up the courtyards of most homes, and he could see families eating their evening meals together. The occasional sound of laughter reached his ears and mingled with the bleating of sheep settling down for the night. It was a simple village with a simple life. He could only hope that it would always remain so.

When he approached the Roman camp, the soldier he had met earlier stepped away from the fire to greet him. Joseph handed him the food.

"May your one God bless you," Marcus said with a pleasant smile.

Joseph only nodded before turning to leave.

"May I ask you a question?" Marcus asked.

Joseph wished to be away, not for fear of this man, but because of his new excitement and purpose. "I cannot stay. I must be in Capernaum by morning. My final marriage ceremony is to take place soon, and I must buy rugs."

The soldier nodded and gave a knowing smile. "I have had some instruction concerning your customs and know how important this time is for both of you. It is the same in our religion. Thank you again for the food." He lifted the bag slightly. "I will be stationed in Jerusalem and will take charge of the training of the garrison at the Antonia. Perhaps we will meet again."

Joseph gave a wan smile and a nod, then quickly walked out of the trees, donkey in tow. He hoped the soldier's statement would never come to pass. Soldiers of Herod seldom came into contact with common Jews such as Joseph unless it was to beat or arrest them for some infraction or disturbance. The thought was unsettling, and he hurried away, firm in the knowledge that he had fulfilled his duty to help even those who might be enemies.

Darkness came quickly, but Joseph had no problem finding the road to Capernaum. He had walked it many times and could do it on the darkest night. By walking most of the night he could be in Capernaum by morning, purchase the rugs that day, get a good night's sleep, and be back the next. The thought excited him. Possibly, he could approach Joachim even sooner than in ten days. Why had he waited, putting it off for doors, shutters, and dishes? He would make Mary his within the week.

CHAPTER 4

As Joachim opened the high gate in the wall of his courtyard, he found his son, Josiah, waiting for him near the door with a torch in his hand. He had never seen such a look of dismay on the boy's face and immediately felt his stomach tighten with dread.

"Josiah, what is it? What is wrong?" he asked with some trepidation.

"I . . . I don't know . . ." his son's voice trailed off, and he looked away from his father, then back again. "Mary is . . . is ill, Father. Very ill."

"What do you mean? How can this be? I saw her only a few hours ago before I went to the synagogue, and she was fine!" He stepped past Josiah and was quickly through the door of the house and into the room where the girls slept. Mary lay on the large bed that the three girls shared, her mother kneeling by her side, pressing a cloth against Mary's forehead. With looks of concern and even tears, the other children watched Mary. Ruth immediately ran to her father and grabbed hold of his leg.

"Father, Father, what is wrong with Mary? Is she ill? Is she?"

Joachim picked up Ruth, hugged her, and calmed her before setting her down on a chair. He then went to Mary's side and got to his knees. Fully expecting her to look sickly and pale, her actual appearance shocked him. Her color was normal, her touch warm but not feverish, but the real difference was in the almost angelic light of contentment and peace that lay across her features.

"This is not the look of a sick girl," he stated.

"She is not sick," Anna replied. "Just tired."

"Tired? But why? And what is this look . . . this difference in her face? Possibly I should call for the rabbi," he suggested with concern. "Prayers should be said for her. We should—"

"There is no need for a rabbi," her mother answered. She softly stroked the forehead of her child. "She has had a vision. This has taken her strength."

"A vision? Mary? But how could this be? Why would God speak with her?" asked her father.

"I don't know, husband," Anna answered. "She will tell us when she can. For now, she will rest."

Joachim felt empty, a stupor clouding his mind. Nothing made sense. He had seen Mary only hours earlier. She seemed fine, excited that Joseph would finally finish making their marriage ceremony. He looked more carefully at his eldest daughter's face. What was this look? Had there been a vision? If so, why? What did it mean? No, no, she was just ill. Anna was wrong. There was nothing miraculous in this, only illness. They must pray for her, that was all. God would intervene and make her well. He gently pulled his hand from Mary's. "I will go and pray."

Anna only shrugged. "Do as you wish, but do not go far. I think she will want to talk to you when she is strong enough. And to Joseph."

Joachim nodded without comprehending, retrieved his prayer shawl, and then looked at Mary once more. He had seen this look, or something akin to it, when his mother and father were near death's door. Peaceful, that's what it was. Ready to die. There was no vision in this, only death. His stomach tied into a tight knot.

* * *

Mary opened her eyes but saw only shadows of light and dark. She blinked several times until her eyes focused on the rough logs holding up the roof. Turning slightly left, she found the face of her mother. Her eyes showed concern but also quiet understanding. Anna smiled and squeezed Mary's hand.

"Good afternoon, daughter," she said gently.

"Afternoon?" Mary tried to clear the dryness from her throat. Her mother reached for a cup of water and lifted Mary's head to give her a drink. The cool liquid felt like velvet in her coarse throat, and she gulped all of it before lying back and closing her eyes, trying to recall what had happened, why she felt so weak and yet so . . . so at peace. Then it all came flooding back.

The angel. The announcement. She was with child. A sudden fear clutched at her stomach.

"Joseph, where is he?" she asked.

"Your father cannot find him, Mary. He left the village last night and—"

"Capernaum. He went to Capernaum." Mary spoke flatly. "To buy a rug for the house." She was both relieved and anguished.

"Then he will be back no later than tomorrow night." Anna's comforting words did not diminish Mary's worry, and she knelt down by her bed before taking her daughter's hand.

"It is all right, Mary. It won't be easy, but God will help them understand."

"You know?" Mary asked. "But how?"

Anna stroked Mary's brow. "A woman understands some things about her children that no others can. I knew something special had happened the moment I saw you. Your face, the feeling in the air around you, I knew." She smiled. "And look at you. You are different; older, wiser, more beautiful. Only angels could make it so."

Mary felt a tear slide out of the corner of her eye and down the side of her face. She had never felt such gratitude for this woman who had borne her! She used her elbows to raise herself and grasp her mother around the waist before the tears flowed.

Her mother held her close, her own tears wetting Mary's hair.

* * *

When Josiah and Joachim came from the synagogue where they had been praying for Mary, they found Anna sitting on the bench just outside the door, Ruth sitting beside her with her head on Anna's lap, asleep. They stood before her with questioning looks.

"Well?" asked the impatient Joachim. "How is she?"

Anna smiled at him. "She is fine."

Both father and son showed relief, and Joachim looked to heaven and silently thanked God for His blessing before sending Josiah off to take the sheep to the fields. "May God be praised," Joachim said, sitting down by his wife.

"Yes," answered Anna with a chuckle, "and may He open Joseph's heart to what he will need to hear."

Joachim looked at his wife curiously. "What do you speak of, wife? This is no time for riddles."

She made sure Josiah was too far away to hear. "She is with child, husband. She carries our Messiah."

Joachim felt the blood drain into his feet, started to totter, and felt the firm clutch of his wife's hand that kept him from falling off the end of the bench.

"Put your head down; catch your breath." She smiled contently.

It took several moments for Joachim to gather his thoughts, his head between his knees. Then he rose up and laid his head weakly against the wall of the house. "You have lost your mind."

"Maybe. We shall see." She smiled again.

"Don't smile like that. I never like it when you smile like that. There is no humor in this. If she is expecting, that means Joseph and she have lain with one another and—"

"And when would this have been?" she interrupted. "You are a fool, husband, especially if you believe those two would ever do such a thing!"

"Others just as good—"

"Stop your words before you regret even thinking them."

"Mother," Ruth said, looking up with sleepy eyes. "What is it? What is wrong?"

"Nothing, dear. Are you rested?" She kissed her youngest on the head.

"Yes."

"Then take the water jar and go to the well. The cistern needs filling."

Ruth got off her mother's lap and stretched, her eyes on her parents. Mary moved inside the house, and Ruth attempted to dash in when her mother gently grabbed her robe and pointed at the jar. "Now, Ruth. You can sit with Mary when you return. She is fine," she said firmly.

Ruth hesitated, then picked up the jar and reluctantly walked through the courtyard gate, looking over her shoulder several times before disappearing from view.

"Answer me truthfully, wife. Has Mary been . . . with another?"

"Of course not."

"Well, if not Joseph and if not another . . ." His voice rose in pitch with each word. He took a deep breath to gain control of his emotions. "Will you please tell me the entire truth?" Joachim pleaded with absolute frustration.

"I told you," Anna replied, facing her husband. "Mary is to have a child, a boy. He is to be called Jesus, and he is to rule our people. The Messiah is coming, Joachim. The Messiah! And he is being born to our daughter!" She stood and went inside.

Joachim didn't know what to think, how to respond. There was no response for such deluded foolishness. How could a woman have a child without having lain with a man? Surely his wife had lost her senses. And yet . . .

His mouth felt dry as desert sand and his tongue the size of a carpenter's awl. He stood and paced back and forth. What did it mean? Was this vision about what was to be? Just a forewarning of a child to be born to Mary and Joseph? After all, both were descendants of David. And yet Anna said Mary was already expecting. If she was already with child . . . He shook his head at the confusion. Surely there was only one answer. She and Joseph had been together.

No, not Mary. How could he think such a thing?

Finally, he stopped in front of the door. He would discover the truth. No more lies and stories of angels. The truth was what he wanted, and he would get it directly from Mary. Taking a deep breath, Joachim stepped over the threshold. When his eyes adjusted, he could see Mary sitting in a chair, a blanket around her shoulders, another across her lap. She looked up at him with those large, dark eyes filled with the innocence of a newborn, and his heart melted.

He tried to regain his resolve by clearing his throat. It was no use. His shoulders slumped, and he spoke in a broken voice of mild frustration. "Mary, I don't understand," he began softly. "Please, help me."

Mary only nodded as he sat down in the chair near her, then told him what happened. When she had finished, she touched her stomach. "I . . . I carry God's Son, our King. I . . . I can't explain how it is so, only that it is."

Joachim stood, then paced again, his mind sober but still racing a dozen directions searching for answers. Mary would never lie, never deceive. But such a story! A child by no mortal, but of God? It could not be possible! He shook his head adamantly. "No, this is not possible. You cannot be with child, Mary. You have known no man. It was a dream, that's all. Just a dream."

"It was no dream, Father," Mary insisted quietly.

"I will hear no more of this!" Joachim said, raising his voice. "You are ill. You have had a dream. Rest and get well!" He turned and left the house.

* * *

"Never mind, daughter," Anna said. "Your father . . . well, he thinks like a man, but he will see, eventually." A wrinkle creased her brow. "It is Joseph who worries me."

"Joseph will be fine, Mother. They both will. They are righteous men. God will help them understand."

Anna only nodded. In the minds of men, there would be a taint to this—the taint of adultery—and though Joseph might love Mary, the prejudices of men would be a powerful counterweight. Joseph was a righteous man—he would not want the stain of what would seem to be an illegitimate son.

"How are you feeling?" Anna forced a smile, changing the subject.

"Well enough, but tired. It is strange how such a thing can make one so weak, so weary."

"Back to bed then," Anna said, standing and reaching for Mary's arm. When Mary was lying down and covered, Anna sat outside on the bench to work. Josiah had taken the sheep to the fields, Ruth was at the well getting water, but where was Dinah? Honestly, the girl was as elusive as the wind. But Anna did not wish to find her now, her mind a jumble of thoughts that took away all desire except to sit and think. Normally a skeptical woman not easily given to fanciful ideas or experiences, she found it interesting that not even the smallest doubt had occurred to her. From the moment she had seen Mary, Anna had felt at peace, and hearing the details had only given her a greater witness. It had happened! She knew it! How odd. And how wonderful! But there were nagging concerns about others, especially Joseph. She must trust God. This was His Son, surely He would look after things, no matter the difficulty.

Joachim came around the corner of the house, pitchfork in hand, but from the look in his eye, it was obvious that he was not thinking of chores. He sat under the large olive tree a few feet away and looked at her.

"What are we to do, wife?"

"Do?" She laughed. "Prepare to welcome our grandson, that is what we do."

"Do you fail to grasp what this means?" he said incredulously. "If she is telling the truth, and even if she isn't, when others in the village learn of it . . . well, some will think she is deluded, crazy, possessed. And if she really is with child, they will . . ." His voice trailed off.

"Accuse her of adultery, wish to stone her? Is that what you fear?" Anna asked.

"Yes. We have seen it." He raised his hand when Anna was about to respond. "And . . . and worse could happen with such a story floating about. The Messiah? A new King? We have lived long enough to see what the Herods do to their enemies and pretender kings. If this story is told by a single member of our village, the child will be considered a threat by Herod. He himself will come here and . . ." He bit his lip.

Anna stood, went to his side, and sat down. Taking his hand in one of hers, she used the other to turn his face toward her and look directly into his eyes. "Joachim, this is not something we tell others. No one, do you understand? Not the rabbi, not the village elders, and certainly not anyone even remotely connected to the Herods." She gave him a kiss on the cheek.

"But when Mary starts to show she is with child—"

"Hopefully Joseph will accept what Mary tells him and they will marry quickly. If not, our neighbors will assume that she and Joseph have lain together, just as you thought. We will tell them nothing different. You spoke of it yourself—it is not the first time a young couple did not wait until after their final marriage ceremony to be with one another. Yes, the taint of sin will bring gossip and some will turn away from her. At worst she will be asked to leave Nazareth, but she and the child will survive, with or without Joseph. God will see to that." She paused. "But I cannot believe it will be without Joseph. God provided him—surely He will help him see. He will not leave Mary alone in this. He will not."

Joachim sighed, shaking his head. "It is so impossible!"

Anna smiled, thinking of something Mary had told her. "With God, is anything impossible?" Joachim blinked, and Anna took his hand. "You have been waiting for the Messiah all your life. Why is it so hard to believe he will come?"

"It is not that I doubt he will come, but in this manner? There is nothing I have ever been taught that helps me understand this, Anna. Nothing."

"Then trust your heart, Joachim. Trust what God is trying to show you!"

"But here, in Nazareth, to our family?" Joachim said, shaking his head in denial.

"You are of the lineage of David, I of Aaron through Jedaiah, remember? Surely that says something. And don't forget your own words. Herod is a butcher. Would you think God would send our Messiah to his household? We know what he does even to his own children! For this reason alone, the Messiah must be born in a place just like Nazareth, where he can come to manhood without the knowledge of kings and caesars!"

Joachim looked into his wife's eyes. He gently touched the side of her sun-darkened face with his hand. "You know, don't you? I mean, you really know." He tapped his chest. "Here, in your heart."

She nodded, a peaceful smile turning her lips slightly heavenward at the corners. "It is in your heart, too, husband. Do not let doubt prevent you from feeling it." Once more she kissed him, this time softly on the lips. "You are a good man, Joachim, or God would not have sent you such a daughter. Promise me you will not disappoint either of them."

CHAPTER 5

Joachim tried to sleep, but by midnight he had given up. Getting out of bed, he went to the door of the girls' sleeping room to find Mary's bed deserted. Hearing someone on the roof, he went outside and climbed the steps to find her in prayer. As quietly as he could, he went back the way he had come.

As he waited, he paced. After dark, his worries had returned, and fears for his daughter haunted him. Joseph was a good man, and that was what worried Joachim. Joseph would not be willing to marry an adulteress, have his name tainted by her, and raise another man's son. His good reputation would be ruined! And the village elders would never stand for putting her away privily. Never. He knew them. They were stern men. There would be punishment of the worst kind, he was sure of it. First, rumor would run rampant, and she and their entire family would be ostracized. Then, as she began showing her pregnancy, things would only get worse. The growth in her womb would be a constant reminder to others of what she had done, and to be rid of the reminder she could be banished from the village, thrown out like some stray dog, or . . . or she would be stoned.

He inhaled deeply, the thought taking his breath away. He had seen one woman at Cana dragged from her home and stoned to death for adultery. It terrified him to think of it happening to Mary! He must do something to protect her, and he must do it quickly, before things got out of control. But what could be done? *What?*

"Can't you sleep, Father?"

He came out of his thoughts to find Mary standing at the foot of the steps, looking directly at him, a slight smile on her face. She had always been a beautiful girl, but she seemed especially so tonight.

He cleared his throat, rubbing his aching head. "If what you say is true, Mary, there is much danger here. We must do something. We have to . . . to talk to Joseph as soon as we can. Somehow he must understand. I . . ."

She smiled in an effort to comfort his fear. "No, not yet." She said it softly. "For now, I must go to Juttah. We should leave in the morning."

"Juttah? But why Juttah?"

"I must visit my cousin, Elisabeth."

Joachim was dumbfounded. Elisabeth was the daughter of his wife's eldest brother, a priest who had lived at Nazareth until his death but had given his daughter to another priest, a priest from the house of Abijah who lived in Juttah, just outside Hebron. Zacharias and Elisabeth had always opened their doors to relatives of Elisabeth's father; Joachim had immediately liked the elderly priest, and they had become friends. They had kept in close contact over the years, and Joachim and his family often visited the home of Zacharias when traveling to Jerusalem for the feasts. Unfortunately, they had not seen one another in more than two years.

"Elisabeth will give birth soon, and I must be there," Mary explained.

Joachim's mouth dropped open. "Elisabeth? But she is well past the age of childbearing!"

She knelt in front of her father. "With God, nothing—"

"Yes, yes, nothing is impossible. So your mother tells me." He sighed. "I do not know what to say, daughter. All of this . . . It is too much for me."

"Just say that you will take me," Mary said.

"But Joseph will be back tomorrow. Surely you should wait and discuss this with him before making such a journey. If you marry now, the people will not question your being with child. Surely it will be much easier."

Mary gave a slight smile. "I am to go now, Father. It is not time for Joseph to know."

"Not time, but why? Surely God sees the need for him to be by your side if there is a child." He bit his tongue as he saw her flinch slightly. "I'm sorry, Mary, but it is still difficult for me."

She smiled. "And it will be even more so for Joseph. Without some physical sign of the child, he will never consider my claim seriously, and he must."

Joachim stared into her face as tears blurred his vision. Such innocence and strength! How could he ever doubt such a girl? Unable to speak, he simply nodded.

"Thank you," she said. Getting to her feet, she went inside, leaving him to think. Possibly it was a good solution. If she was just dreaming, time would show her—show all of them—and they would have no further concern. If it was not a dream, another few months might make the difference Mary felt Joseph would need. Then again . . .

Joachim took a deep breath, closed his eyes once more, and prayed for strength. He sat for nearly another hour, thinking, wondering, then got to his feet and went back to his bed. He was exhausted and would need rest.

* * *

Leaving Nazareth a little after sunup the next morning, Joachim and Mary took turns leading their small but sturdy donkey south through the valley of Esdraelon then east until Scythopolis, where the road turned south toward Jerusalem. They camped just south of Scythopolis, along the banks of the Jordan. The next two days were spent traveling between there and Bethany, just east and on the back side of the Mount of Olives. They rose before dawn on the fourth day, passed through Bethany, and climbed the Mount of Olives, descending a few hundred yards before the sun cast its rays over Jerusalem. The smoke of the sacrifices, mingled with the smoke of incense and hundreds of cooking fires, filled the deep valley of Kidron and the city of Jerusalem like a thin cloud. The high reaches of the temple and its surrounding walls poked through the layer of smoke, and the sun's rays glinted off the sanctuary's glistening walls.

"The temple of our God," Joachim whispered. He had always been in awe of this holy place, but new thoughts came to him this time. Thoughts about the Messiah. If it was time, if Mary did carry such a child, how would he view this place? What would he do to change it? The place was not perfect, its high priestly families corrupt, the Romans in control, wealth and power more important than humility before God. Surely he would take action against such wickedness! Would this grand structure be destroyed in the wrath that must surely come? The thought made Joachim's blood chill. War. Destruction. Blood would run in the streets! How could Mary prepare a King for such a rule?

His eyes fell upon the high towers that surrounded the palace of Herod. He had been past those towers on a number of occasions. One could not enter the city from the west without passing by the fortressed palace of the king, but it had always been a hurried passing. Joachim feared the house of the Herods and always had a deep foreboding about its inhabitants, that somehow this king would try to harm his family. Today, he realized how that might actually come to pass. He glanced at Mary furtively while biting his lip. If Herod knew of this child, he would surely seek to kill him.

The fear in the pit of Joachim's stomach would not diminish, forcing him to his feet. "Mary, come! We must hurry," he said.

She tried to catch up. "What is it?" she asked. "What did you see?"

"Don't you see? If you carry our Messiah . . ." he answered anxiously. "If the Herods were to learn of him . . . If they knew . . ."

She put an arm through his to slow him. "They will not be able to harm the child, Father. God would not put him among us only to let such a vile man snuff out his life."

Joachim glanced over his shoulder at the city. Why did her words give so little comfort? Why did he feel this sudden panic when he wasn't even sure she was with child? But he could not help it. Something inside, some fear, pushed him forward.

Their pace was such that before the city faded from view, Joachim was out of breath. Though they needed a rest, he pushed on until Mary gently pulled him off the road into the shade of a gnarled olive tree, where they sat under its silver green leaves.

Mary removed a waterskin from the donkey's traveling saddle and handed it to Joachim. After he finished drinking, she poured a little water into her own throat, then dabbed a cloth, handing it to her father to cool his brow and wipe away the dust and sweat. These things did not give him much comfort. He watched every stranger passing along the road as if he might be an enemy, someone looking for them, waiting to take them.

Mary sat down beside him and touched his arm. "Father, you mustn't fret like this. I worry that you might—"

"You worry about me when it is you whom they might harm? Mary, don't you realize—"

"Yes, I know the power of the Herods, Father, but I have been touched by the power of God, and believe me, the Herods can do nothing to harm Jesus. Nothing."

Joachim looked into her dark eyes, and what he found there immediately began melting his fears. Mary had always been close to God, a great comfort in their home. Even scripture had become almost an obsession for her. From the time her elder brother first started reading the few scrolls Joachim had managed to buy or the scrolls he had borrowed, Mary had wanted to read them. He had been a bit reluctant to allow such a blessing because it took time away from chores and because the idea of women studying the Torah was frowned on by many local men, but Mary had always known how to soften his heart, and he had finally given in. It had changed her and had brought a special feeling to their entire house, a feeling Joachim, not one given to much study, had secretly been thankful for. He took a deep breath. "I have always known you to be a special child, Mary, but you truly amaze me now. Your strength, your faith . . ." He shook his head. "Oh, if only I could believe half as much!"

She gave him a warm smile. "A child is the creation of her parents. If I am even close to what you say, it is your doing, and mother's. Now, come. I am eager to see Elisabeth."

Mary got to her feet and went to the donkey. Removing a small cloth of wrapped dates from their pack, she handed them to him. After he took several, she did the same and put them back while he untied the animal. Starting down the path, she put her arm through his, and both ate their dates.

"Maybe you should ride the donkey," Joachim suggested. "It has been a long journey, and you are tired. I can see it in your face."

"No, no, I am fine," Mary responded. She clung even tighter to his arm. "I love you," she said softly.

Joachim felt his heart swell. Though a deeply emotional man, he had learned to hold back the outward signs. He choked back the tears that tried to push out of the corner of each eye. When finally under control, he croaked out the words "I love you too, daughter."

Nonetheless, fearful thoughts still nagged at him. If she *was* expecting a child, Joseph would divorce her. She refused to consider such a thing, but Joachim must, because it would fall on him to help her through it, even if it meant leaving Nazareth, leaving everything they loved for someplace where she could find peace. Divorced and without Joseph, she would have no one else. The thought was nearly overwhelming. A sudden prayer entered his heart before he could stop it. *Could she be mistaken? Was it all just a dream, nothing more?*

The guilt at even considering such a thing struck him hard, a deep pain in his stomach that threatened to make him bend over in anguish. A chastisement. He recanted and asked for forgiveness immediately before God struck him with more than guilt.

* * *

Continuing the journey, they were outside Bethlehem a few hours later. Sitting atop a hill along one of the main roads, Joachim surveyed Bethlehem, the traditional burial site of Rachel, the wife of the prophet Jacob, head of the entire house of Israel. But the village was best known for its messianic connections. Ruth, ancestress of David, lived here with Boaz, and David's father Jesse called Bethlehem his home. It was here that David acted as shepherd for his father and where he was anointed king by the prophet Samuel. And it was through David's lineage, Joachim knew, that the Messiah would be born. *My and Mary's ancestor,* he thought, *and Joseph's.* If Mary was with child, at least the child would be born into the proper lineage. But why not Joseph's son, his blood? Why this . . . this miraculous birth? It made Joachim's head spin.

As they gazed at the city's western side, they looked upon remnants of the ancient walls and fortifications. Bethlehem had been fully fortified by Rehoboam to protect the people of the area from enemies living in the south. Though most of the ancient walls had crumbled or fallen into disarray, one could still tell that it had once been a large city. Now it was little more than a village where farmers, shepherds, and local tradesmen lived, though there were half a dozen caravansaries located at the edges. So close to Jerusalem and on the main road to Egypt, travelers needed places to stay, especially at the times of major feasts when the entire region was overrun with visitors.

"Look." Joachim pointed to a large herd of sheep grazing in a valley that ran west to east along the western side of the town.

Mary had seen them before. That first time, she had thought they must belong to a very rich man, but her father had explained that they were herds raised for the temple by the priests, bred and cared for here until old enough for sacrifice. There were a dozen such flocks in the region, cared for by shepherds paid by the temple. A few were even from families connected to the priestly courses that offered the daily sacrifice. They were a special breed, righteous men dedicated to raising lambs that would be proper sacrifices. A large pen filled with lambs stood near the road, a few shepherds watching over them.

"These are going to be taken to the temple soon," Joachim said. "See how they check them for spots and blemishes."

Mary nodded. She knew that the sacrifice must be clean, but so many of these were imperfect. She noticed that even a few of the blemished were being selected.

Joachim noticed as well and frowned. "It used to be that you would find no sheep with blemish among the temple flocks. Now," he continued, "they are not so careful. But it is hard. The demand is so much greater than the supply. It takes many sheep to feed the fires of the temple each year, especially at Passover."

They turned down a road that ran west into some low hills, then went north again, toward the village of Juttah. The sun was in the afternoon sky when they reached the top of a hill. In the distance to the south, they could see Hebron, the village of the patriarchs. Hebron was also fortified by Rehoboam, for the same reason as Bethlehem, but unlike that village, it had been kept intact by succeeding kings. As the ancient home of Abraham and the resting place of the patriarch, his son Isaac, his grandson Jacob, his great-grandson Joseph, and even some of their wives, it had been revered by their descendants for generations. Kings would be fools not to care for it. Herod seemed to understand this more than his predecessors, and the city not only had a garrison of soldiers but was being beautified with a great enclosure over the cave where the bodies of the patriarchs lay.

But then Herod was using every device he could think of to be accepted by his Jewish subjects. Feeling that being one of them would make the Jews more manageable, the Idumean had become a Jewish proselyte, which, at best, made him a half-Jew. Then he married Mariamne, granddaughter of Hyrcanus II, leader of the Hasmonean royal family, in hopes that it would complete his acceptance. It did make him more acceptable to the Jewish elite, who supported him and were looking for anything that would justify that support, but the Pharisees and most of the rest of the populace still thought of him as nothing more than an interloper. Of course, he silenced such critics when he could, especially the ones foolish enough to speak against him openly, while trying to impress all others with his bold building projects—the temple complex at Jerusalem and this enclosure of the tomb of the patriarchs being the most noted. Unfortunately, he built them by raising taxes and confiscating property of both the rich and the poor. In the minds of most, his efforts added only to the seething hate most held for him and his family. The sudden thought that her son would remove such a man pleased Mary.

It was a thought she immediately regretted. The very picture of her child growing to manhood only to wield a sword, of killing, destroying, made her shudder, and she prayed for forgiveness for entertaining it while at the same moment feeling it must be! The prophets, the rabbis, the psalmists all testified of it.

See, Lord, and raise up for them their king, the son of David, to rule over your servant Israel . . . Undergird him with strength to destroy the unrighteous rulers, to purge Jerusalem from Gentiles who trample her to destruction; in wisdom and in righteousness to drive out the sinners from the inheritance; to smash the arrogance of sinners like the potter's jar; to shatter all their substance with an iron rod; to destroy unlawful nations with the word of his mouth; at his warning the nations will flee from his presence; and he will condemn sinners by the thoughts of their hearts.

Even though only written in the last hundred years as part of the Psalms of Solomon, a book of verses created by some unknown rabbi, it held great hope for Mary's people and for her. Like everyone else, she was tired of oppression, of rulers without morals who refused to follow God. It was time to be rid of them. Wasn't that the reason he was God's Son as well as hers? Would not this combination give him the power to defeat such men?

Then why did Mary feel there was something more? Something she was missing? That somehow this would not be a child of violence? Surely it must be her instincts trying to suppress the thoughts of blood and mayhem!

They followed a road down the side of the hill into a gorge that quickly widened into a peaceful valley. At its center was the village of Juttah, the village where Zacharias and Elisabeth lived.

Elisabeth was much older than Mary, but they had been close ever since Mary was a baby. Her mother had taken quite ill in giving birth to Mary, and Elisabeth had come to Nazareth to help. She had grown very attached to Mary and had made the journey to Galilee for a few weeks every few years to spoil Mary.

And now Elisabeth was expecting a child of her own! Mary was nearly as excited for her as she was for the special child in her own womb. With only a few months between them, surely the two children would grow up knowing each other as dear friends!

Most of the houses of Juttah sat on slopes that climbed steeply from the valley floor. The focal point of the village was the spring that emerged from the rocks of the east hill and cascaded down a manmade ditch into a small pool at the center of the village square. Considering it to be pure water, priests of the courses of Abijah and Jedaiah gathered here before going up to the temple to work, cleansing and preparing themselves for their week-long service in Jerusalem. To accommodate them, a mikveh, or purification pool, had been built and enclosed by a small building attached to the synagogue, so all could perform their preparations privately.

Mary and her father passed the well and mikveh under the watchful eyes of villagers, a few of whom nodded recognition from previous visits by Mary's father and his family. Leaving the village, they walked for another five minutes before approaching a small home built partially into the hillside. There were the usual pens for animals and a large garden where Zacharias and Elisabeth raised their own vegetables. Though a priest, Zacharias derived very little of his living from his work at the temple, even though priests were given the hides of the sacrifices to clean, tan, and sell. The sheer number of priests limited them to a few hides each year and required that they either live in poverty or find other means to meet their families' needs. Zacharias sold vegetables and built furniture to sell in the marketplaces at Hebron and Jerusalem.

A man in a nearby field recognized them, quickly stopped his digging, and ran in their direction, jumping over and around various plants to keep from squashing them.

"Joachim," he yelled. "It is I, Jeremiah."

Mary noticed that her father was unsure of the man's identity, then a sudden recognition crossed his face. "Ah, Jeremiah. I remember now! You are the priest who helped me find a suitable sacrifice at the temple, a friend of Zacharias."

"Yes, yes, when the guards would not allow your own to pass through the gates. They claimed it was unclean." He frowned. "Of course, they were wrong, using it as an excuse to force you to buy one of the animals offered for sale." He shook his head woefully. "It happens more often than it should." He waived a dismissive hand. "Never mind, God will judge them. You have come to see Zacharias, and I must prepare you."

"Prepare me?" Joachim said.

Jeremiah's lips and face sagged into a serious frown. "Something has happened. Something wonderful and yet . . . How shall I say . . . Yes, mysterious, beyond anything of this earth."

"You mean that Elisabeth is to have a child?" Mary interjected with a slight smile.

Jeremiah looked toward her as if seeing her for the first time. "Why, yes, but how . . . Did he send messengers? Is that why you have come?"

Mary looked at Joachim, who glanced at her but was unsure of what to say. "Yes, a messenger came," she responded, "but your words say there is more."

"A vision. Zacharias had a vision at the temple. He . . . he cannot speak of it and refuses to write and tell even me what he saw, why he cannot speak, cannot hear."

Joachim cleared his throat and spoke. "Cannot speak or hear?"

Jeremiah looked a bit confused. "Why, he is deaf and dumb! Surely he spoke of this in his message to you. It has everyone talking, wondering what really happened in the Holy Place. Was it an angel? Did God appear? One of His prophets?" He sighed. "But, alas, Zacharias writes nothing. Instead he takes his wife to the desert to see her people for five months!" He threw his hands in the air and rolled his eyes toward heaven. "God be kind to them in their old age! Anyway, they only returned yesterday, and everyone sees that Elisabeth truly is going to have a child and the whole village is gossiping again!" He shrugged. "I was hoping that he might have given you some idea of what happened—that you were here because of it." He exhaled slowly. "But I see that you know less than I do. Than all of us do!" The last sentence was said more loudly and with some frustration.

Joachim's face flushed with excitement. "You're sure? He had a vision, and Elisabeth is expecting?"

"Of course I am sure," Jeremiah replied, a bit disgruntled at the challenge.

"Yes, yes, forgive me," Joachim said, his lips in a wide grin. "Thank you, Jeremiah. It is good to see you again! We must be going. Mary is tired, and so am I."

"My apologies," Jeremiah stated with a bow. "But if you learn anything . . ." he added weakly while shaking a pointing finger at a house across the fields, "my humble house."

Joachim touched Jeremiah on the arm. "Zacharias spoke of you as his dearest friend. If he were free to tell about what happened, I am sure he would have given you every detail."

Jeremiah looked embarrassed, his face turning a crimson red. "Again, I must apologize. My curiosity has once again overcome me." He bowed. "Please forgive my inquisitive nature. You are right. When Zacharias is ready, he will speak to me." Another bow. "May the God of Israel go with you."

"And you," Joachim responded while anxiously tugging on the rope of the donkey, Mary just a bit ahead of him.

* * *

Elisabeth squinted at the man standing a few feet from her doorway in the gray of evening, a look of curiosity in her eyes that suddenly changed to one of recognition. "Joachim!" she uttered with enthusiasm. "Come in! What brings you such a distance? I . . ." As she pulled him into the house, she glanced over his shoulder and saw Mary. "Mary! Oh, dear girl! You look so tired! Come in, come in! Quickly!" She moved Joachim to the side and reached for Mary's arm and brought her inside where they hugged one another tightly.

Mary pulled away slightly and could not help but look at the belly that had so firmly touched her own. "Oh, cousin," Mary said. "It is true! You are with child!"

Elisabeth grinned, her hand softly caressing her stomach. "Yes, it is—" Her eyes suddenly lit up, and she laughed lightly. "Oh, the baby! He . . . he moves! And it is no small movement either!"

Then her eyes settled on Mary's face, and it seemed to Mary as if she were searching her very soul. "Mary," she said with a soft smile. "Oh, Mary, blessed are you among women!" Her long fingers reached out and touched Mary's stomach. "And blessed is the fruit of *your* womb." Elisabeth knelt before her. "And what caused heaven to bestow this blessing upon me—that the mother of my Lord should come to me?" She bowed her head and touched her own stomach reverently. "As soon as I heard your greeting, the babe leaped in my womb for joy." She looked up at Mary, a curious look of understanding crossing her face. "And blessed are you for your belief, for all of God's words will be fulfilled."

Mary felt the strength of the Spirit cascade through her as she lifted the tall and stately Elisabeth from her knees, her heart nearly melting with feelings of gratitude to God for this second witness. "My soul does magnify the Lord," she replied softly. Her right hand touched her stomach as she looked down. "And my spirit has rejoiced in God my Savior. He has overlooked my imperfections and greatly honored me." She took Elisabeth by the hands as the Spirit flowed into her like a river of warm water, her mind reeling with words of praise that her tongue thrilled to speak.

"He that is mighty has done great things to me; and holy is His name. His mercy is on all of us who reverence Him from every generation." She turned to her father, touching the tear that rolled down his cheek, then gave him a smile. "God has shown us the strength of His arm, Father. With this child He scatters the proud in heart. He removes the mighty from their high seats, and He exalts those of low degree. He fills the hungry with good things. He will help His servant Israel and is showing us mercy just as He promised to our fathers, to Abraham and his seed forever."

Joachim bent his knee to the floor, where he could only bow his head in abject humility. "Mary," he whispered. "Mary, I do not deserve . . ."

Mary reached down and lifted him up, then wrapped her arms firmly around him, tears rolling down her cheeks and falling freely onto his robe. Her heart was overflowing with a joy and warmth of love that she had not even felt with the angel! How could such a feeling grasp one's heart so deeply?

Finally, Joachim looked into her eyes and gave her a smile. "All my life, I have prayed for our Messiah. All my life I have felt he would come and I would see it, but never, never, did I dream . . ." His lip quivered with gratitude and he could say nothing more.

Mary squeezed him once more, then kissed his cheek gently, holding him close.

After a moment, Elisabeth touched each on the arm. "Come, it has been a long journey, and you both must eat something and rest." She directed them toward the cooking area.

"First thing in the morning, I must go to the temple. I . . . I must offer sacrifice. A bullock at the very least!" Joachim said with excitement. "I must thank Him, celebrate! I . . ."

Mary smiled at her father while putting a finger to his lips. "In time, all men will celebrate with us, Father. For now, it must remain our secret."

"Yes, yes, of course. It is just that . . . Oh my, the Messiah, Mary! And His prophet! I am to be . . . You are to be . . . Elisabeth is to be . . ."

Mary and Elisabeth laughed lightly as Joachim chattered and stammered on with excitement. Then Mary had a sobering thought as she recalled her father's earlier concerns. All men would not celebrate the coming of this child. All men would not welcome him with open arms and be glad at his coming. Some truly would seek his life.

The chill ran the full length of her backbone.

CHAPTER 6

Joseph learned of Mary's departure shortly after it occurred. He had returned from Capernaum with the rugs, and while he was placing them in their house, Matthias entered to tell him that Mary had left the village to care for an ailing cousin.

"But this cannot be," Joseph replied quickly. "Just . . . just two days ago . . ."

"She is gone, Joseph. I saw her leave the village with Joachim. Anna has been telling everyone she went to Juttah."

"Juttah? But the only people they know in Juttah are Zacharias and Elisabeth."

"I remember meeting them at the temple. He is a priest, isn't he?"

"Yes, a cousin of Mary's mother. I will talk to Anna."

He left immediately for Mary's home with the horrible feeling that something was wrong, that Mary had run away. He found Anna busy with the evening meal, the other children sitting around the outside cooking fire. She gave Joseph a brief smile, then busied herself making flat bread while speaking to him.

"You have come about Mary."

"Yes," he said softly.

"She has gone to help my cousin Elisabeth."

"Yes, I know, but she left so quickly . . ."

"Elisabeth is quite old, thought to be beyond her years for bearing children, but this blessing has come to her. Mary went to take care of her and will return as soon as the baby is born." She kept her eyes on her work.

Joseph stood speechless, nodded, and turned to leave.

"Are you hungry?" Anna asked.

Joseph turned back. He had no appetite but wanted to stay. "A bit, yes."

Anna placed the flat bread on the rounded surface of the iron oven. "Then sit. The bread will be ready soon."

"When will Elisabeth deliver?" he asked after sitting.

"Three, maybe four months." She smiled. "You wanted more time to finish the house, prepare for Mary. Now you have it." A sudden cloud seemed to cross her face, and she looked away.

"What is it, Anna? What is wrong?"

She forced a smile as she used a flat, wooden cooking tool to flip the bread over. "Joseph, you are good man, and Mary will need you to be strong for her when she returns. Very strong."

She handed him a piece of the freshly cooked bread. He watched her carefully, mystified by her words, hardly noticing the bread. She offered it again.

"Eat, Joseph."

As he lifted the bread to his mouth, she spoke again. "And keep word of Elisabeth's baby to yourself. No telling what gossip would go around about the child of an aged priest whose wife is beyond the years of childbearing." She smiled.

He had lain awake that night, wondering at it all, then finally given up, forcing himself to concentrate on what to do with the next three or four months. By morning, he had slept little but had decided to finish the house, then go to work for the governor in Capernaum who was adding on to the local synagogue in an effort to gain favor with the Jewish population. He was offering to give credit for the payment of taxes to everyone, and to artisans working in stone and wood he would pay a good wage as well.

* * *

It took Joseph a month to finish the house, and then he had come to Capernaum, where he had worked nearly three more months. His taxes were paid, and he had put away a few coins for the future, but it was less than expected. The governor, a distant relation to Herod, had not been as generous as he had promised, but Joseph was not complaining. It had kept his mind and spirit occupied in Mary's long absence.

He scratched his sweat-beaded beard as he examined the stonework he was laying. The mortar was even, but the border channel on the outside of the stone hadn't been carved deeply enough. Upset at himself for such slipshod work, he tossed his trowel aside and picked up hammer and chisel, took a deep breath, and began correcting his mistake. Such things had happened too often lately, and even the steward, a man who respected Joseph's work, had been forced to point out several errors. What could they expect? His mind was on Mary more and more as the hoped-for time of her return neared. He simply could not help it. They had all chided him many times about his thoughtless stupors, but he did not care. According to what Anna had told him, she would return soon, and it was hard to think of anything else.

"Take a rest, my friend."

Joseph turned to find Matthias standing below the scaffolding, a smile on his face. "Another love moment, I see," he quipped, looking at the stone. "If you have many more of those, you will destroy any reputation I may have secured for you." He laughed loudly. "Come, let us go for water. The sun and the daughter of Joachim and Anna are getting the best of you."

Joseph turned back and began chiseling, a slight smile creasing his lips. It was hard to be upset with Matthias, but he was in little mood for humor this morning. "When this is as it should be, I will go for water, not before," he replied, forcing a frown.

"And something to eat while we sit by the sea," Matthias added. "We could both use some time away from the heat put off by these miserable stones."

Concentrating on his work, Joseph only nodded. A few moments later, he finished the border and laid his tools in the box before climbing down the ladder to clean his trowel of already dried mortar. Then he sat next to Matthias in the shade of a tree. Joseph reached for the goatskin bag and took a mouthful of water, rinsed, and spit it on the ground before drinking his fill and handing it back to Matthias, who slung it over one shoulder. The two of them then stood and walked down the street toward the harbor.

As they passed the market, Joseph picked out two handfuls of dates and a pair of pomegranates while Matthias purchased bread and cheese. After paying the vendors and placing the food in their bags, they continued to the harbor before deciding on a place to eat.

Capernaum had been a small fishing village until just a few years earlier, when the Romans built a main road from Damascus that ran past the village. Since then, it had become a busy town and was quickly growing into a city. A center of rule for the provincial governor, who felt a need for some protection, the Herods had sent a garrison to be housed here. It was not a popular idea with most of the villagers, but the Herodian centurion had appeased them by having their synagogue enlarged and the harbor area remodeled with docks of paved stone that launched into the sea like the fingers of a man's hand. Some degree of prosperity had followed as travelers used the town's inns and purchased food, and as the fishing industry shifted many of its boats from the aging and dilapidated docks of Bethsaida and Magdala. Carpenters and other artisans like Joseph had found work building the synagogue, new homes, and warehouses and stores for the elite who controlled commerce and came to live in Capernaum—or who provided lesser homes for their hired stewards, who acted as over-seers of their business interests. Farms from the surrounding villages also experienced some increase in profits as more food, wine, and other goods were needed for travelers and the growing population. But few of the average citizens experienced any significant increase in wages and profits, as the brokers and tax collectors were ready to open their purses and take most of the excess, either for themselves or for the elite rich who controlled them.

There were at least a dozen fishing boats tied alongside various docks, their owners unloading and selling the morning catch to village women and vendors alike. A few had already finished and were washing decks, doing general repairs, mending sails and nets, or talking with others about the day's catch. The place was awash with the excitement of a good day on the sea, and the sound of laughter and good-natured jabs at one another filled the air. Even around the booth of the tax collector, the men seemed in high spirits. This day there would be a profit.

Matthias pointed at a large gathering of men a hundred yards off the west end of the dock. A man stood on a boat beached on the stones of the open shore, preaching to a small group of men.

"I know this man," Matthias said. "A zealot, and a friend in my wayward days. Come, let's see what he has to say."

As they walked toward the gathering, Joseph could hear the passionate words that accompanied the enlivened gestures of the speaker. Matthias was right, he was a zealot, denouncing the Romans, the Herods, the priests of Jerusalem, and the publicans safely behind the locked doors of the tax collectors' booths. Joseph stopped in his tracks. Herodian soldiers were coming onto the beach, and the crowd was scattering. Joseph pulled Matthias into a boat tied to the last dock and sat down to get himself out of view, but Matthias kept himself aloft, his eyes on the capture of the rebel. "They are beating him," Matthias declared angrily. He got ready to jump from the boat, but Joseph already had a firm hold on his friend's tunic. "Sit down, Matthias, or he won't be the only one they beat and imprison today."

Matthias glanced down at Joseph with fire in his eyes, about to respond, then sat down, his shoulders in an angry slump. "Someday . . ."

"Yes, I know," Joseph said, "but not today." He continued in jest, "After all, there are only twenty of them. They would not have a chance." He tried a smile.

After a moment, Matthias smiled back, then looked over the edge of the ship toward where the man was being dragged away. The smile quickly disappeared.

"You wish to see them dead."

Joseph and Matthias looked up to see a large man standing on the dock next to the ship. His clothing and the net he held in his hand revealed him as a fisherman. A young woman stood next to him, her dark arms glistening with sweat in the hot sun. She carried several baskets used for hauling fish from boats to the holding pools along the docks. Tall for a woman, her frame was large though well proportioned, and her arms and legs were muscled, apparently from hard work.

"Would it be a bad thing?" Matthias asked sarcastically. The question was for the man, but the woman had Matthias's eye. She met his look of admiration with a hard stare of challenge that forced him to avert his eyes. She went to the front of the boat and stored the baskets under the shelf built over the tip of the vessel, then pulled netting from the ship and began arranging it for the next day's use. Neither Joseph nor Matthias had ever seen a woman of such stature or physical ability.

The fisherman smiled but kept to the argument at hand. "It depends." He stepped into the boat and sat down on one of the benches that connected the two sides. Joseph smiled as he saw that Matthias's eyes remained fixed on the girl. This was unusual for his friend. Very unusual.

The man waggled his head toward the soldiers and their captive. "The man is a fool. He deserves prison."

The words brought Matthias's head around, his body stiffening. "He is a patriot," he retorted firmly.

The man looked directly at Matthias with cold eyes. It was obvious that he was not intimidated by Matthias's unusual size—but then he was nearly as large himself. "Maybe, but a fool just the same. Now, if you don't mind, you are in our way. We must prepare for tomorrow's fishing."

Matthias stood and jumped to the dock. His attention going back to the woman.

"Your daughter?" Joseph asked.

"Yes, and as you see, a good worker."

"You have no sons?"

"We had one. He was killed by the Herods."

Matthias forced his attention back to the fisherman. "Then you of all men should fight for that man," he said angrily.

"You do not fight the Herods or the Romans with words," the fisherman answered. "Now we have one less pair of hands to wield a sword when the Messiah is ready for us." The look was a hard one, filled with controlled hate that made the hair on Joseph's neck stand up.

"You speak as if the Messiah is already among us," Joseph said.

"He is."

"You know this?" Matthias asked.

"Yes, I know it. He is gathering a force in the mountains north of here."

"You mean Judas ben Hezekiah," Joseph replied flatly.

The man looked up, "Yes, that is who I mean."

"But he does not claim to be the Messiah," Matthias pointed out.

"He will," came the reply.

"He is nothing but a brigand," Joseph added, "and will get a lot of people killed needlessly." He stepped from the boat.

"The Messiah is one who will lead us to victory over the Romans and the Herods. Judas has strength, and many men are willing to follow him, and as a son of David, he has the lineage. Do not sell him short," the fisherman answered.

"His claim to be a son of David is unfounded," Joseph stated. "Besides, there is more to our Messiah than his lineage."

"You speak as if you know Judas," the man replied.

"I know his reputation, and I know that his claim of lineage in the house of David is questionable."

"And how do you know this?" the man asked.

"Because I am of David's lineage, and I know my forefathers and their descendants like I know the tools of my trade." He paused. "Beware of pretenders to the throne of David, fisherman; they will get you killed." He strode away. Matthias followed but stumbled over some netting, nearly falling, his eyes still on the woman.

Joseph smiled as he reached out and steadied his large friend. "I have never seen you so clumsy before, Matthias."

"I have never seen a woman like that before, Joseph! A woman like her could make a man's life worth living!"

Joseph laughed loudly. "And if you were late to supper, she could give even you a beating! I thought you were going to see the world."

"Why look further—God has sent her here! And from her, I would take any beating gladly." He stopped, a sudden firm determination in the set of his jaw. "I will make her my wife."

Joseph stopped in his tracks and turned around. "Just like that." He shook his head. "Don't be foolish. You don't even know her. She may be betrothed, she might have a temper worse than Herod's—"

"She is not married, or she wouldn't be here. About the rest, I don't care. I will ask for her hand."

Joseph was dumbfounded. He had never seen his friend so taken by anything, especially a woman. "Matthias, you cannot . . .You don't even have a bride gift. How can you possibly—"

"I have saved money, nearly ten shekels. I will pay it all if I must." He turned back.

"But you don't know her! And she certainly doesn't know anything about you! What makes you think she will even agree?"

Matthias became thoughtful. "I will talk with him."

Immediately, he turned back and marched down the dock toward the fisherman and his daughter. Astounded, Joseph hesitated, and by the time he recovered, Matthias was already speaking to the fisherman. He reached the two of them just as they shook hands.

"Tonight then?" Matthias said.

The girl stood a dozen feet away, a curious look on her face, a look Joseph thought held both admiration and amusement.

The fisherman nodded, giving Matthias directions to his house. "My name is Simon. If you cannot find it, just ask. Everyone knows me."

Matthias nodded, glanced over his shoulder at the woman, then walked away, Joseph quickly catching up. "He has invited you to his home," Joseph said with awe.

"Yes, and before the night is finished, I will be betrothed." Matthias grinned.

Joseph grabbed his friend by the arm and turned him so that they faced one another. "No, you mustn't ask for her tonight. You must talk, get to know one another a little, learn more of the family. You are moving too quickly, Matthias! What do you know of Simon? Of this girl? She looks older, and yet she is not married. Don't you wonder why? Has it occurred to you that . . . that she might have a temper . . . or possibly it is her cooking. For all you know, she burns everything she touches!"

Matthias smiled. "Then I will eat it burned. I know what I want, Joseph." Matthias slapped his friend jovially on the back. "Did you not see how strong she was? She could outwork most men! And the children she could bear! Sons to work beside me at last! And those eyes! Did you not see her eyes? They are as dark as the sea itself! What beautiful eyes! To look into those eyes for the rest of my days? This alone would be worth every shekel Simon may ask!" He started to walk again, smiling widely. "No, Joseph, I will not waste time. Salome, that is her name—and what a beautiful name it is—Salome will be mine tonight!"

They had moved up the street so quickly that they were back at work when Matthias finished speaking of the girl. The rest of the day, the man was a whirlwind of activity, had smiles for everyone, and proceeded to tell all of his good fortune. Joseph thought that by the end of the day, surely the whole city would hear the news.

"Watch him," one worker said with a smile. "Surely he has lost his mind!"

"There is no fool as bad as one who has become a fool over a woman," laughed another. "Better go with him, Joseph. Simon will have his house and all his money before the night is over! And for what? A woman who works like a mule and probably kicks like one too!"

When the sun disappeared below the hills to the west, they picked up what little pay they were given for food and retrieved their bedrolls from the overseer's back room. Joseph started for the gate that would take them to the workers' sleeping quarters, but Matthias grabbed his arm and pulled him toward the city center.

"We cannot have the smell of a week's work on us when we go to Simon's house tonight. We must go to the public bath and put on clean clothes."

"We? I refuse to be involved in this madness, Matthias," Joseph said seriously.

Matthias faced Joseph, concern now etched in the wrinkles around his eyes. "You are my friend, Joseph, possibly my only real friend. I am a bumbling fool when it comes to delicate things, you know that. You must come and be my spokesman!"

Joseph searched his friend's eyes. "You are that determined?"

Matthias only nodded, pain in his eyes. He had bitten off more than he could chew, and he was beginning to feel the horror of it creep up his spine.

Joseph sighed. "Very well, Matthias, I will go with you, but you must let me do the bargaining. Agreed?"

Matthias thought a moment before answering. "All right, Joseph, but only if you promise that you will not give up easily. I must have this woman as my wife."

"I will do my best," Joseph answered. He was resigned to it. He had never seen Matthias like this, and arguing would only make him angry. He would do his best to make something good come of it, even though he feared the worst.

"We will go to the sea for bathing." Joseph smiled. "If the woman is worth as much as you say, you must save every penny."

They walked to the sea then along its shore until they were away from the fires, lamps, and prying eyes of the city. After bathing, they dressed in clothes washed the night before. They were nearly ready when a boy approached them along the beach. He had a message for Matthias, who held his breath, afraid it was a retraction of Simon's invitation. Joseph thanked the boy and sent him on his way with a small coin, then read the letter handed to him by Matthias. It was an invitation from the local rabbi to visit him before they went to Simon's home.

"What does it mean, Joseph?" Matthias asked.

"It means the rabbi wishes to speak to us, nothing more."

"But it must be about Salome," Matthias said agitatedly. "Simon must wish to break his invitation." He began pacing.

"I won't lie to you, Matthias, that is possible, but we won't know until we go to the synagogue, will we?"

Matthias's shoulders seemed to slump, and he hardly said a word as they gathered their things and hurried back toward the town. Joseph knew how he felt. He had felt such fear when trying to earn the money and ask for Mary. Losing something you wanted so badly was a fearful thing.

They reached the synagogue, covered their heads with their prayer shawls, and entered. Several groups of men were sitting on different benches along the walls, speaking quietly within their groups. Joseph knew that some would be discussing politics, others community affairs, while still others would argue over the law and the words of the rabbis. Most would pray and invoke God's blessings on their personal lives at some time during the evening, and all would go away with news of the world as learned from caravans passing through.

As Joseph and Matthias finished a short prayer, a man in one of the groups noticed them, nodded a welcome, then continued his discussion, finally excusing himself and approaching them a few minutes later.

"Brethren," he said with a slight smile.

"Rabbi," Joseph responded after both he and Matthias stood to bow slightly at the waist. They had both come to know the rabbi while working on the synagogue, and Joseph had spent some evenings discussing the Torah and the sayings of the prophets with him. He was a follower of Hillel; in fact, he had learned at the feet of the great rabbi. Joseph found his interpretations much the same as his own and had learned to respect his views even more than those of his own rabbi in Nazareth.

The rabbi turned to Matthias and smiled broadly. "So you think you want to marry the daughter of Simon the fisherman."

Matthias nodded with a bit of a pained smile. "Simon spoke to you?"

"Yes, of course. He had seen you both here for Sabbath and asked about you. He also knew you would have questions before your visit tonight." Seeing the worried look on Matthias's face, the rabbi touched his arm lightly, then patted it. "Do not worry. I do not bear bad news. My only duty is to answer questions and make sure this is what you wish to do. Simon does not want to take advantage of a man, nor does he want to embarrass his daughter by entertaining a suitor who is neither willing nor capable of making a fair but lasting contract."

Matthias's shoulders lifted a bit, but the worry did not leave his eyes. "Take advantage? But how can this be? Salome is a beautiful woman with much to offer. My eyes tell my heart she will make a good wife and bear me many children." He bowed slightly. "For this honor, I am willing to pay a substantial bride gift, even though I am but a poor carpenter."

The rabbi gave Matthias a comforting smile, then glanced around the room to find all eyes on them, several men whispering to each other. "Come," he said, motioning toward a far corner. "We can speak more privately over here."

When Matthias and Joseph were seated on a well-worn bench near the wall and the rabbi on a chair he pulled in front of them, the rabbi spoke.

"Simon is a good man who works hard and has a good family. Though we do not see him here very often, he fears God and lives the law. Though he is a poor fisherman, I know I can always go to his ship when I need food for the hungry. He is of the lineage of Judah but not of the royal line. It is said that his ancestors served King David as well and were among the king's cherished friends. When the Hasmoneans came to power, his great-grandfather feared for his family and went into hiding at Cana, where Simon's family lived until his father's property was taken. As the eldest son, he moved his aged parents to Capernaum and cared for them until they died. His wife followed them to the grave a short time later, and he has raised Salome alone."

"He has never remarried?" Matthias asked.

"No," the rabbi paused, then leaned forward. "He is a zealot, a fighter. Some say he trains others with the sword. He does not feel to marry because he may have to go and fight for our freedom. Simon's family has looked for the Messiah for generations. Like his forefathers, he wishes to serve the house of David and bring Israel out of bondage. If the Messiah came, Simon would willingly lay down his life for him."

"His is an honorable lineage," Matthias said, a wrinkle to his brow.

"And what is yours, Matthias ben Levi?" the rabbi asked.

"I am of Benjamin," Matthias answered.

"Also warriors. They did great service in resisting the Philistines. And Saul, our first king, was of Benjamin. It will suit Simon."

"Simon speaks of Judas ben Hezekiah as if he might be the Messiah," Joseph pointed out. "If this is so, he is a fool."

The rabbi frowned slightly. "Possibly." He looked at Matthias. "Do you agree with your friend?"

Matthias glanced at Joseph with a bit of a hard look, as if to chastise him for bringing this up. He then stiffened his shoulders. "The Messiah will need no one to argue for him. When he comes, we will know him."

"But you would fight for him," the rabbi said.

"Yes, I would fight, and if Simon is of the same mind, I would be honored to have his daughter to wife."

The rabbi leaned forward. "Ah, now we get to the subject that really matters and the reason Simon and Salome asked that I talk to you." He sat back, searching the anxious face of Matthias. "It is essential that you know now, before you go to Simon's home, that Salome is divorced, at least technically. And she has a child."

Matthias blinked several times, and Joseph sat back in his chair, a bit startled.

"Technically?" Joseph said.

"As you know, when a man takes a vow of marital abstinence, the woman can ask for a divorce. This is the case with Salome. Her husband deserted her and the child to follow after the sect we in Galilee call the Herodians."

Joseph cringed. The Herodians were a small party of the larger sect known as the Essenes. The Essenes were one of three groups that developed during the struggles for power during the Hasmonean period. The other two were the Sadducees and Pharisees. The Essenes fell into disfavor with the Hasmonean hierarchy, but when Herod decided to overthrow the remnants of the corrupt dynasty, he astutely curried the favor of the Essenes along with disgruntled Sadducees and Pharisees. Though their support was of little value militarily, and it was Rome who ultimately lifted him to power, Herod knew he would need the support of all three of the most prominent sects. The Essenes supported him in a much greater degree than either the Pharisees or the Sadducees, and when he came to power, Herod freed the Essenes from the oaths of loyalty imposed on all others, including the powerful Sadducees and Pharisees—a slap in the face for their lukewarm support. This gave the Essenes, thereafter called the Herodians, an unprecedented degree of religious freedom. They used it to carry out a missionary expansion that founded Essene communities in nearly every village in Palestine until they finally became the second largest sect in the Jewish religion. Only the Pharisees outnumbered them. The Sadducees, though smaller in numbers than either of the others, still held more power because of their wealth and position, but Herodian leaders were working hard to change that through continued appeals to Herod.

Matthias spoke. "Some may think of the Essenes as pious men because they withdraw themselves from the world and pray nearly every hour, but they carry things too far. To think a woman and children can make one unclean is an abomination in the sight of God. And to leave them helpless . . ." Matthias's face went red, and he took a deep breath to control his anger. "The man should be whipped."

"I agree that they have taken a wrong path, but do not be too harsh on them. Piety is a blessed state and—"

"God commanded Adam and Eve to multiply and replenish the earth. It was the first commandment given to men by God," Joseph interjected. "To leave a wife without a cause allowed by the law is to leave God. No amount of self-imposed silence, self denial, or study of Torah can overcome such an act, and if it is allowed in Israel, God will punish us as surely as He lives."

The rabbi's lips drifted to a frown. "You require even more than the rabbis."

"It is not I who requires it. It is God, and He has said so through Moses. For men to twist His words so that they can break His rules is an abomination."

Matthias touched Joseph's arm. "None of this matters to me. Are you telling me that because the law does not justify divorce except when adultery is committed, that Salome is still married?"

"Yes, but . . . but there is a way, now that she has a suitor in place, but it will take a little time."

"How long?" Matthias asked.

"A week, maybe two." He leaned forward. "The rabbis have clearly stated that a wife can have a divorce when her husband deserts her. Based on these laws, we will convene a court of elders and compel her husband to give her a writing of divorcement. This is Israel's religious law today and cannot be disputed."

"Then we are agreed." Matthias smiled. "I am willing to wait."

"And you do not mind the taint of divorce?"

"As Joseph said, her husband is the sinner. She has done nothing wrong. There is no taint."

The rabbi nodded. "But there are those in Israel who may think her less because of it. Are you prepared to deal with such people? This is Simon's concern."

"If others wish to judge us less, though God does not, they are fools and put their own souls in jeopardy. As far as I am concerned, they can go to the devil." Matthias stood. "Is this all that stands in the way of her accepting me as her husband?"

"There is still the matter of the bride gift," Joseph said, looking at the rabbi. "I assume you have instructions concerning this as well."

Matthias sat back down, his eyes expectantly upon the rabbi. "Do you?"

"Simon did well by Salome. Reuben, her husband, paid a handsome bride price for her as well as contracting to give her a sum of money if there was ever a divorce."

"Then there was a Ketubah, a marriage deed?" Joseph queried.

"Yes, and all of her husband's goods were sold to try and pay the contract, but there was little of value and the full amount is still wanting." He looked at Matthias. "You are to pay the remainder to Salome."

"And the remainder is how much?" Joseph asked.

"Ten shekels."

"Done," Matthias said loudly, slapping his leg at the same time. Once more he started to stand.

The rabbi smiled. "Sit. There is one other condition."

"Speak, then!" Matthias sat hard on the bench, a hand throwing his long hair back out of his eyes. "I wish to see my bride tonight."

"You must build her a home, and it must be here, in Capernaum."

Joseph and Matthias looked at one another.

"It is not a bad place, and there is plenty of work," Joseph urged.

"It is not Nazareth." Matthias stood and walked to the far wall and back, his hands clasped behind him.

"We will go to Simon's now. I will discuss this with him."

"It is not his condition. It is hers," the rabbi replied.

"Then I will talk to her," Matthias said firmly. He grabbed the rabbi by an arm and had him standing on his feet before the rabbi knew what was happening. "Lead the way, Rabbi. I wish to see my future bride." He grinned while brushing off the spot of clothing he had grabbed hold of.

The rabbi, appearing quite overcome, only nodded while shuffling toward the door. A slight breeze blew from the sea and cooled the night. It would not be a horrible place to live, especially in summer. It was very hot in Nazareth, and when the southern winds blew off the desert, there was no fresh sea air to dull the bite as there was here.

The walk was a short one. The synagogue was near the sea, and Simon's home lay only a block away and near the shore. Simon was sitting on a bench near the front door, sharpening knives by the light of a large clay lamp filled with fish oil. He did not move as they entered the gate.

"You have agreed to our conditions?" he asked, his finger running along the edge of the knife.

"There is one matter of importance that he wishes to discuss with . . . your daughter," the rabbi said.

"The house and its location," Simon said assuredly. He looked at Matthias. "She is not here."

"Where is she?" Matthias asked.

"Mending nets."

Matthias left without another word. Joseph watched him go and wished him luck. Simon handed Joseph a sharpening stone and a knife. "You had better busy yourself. It may be a while. Rabbi, you are free to go inside and start writing up the contract. Even though it cannot be made official until the divorce, she wants it prepared. It will be needed before morning."

"But I don't know what to—"

"Ten shekels and a house in Capernaum. It won't change," Simon said with a knowing grin. "Matthias does not know Salome like I do."

* * *

Matthias found Salome sitting on the stone-and-mortar dock, a large, brightly burning clay lamp lighting her work. He watched her from the shadows for a moment, trying to get up the courage to actually approach her. He had never been good at speaking to women, and though he felt strongly to have this one as his wife, his courage had begun to wane on his walk here. He had never wanted anything more in his life, and if he said the wrong thing . . .

She looked even more beautiful in the light of the lamp, and when she tipped her head, the light glistened in her dark hair and lit up her eyes. Those beautiful eyes.

She stood and began folding the net. "I could use your help," she said without looking his direction. Matthias was startled that she had sensed his presence but found he could not move. His feet seemed to have turned to lead and his mouth had gone dry, but he needed to rub the sweat from his palms. Licking his lips, he stepped onto the dock, stumbling once on its uneven surface, then twice. He cursed his clumsiness under his breath. Surely this was no way to begin!

"I am no fisherman. I—" he began lamely.

"Take hold of that corner and hand it to me," she ordered.

He picked it up and did as he was told.

"Now that one." She pointed.

He did as he was told again, and she deftly began laying the net in order. Before he could figure out exactly what she had done, it was folded and ready.

"It goes there," she said, pointing to the front section of the boat.

Matthias picked up the net and stepped into the boat. The net was not light, and he struggled to keep his balance as the boat moved under his weight.

"You will get used to it," she said.

Her voice was deeper than most women's but still very feminine, at least to his ears, and he fell in love with the sound of it.

"Get used to it?"

"If I bear your children, my father will need you to fish with him." Her smile showed two rows of even teeth, though there was a slight separation between the top middle teeth. Another thing to love.

"I am a carpenter, not a fisherman," Matthias explained.

"You can be both and make us rich." She smiled again, her arms folded across her waist as she stood on the dock and watched him.

He couldn't help the smile. "I live in Nazareth."

"You have a house in Nazareth, but we must live here, in Capernaum. I will not leave my father alone."

Though he cringed slightly at the thought of leaving Nazareth, he knew from her tone that this was not negotiable. He did like Capernaum, the sea, and she was probably right—he could make a better living here. With a wife and child to care for, it was probably best. "How soon can we marry?" Matthias asked.

"There is the divorce, but after that . . ." She shrugged. "I have been through the formalities and see no need to go through them again, but family will want to honor us. A week, maybe two. You can get a good start on a house."

He wondered if she and her former husband had made a home, if she still lived in it, but decided it did not matter. He would not want to share another man's house with her.

"What is our daughter's name?" he asked.

Salome smiled at him. "Mara. She saw you today. She thinks you will make a good husband."

"I like her already." He stepped from the boat to stand directly in front of her.

"You know why my husband left me?" she asked, looking into his eyes.

"He followed after the way of Essenes."

"And will you follow after such fanatics?" she wondered stiffly.

"God teaches that a man and woman should become one in the Lord. How we worship and whom we follow will be decided together." He wet his lips and cleared his throat, forcing the words from his heart into the cool air of evening. "I will love you for your life. There will be no following after other gods, no desertions for fanatical reasons, no divorces."

"Take my hand," she said, extending hers.

Matthias hesitated, then wiped his hands on his linen tunic before taking her hand.

"Your size puts people off, but today I saw your eyes. You are a gentle man, a man whose heart is bigger than both his fists. When you returned to speak with Father, I knew what you wanted to ask, and I knew, even then, that it was God's will that I agree to marry you. I will honor you, Matthias ben Levi, but I will not be your servant. I will be your equal, or we will go our separate ways tonight."

Matthias could not believe how hard his heart pounded, how much he ached to take her in his arms! He had never felt such emotion and choked back a shout of joy that threatened to escape his trembling lips, leaving him with nothing to do but nod, then clear his throat and croak an answer. "Then we will marry."

She quickly looked around, found no one, and stepped forward and planted a light kiss on his lips before pulling away to speak. "Come then, the rabbi will be waiting to make arrangements."

Matthias walked beside her. Was love this easy for everyone? Could it be that this was what Joseph felt and had spoken of so many times and that he, Matthias, had made light of? Never again. He understood now. There was nothing as wonderful as this. Nothing.

CHAPTER 7

They returned to work the next morning, Matthias hardly able to contain himself. The news quickly spread, and everyone congratulated him or mocked him in jest. Just after they began their work, the foreman's assistant handed Joseph a small parchment tied with a leather cord. "A man who passed through Nazareth was asked to deliver it. He dropped it off here early this morning before going north."

Joseph nodded his thanks but was already breaking the seal on the scroll and unrolling it with shaking hands.

"What is it?" Matthias asked.

Joseph searched for the signature, then smiled. "A letter from Mary. She has returned from Juttah!"

Matthias slapped him on the back, making Joseph wince. "Ah, God has blessed us both this day, hasn't He?"

Joseph hardly heard Matthias, his eyes on the carefully scribed words of the page.

Dearest Joseph,

I have missed you these long months, but going to Juttah was required by God and has helped me accept what has happened to me. There is much we must speak of. Come home soon.

Mary

Joseph's eyes focused on a few words. "There is much we must speak of." He wiped the dust from his palms. The wedding. It must be the wedding. His eyes went to another part of the letter. "Accept what has happened to me." What did she mean? What had happened?

"What is it, Joseph?" Matthias queried.

"I don't know, but I must go to Nazareth immediately."

"She is well? There is no trouble?"

"No . . . I don't know . . . The letter . . ." He took a deep breath. "No. Everything is fine, but I must go back to Nazareth tonight."

"Yes, I see it in your eyes, and I can see that it is not nothing." He paused. "I will go with you—"

"No, no. You have your own wedding to prepare for now and a house to build. I will return to help you as soon as I can." He began putting his tools into their bag. "Tell the overseer that I had to leave and don't know when I will be able to return. Tell him why." Joseph was already heading for the western gate and spoke over his shoulder. "Shalom, Matthias, and God be with you and Salome. I will tell the village of your good fortune." He stopped, then went back and gripped Matthias firmly by the hand, then they embraced. "Let us know when the wedding will be."

Matthias grinned. "Go, and God go with you." With that, he gently pushed his friend toward the west gate.

* * *

The bath was both refreshing and cleansing, and Joseph removed himself with some reluctance. A sudden storm had come up during the night, forcing him to take refuge in a stand of trees near a dried-up spring. By morning, the spring was flowing clean and had formed a pool in the basin below it. Wet, tired, and dirty from travel, he had removed his clothes, washed them, and lay them on the rocks to dry while he bathed. He could not approach Mary in filth and looking like a half-drowned rat, exhausted from his journey. He must prepare himself, get some rest, and be presentable.

During his walk, Joseph had thought things through, convincing himself there was nothing to worry about. Though the message raised questions, he was sure there was a good explanation. He would go to her home, announce his plans to finish the wedding in a week's time, then talk about her trip. Everything would be as it should be.

His clothes were still damp from washing, but knowing the hot sun would dry them even as he wore them, he dressed anyway, picked up his toolbox, and began the climb up the slope leading to Nazareth.

Halfway up, he saw a man with a young boy, their flocks grazing alongside the hill below. Nostalgia rolled over him as he watched the man pull a scroll from his pack and unroll it to read and to teach his son. It seemed like only yesterday that he and his father were on these slopes, their sheep grazing peacefully on rich grasses while they talked of their care, then studied together. How he missed him! And his mother!

His father had a particular passion for the Torah—a passion Joseph saw in few others, and a passion that he had passed on to his only son. He owed his father more than he could ever repay.

"You are a son of David; you should know the law better than any other," his father would say. But, at first, Joseph had been a reluctant believer in study. His love lay in working with his hands, herding his father's small flock in the fields or pruning the trees and harvesting the wheat of a neighbor's fields so they could share in the bounty. Going to synagogue school was not something he enjoyed, but he had been obedient, and a love for scripture had followed. Even greater was the satisfaction that it was his knowledge of the Torah that Joachim had seen and admired when selecting a husband for his daughter.

There had been other blessings as well. Through study, Joseph had discovered the wonder of God's presence in the Torah. He also learned that the interpretation sometimes placed on God's laws by scribes and rabbis was not always in keeping with the spirit of what God told Moses and His other prophets. While respecting the words of the rabbis, Joseph carefully noted when some strained at the letter but ignored the deeper intent. From this knowledge had come a deep desire to seek to please God, not just obey rules that pleased men.

He trudged on, the sun's rays replacing the cool morning air with their heat. Joseph was only a mile from the village now and thought he could smell the cooking fires. He had never known any other home than Nazareth, and he relished each return. Even after his father and mother died, he hadn't considered living any other place, especially with a sister to care for.

When his parents died within two years of one another, Joseph had taken over his father's carpentry shop and cared for his younger sister until he could arrange a marriage for her. His sister was pretty, a good worker, and religious, so it was easy to find her a good husband. For some time, his sister and her husband lived in a neighboring village, where the husband worked as a steward for one of the large landowners, making a better wage than even Joseph, but the landowner had purchased other properties in the north, and they had been moved there. His sister's husband was a good man, an honest man, and he treated his wife with love and respect. They had two children now, both boys, strong, a bit spoiled by their father and their uncle Joseph when he saw them, which wasn't often now. He hoped the little family could come to his wedding. If not, then as soon as Mary and he were married, they must travel north and see them.

His heart pumped a little harder as he thought of the wedding. All was ready. The house was as good as any in the village; he made good money and had even saved a little. Mary would be able to hold her head high.

Finally, he reached the top of the hill and looked down on the village, his eyes immediately falling on Mary's house. The walls prevented him from seeing into the courtyard, but Anna was sitting alone on the roof grinding grain.

"Hello, Joseph."

Joseph looked to his left to find Lebbaeus sitting on a rock and smiling. Joseph greeted the boy with a wide smile of his own. "Lebbaeus! Good to see you. How is the carving going?"

Lebbaeus withdrew his hand from behind his back and extended a wooden object to Joseph, who took it. It was a plate with detailed flowers carved around its edges so intricately that Joseph had to rub his eyes and focus more carefully.

"Beautiful, Lebbaeus. Well done!"

The boy beamed as Joseph handed the plate back.

"Have you come to arrange the final celebration?" Lebbaeus asked.

Joseph smiled back. "Yes, I have. It will be in one week, and you, my young friend, are invited as our special guest."

The boy brightened even more, then a dark look crossed his face. "She is at home, Joseph. Her sister says she . . . she is not well."

"I'm sure all is well," Joseph replied. His stomach felt a twinge of pain once again, and he began walking down the hill. "Keep working on your carving, Lebbaeus. You will be a great artisan someday." He forced a smile back at the boy.

Illness! So this was the trouble. His heart pounded against his rib cage as he hurried down the road, his mind already pleading with God that whatever it was would be a simple thing, something easily taken care of, something he could resolve, even as his stomach wrenched with the deeper knowledge that there was more.

* * *

Mary sat on a stiff-backed chair in front of the fireplace, her father pacing near the door. Having sent the other children to the fields or to other chores away from the house, her mother sat outside grinding grain. The three of them knew Joseph would come today, and they waited anxiously for his arrival.

Mary's time at Juttah had been a mixed blessing. Although Elisabeth and Zacharias rejoiced along with her at the first signs of her pregnancy, it had become a time of sickness that she thought would never end. Though she knew God would never let anything happen to the baby, she was confined to her bed by an inability to keep her food down. Her aged relatives had taken care of her every need as best they could, but it was still a difficult time. She had thought of sending for her mother, but a calm reassurance had come that told her everything would be all right—and that having Anna make the journey to sit by Mary's bedside and watch her go through what every other woman went through would be foolishness. With God's help, Mary would deal with it, and they need not worry. She carried Israel's future King and the Son of the Most High God. Such a child would never lose his life in the womb. God simply would not allow it, but He would not take away Mary's discomfort, either. She was mortal and would suffer the mortal pains of giving the child life, but God would look after the baby.

In Mary's third month, her nausea lessened, and she returned to a somewhat normal routine, although Zacharias insisted that neither Elisabeth nor Mary work at any strenuous chore that might endanger their children. Zacharias had taken in a woman and her two sons who were left destitute when her husband had taken ill and died. The boys worked the large garden, took care of the animals, chopped wood, and carried water, while their mother did the household chores. For their services, they were given shelter, food, and clothing, and they were happy for it. Zacharias also taught the boys reading, writing, and the study of the Torah, and treated them as if they were his own kin.

Knowing all was cared for, the two expectant mothers had sat together under the old olive tree in the side yard or on the roof in the afternoon sun and prepared yarn or knitted clothing for the two boys they carried. They also helped prepare meals and labored at light chores while they visited. In the evenings, Zacharias would open his scrolls and show them scripture, then write his interpretation on a wax tablet. Some were about their two sons, but most were about the future of Israel under the Messiah, His mission, and the reign of peace that would surely follow. It was overwhelming for Mary and a bit frightening, especially when the scriptures talked of the cleansing of Israel and the destruction of the wicked. How could an earthly king, especially one raised as a peasant, possibly bring about such things? It was simply too great for her mind to grasp, leaving her to ponder it all in her heart. She realized that only time would bring true understanding.

Finally, Elisabeth's son had been born. Though he had more than enough hair and a ruddy complexion, the child was perfectly formed and immediately alert to all around him. It seemed like the entire community came to see him, giving congratulations to Elisabeth and Zacharias, celebrating with them in a glorious event that all had thought would never come. On the eighth day, Zacharias's good friend, Jeremiah, led a small procession of priests and their families to the house for the boy's circumcision. It was a glorious and happy time as they paraded into the yard, singing a song of devotion to Israel, then took on a more somber tone as the procedure began.

The cutting and the shedding of blood elicited painful cries from the infant that made even Mary want to step in. She knew it was worse for Elisabeth, who kept her place, allowing the ceremony to proceed until the rabbi placed his hands on the child's head and gave him a blessing and called him Zacharias.

"No, no, his name is to be John," Elisabeth said adamantly.

"There is none of your kindred that are called by this name," answered a surprised rabbi. "Surely the name should be that of his father, or at least his grandfather." He glanced at Zacharias, who could not hear, but who was straining to understand the problem, concern etched in the aged lines of his face. Finally, Elisabeth stepped to her husband and patted him gently on the arm, while taking a writing tablet and quickly putting words on its waxen surface. *They want to call him after you. I told them—*

Zacharias stopped her writing and nodded, then took the tablet, pressed out Elisabeth's writings, and used the stylus to write some of his own. *His name is John.*

Of course, all marveled at this. Tradition indicated using the names of the family. It was a way of passing on one's heritage, especially in the case of the eldest son, and for Zacharias to break this tradition, especially since he was a priest and his son would surely follow in his footsteps, was difficult for them to understand.

The rabbi took a deep breath, "Are you sure?" he asked rather loudly.

Zacharias seemed stunned by his words, then touched his ear with a smile while clearing his throat. "Yes, I am sure. It is God's will."

The shock of hearing his voice caused a wave of muttered speech to fill the room. The rabbi, frozen by this sudden turn of events, did not move.

Zacharias smiled. "Go ahead, Rabbi. It is all right." He smiled while putting an arm around a stunned but relieved and happy Elisabeth.

The rabbi carefully completed the ceremony. When he was finished, Zacharias gently took John in his arms, tears in the elderly father's eyes. "And now I will bless my son."

The room echoed with the murmurs of amazement, then grew very still as Zacharias looked down with gentle kindness at his new son and spoke words Mary would never forget.

"Blessed be the Lord God of Israel," he said. "For he hath visited and redeemed his people." With wet eyes, he had looked at Mary and with clarity spoke words that went straight to her heart. "And hath raised up an horn of salvation for us in the house of his servant

David; as he spake by the mouth of his holy prophets, which have been since the world began; that we should be saved from our enemies, and from the hand of all that hate us; to perform the mercy promised to our fathers, and to remember his holy covenant; the oath which he sware to our father Abraham, that he would grant unto us, that we being delivered out of the hand of our enemies might serve him without fear, in holiness and righteousness before him, all the days of our lives." He paused, his aged eyes focused on Mary, tears flowing down his cheeks to match her own. He spoke of her son, of the glorious Messiah. She felt Elisabeth's arm enfold her waist, felt the warmth and comfort of her cousin against the womb where lay the Son of God. It was so wonderful and yet so strange.

In the next moment, Zacharias had looked down at his son again, speaking directly to the child as if he could surely understand. "And thou, child, shalt be called the prophet of the Highest: for thou shalt go before the face of the Lord to prepare his ways; to give knowledge of salvation unto his people by the remission of their sins." He looked at Elisabeth. "Through the tender mercy of our God; whereby the dawn from on high hath visited us, to give light to them that sit in darkness and in the shadow of death, to guide our feet into the way of peace." With that, he had lifted the child to his chest and bent to kiss him tenderly on the cheek.

The room erupted with praise and wonder at the words, and for days the miracle of Zacharias's renewed voice and the wonder of his blessing was on everyone's lips. As she listened to the gossip, Mary discovered that few of them truly understood what it all meant, how miraculous it all really was and would be. Though all Israel expected their Messiah to come someday, it was nearly impossible to believe he would come now and even more difficult to understand that another, a child that would surely grow up in their midst, would prepare his way.

On the third day after the blessing, the sudden knowledge came to Mary that she must go home, back to Nazareth, back to Joseph. It was time to face the coming of her own son.

It had been hard to leave. She had found safety and peace at Juttah, and she knew that would now end. She needed Joseph, his support and strength. To hide here longer, to put off the inevitable, would only make things harder. She was beginning to expand at her waist, and he must be told. Only then could he decide.

As she returned with the help of Jeremiah and his son, Ebenezer, it was with some apprehension. Though she prayed for God to show her what to say, how to approach Joseph, no real answer came. Even now, as she sat here waiting, she did not know. God would surely have to help her, tell her what to say, because her mind was as empty as a clay jar!

"He comes," Anna said from the doorway. She motioned to Joachim. "Come, they must be alone for this."

Joachim seemed paralyzed, sweat on his brow, his eyes firmly fixed on Mary.

"Joachim, did you hear me?" Anna asked.

"Yes, yes, I heard you." He forced himself to his feet and stepped hesitantly to the door before glancing back at Mary. "Daughter, I . . ."

She blinked, then smiled. "It is all right, Father. God will help us."

He gave a concerned smile, then forced himself to leave the house.

* * *

As Joachim walked into the sunlight, he saw Joseph opening the tall gate of the outer wall of the courtyard and quickly used a rag to wipe the sweat from his brow.

"Joseph," he said, forcing a pleasant expression and extending a hand of welcome. "It is good to see you. How are things in Capernaum?"

Joseph glanced nervously at the house, then back at Joachim. "Growing," was all he could think of to say. "Mary is . . . Is she here?"

Joachim's smile turned to a furrowed brow of concern. "Yes . . . but—"

"She is in the house, Joseph," Anna said while eyeing her husband darkly. "She waits for you, and we will keep you no longer."

Joseph tried to step forward but was prevented by Joachim's firm grip on his arm.

"Joachim," Anna said firmly, "let him go."

Joachim released Joseph as if the young man's arm were hot, and nervously chuckled before turning quickly toward the pens. Anna watched Joseph go inside, then closed her eyes and said a quiet prayer.

"Dear Lord, help him believe." With that, she sat down on the bench near the wall and waited.

* * *

"Shalom," Joseph said at the door, his eyes trying to adjust to the darkness of the room.

"Shalom, husband," Mary said softly. She rose to her feet and walked to him. "It is wonderful to see you."

She was standing so close that he could smell the soap she used to wash her hair, could feel her breath wafting against his clothing. He wanted desperately to reach out, to hold her in his arms, but he could not. His eyes searched hers. There was something wrong. It was there, in her face, and it made his stomach churn.

"And . . . and you," he said. His voice sounded scratchy, and he cleared his throat as his eyes continued to search her face for answers. It was as if she had aged several years. Her face—different somehow but even more beautiful! This was not the face of a sick woman, but there was something . . . "You . . ." His voice broke, and he cleared his throat again. "You are well?"

She laughed lightly. "As well as I can be."

"Your journey, it went smoothly then?"

She nodded. "Yes. Zacharias and Elisabeth have a new son. His name is John."

"John, but—"

"It is not a family name." She smiled. "Yes, I know, but it is the name given him by God."

He felt the sweet touch of her hand on his arm, felt her pull, coaxing his own hand from his side. She lifted it and kissed it softly, then looked into his eyes. He could see concern in her face. "Joseph . . ."

She looked down as if losing her will, then regained her composure and looked up again. "Joseph, Elisabeth isn't the only one promised a son." She paused, watching his look change to that of bewilderment, then took a deep breath and spoke the words she knew he would hear with difficulty. "We are to have one as well."

CHAPTER 8

Joseph would not remember leaving the house, nor would he remember wandering in the fields, his mind fully occupied with Mary's words, then the touch of her stomach when she placed his hand there. He tried to understand, tried with all his heart, but the more he tried, the worse he felt. How could she expect him to believe such a story? How? Did she think him a fool? And to blame her . . . her . . . lust upon God! Blasphemy!

Oh, how his heart ached! It could not be! And yet it was. He looked at his fingers. He had touched her. She *was* with child. He had felt the blood drain from his head as if someone had opened a spigot in his knees. It had been all he could do to stumble from the room. She tried to hold onto him, her sobs filling his head as he tore away and ran into the fields, where his tears drenched the parched earth and his anguish forced cries to heaven.

Then his pain turned to betrayed anger. A child! And it was not his child! She had lain with another and had made up this desperate story to cover her sin. He would not let her pull him into such a disgrace. Never!

Leaving the fields, he went to the synagogue to find the rabbi. He would divorce her. She left him no choice.

The rabbi was not at home. Leaving no message, Joseph trudged home, then to his shop, angry, confused, dejected. He aimlessly busied himself by slapping a board into the wooden vise and clamping it tight, then picking up his shaving tool and mindlessly attacking the wood. After a dozen strokes, his anger and frustration overcame him, and he threw the shaver at the far wall, where it hit with a bang before falling to the floor.

A vision? The Son of God? How could this be? It could not. His heart ached even worse.

He heard someone on the path and turned to see Joachim standing at the door. He grabbed a saw and busied himself cutting the board, hoping Joachim would go away.

"Joseph, I . . ."

"I have no time to talk, Joachim. Please leave."

Joachim sighed as he turned to leave, then hesitated and finally turned back.

"She is telling you the truth, Joseph," he said firmly.

"Ah, then this . . . this angel appeared to you as well," Joseph exclaimed.

"No, he did not, but—"

Joseph removed the saw from the cut and threw it onto the workbench while trying to keep his voice calm. "It is impossible, Joachim! We both know it." He released the vise with a violent twist of his hand.

Joachim stepped inside and closed the door. "Mary has not betrayed you, Joseph."

"She has been gone for more than three months. Were you with her all that time? Do you know for sure that . . . that nothing happened while she was away?"

Joachim did not answer immediately, his mind searching for words. "I . . . I don't know what to say," he murmured weakly.

Joseph turned, his face flushed with anger. "She has betrayed me for another, and you have nothing to say?" He turned away and grabbed the wood from the vise, throwing it aside in disgust.

"Silence, you fool!" Joachim ordered through clenched teeth.

Joseph was startled by the strength in the voice of the usually timid Joachim, and he winced at the power in the rebuke.

"Mary could never do such a thing, and if you believe she could, then you do not deserve her! Do you honestly think Mary could make up such a story? Can you believe, even for a moment, that such a deception could force its way into such a pure heart?" He stepped closer to Joseph as if he might strike him with the back of his hand. In reaction, Joseph stepped back, then turned away.

"Leave," Joseph breathed. "Before one of us does something he might regret."

"I already have such a regret! I am the one who chose you as my daughter's husband, and here, at the moment she needs you most, you run away like . . . like some ill-tempered, spoiled child!"

Joseph turned, his face flushed with anger, but he bit his lip against the words that leaped into his throat. He grabbed a nearby half-finished table leg and slammed it onto his work table, then into his vise.

After a long moment, Joseph leaned against the table, his head down. "I will see the rabbi as soon as I can control my feelings. I will put her away."

"Divorce her? But they will stone her for adultery! You cannot—"

"Joachim, you know the law. I will do it secretly, before two witnesses. There will be no stoning, but I will not take her to wife. Adultery is a great wickedness and a sin against God. I will not live with such a woman. Now leave me, Joachim. Leave me alone!"

Joachim turned to the door and was ready to pull it open by its wooden latch, but his hand would not, could not, lift the handle. He took a deep breath. "Don't do this, Joseph. If you do, you will regret it the rest of your life. She is telling you the truth. I know it!" He opened the door and left, closing it firmly behind him.

Weak and weary to the bone, Joseph collapsed into a nearby chair, his shoulders slumped, his face in his hands. The sun set, and the dark of night encircled him, but still he did not move, his mind a jumble of thoughts and emotions, his heart aching with such pain that he thought surely death would come, wanted it to come. Always his mind returned to the same fate. He must put her away. Privately, but it must be done. There was no other choice. He could not live with a woman who had done such a thing.

Tears sprang to his eyes and he wept, the weight of this final decision falling heavily upon his shoulders and flowing into his heart, nearly breaking it. Finally, a few hours before dawn, exhausted, he fell into a leaden sleep.

Tomorrow he would see the rabbi.

* * *

Mary had just drifted to sleep when she heard pounding on the front door and immediately awoke. Her father was already up, struggling to get to the door, as she tried to make sense of this sudden chaos. Was that Joseph's voice? What would he be doing here this time of night? Or was it morning? What was happening?

She sat up and tried to blink the fog from her eyes when suddenly Joseph's face appeared very close to her own, the dim rays from a lamp ignited by her mother lighting up his dark eyes, and glistening in the tears that ran down his cheeks. He was kneeling at her bedside. Reactively, she pulled the blanket to her chin.

"Joseph? What is it? What can this mean?"

He took her hand with both of his and kissed it lightly, then began sobbing, his chin humbly resting against his chest.

She glanced at her mother, who gave her a slight nod in return, then a shrug. "With God, nothing is impossible," Anna said softly.

Mary ran her fingers over Joseph's hair, then kissed his head lightly.

The other children slept in the same room and were trying to make sense of what was happening, even as they rubbed the sleep from their eyes.

"What is it, Mother?" Ruth asked while blinking against the light of the lamp.

"Is that Joseph?" Dinah asked with a pained voice. "Can't he see it is not even sunup yet?" she groaned.

"Turn off the lamp!" Josiah moaned.

"Hush, all of you," Anna demanded. "Get up! Out, out!" she said, grabbing each child, bringing them to their feet. "Mary and Joseph need a moment. Out with you!"

"But—" protested Josiah as he was prodded to his feet by his mother's strong hands.

"Go!" Anna said forcefully. "To the roof. You can sleep there for now! Out with you!"

"But, Mother," Josiah whined, "it is too cold on the roof at this time of year, you know that."

"Then to the barn! Sleep with the animals, sleep . . . sleep in the hay, but out! Now!"

Mary's brother hesitated, and their mother pushed him harder. Reluctantly, he stepped across the threshold and into the darkness, Ruth and Dinah stumbling after him, with Joachim shushing and herding them toward the steps to the hay stall. Anna smiled and quickly thanked God for His miracle as she closed the door behind her and the rest of the family.

It was a few long minutes before Joseph finally got control of his emotions and lifted his head to look into Mary's eyes. "Please," he begged in a whisper, "please forgive me. I . . . I doubted you and—"

She placed a finger gently against his lips. "Shh, it is all right." She smiled lovingly at him, then stroked his cheek with her hand. "God has shown you, hasn't He."

Joseph nodded. "A dream. It . . . it was so clear, Mary! An angel . . . his message . . . I . . ." He bit his lip against the tears that once more flowed from the corners of his eyes.

"I love you, Joseph," Mary managed, getting to her knees and taking his face in her hands. "God has chosen a good man to raise His Son."

Joseph took her gently into his arms and held her close. "I will not fail you," he said softly. "I will not fail either of you."

"Yes, I know," Mary answered. "I know." She wrapped her arms tightly around her husband and slowly closed her eyes. Nor had God failed her. Joseph knew.

CHAPTER 9

Joseph and Joachim made arrangements for the final wedding ceremony the next day. Six days later, the celebration was held with nearly the entire village of Nazareth in attendance. Even though Mary had been with child for more than four months, her slight build and the loose layers of clothing she wore—as all Nazarene women wore in the colder months of fall and winter—concealed her condition. The wedding was a happy event neither Joseph nor Mary would forget. The angel Gabriel's promise had been fulfilled, and Mary had become Joseph's wife.

But the wedding required one small deception. For the marriage to be more than an espousal, consummation was required. The entire village assumed that this took place the night of the celebration, but Joseph did not touch Mary. She was with child, and there would be no physical intimacy between them until the baby was born and until at least the initial seven days of her purification had passed.

After the ceremony, Mary's waistline continued to gradually expand, but she did not grow large, giving little reason for rumors about the actual timing of her pregnancy. Joseph hoped it would remain so, but the last month of her pregnancy, she suddenly blossomed, raising a few eyebrows. He cringed to think what might happen when she actually gave birth months before she should. Surely he and Mary would be accused of consummating their marriage prematurely, and they and the child would have to bear the stigma for the rest of their lives.

But the angel had come. Whatever they must suffer for this child they would suffer. It would please both of them to do so.

He thought back to that night. After hours of battling his feelings and a determination to put Mary away, he had felt the weight of exhaustion nearly smother him in a deep sleep. Then the dream had burst into his mind with an explosion of light unlike anything Joseph had ever experienced. In the midst of what seemed to be the sun, he had beheld a personage. Quickly, the light subsided and the image appeared more clearly—clearly enough that Joseph realized it was not just a man, at least not like any other man, but someone greater, someone sent from the very presence of God. Joseph would never forget the sublime look on the angel's face or the sound of his voice. It filled him from head to foot, and the words squashed his doubts more easily than a gristmill turned hard wheat to powder. Mary had not lied. The child she carried was a very special child—a child conceived by powers beyond Joseph's ability to even begin to understand. But he did understand that the child was not his son but God's, and that he would be Israel's Messiah. In fact, in all his life, Joseph had never understood anything so deeply! Nor was there any doubt what his role must be—protector, earthly father, guide, teacher—he must be all these to God's child.

Joseph had also been chastened by his own guilt. Even though he had felt enfolded by a spiritual warmth he could not explain, he had also felt self-loathing for his thoughts and his treatment of Mary, a guilt that still pinched his heart on occasion. Even though he knew that both God and Mary had forgiven him, it was not so easy to forgive himself.

But over the last few months the weight of guilt had given way to fear. What if he failed? How did one protect such a child? Teach him? Prepare him for what lay ahead? Joseph had spent many hours, both at the synagogue and in his own house, reading the Torah and the prophets, not only learning all that was said about the child, but praying that he would be led, taught, and shown what to do to protect and teach him. His fears had slowly subsided, and the Holy Spirit had comforted him. There had been no further dreams, no revelations; but inside, in the depth of his soul, he had come to know that those would come if needed, that God would make him equal to the task if he would do all he could. This knowledge gave Joseph some peace of mind, but he also understood that God would not do all the work for him and Mary. They would need to be prepared, to watch over and protect the child, just as he was currently doing by trying to keep the child's identity a secret. But Joseph knew God would watch, and if the child were threatened by something Joseph and Mary could not control, Joseph knew He would send protection. Nothing would prevent this child from completing his appointed mission. God would see to that.

"Joseph?"

Joseph snapped out of his thoughts and turned to find Mary in the doorway between the house and his shop. She grew more beautiful each day! She was such a blessing to him, while her calling as the mother of the Messiah also kept him in awe. At first, he had felt that even to touch her would be wrong, but she made it clear that though her womb housed the Messiah, her divine calling had not changed her. She was human and needed affection, and she needed to be held. It made him love her even more.

"Yes, my love, what is it?" he answered.

"While at the well, I saw Salome. She says that you asked her and Matthias to dinner."

Joseph's eyes opened wide, and he turned to Mary. He had completely forgotten. "I . . . I am sorry. I should have remembered to tell you. I—"

Mary chuckled. "Never mind. I would have been disappointed if you had not asked them to come. Salome is wonderful company, and to see Matthias such a changed man . . ." She rolled her eyes. "My goodness, what marriage can do to a man!"

Joseph laughed. "Indeed!"

Since his final marriage ceremony three months earlier, Matthias had truly changed. The long, wild, unkempt hair and beard were now well trimmed and neat. His clothes, seldom washed when he was single, were not only clean, but also free of cuts and tears and ragged edges. And he had become a fisherman! A rather good fisherman, from everything Joseph heard.

"You know that Mara is not with them this time?" Joseph asked.

"Yes, she was ill and they did not think it wise to bring her along. She is staying with her grandfather."

Joseph sensed the sadness in her voice, feeling the same in his own heart. Mara was a joy to have around. Helpful, inquisitive, and very opinionated, she was always a flurry of action, and she loved Matthias like he was her real father. Five years of age, she would sit atop his large shoulders, pointing out this and that while asking questions about everything from people to flowers and bugs. But Matthias never seemed to grow weary of her questions, or of carrying her about. Joseph saw in his friend's eyes that it was not just Salome who had captured his heart. Mara held it in her tiny hands as surely as Salome held it in hers.

Mary came to the door. "They have good news."

Joseph grinned. "Yes, I know."

Mary seemed surprised. "But Salome told him not to tell a soul."

"And according to Matthias, Salome was to tell no one either." He grinned. "Do you remember when we first started telling others about your pregnancy, how exciting it was?"

She chuckled. "I remember you journeyed to Capernaum to tell Matthias yourself. Then off to half a dozen other villages to tell your friends."

"And it was all over Nazareth before breakfast. One trip to the well, and you left me no choice! If I wanted to tell someone who would say something other than 'Yes, Joseph, Mary has already told us,' I had to go to Capernaum!"

They laughed lightly, then Joseph sobered a bit. "I remember how hard it was not to tell everything, to shout it from the housetops."

"I felt the same, and so did Mother and Father," she said, touching her stomach gently. "You know, it is quite an amazing thing that Mother has kept quiet. She has always been one of the worst when it came to gossip, and to stay silent while having in her grasp such knowledge must be difficult for her, and yet it was my father who nearly gave the secret away."

Joseph grinned. "I remember."

They had been at Sabbath meeting when Joachim suddenly went up to the podium to read. Joachim did not do such a thing often, and all were curious as to which scripture he might read. The room had grown very quiet. He had turned the scrolls again and again, his eyes carefully searching for a verse. Then he had read from Isaiah—"And there shall come forth a rod out of the stem of Jesse, and a Branch shall grow out of his roots: and the spirit of the Lord shall rest upon him, the spirit of wisdom and understanding, the spirit of counsel and might, the spirit of knowledge and of the fear of the Lord."

At that point, Joseph had felt a sudden anxiety and exchanged a desperate glance with Mary as Joachim continued. "And shall make him of quick understanding in the fear of the Lord: and he shall not judge after the sight of his eyes, neither reprove after the hearing of his ears: But with righteousness shall he judge the poor, and reprove with equity for the meek of the earth: and he shall smite the earth with the rod of his mouth, and with the breath of his lips shall he slay the wicked."

Joseph and Mary both knew Joachim was about to tell all, and they were near a state of desperate panic, nearly paralyzed by his incautious act. Joseph managed to catch Joachim's attention and shake his head slowly left and right, the look of fire in his eyes warning of the horrible result if his father-in-law went further, but it seemed only to strengthen Joachim's resolve. Even when Joachim looked up at the balcony where his wife sat, her dark brown eyes threatening a storm he would never see the end of, he seemed determined to speak of Mary's child.

But in the end he could not, and the crowd began to whisper. After a few seconds of silence followed by muffled chuckles and prayers from Joseph and Mary, Joachim finally gave up and left the podium without saying a word more.

Joseph had nearly collapsed with relief and gently pushed his way through the crowd surrounding the Torah stand to find Joachim sitting on a bench near the door.

"I nearly gave it away," Joachim had mumbled weakly.

"Yes, I know, but you stopped yourself."

"No, no, you saw me! I would have said it if . . . if God had not stopped me. I tried to speak. In my pride, I wanted to say it, felt I must tell them, that I had a right to tell them, but God had me by the throat, Joseph. He would have strangled the life out of me if I had spoken even one word."

Joseph saw the fear on his father-in-law's face and knew. There was no need to scold him. He had learned a hard lesson, one he would never forget, and except for some scathing words from Anna after the meeting, it had been left behind.

Mary chuckled. "Mother threatens him every day now. If he told a single soul, I am afraid she would make him very miserable."

Joseph grinned. "Of that I am sure." His look sobered. "Fortunately, he has not been tempted again." He fingered a piece of wood, his eyes on Mary. "Are you sure you feel up to company?"

"I feel tired, and, at the moment . . ." She gave him a wicked smile, then poked him in the side with a stiff finger, "a bit mean." She tried to dart away.

Deftly, he caught her hand and swung her around and into his arms, where he held her tightly against him. "You won't get away that easy." He looked into her dark eyes, then felt her stomach kick against his own. "The boy protects his mother."

Mary sighed as she laid her head on his shoulder. "Lately he seems to push on all sides. I know I have bruises."

"He will want his freedom soon."

"And rightly so. It has been more than eight months."

Joseph's face showed his worry. "Are you determined . . . traveling to Bethlehem . . . It is such a long way, Mary, and not easy at any time, but now, in your condition, possibly . . . possibly you should stay and prepare for him."

She looked up at Joseph, the set of her chin showing her determination. "We have talked of this before. You know I will not stay here alone."

The edict had been read to the village by a tax collector from Sepphoris. The Romans had declared a census, and all male members of families must be counted. To make matters worse, for political reasons, the great Sanhedrin at Jerusalem had required that the counting be done in the city of one's ancestors so that they could number the members of each tribe. For Joseph, that meant a long journey to Bethlehem, one he had felt they must delay because the child's birth drew near.

But Mary insisted they go. The village gossips were speaking of Mary's sudden growth in size and what it might mean. The word *adultery* had been whispered about, and Mary had heard it. She had been in tears when he returned home that day, and it had been hard to comfort her. That night, she said she felt that they must leave Nazareth, at least for the present time. Deeply saddened for her, and angry at the village women he knew would never accept what had really happened even if he told them, Joseph had agreed.

Their decision to go had quickly stopped some of the gossip. After all, why would a woman expecting a child right away, especially her first, travel such a distance? Added to Mary's reputation as a faithful daughter of Israel, even the die-hard know-it-alls were forced to leave it alone, at least for the moment. Joseph had begun to see wisdom in the child being born in Bethlehem. At least it could happen in peace. Joseph had not grown totally comfortable with leaving, even though he had the strange feeling that God wanted it this way. Thus his feelings fluctuated between whether they should or shouldn't make such a long journey.

He sighed, looking into Mary's dark eyes. "Very well, but it still worries me, you know that."

"Yes, I know." She put her arms around him and placed her head against his shoulder. "Thank you for considering my feelings, Joseph. I know it will make things more difficult for you."

"For me? It is you . . ."

She kissed him quickly. "I will be fine." She rubbed his cheek with a finger. "I love you, and soon . . ."

"Shh," he said into her ear. He kissed her on the forehead, then pushed her gently toward the living area of the house. "Now, off with you. I must finish this bench before our guests come." He watched her until she busied herself at the table. From the very start, he had longed for her, and each night as they lay next to one another, his desire seemed to grow stronger. Only prayer and God's help had saved him and kept him in compliance with what he knew must be.

* * *

Mary busied herself with dinner. Pouring water into a kettle, she hung it over the fire before sitting at the table to peel turnips and onions and clean a dried and salted fish brought to them by Matthias. She stopped for a moment, touching her stomach as the baby kicked or turned inside her womb.

"Patience, my son. You must wait. Just a few days, until we get to Bethlehem." Her abdomen was very tight and, contrary to what Joseph tried to make her believe, it seemed enormous. It was becoming more and more obvious that she had been with child for more than five or six months, and she would be glad when they could finally leave.

Not that she didn't worry about the trip. It would take its toll, and the child might be born along the way, but it did not matter. She was eager to be out of the village and would endure any pain it might require.

She heard footsteps in the courtyard and knew immediately who it was. She came every day at this time to check on her daughter and grandson.

"Hello, Mother," Mary exclaimed happily as Anna unlatched the door and entered.

"Hello, Mary," Anna replied, removing the shawl from her head and shoulders and shaking off the water before greeting Mary with the traditional kiss on each cheek. "It is warm in here. Good, you do not want to catch a chill. Not now, not when the child is getting restless."

"You are wet. It has started to rain again." Mary could not help the tinge of disappointment in her voice. Continuing rain would only make her and Joseph's trip more difficult.

"A slight drizzle, nothing more," her mother soothed.

The rainy season was well past, but this spring they had been both blessed and cursed with an unusual amount of rain that kept the crops wet and growing but made the streets and roads muddy and the temperature a bit chilly.

"At least it will be a good harvest," Mary pointed out. "Has Father returned from Sepphoris?" Her father had taken wool from their sheep to the city market.

"He will be here tomorrow." Anna smiled. "You look uncomfortable. Why don't you lie down and let me—"

"I am fine," Mary insisted. She cut the shaved turnips into pieces and dropped them in the heating water. Her mother and father had been agreeable to Joseph and Mary's travel to Bethlehem. Anna had heard more of the gossip than Mary had, and like Mary, she saw the trip as a relief from the wagging tongues of gossips. "How is Josiah?" Mary asked, changing the subject.

Her mother's shoulders slumped, but she shrugged it off and went near the fire for warmth. "He is much better. He will come and see you before you leave."

Mary heard the worry in her mother's voice. They were all worried. Josiah had gotten a cold that had turned into something worse. They had nearly lost him in the month of Tebeth. Even now, he breathed with difficulty, and only two weeks ago he had worsened once more. Though Anna spoke positively to others, she still worried about her son. At best, such a sickness was difficult to recover from. At worst, one never did. The ailment could slowly weaken a person until the body finally gave out. Mary and Joseph had said many long prayers for Josiah, and she would remember to do so again tonight.

"I was hoping that . . . well . . . he would be better, that we could travel with you, help when the baby comes. Your father has never missed Passover. And now to miss being with you as well hurts us both." Passover was only a few days away. They had planned to travel in time to attend all of the celebration, but because Josiah had worsened, they had delayed until the fever cleared and the danger passed.

"Do not worry, Mother. I have a good, capable husband, and though the baby is getting more anxious, he gives me no pain that would herald his birth." Anna had sat on a chair, and Mary knelt down and looked up into her mother's eyes. "God is with us. We will be all right."

Anna smiled, then stroked Mary's hair lightly. "You are a wonder, child. God chose very well."

Mary stood and kissed her mother's forehead, then returned to her work. They chatted over the latest news until Anna felt she must leave.

"I must hurry home. A meal for the children must be prepared, and though I left Dinah in charge . . . well, your sister isn't the most dependable child, is she?" She put her shawl over her head and shoulders, then kissed Mary before laying a gentle hand on her daughter's stomach. A kind, loving look crossed her face as she felt the movement in Mary's womb.

"Dear Lord of heaven and earth, bless him to wait a little longer," she said, closing her eyes while lifting her head heavenward. She rubbed Mary's cheek. "I love you, daughter, and I wish I could see his birth, but both of us know it is better he be born away from here." Her eyes misted. "I will miss you very much." Anna forced a smile, quickly gained her composure, stood straight, and went to the door. "I will come again tomorrow." She closed the door behind her.

Mary stood still for a moment, dangerously close to bursting into tears. Her mother had always been a strong woman, some would even say a hard one, but she loved her children deeply, and Mary had always felt it. The thought of leaving her behind, of not having her there when the baby was born, made Mary ache inside.

She quickly wiped away a tear, then busied herself preparing the fish. Her emotions were always close to the surface these days, but she had no time for tears. Matthias and Salome would arrive soon.

Mary had just finished making the soup and removed the bread from the oven when she heard a knock at the door. She opened it to find a soaked Matthias and Salome. Giving them both a warm-but-hurried greeting, she quickly brought them inside where they removed their head coverings and hung them from dowels.

"Shalom," Matthias intoned with a pleasant grin. He smiled a lot these days. And why not? Salome was a wonderful, strong woman who cared for him, loved him. How could he be unhappy? He helped her remove her cloak as she also spoke a greeting and then hugged Mary.

"How are you feeling?" Salome asked. A look of worry mingled with confusion furrowed her brow.

Salome had not seen Mary for several months, their last visit to Nazareth coming in the month of Shebat, when Mary's abdomen had not yet swollen like a great melon. Mary glanced at Matthias, whose eyes were also fixed on her stomach. There was also a question in them.

"Like I might have twins." Mary smiled. They glanced at each other but did not question Mary further. She was grateful. "And you? How are you feeling this afternoon? How many months is it now?" she queried.

"Nearly three, but I feel fine," Salome replied nonchalantly. "Sickness does not seem to follow me in childbearing."

"Then God has given you a special blessing." Mary laughed, remembering her own sickness.

"You have told her?" Matthias asked, with a raised eyebrow.

"And you haven't told Joseph?" Salome wondered aloud without even looking over at him.

Matthias flushed red and mumbled. "Where is he?"

"In the shop finishing a bench for someone. Over to the fire, Salome! This is no time for sickness," Mary ordered kindly. "The food is ready, and I have only to place it for eating." She turned back to her preparations as Salome drew closer to the fire and Matthias slipped into the shop.

* * *

Matthias and Joseph greeted one another with a hug and a kiss on the cheek.

"Ah, hard at work as usual," Matthias declared, grinning at the hand plane Joseph was using, then at the piece of wood he was trying to smooth. "Let me have at it now! It's been some time since I worked at such a delicate piece."

Joseph gave him the tool. "Surely you have started on your own furniture," Joseph reproved.

Matthias shook his head to the contrary as he put the plane to the wood. "Soon. The house has been delayed because of the need to build another boat."

Joseph shook his head lightly at the idea. "It is still hard to see you handling nets instead of hammer and chisel."

"It took me a month to learn enough just to salvage my pride, but the worst was the humiliation of sickness." He rolled his eyes. "The waves! Do you know I lost thirty pounds? It is one thing to stand on such a boat near shore on a pretty day imagining yourself in the midst of a calm sea, but quite another to be tossed about like a cork on the waves of a windblown Galilee! I couldn't keep a thing in my stomach!" He looked up. "Now, after four months, I fish with the best of them, and I enjoy it," he said proudly. "And, if you plan it right, if you build your own boats, you can make a little money even with the Herods taking such a terrible toll through their miserable tax collectors." He took a deep breath. "You should come. You would make a good fisherman."

Joseph laughed. It was good to see his friend happy with his life. "You have finally found your place, haven't you, Matthias?"

Matthias looked a bit sheepish. "Yes, I think I have." He put down the tool and looked up at Joseph. "It is hard work, but the air is cool and fresh and Salome is at my side much of the time." He shook his head lightly. "She is quite a woman, my Salome," he averred with admiration. Then he sighed. "But we still struggle. The Herods, the

Romans, the temple hierarchy, all must have their fancy houses and silk gowns. As with everyone else, they tax us heavily for leases the Herods say they control. Without these we cannot fish at all. To get them, we must give another eight percent of what we catch. This is in addition to all the other taxes! Nearly fifty percent, Joseph. We are lucky they leave us enough fish to feed our own families." Another deep breath. "But we work hard, and some of us are banding together in an alliance. This should help."

"Alliance?" Joseph asked.

"These days, the rich have a great taste for fish and the sauces made from them. This creates a great demand. By banding together, we can control production. If we do not catch a lot of fish, the distributors cannot produce what the rich want. The rich, always ready to complain when they are denied their luxury, begin to make noise. This puts pressure on the tax collectors, and though they grumble, they are more willing to take less of our profits in order to keep the rich happy and, of course, the collectors from being replaced. Everyone is happy."

Joseph saw the genius of it but also the danger. "The tax collectors could decide to put you out of business, take your boats, and get others to catch their fish."

"Because we all band together, they could not get others who are skilled, and it would take too long to train those with no skill. Believe me, though I have learned quickly, there is still much I do not know about the sea and catching its fish. I would never try on my own. Nor will others." Matthias handed Joseph the plane. "Now, to more important matters. When is Mary to give birth?"

Joseph turned away, putting the plane in its proper place to avoid his friend's stare. "There is still plenty of time, Matthias."

"And yet Salome thinks she is ripe for delivery even now. Mary explains it by alluding to twins. Is it possible?"

"Anything is possible, I suppose," Joseph answered, tinkering with the placement of the plane.

"You're lying. I can always tell when you lie. You look away, you busy yourself, and you cannot look me in the eye. I am good at lying, Joseph, but you, you are horrible." He paused again. "The village is talking. 'She is too big,' says one. 'They must have lain together before the final ceremony,'" he said, mocking the voice of a woman so well that Joseph knew immediately who it was.

"Very good," Joseph said with a chuckle. "You sound just like the rabbi's wife."

Matthias sighed. "They say a lot of things, Joseph, but I do not listen to their idle chatter. I wait for my friend to tell me the truth."

Joseph lost the smile while wiping his dusty hands on a rag. "I did not lie with her," he said quietly, looking directly at his friend.

Matthias searched Joseph's eyes. Other than twins, there was only one other possibility. Mary had lain with another man, either willingly or by force. He would never believe the first, not of Mary. And the second . . . Joseph would tell him if a man had done such a thing. They would hunt down the pig together! "Very well, Joseph. Twins it must be." He stood and placed his hands on Joseph's shoulders. "There are still rumors. Possibly you should consider coming to Capernaum, maybe even live there until after the child . . . um, children are born. Work is plentiful," he smiled, "even for a carpenter with so little talent as yours."

Joseph smiled. "Your offer is kind, but we are leaving for Bethlehem in two days."

Matthias was surprised. "Bethlehem? But why?"

"For one thing, to get away from those gossips you talk about," Joseph said. "For another, we go to be counted. You remember, there is a census and we have been called to the towns of our forefathers?"

"The Herods do not let one forget." He picked up the adze lying on the workbench and put it in Joseph's toolbox.

"Joseph, Matthias, it is time to eat," Mary called from the other room.

The two men stood and joined their wives, already seated on cushions placed on the rug around the low eating table.

The meal was simple but tasty, and they talked of many things as they ate. When they discussed Salome's pregnancy, Matthias beamed. When Mary's giving birth was about to become the subject again, Joseph deftly turned the conversation toward Capernaum and what was happening there.

According to Salome, the town was quickly becoming the center of commerce and trade for northern Galilee, especially for the fishing industry. There was a good deal of building going on, and all kinds of people stopped on their way from Syria to Jerusalem.

"And you, Matthias, how do you feel about what is happening in your new home?" Joseph asked.

Matthias's eyes were focused on the bread he was lifting from a plate in the middle of the table as he spoke. "Noisy, too many people, and the garrison of Herod's soldiers makes it unpleasant." He glanced at Salome and smiled. "But with Salome and Mara, with boats and the sea to fish, well . . . the rest seems of little importance."

Salome blushed, and Joseph could see that they had found something special. "Does Judas ben Hezekiah still call for revolution?" Joseph wondered.

Matthias glanced at Salome, who only shrugged. "Nothing has changed. He has a considerable following, and rebellion is sure to come. They say that Herod has an illness that will take his life, slowly but surely. God's retribution, if you ask me. Anyway, there is chaos in Herod's house—each son, each wife, each daughter positioning for advantage when he dies. In the minds of rebels and patriots who hate the Herods and the Romans, his death will be a good time for revolution."

Salome spoke. "Judas ben Hezekiah has already received the support of one of the priestly families who were forced into exile. They think it is time to replace the corrupt priesthood in Jerusalem. This appeals to even more of our people. Men like my father." She looked at Matthias, then added evenly, "And my husband. Men who would never consider fighting with Judas before are more inclined to support him."

Joseph sat back, a solemn look on his face. "They cannot win. Only the Messiah will free us, and all of us know it."

"Maybe he is the Messiah, Joseph," Matthias stated softly. "Maybe it is finally time to fight for our land and for our God."

Joseph looked at Mary to find her eyes wide, her face pale with concern. She swallowed hard, then forced herself to speak.

"You must wait. The Messiah is coming, but it is not Judas." Her words were soft but firm, full of conviction, her eyes gazing first into those of Matthias, then into Salome's.

Matthias and Salome looked at one another, unsure of what to say.

"Mary speaks the truth," Joseph said.

"God has made this known to you?" Matthias asked, his voice tinged with doubt, a slight smile on his lips.

"Have I ever led you astray, Matthias?"

Matthias shook his head slowly. "No, Joseph, but how could you know such a thing?"

Joseph leaned forward, his face sober. "I just know, that's all. Do not follow Judas, Matthias. It will only lead to sorrow. You will lose Salome, the child she will deliver to you, and Mara."

Matthias leaned forward, frustration in his face. "If you have some knowledge that gives you this absolute conviction, then share it with me, but do not play with my feelings, Joseph."

Joseph sat back. Though he wanted to tell Matthias everything, be as open as his friend had been earlier, he knew in his heart that he must not. Not now, possibly not for many years to come. He would find another way to convince Matthias, but he must not tell even his closest friend the sacred knowledge he held.

It seemed like a long moment as Joseph struggled to find a way, but finally a thought occurred to him. "Do you believe the prophets, Matthias?"

"Of course. You know I do."

"Then search their words. See if Judas ben Hezekiah is the Messiah the prophets speak of. If you find him to be, then follow him. But search, Matthias, and search carefully, for the lives of you and your family rely on what you discover."

"You have read them. Tell us now," Matthias stated firmly.

"No, it will not be the same," replied Joseph evenly. "You must search the scriptures for yourself. Only this way will you know for yourself when you truly see the Messiah. Only then will you know whom to follow."

Matthias sat back. "Once more you avoid answering me directly."

"I have answered you as best I can. You need a witness from God, not from me, Matthias. And such a witness demands the price of study. Pay that price, or you will be led astray. It is as simple as that."

"You know I read with difficulty. You ask a lot."

"Yes, I know, but it will be worth it, my friend. You will see what I see, and you will see it for yourself. Isn't this enough to make you want to search the scriptures?" Joseph asked.

Matthias put up his hand as if to stop Joseph from speaking further. "Yes, yes, I suppose it is."

"Then you will study?"

"Yes, I will study." Matthias smiled.

"And you will not fight with Judas unless the scriptures show you he is the one?" Mary asked.

"Again, yes, I will wait!"

"Good." Mary sighed.

Even Salome showed relief. "When do you leave for Bethlehem?" she asked, glad to change the subject.

"In the next few days," Mary replied.

"But the Passover crowds will still be very large," Matthias declared. "It will be nearly impossible to find lodging, even in Bethlehem."

"We have relatives there who will shelter us," Joseph explained.

"And when will you return?" Salome queried.

Mary looked at Joseph, unsure of just how to answer the question. They intended to stay until after the baby was born, but that reply would only give rise to other questions she could not answer.

"If there is work there, we may stay until fall, possibly through the winter. It depends on when the child is born."

"Then when you return, come to Capernaum and visit us. God willing, we will have boys, both of us, and we must share our happiness at such blessings! Besides, it is time we repaid your hospitality for the meals you have fed us on our trips here." He got to his feet. "It is late, and our wives need their rest. Come, Salome, we must pull ourselves away and leave our friends in peace to prepare for their journey."

Salome took her husband's offered hand and got to her feet, while Joseph stood and helped Mary.

Mary spoke in genuine protest. "Surely you can stay a little longer."

"Matthias is right. It is late, and the journey here took its toll. I am quite exhausted. We need to get some sleep before leaving in the morning," Salome responded.

It had stopped raining, and Mary and Joseph accompanied their friends to the gate of the courtyard, where they spoke heartfelt good-byes.

"May the God of Israel bless you in your journey," Matthias said to them. He looked at Mary. "I worry for you."

"God truly is with us, Matthias. We will be safe. Take care of Salome, and remember your promise to study before—"

Matthias chuckled. "You are even more persistent than your stubborn husband!" His eyes softened. "There is more to this persistence than meets the eye, isn't there?"

Mary only smiled and stood on tiptoes to kiss him lightly on the cheek. "Promise me, Matthias."

Matthias blushed at Mary's sudden show of affection but promised, then turned to Joseph. "Someday you and I will talk more about this. This I also promise."

Joseph smiled as Matthias turned away, Salome holding tightly to his arm, the soft light of a full moon showing them the way. Mary and Joseph watched them go.

"Will we see them again?" Mary asked as they disappeared in the shadows down the hill.

"Yes, of course."

"Should we have told them?"

"No. God will tell us when, and it is not now. Come, let's go inside." He closed the gate, and they went back to the house to prepare to leave for Bethlehem. Tomorrow they would begin the journey.

CHAPTER 10

Joseph closed the door to the house with some reluctance, wondering if they would ever see it again. Joachim promised to watch over their property, but still Joseph worried. It was all he and Mary owned in this world, and if it were lost . . .

But he could not think this way. He must trust that it would be safe until their return.

Mary's family waited in the street as he latched the door and tenderly touched the mezuzah he had carved and attached to the doorframe. "Please Lord, protect this house for us," he said quietly.

"You will be back before you know it," Joachim said, gently pulling Joseph away. "God is in what you do, Joseph. Do not worry—He will not let anything happen to either of you."

Joseph nodded as Joachim handed him a small leather purse. "This is to be used as you see fit. It is not much, but you will need a sacrifice when the boy is presented to God, and there is enough for an inn if Mary . . . well, if the child should come too soon."

"No, no, I have enough for the offering, Joachim," Joseph insisted, shoving the purse toward his father-in-law.

Joachim put both hands on Joseph's shoulders and looked him directly in the eye. "My dear Joseph, would you deny me this blessing?" He paused. Seeing that his question had its desired effect, he smiled. "Do not forget, you need money for Mary's purification, for a house, for many things. Now, go, and take care. There are robbers on the roads in the hills of Samaria, especially this time of year." He gently pushed him toward their fully burdened donkey.

Joseph sighed. He did not like taking charity, especially from his father-in-law, who had many mouths to feed and a sick child besides. But neither could he turn away his kind offering.

"Thank you, Joachim."

"You must go." He stepped closer so as not to be overheard by others who did not know of their secret. "Josiah will be well soon, then we will come. I only wish we could come now! The birth of such a child . . ."

Joseph saw the anguish on Joachim's face. He knew whose son Mary carried, knew it deep in his heart. Like Joseph, he was in awe of the miracle that could not be explained, and he wanted to see it, to watch such a boy come into the world. It was painful to think of it all happening without him.

"I will send word as soon as he comes," Joseph assured him. "I will tell you all about it." The words were inadequate, and he knew it. He looked down at his feet.

Joachim clutched both of Joseph's arms. "I have not told you since your marriage, but you are a good man, Joseph. God chose well. There will be many things to see, to know. I will try to be patient." He stepped back and blinked to keep the tears away.

Anna stepped up and kissed Joseph on both cheeks, whispering in his ears as she did. "My husband is right. God chose well. Send us word, my son." She turned to Mary and kissed her as well, then hugged her warmly. Mary hugged Joachim and each of the others, and the flow of tears increased until Joseph finally put an arm around Mary's shoulder and gently eased her up the road that led south out of the village. They stopped at the top of the hill and waved one last time.

"I have this awful feeling . . ." Mary spoke softly.

Joseph felt it as well but said nothing. Instead, he held her close for a moment before turning her away from the village to begin their journey in earnest. Though he had his share of fear, he also felt a comfortable calm that they were doing the right thing.

Mary nodded, drying her eyes and stiffening her back with resolve.

There were three major roads to Jerusalem. The less-traveled, longer but safer one went east to the Jordan River Valley, then south to Jericho. After that, one had to climb a steep road into the mountains of Judea to Jerusalem. Mary had taken this one to see Elisabeth.

The second road ran west to Megiddo, then to the shores of the Mediterranean Sea, where it turned south to Joppa. From there, a traveler going to the Holy City turned east and climbed the hills of Judea to reach his destination. It was a much longer route and heavily traveled by gentile caravans from Rome to Egypt. Joseph did not care for the company or the extra miles.

The final route, and the one they chose, was known as the Way of the Patriarchs, and it ran directly south through the Judean mountains to Shechem, past the ruins of ancient Shiloh, and on to Jerusalem. Though more dangerous because of robbers and other unfriendly people—sometimes bothersome Samaritans—it was cooler this time of year and would save Joseph and Mary two days over either of the other routes. It was also dotted with many more villages in case Mary delivered prematurely.

Donkey in tow, the couple descended the hill into the Plain of Esdraelon. Going south, Joseph stopped whenever Mary requested a rest. They passed Nain about sunset and made their first camp just south of a small house nestled against the edge of the hills. There were at least a dozen other groups here, both large and small, and most were already camped and preparing their meals or entertaining each other with music and dance. Joseph and Mary listened as they unloaded their possessions. Joseph gathered some dried wood higher up the hill while Mary rested, then he pitched their tent while she prepared a fire and fixed their evening meal.

"It will be more difficult tomorrow," Joseph said worriedly as he sat to eat. "How do you feel?"

"Fine." Mary smiled.

Joseph finished his food and stoked the fire. There was a chill in the air. "A storm is coming," he stated.

After talking and enjoying the warmth of the fire and the music of harp and flute from a nearby camp, Joseph retrieved his prayer shawl and went to find privacy. Mary did not wait long before slipping into the tent, saying her prayers, and sliding between her blankets. When Joseph returned, he slipped in next to her and was nearly asleep when he heard the sound of distant thunder. Fifteen minutes later, water poured down on them as the sky lit up again and again with lightning. Thunder clapped so loudly that Joseph had to cover his ears, and the rain fell so hard that even the dense camel's hair of the tent could not keep it all out. Their blankets were wet in only a few minutes.

Then came the wind.

Joseph felt the tent lift and held his breath until it settled again. Another strong gust lifted one corner and pulled out the stake, and he scrambled from his bed, grabbed the tent, and pulled it back into place. With the wind and rain pounding his face and shoulders, he used his mallet to drive the stakes deeper into the ground just as lightning struck so close by that it made him flinch. He heard the donkey bray and sensed that it was in trouble. Putting up a hand and arm to shield his eyes, he moved carefully through the pouring rain, violent wind, and darkness to find the animal.

He found it in a small thicket of underbrush where the hobble rope had become snagged; the donkey had gotten entangled in the rope and fallen. Its legs thrashed violently as it tried to get free, but its head was caught under the ropes and between its legs. Joseph spoke soothing words as he tried to quiet the donkey so that he could get close enough to help without getting injured by its thrashing hooves.

Joseph felt something touch his back and turned quickly to find Mary standing behind him, rain dripping down her face.

"I will talk to him. You try and get around to the other side and cut the rope," she shouted over the wind and storm.

Joseph worried for her safety but knew he would only waste precious time trying to convince her to get back inside the tent. Nodding reluctant agreement, he quickly went around the thicket, removed his knife from its sheath, and began cutting his way through the low branches. When he reached the donkey, Mary's soothing touch had quieted the animal enough that it had stopped struggling. Joseph reached through and quickly cut the hobble rope. As the donkey flailed around once more, trying to get free of the thicket, Mary lurched away, tripped, and fell onto some rocks. As the animal struggled to its feet and bolted away, Joseph scrambled to where Mary lay, pain etching her face and her hand gripping her backside where it had obviously come in brutal contact with a stone.

"Are you all right?" he yelled above the sound of the storm.

She gritted her teeth and nodded firmly as she spoke and grabbed his arm. "You must find him, Joseph."

Joseph nodded, then stood and helped her to her feet. She put a hand on her bruised backside as he helped her to the tent. "Stay here, Mary. I will look for him, but you cannot get ill. Not this close to the baby's birth."

She nodded and went inside, closing the flap of the tent against the wind.

* * *

Some distance up the hillside, Joseph came upon a camp that had lost their tent to the wind. Two of their six people appeared injured, and all their animals had fled.

"You looking for a donkey?" yelled a man helping pull the tent from the mud.

"Yes."

"He ran through here. Nearly knocked me over. Frightened. Strange for a donkey—they are usually calm in such times. But then this was no normal storm, was it? As if the devil himself were in it! All of the animals are frightened. I have never seen such wind and noise! The animals will run for hours. You will never find him." Visibly shaken, he pointed a direction and turned his attention to a frightened child.

Joseph felt his way through the trees, the only light coming from the strikes of distant lightning. He found a stream flowing over its banks with such a rush of current that he knew he could never cross. Stooping low, he searched for tracks, finding them a moment later. The donkey had not crossed; its tracks led farther up the hill.

Joseph climbed until he reached a small, manmade plateau. A dozen ancient olive trees ran along its rim, and he found the donkey and a mule under the largest tree, their heads hanging limply in exhaustion.

Fortunately, the donkey did not bolt when it saw Joseph, instead turning to the mule as if to tell it they had company. The mule was apparently too tired to care and looked away, allowing Joseph to approach and stroke his animal in an attempt to calm him.

"There now, Saul, it is over, and you have nothing to fear." At that moment, a rod of lightning struck in the distance, and Saul tensed but did not move, though the mule bolted backward nearly to the edge of leveled ground. Another step and he would tumble over the precipice.

"Whoa, mule!" Joseph ordered, stepping carefully toward the rain-soaked animal. "Careful, or you will end up at the bottom of the gorge with all your legs broken."

The mule must have sensed that Joseph was a friend, and it looked behind at the slanting hillside. The mule moved forward, and Joseph grabbed the rope. He gently stroked the mule's wet hide as Saul nuzzled his shoulder. Saul was large for a donkey, but the mule seemed to dwarf him. Mules were animals that only the rich could afford, and Joseph wondered who the owner might be.

Joseph started for a mud-covered trail that led from the olive grove down the hill. "Come on, then, let's find your owner."

Knowing Saul would follow, Joseph led the mule, taking it slowly. With the path slick and the forest dark, it would be easy for both man and beast to fall and break a leg. The storm had passed when they reached the camps, now well lit with fires, everyone trying to get things cleaned and dried. Joseph stopped at the first camp and asked if the mule belonged to them.

"Fine animal, take at least a year's wages to purchase," said a middle-aged man. "One like me can only afford a mule in his dreams."

Joseph asked at the next camp and received a similar answer, but at the third, he found the mule's owner.

It was a large camp with several tents, the central one of fine quality and of a size Joseph was sure could house half a dozen families. Seemingly unscathed by the storm, this tent was lit with lanterns, allowing Joseph to see through the open flap. The ground inside was covered with fine rugs, now coated with mud and soaked through. By the light of at least a hundred lamps, servants worked to clean the rugs. One servant, seeing Joseph approach, set aside the items he was carrying and came to meet him.

"Does this animal belong to your master?" Joseph asked.

"He does," the servant answered, stroking the mule's neck.

It was then that Joseph saw the owner and nearly stopped breathing. It was the governor's steward, whom Matthias had so incautiously insulted and who would surely recognize Joseph. The steward was standing at the tent door looking their direction.

"Who is it, Mensos?" the steward demanded loudly.

"A friend has found your mule, sire."

"Well, don't just stand there! Get the animal cleaned and dried before he dies from this . . . this mess!" He turned and went back inside the tent, commanding several others who apparently were not working at their tasks hard enough.

The servant seemed a bit ashamed and bowed slightly in apology. "Many masters would pay you for your help, but—"

"It is not necessary," Joseph replied. "God go with you." Joseph started down the hill, anxious to get away.

"And you," the servant called.

Joseph hurried back to his and Mary's camp, his stomach churning and the thought pressing on him that they should leave immediately. But why? What possible threat could this man be to them? He did not know, but he would not ignore this feeling either. He could not.

Mary was warming herself by the fire, standing as close as good sense would allow. She had already changed into dry clothes, the others hanging in a tree, dripping. She ran to greet Joseph with a hug and a quick kiss.

"Are you all right?" he asked as he picked up the halter and put it on the donkey.

"Except for a bruised backside, I am fine. But look at you! Soaked, muddy. You will catch your death of cold. Quickly, you must remove your clothes and let me dry them by the fire.

"We have to leave, Mary," Joseph said, handing her the donkey's lead rope.

Mary looked flabbergasted. "Leave, but why? What has happened, Joseph?"

While he began taking down the tent, Joseph told her about returning the mule to the unfriendly steward.

"But surely this steward would not remember you as an enemy. It was Matthias who spoke—"

"Men like this do not forget. Now, please, I cannot tell you why, but I feel we must be away from here."

They hurriedly packed and loaded everything onto the donkey. Joseph prepared a torch from rags doused in oil, and they began their journey. At first, the road was muddy and slick, but after nearly an hour of walking, the earth turned dry again. Though violent, the storm had obviously covered only a small area.

"I must rest soon, Joseph," Mary said.

Joseph saw a fire on the side of a nearby hill and helped Mary move in that direction. They found a camp with half a dozen people talking and singing around the fire and asked if they could pitch their soaked tent nearby. Given permission, Joseph removed the tent and blankets and made them a bed under the stars with their driest blankets. He could see that Mary was exhausted, and he helped her slip between the covers before retrieving his prayer shawl and saying his prayers. Tonight, they were short ones, and soon he was beside Mary and fast asleep. Though they would be in the mountains of Samaria, tomorrow would surely be an easier day.

CHAPTER 11

They slept until after sunup, and by the time Joseph forced himself up and into his own clothes, the other travelers in the camp had already packed and left. Joseph woke Mary and unpacked some bread and dried meat, and they ate before repacking their donkey.

The road climbed onto the ridge of the Samaritan mountains at Ginae to wind its way south to Sebaste. Many travelers were journeying to Passover, more than Joseph had ever seen, and it did not bode well for finding room, even in Bethlehem.

The young couple stopped several times before reaching Sebaste, the city built by Herod for his gentile friends, where it was rumored that he imprisoned two of his sons until receiving permission from the emperor to have them slain for conspiring against him. Joseph and Mary circumvented the city, then rested briefly at a well in the valley just north of Neapolis. During the descent to the well, Mary felt her third and most disconcerting contraction and asked Joseph to prolong the rest.

"We can stop here for the night," Joseph answered with some anxiety. "We have gone nearly a day's journey anyway, and the tent needs to be dried."

When Mary did not argue, Joseph grew even more anxious and quickly helped her down a path to the edge of a normally dry streambed, now filled with small pools from the previous night's rainfall.

Removing a blanket, he laid it on the grass near a fallen log so she could lie down. "Take your rest. I'll see to the fire and get us something to eat."

Once more, Mary did not argue, but carefully stretched out her legs and braced her back against the log.

"Is the baby coming?" Joseph asked apprehensively.

She shook her head. "No, but he is sending us a warning. I suppose we must slow our pace," she said with some despair.

Joseph removed the packs from the donkey's back. "There is no hurry, Mary." He dug into the first pack and found a small cushion used for sleeping and placed it behind her back.

"I can mix the bread while you—"

He pushed back her headscarf to reveal her hair, then stroked it back. "You will do nothing of the sort," he said tenderly. "You will rest. I have been on my own long enough to know how to fix a meal."

Mary did not object, and by the time he finished unloading the donkey and laying the still-damp tent out in the sun to dry, she was asleep.

Joseph rubbed down the donkey with grass before leading him to an area where more of it grew tall along the creek bed. Once more, he hobbled the animal, stroked him with a few kind words, then returned to camp. Mary was curled up on the blanket, and Joseph quickly unpacked the sleeping blankets, placing the driest one over her before hanging the others over tree limbs to finish drying.

He looked around for dead wood but once more had to search along the higher hills to find enough for a fire. At one point, his view opened on the valley and the mountain where Sebaste sat. The once-proud city of Jeroboam the Second had been nearly destroyed when the Assyrians fell on the rebellious northern tribes of Israel, killing thousands and taking many more captive into Assyria. Because they had refused the prophets' warnings, the tribes had become scattered among the nations to the north. But there were also prophecies about their return under the power of their Messiah.

The thought took Joseph's breath away. How could Jesus bring such a thing to pass? How could these cities, filled with the powerful Romans and thousands of other Gentiles, fall in battle, then be rebuilt and filled with the descendants of those ancient tribes who had disappeared? And yet had it had been declared by Isaiah.

Joseph spoke the words softly. "Unto us a child is born, unto us a son is given: and the government shall be upon his shoulder: and his name shall be called Wonderful, Counsellor, The mighty God, The everlasting Father, The Prince of Peace. Of the increase of his government and peace there shall be no end, upon the throne of David, and upon his kingdom, to order it, and to establish it with judgment and with justice from henceforth even for ever."

The words were clear, and Mary would bear the very Son of God. He would sit upon David's throne and govern all Israel, and he would do it because of the power vested in him as God's Son. Joseph took one last look at Sebaste. He had been in the city, knew of its people and their sins. He also knew that Herod and the Roman Emperor were not likely to give up their power easily to a man of Galilee, the son of a lowly carpenter. The thought of what such pride would mean made Joseph's skin crawl.

He shoved the thought aside and hurriedly picked up more sticks until he could carry no more. Returning to camp as deeper shadows began creeping across the valley floor, he was pleased to find Mary still sleeping. It could only mean that the pain had subsided and the baby's coming was not nigh.

Travelers had begun to pull off the road to search for the best spots to set up camp for the night, and the small valley teemed with camp preparations, fires, and food. The smells made Joseph salivate, and he prepared a place for their own fire, delicately nurturing a flame to life with the use of knife, flint, and dried brush fibers, adding shavings, then dried kindling. The orange and yellow flames gave comfort against the coming night, and Joseph allowed himself a moment's relaxation before placing a pot of water on the newly formed coals.

"May a traveler unfamiliar with your country join you?"

The voice came from the shadows, and Joseph stood, one hand on the short sword tucked under his robe. "Come into the light so that I can see if you are friend or enemy," he replied cautiously.

A man about ten years older than Joseph stepped out of the dark shadows. "I apologize. I did not realize I was standing in the shadows."

Joseph looked at the fine clothes. "You are a foreigner."

"Of Athens. I have come for Passover, and for business, at Jerusalem." The man lifted his hand to reveal two dead game hens. He bowed at the waist. "If you will allow a humble Jew of Athens to cook these over your fire, we can share them."

Joseph took his hand from the hilt of his knife and looked at the two sand grouse. They were not among the fowl forbidden by God, and this Greek was obviously sincere. The fresh flesh would be welcome when compared to the dried meat that Joseph and Mary had brought, but he still hesitated.

"Then you are not only Greek but also Jewish?" Joseph asked tentatively.

The man nodded. "In the past, more Greek than Jew, I am afraid. But my heart and my studies . . . they bring me back to find my people . . . and my God."

"Your gift is welcome," Mary interjected, "but I will see to its cooking." She had been lying outside the light of the fire, and Joseph had not noticed her approach. She stood and stepped toward the stranger, her headscarf in place and her hand extended to take the birds, which he gave to her with a slight bow, worry in his eyes as he saw her condition and how tired she looked.

"You are tired and . . . the child."

"You are kind to be concerned, but I am quite strong enough to prepare birds for roasting." She turned to Joseph. "Cut sticks on which to skewer them, Joseph, and invite our benefactor to dine with us. The grouse are fat for cooking and will feed us all very well." She went to the packs to retrieve her knife and other items needed for skinning and preparing the grouse.

"I do have several animals. May they share the fresh grass with your own?"

Joseph only nodded, and the man disappeared but reappeared quickly, a fine horse at his side. Another man appeared with two mules. After they unloaded the animals, the servant deftly hobbled each in the tall grass near Saul and then dissolved again into the darkness only to return moments later with two camels. The donkey and horse sniffed at one another, but both ignored the camels as the servant led them farther down the stream.

"May I sit?" the Greek asked, pointing to the grass near the fire.

Joseph nodded. "You ride a fine horse." He picked up his knife and hacked down a thick, green branch from a tree a few feet outside their camp.

"Yes, we have been friends for a long time. My wife rides his brother. If you saw them together, you would not be able to tell the difference."

"Then you are married," Mary commented.

"Yes, and we have a daughter. I miss them more than I can say. Fortunately, they will be joining me in Jerusalem. They come by ship. I had business in Damascus, then with the governor at Sepphoris."

Joseph's knife stopped in midair before he began forcefully whittling points on each end of the stick. "You know the governor."

"It was business, nothing more."

"And the governor's steward, you know him as well?" Joseph asked, trying to hide his anxiety.

"He was there, but I spoke little to him, despite his attempts to get my ear. Though they say he is destined for the king's house, I saw little to commend him to that kind of power. You know him?"

"We met. I did work on the great room at the governor's palace. The columns—"

"Magnificent work!" approved the Greek. "You are a talented carpenter. When I build a home in Sepphoris, surely you will come and work for me!"

"We go to Bethlehem to live. I don't know when we will return to—"

"I have no immediate plans. Did you live at Sepphoris, then?"

"In a village nearby. Nazareth."

"Then if things work as I hope, I will look for you."

Joseph laid the skewers aside for Mary's use, then sat down across the fire pit from the Greek. "And your name?"

"Seth, son of Aristamaeus. We live in Athens at present, but it is time my family returned to our homeland. My shipping business is doing well in this region, and I go to make arrangements for my family in Jerusalem until I can do something about Sepphoris."

"But why Sepphoris?" Joseph wondered.

"It is halfway between Damascus and Jerusalem, there are many olive groves from which to glean the best oil known to man, and it is beautiful country. Does a man need more reasons?"

The servant returned and began pitching a travel tent, Joseph watching him.

"His name is Phillip. Though a servant, he and I eat at the same table. We have been friends since the day his father brought him to us."

"And his servitude, what was its purpose?" Joseph queried.

"His father could not pay his taxes and was about to lose his property to Rome. My father paid them. For three years, Phillip worked to pay the debt. Now he works for wages because he desires to start a business of his own."

"Are all Athenians so generous as you and your father?"

"It would please God if it were so. Unfortunately, there are few like my father."

"Then in some things, Athens is not so different from Israel. And what cities have you seen since leaving Athens?" Joseph inquired. He had heard of Athens, of Rome, of so many places and had often wondered what they and the other great cities of the world were really like.

"Rome, Antioch, and, as I mentioned, Damascus, to purchase spices. We sell them in Athens."

Joseph marveled that it was all said matter-of-factly and without pride. This was not a man who exulted in his own accomplishments or considered himself a better man because of his wealth or access to the world.

"Tell me of Jerusalem," Seth said to Joseph.

Joseph smiled slightly. "You have been to so many places. You are a Jew, and yet you have not been to Jerusalem! Surely the feasts, the call to return for them . . ."

"Yes, I am guilty of negligence when it comes to our religion, but as you see, I have repented." He grinned. "Now tell me, is it as beautiful as they say?"

Joseph nodded. "I have not traveled to your Athens, or to any of these cities you mention, but I have been to the temple many times. I think it would be very hard to match its beauty and majesty. But on a fast horse you will soon see for yourself."

Seth sighed. "Yes, I have dreamed of it for some time."

"And yet you delayed," stated Joseph.

Mary put her cooking utensils near the fire and knelt to prepare the birds by soaking the meat in salt to draw out the blood, as Seth responded. "I have only recently found our faith of any interest." He picked up a leather pouch that lay on the ground by his side. "Here, look at this." He pulled out a scroll. "This is a writing of Isaiah."

He handed the scroll to Joseph, who saw immediately that it was written in Greek. "I have heard of scrolls like these, but the chief priests, the scribes of the temple, have denounced them."

Seth smiled. "Because they are not written in Hebrew but in Greek. So I was told, so many are told, but they will have to change their minds. There are many Jews who live in the Roman cities, just as I do. In Athens alone there are thousands, more in Ephesus and Rome. One quarter of the city of Alexandria is filled with Jews, and few of them read or speak your Hebrew anymore. They are educated in the Greek language, the language of the Empire. Even here, in your country—"

"Yes, yes, I know. Greek is the language the Romans force upon us. We try to learn a little, even though Aramaic is the language we speak here. But Hebrew is a sacred language, and to defile our scriptures with common Greek or Aramaic is not popular with our scribes or with us."

"Even though it could be of great benefit to our people?" Seth asked. He leaned forward again. "Is it not true, Joseph of Nazareth, that to be understood, the prophets must be read and studied? If Hebrew is no longer used by many Jews . . ." He shrugged. "Soon we lose sight of God. Then we find other gods. Even now, some do so, straying from our ancient religion simply because they do not know it." He took a deep breath. "I was one of these. I worshipped Diana and a dozen other gods because I was not raised with Hebrew as my language."

"And yet you speak it now."

Seth smiled, lifting the scroll. "Only because of this. I was curious and bought this in Alexandria while on business there. I believed these words and bought many others. Eventually, I was converted and learned Hebrew as part of my decision to bring my family home to this land. So you see, having this in Greek saved my life. Many others will follow because they read many things in Greek now. The writings of philosophers, of politicians, of religious leaders and poets. Why not our Torah?" He sat back.

Joseph blinked at the question. It confused him. All his life, his study of the Torah had been in God's language, given to the children of Israel from the Tower of Babel. To think that some of Joseph's people were deserting the language of their fathers did not make sense to him and was a bit frightening.

Seth took the scroll and rolled it closed, then looked at Mary, who had just finished putting the first bird in salt water.

"Your child," he said to her, "and other children who come to you, will live in a Greek-speaking world. Do not neglect their education by teaching them only Hebrew or the Aramaic you speak every day. If they are to know all they must know of this world, if they are to understand what their own people outside this small place in creation understand about our scriptures, you must teach them Greek and make such scrolls as these available to them."

"Tell me, Seth, how much does such a scroll cost?" Mary inquired.

Seth thought a moment. "A hundred denarii."

"And how many denarii do you think my husband, who is as fine a carpenter as lives in all Israel, makes in a single day in this land where kings and their rich clients require heavy taxes or in many cases take the fruit of one's labor for free?"

Seth got the point, sobered, and did not answer.

"When Joseph is paid in money—and he is paid in money more often than most—he makes a denarius a day, hardly enough to pay our own taxes and buy things he cannot provide through his own labors for us, not to mention this child and our future children."

Seth leaned forward and handed the scroll to Joseph. "Then let this be his first book. May God grant him wisdom and a knowledge of the Greek language through this simple gift."

Joseph was stunned. "But, I cannot . . . It's worth . . . I cannot repay."

"It is not for you, Joseph, but for the child." Seth hesitated. "I sense . . . well, never mind the foolish ranting of a man in need of redemption for a life of neglect of the one God. I am rich enough to replace this and buy many others. Your children will be a help to their peers by having some knowledge of it."

Joseph handled the scroll gingerly. "It is too much . . ."

"Then we will make a deal. When I build my home in Sepphoris, you will work off the purchase price by building me beautiful columns and doors, even better than those of the governor." He smiled and extended his hand. "Is it a deal?"

Joseph grinned. "It is." He reached out and shook the hand of his new friend.

"Thank you, Seth," Mary said quietly. "It will be a wonderful blessing for our child and for us."

"Now, I must help Phillip put up our tent." He stood and joined his servant. Joseph was impressed as he watched the two men. Though one served the other, they truly were friends. An hour later, the four travelers ate, spoke of faraway places, and went to bed. Joseph thought of a thousand things until his mind finally drifted into a dream-filled sleep.

* * *

Mary heard Joseph's heavy breathing, slipped from the covers, and retrieved a lamp. After lighting it, she removed the Isaiah scroll from its pouch. Though she knew a little Greek, she could not read the strange letters, but she reverently admired them just the same. She would see that Jesus read them someday, and he would read them to her and Joseph and the rest of their children. God's Son would not be lacking in education. After a few moments, she rolled the scroll and put it in the pouch, blew out the lamp, and lay back. A few moments later she drifted into a sound sleep.

* * *

When Joseph and Mary awoke the next morning, their new friends were packing their tent and preparing to leave. Business would take them to Caesarea Maritima on the sea before they traveled south to Jerusalem. After a quick breakfast that Phillip had prepared for all of them, Joseph and Mary said their good-byes and watched the two men disappear down a valley leading west.

The young couple did not arrive at Jerusalem for four more days. The Passover and the Feast of Unleavened Bread were in full celebration, and the city was full to overflowing, the camps around it bulging at every valley and hilltop. Like thousands of others, Joseph usually stayed in one of these camps when at Passover, both because the city was too expensive and because of tradition. He had done it from childhood and had friends from many places both inside and outside Israel who returned each year. They would rekindle friendships and discuss the Torah, offer their Passover sacrifices together, and then celebrate the Feast of Unleavened Bread the following week.

Joseph wondered if any of his friends were here but shoved the thought aside—he had no time to look for them. Mary's pains had graduated from warnings to the imminence of birth, and Joseph had carried most of their packs on his own back so that she could ride the donkey. Even then he had to move slowly. Though Saul was a large donkey, he was still a donkey, and his gait not the most pleasant for any rider, especially one expecting a child.

It was mid-afternoon when they left the Sebaste-to-Jerusalem road just north of the city and went west around its high walls. The road from Joppa intersected with theirs at Tower's Pool, but they passed by it and got on the road to Bethlehem that ran under the shadow of the three tall and overpowering towers of Herod's palace. There were dozens of soldiers atop the walls that ran from tower to tower, and though the road was crowded and he knew the guards would give little heed to him and Mary, Joseph felt a good deal of anxiety until they were well past the palace.

Of the camps around the city, the largest blossomed along the hillside that lifted gently west of the Bethlehem road. There were trails between tents running north and south, east and west, but most ended up feeding into a main artery leading to Serpent's Pool, the largest source of water on the western side of the city. Joseph stopped there to fill their water bag and let Mary rest.

Crowded, hot, and dusty, the place smelled of animal dung, cooking, and the sweat of men under the midday sun. Joseph had never felt it oppressive before but found it so now and was eager to get into the hills south of the city and on to Bethlehem.

He helped a tired Mary down from her perch atop Saul just as a man finished watering his animals in one of the troughs fed by the pool. Joseph did not need to urge Saul into the space left vacant, and the donkey drank its fill while Mary sat on the edge of the trough next to it and washed her face and cooled her neck, then dried off with her headscarf.

"There are so many people," she exclaimed.

"I have never seen anything like it," Joseph replied. "Did you see the soldiers, how many there are? It is strange, but I never realized before just how afraid King Herod is of our people."

Mary smiled ironically. "Herod, afraid of us?"

"Yes, I know it seems odd, but he is. He must be. He surrounds himself with high walls, towers, and hundreds of soldiers and never walks freely among us. What else could it be but fear?"

Joseph could see that Mary was exhausted and wished once again that he had insisted she stay in Nazareth. A woman whom they had passed on the road near Shiloh had berated him for bringing her in such a condition, declaring that the child could be stillborn because of it. Since then he had fretted, fearful of the retribution that would surely come if he had endangered the life of God's Son. He placed a hand on her stomach. "How is he?"

"Active." She smiled. "Do not fret, Joseph. The child is well enough, believe me." When a space opened up next to her, he sat down and used a rag to clean and cool himself.

"I wonder what it will take to conquer those walls. Even the Romans would be hard pressed to take this city. Surely it will take a great warrior to remove the Herods from it," Joseph said. He wiped the back of his neck and let the water trickle under his clothing. It felt good but also made him wish for a wide stream in which to remove the dust and dirt of nearly a week's travel. "Isaiah says the Messiah will tread down his enemies with anger and fury, that he will feed those who oppress us with their own flesh until they are drunk with it as with sweet wine. He says this is the way that all flesh will know that the Lord is the Savior and the Redeemer of Israel. I suppose these walls will be nothing when the time comes."

Mary wrung out the rag she was using to cool herself. "But he also says that our Jesus will grow up as a tender plant just like other children in Israel, that there will be nothing that will make him stand out." She took a deep breath. "In fact, he will be despised and rejected of men, know sorrow and grief because of our rejection of him; that he will be wounded for our sins, oppressed by us and . . . and finally killed."

For a moment, Mary couldn't speak. Finally, she cleared her throat. "Then Isaiah tells us that out of his death will come our salvation, Joseph. Out of this will come peace to this land and the entire world." She shook her head slowly. "I have tried to see how he can do both, what kind of man he must be, what it will mean for you and me and other children who come to us, but I cannot. It is . . . it is as if our Jesus will be two people, one a warrior, one a man of peace who will declare himself, be rejected, and never lift a finger to stop his own death. It is hard for me to bear the thought of either."

She touched her stomach reverently. "But one thing I do know is that he will never have to hang his head in shame for what he does. He will never butcher the innocent as Herod has done, and when it is finished, all mankind will bow in reverence before him, for in the end, God's Son will save them, Joseph. Jew and Gentile. He will save those who want to be saved." She laid her head on his shoulder and clutched his arm tightly. "I can only pray for the strength to endure whatever it is he must do to accomplish such a thing."

Joseph put an arm around her shoulder and leaned his head against hers. She was a marvel, and at times like these, when she laid bare her heart to him, he loved her more than he thought possible. After a moment and a squeeze of his hand, Joseph stood and let more water into the trough.

"I heard someone selling dates. I will see if I can buy some for us while you fill the water bag." He turned into the crowd just as someone knocked him back into Saul. The donkey slipped to the side, braying loudly as a man fell to the ground behind him and at Joseph's feet. Saul kicked at him, grazing the man's shoulder. He scrambled out of the way before Saul got in a second strike. But he was not so lucky in escaping a larger man who pushed through the crowd, anger etched in every line of his face. Joseph had never seen anyone so filled with hate, and quickly placed himself between the angry man and Mary.

"Got you now!" said the brute to the man who had scrambled away from Saul's flailing hoof. The large man grabbed for him, but the scrambler was too quick and dodged his grasp. Unfortunately, he was hemmed in by the trough and by the growing circle of onlookers. Another grab, this time successful, and the scrambling man was dangling in the air several inches off the ground.

"Try to cheat me, will you?" the large man threatened. He was about to swing a rock at his victim's skull when Joseph reached out reactively and grabbed his thick arm to prevent the blow. The attacker spun around and cast his prey into Joseph, sending both of them to the ground. Being closest to the assailant, Joseph was the first to feel his wrath and found himself lifted, then tossed toward the crowd, which shoved him back toward the pursuing madman.

Suddenly a soldier appeared and rammed the blunt end of his spear into the back of the attacker's neck. The assailant fell forward as if he had no legs, and his head hit the hard ground with such impact it made Joseph cringe. The soldier tied the stunned man's hands behind him as Joseph quickly returned to Mary, who grabbled tightly onto his arm.

"Clear the way! Back up there!" yelled a voice just beyond the inner part of the circle.

The crowd parted as if it were the Red Sea, and several of Herod's foreign soldiers pushed them back even farther as two men on horseback entered the circle. The foot soldiers making way for them were fearsome looking—large, solid men with arms of stone and eyes to match. Most were Gauls and Thracians, but Joseph knew there were Armenians and Celts as well. Rome had captured much of the north and these men had fought them, then become a part of the empire, plying their trade as fighters and mercenaries. They suited Herod because they had no eye on the throne and were vicious fighters who put fear into every opponent.

The two horsemen approached, and Joseph saw that both wore Roman attire and that one was a centurion. Their helmets were not of brass but polished steel and their uniforms and saddles of the finest quality.

"What's going on here?" asked the centurion.

"Just a fight, sir," answered the soldier tying the madman's hands.

"There are usually two involved in a fight, soldier. Where is the other one?"

The soldier looked around, his eyes settling on Joseph. Joseph's heart thumped hard against his chest as he saw that he was about to be accused, and he nearly fainted with relief when the crowd pushed the real brawler forward. The soldier eyed him as he stumbled into the circle.

"That's him, sir," the soldier said.

"Are you sure?"

"Well, sir, it happened so fast, and I was busy with this big one sir, and . . ."

The soldier dismounted and removed his helmet.

"We know that man," Joseph whispered to Mary.

Mary looked at him carefully then nodded. "The man in Nazareth. The one who kept the Gaul from me and tried to return the water jug."

The centurion walked around the circle. "Did anyone see what happened?"

There was no response.

"My name is Marcus Vitellius, a Roman and centurion of Herod's army in Judea. I do not wish to punish anyone unjustly. If you have anything to say in their defense, now is the time." He halted in front of Joseph, studied him, then smiled. "How about you, man of Nazareth? Did you see anything?"

Joseph nodded. "The big one attacked the other. Tried to bash his head in with a rock."

"Do you know why he attacked the other one?"

"He said something about being cheated."

Marcus nodded, then faced the brute, now on his feet between two soldiers. "Were you cheated?"

"Yes, this one used bad scales to measure out grain. He was cheating everyone. When I challenged him, he drew a knife and tried to slice off my hand. If I had not been quick enough . . ."

"And you retaliated."

"Yes, sir, it's true I came after him, but only because he's a cheat and he tried to cut me! No one does that to me without a fight!"

"It's a lie. I never cheated anyone," the other man insisted.

"Your scales will tell us if you lie," Marcus turned to his soldiers. "Take them both. Find this one's shop. Check the scales. If the owner is lying, arrest him and set this one free." He turned to the large man. "If you're lying, I'll see you sent off to the galley ships for the rest of your life. If you're telling the truth, you will only be punished for violence against another man. We have laws. Because you didn't turn to us to solve your troubles, it will be twenty lashes before any release."

The large man stiffened his back. "I'm telling the truth, and I'll take the twenty gladly if this man is punished."

"If he's a cheat, he will be." Marcus the centurion turned to the other horseman. "Banat, take them, and see that my word is kept."

The soldiers called for others behind them, and the two fighters disappeared through a crowd that once more parted like the Red Sea. Marcus turned back to Joseph.

"Well, Joseph of Nazareth, nice to see you again," Marcus said kindly. He looked at Mary and bowed slightly. "Even more lovely than before. A son, I hope."

Mary did not look at him directly, her face mostly covered with the tail of the headscarf. She said a quiet, "Thank you," then turned to finish filling the water bag.

"You judged them well," Joseph said. "Though the galleys would be a little stiff for fighting."

"For lying to a soldier. I can only do the right thing when I know the truth. You are here for Passover?"

"For the Emperor's census. We go to Bethlehem."

"The city of David. I have been there. A band of robbers tried to steal a herd of sheep belonging to one of your priestly clans. It falls under my jurisdiction. It is an old village, peaceful but small. I only hope you can find a place to stay." He looked at the camp. "As you see, we're already full and overflowing." His face clouded a bit. "But you shouldn't even be here. The census is foolishness enough, but to have you register in your own towns only makes it worse. Sometimes I think Herod's advisors . . . Well, enough. It is a sour subject with me." He looked at Mary with concern. "She is tired, and with her delivery close, you should probably stay in Jerusalem tonight."

Joseph was tempted, but Mary shook her head in the negative.

"No, thank you," Joseph answered. "Just a few more miles, and we will be comfortable enough."

"Very well." Marcus smiled. "Good to see you again. May your God bless you with a beautiful son."

"Thank you," Joseph said.

Marcus returned to his horse, mounted, and headed toward the city. Once more, Joseph was grateful for their meeting, but he was also glad it was over.

"He has a good heart," Mary said as she stepped to Joseph's side.

Joseph nodded, "But he is still a Roman. And a soldier." He turned to adjust the donkey's baggage saddle. "Are you rested enough?"

"Yes, and eager to be free of this place," she said.

Joseph took Saul's lead rope, and they started south. The road was very steep and winding, and before they reached the top of the next hill, Joseph asked if she needed another rest. Though she was obviously hurting, she shook her head adamantly. "But I will ride Saul."

He removed one of the packs to carry, then lifted her onto the donkey, and they trudged on slowly, finally reaching the top, where Joseph insisted they rest. He led Saul off the road to the shade of a small cypress tree before helping her down. As she sat, she grimaced against the pain. He quickly grabbed a blanket and laid it on the ground, then helped her to lie down, holding her hand until the pain subsided. Once more, he felt helpless and looked at the distant skyline of Bethlehem and quietly wished it were closer.

When the pain subsided, Mary squeezed his hand. "I must rest a few moments, then we can go." She forced a slight smile, and Joseph stroked the dampness from her forehead with the sleeve of his robe as she closed her eyes. He released her hand and returned to Saul to retrieve the water-skin. It was then he discovered that he had left it behind.

Cursing himself for his thoughtlessness, he considered returning for it but knew it would do no good. It would be gone by now, confiscated by someone for their own needs, and he could not leave Mary alone anyway. Nor could he ask her to make the return journey. He removed a small bag of dates and sat down near her, his back against the trunk of the cypress. After eating a few and admiring the view of Jerusalem from the hilltop, he grew drowsy and allowed himself a moment's nap. He awoke with a start to find Mary leaning over him, gently shaking his shoulder. He sat upright to find that the sun had begun to set.

"We've slept too long," Mary pointed out.

"How do you feel?" he asked, getting to his feet.

"Rested, and the pain is gone. I think I can make it now."

Joseph jumped to his feet and untied Saul's lead rope.

"I left the waterskin, didn't I?" Mary asked worriedly as they reached the road.

"It was mine to remember, but you are right, it was left behind."

"May I offer you a drink from this one?" Overhearing their conversation, an old gentleman climbing the hill below them held out a small water bag. Touting a white beard and dressed after the manner of a Jew, he seemed of little threat to Joseph.

"My wife could use a drink, but I am fine."

The old gentleman handed the water bag to Mary. "You go to Bethlehem."

Joseph nodded. "To be counted for the census."

"I have just come from there. It was also the village of my fore-fathers."

Mary wiped the moisture from her lips and handed the bag back to its owner with a thank you. The man extended the bag to Joseph, who declined.

"Drink. It is another hour to Bethlehem."

Joseph took the bag and drank briefly before giving it back. "We thank you for your kindness," he stated.

"The village is full. I suppose you have relatives who can take you in."

"Yes."

"And a midwife," he said, smiling. "In case you cannot find someone, there is a woman, a kindly one who has delivered many children in the village. Her name is Abital, and her house sits near the old fortress gate on the south of the village."

"Once more, we thank you. And where does your journey take you?"

"Only to Jerusalem. It is my home, and my son and his family are there for Passover. They brought others, and it is crowded. I decided to take this day's journey." He smiled. "I am too old for such chaos." He put the strap of the waterskin over his shoulder and gave another slight bow. "To have a child born in the village of David would be no small honor. May God grant you such a blessing."

He walked down the hill, and Joseph looked after him a moment. The words spoken pushed something to the edge of his memory, but he could not quite grasp it. A scripture . . . What was it?

"Joseph."

Mary's voice brought him out of his thoughts. "Yes?" he answered.

"We must go."

CHAPTER 12

Joseph lifted Mary onto the donkey's back once more. She braced herself against the horn of the pack saddle, and Joseph carefully picked the easiest way along the trail toward Bethlehem. It was dark when they reached the old fortress walls of the village and passed through the northern gate. As they passed by a large inn that was overflowing with men and animals, Joseph said a silent prayer. He cringed at the thought of staying there.

Joseph hoped to find a kataluma. The word was often interpreted as *inn* by the Greeks and Romans who did not understand Jewish language and customs, but in reality it was a private room in a home that was let out by its owners to visiting family members or close friends. Travelers who stayed in a khan, or caravansary, obviously had no relatives in the village or city, or the rooms held by relatives were full. But the khans were horrible places where thieves mingled with honest men and the stall-like quarters offered no privacy. Joseph dreaded the idea of Mary sleeping in such a place, let alone delivering the child there.

Joseph's stomach churned as they worked their way through narrow streets to the center of the town, streets made even narrower by animals tethered outside homes and courtyards to make room for guests. He had never seen even Jerusalem so crowded!

The central square was filled with men and families camped around the well, preparing their evening meals and rolling out their blankets and sleeping mats under makeshift shelters. A woman carrying a water pot on her head weaved her away around these, and Joseph excused himself and asked her if she knew where the Street of the Kings might be.

"Humph! Another traveler! If you expect to find any room, you have lost your senses!" She looked at Mary, and her harsh tone softened. She pointed toward a street that went back to the north. "That is the street you look for." She started to leave.

"The house of Abel, son of Bethuel. Do you know which one—"

"The last one before you reach the ancient wall," she replied. Then she hurried away, nearly colliding with a man who stumbled into her. After the two exchanged words of derision, the woman disappeared into the street from which Joseph and Mary had just emerged. Joseph's anxiety increased as he guided the donkey carefully through the crowd, then into the Street of the Kings. A less-congested area, the street was bordered by a few large, communal homes with small courtyards just inside their gates. Unfortunately, even these seemed filled either with animals or with people cooking around open fires—or both. Finally, Joseph and Mary came to the last house. It was small, its shuttered windows open, light mingling with numerous voices cascading onto the street. There was no courtyard, and Joseph took a deep breath and knocked, then waited for the cousin he hardly knew to come to his door.

It opened and an elderly man stood before him.

"Shalom. I seek Abel, son of Bethuel." Joseph bowed slightly.

"I am Abel, son of Bethuel," the man responded.

Joseph could see a room filled with men, women, and children just behind him. They had just finished a meal. "My name is Joseph, son of Jacob, and this is my wife, Mary. We are from Nazareth, come for the census and for Passover. I am your kin, and Mary is expecting a child. We hoped that you might have a room."

Abel frowned and stepped to one side to reveal those behind him. "As you can see, my house is full. I have no room. Possibly the khan . . ."

"My wife is expecting. The pains already give us warning, and a khan would be the worst possible place for a child's birth. Do you know of anyone who might still have a room? I can pay if necessary, but we need privacy."

Abel's countenance softened, and he thought for a moment. "I am sorry, Joseph, but I have no room."

"Grandfather!" A voice came from behind Abel, and he turned to one side. A young woman about Mary's age stood behind him.

"Yes, Adah, what is it?" he asked.

"You have the stable. It is warm enough and will give some privacy."

"She is right, Father," added one of the men. "Some of us can sleep on the roof."

"Or in the tower overlooking the fields. The sheep and vineyards need watching against thieves anyway," said another. "Give them the stable."

Adah spoke again. "It will be even better than here if the baby does come. They will have privacy, and I can help Mary care for the child."

Abel sighed while smiling gratefully at her and the others. "Yes, you are right. Thank you." He turned to Joseph. "It is only a cave, a stable where I house animals. You are welcome to it if . . . if you think it would serve your purposes."

Relieved, Joseph smiled. The house was crowded, the city overflowing, and to find a place away from it all seemed like a very great blessing. "We would be pleased, yes, thank you," Joseph said, putting an arm around a grateful Mary.

Abel lifted his head and smiled. "Then we shall go and see what can be done." He picked up a large lamp, already lit.

"But Grandfather, you should introduce them to all—"

"Yes, yes, of course." He did so, quickly giving the names of all those in the room. Joseph counted twenty-two names. For such a small house, it would be very crowded.

"Now, off to the stable," Abel declared. "I can see your Mary is quite exhausted." He stepped outside and led the way through an opening in the crumbling city wall where a path led down the hillside. They saw numerous campfires in the valley and across the hills.

"Some of these belong to our shepherds, now watching over their flocks, not just because it is time for the lambs, but because there are so many people, and a free lamb . . ." He shrugged. "It is tempting to some. But most of the fires are those of guests. As you see, our little village could never house them all." He pointed to a fire along the hill. "That is where my sheep graze. They have already begun to drop their lambs, and though my grandsons are quite good shepherds, my son is also with them. My grandsons have little experience in helping the ewes give birth, and we cannot afford to lose even one lamb."

Abel moved farther along the path to an opening in the side of the hill. "I hope this will do."

Wide enough for a large horse to enter, an opening in the hillside sloped downward, then flattened out and widened into a small room with a low ceiling. Four donkeys stood tied to heavy stones lying on the floor, a hole drilled through the center of each stone. The donkeys all looked at the old man and the young couple as they entered, and several snorted when Saul appeared. He brayed as if happy to see some of his own kind, and a female returned the gesture with a bray of her own.

Abel pointed to her. "The small one is mine, the others belong to my sons and a cousin here for Passover. You can put yours there, at the end. Grass is not so plentiful now that the goats and sheep graze the fields, but we find a load each day. For tonight, there is enough left for your animal. If you keep the place clean of dung, I will see that they bring extra for you."

Joseph nodded. "If you need your sons for the care of the sheep and the new lambs, I can cut the grass and feed the animals."

"Yes, that would be most helpful. Thank you," Abel said, sounding impressed with Joseph's offer.

Joseph searched the room, looking for a place to make a bed. Abel turned the lamp around to reveal the back section of the cave.

"As you see, there is a small upper level where we store straw and the implements of harvest and planting. This is the part Adah spoke of. It is quite small, but there is room enough for a comfortable bed and then some."

Three steps were carved into a lower portion of the cave wall, then an opening reached back into the rock another four or five cubits. The ceiling was sufficiently high for comfortable movement, and the area gave them separation from the animals.

"I will take my donkey and those of my two sons with me tonight. We will need them in the morning. The other must stay but will be good company for your own."

"It is not necessary to remove them," Mary replied. "They will provide warmth and—"

"And a pungent odor," Abel interrupted, smiling. "As you see, we have not had time to clean out the dung lately. I apologize. And these animals will only make it worse."

"I will see to it tomorrow," Joseph declared. "And we need no apology. We thank you for your kindness and will ask God to bless you with beautiful lambs. And Mary is right; you do not need to remove the donkeys."

"I will take them to the fields just the same. They can graze on fresh grass and will be there when I need them. Along with caring for new lambs and the sheep, our barley has become ready for harvest early this year. They work carrying the sheaves to the threshing floor." Abel pointed to a crack in the ceiling. "Air flows through the crack for ventilation, and there is a fire pit just outside the cave entrance." He placed the lamp on a ledge carved in the rock. "The threshing floor is just above us, and there is straw there. A trail goes to it directly from the cave. How long will you stay in Bethlehem?"

"We aren't sure. At least six months, maybe longer."

"When Passover is finished, we can find you a better place. And your work, what is it you do?"

"I am a carpenter," Joseph answered.

"The best in all Israel," Mary added.

Abel chuckled. "We need a good carpenter here. Herod and the chief priests take ours for their own purposes and for the temple. This may be your fate as well, especially if you are as good as your wife says. Do you have a lamp?"

Joseph removed one from the pack on Saul's back, and Abel poured some oil from his large one into it. Joseph then put a wick in the oil and used the flame from Abel's lamp to light it.

"I will check on you in the morning." Abel looked at Mary. "If you need a midwife, there are many in the village."

"We learned of a woman named Abital while coming here. Is she—"

"A very good midwife who delivered all my own children. Her house is near the edge of the village."

"Then tomorrow Joseph or I will visit her."

Abel bowed slightly. "Sleep well, then." He untied two of the animals and led them toward the front of the cave.

"Where does one register?" Joseph asked.

"Ah, yes, the census. At the market near the town gate that leads to Jerusalem. You cannot miss it." He walked toward the cave's entrance, then disappeared into the night.

"We are blessed," Mary said. "When we came into the village . . . the khan, the streets. I did not think we would ever find anything so good as this."

"Nor I."

"Bring straw while I get us a bite to eat before we sleep."

They busied themselves, glad to have the long journey over. Mary's labor pains seemed to subside, and relief replaced her fear of giving birth on the trail. Joseph removed the packs from his and Saul's backs, removed another lamp, lit it, and led the animal up to the threshing floor. He found plenty of straw and loaded Saul until the animal looked small under the stack tied to the work pack. Returning to the stable, Joseph spread the straw in the sleeping room before tethering the donkey and giving him some grass.

As Mary and Joseph finished their broth, bread, and cheese, a light appeared in the tunnel, and Adah entered. She had a water jug on her shoulder and presented it to Joseph. "Grandfather said you might need it."

"Yes, very much. Thank you," Mary responded. "And thank you for reminding your grandfather about this place. It will do very nicely."

Adah smiled. "I am glad of the baby and wish to help when he comes."

"Then you live here, in Bethlehem?" Joseph asked.

"My father watches the sheep tonight. We live in a house outside the village, near the olive groves."

"And all of the other people in the house?"

"My grandmother's brother and sister and some of their families. They live in northern Galilee, south of Caesarea Philippi. They come when they can for Passover. This year, they brought everyone because of the census." She bowed. "I will come and bring more water tomorrow."

They thanked her again, and she disappeared down the tunnel.

Mary placed the remainder of their food inside a pack and pushed it back onto the upper ledge where they would sleep, then began laying out their bed mats and blankets.

Joseph used his lamp to inspect the cave. His search revealed a crack in the wall where he could feel the flow of fresh air—a good place for a small fire when the baby came. Though the cave was warm enough for them, it would be chilly for a newborn.

He saw Mary kneeling in prayer and quietly removed his own prayer shawl from the pack near the steps, walking up the tunnel and outside. Putting the prayer shawl in place, he knelt facing the holy sanctuary of the temple, but looked up toward heaven. In a quiet tone, he gave thanks for their safe arrival and for a comfortable place to sleep, for Abel and especially Adah, who seemed touched by the finger of God to help them. Even the stranger on the road was a blessing for his offering of water, as was Marcus for being there when things could have gone badly for Joseph.

Then, as he had done every day, several times a day since his dream, he asked for strength to protect Mary and the baby.

"Enlighten my mind, Father, that I might know Thy will and follow it."

He closed the prayer, then stood, enjoying the fresh mountain air mingled with smoke from the fires dotting the landscape before him. In the distance, singing was accompanied by flutes and other instruments; Joseph could vaguely see dancing and celebration around a large fire on a hill to the northwest of him. Beyond these camps, the subdued dome of light over Jerusalem—emanating from hundreds of lamps and fires burning there—reflected off the high walls of the temple itself. God's house. Joseph would go as soon as he could and give a peace offering, one of sincere thanks for his many blessings.

Joseph felt very tired. Picking up his lamp, he went inside to find Mary snuggled beneath the blankets. He watched her a moment. How beautiful and vulnerable, yet so strong. Once more, he knew that God had chosen well for His Son. Joseph put out the lamps, removed his outer clothing, and slipped in next to his wife. Sensing his presence, she turned and put her head on an arm he automatically extended for her, then snuggled in close.

"I love you, Joseph," she said softly.

"And I love you."

The darkness was absolute, the silence deepened by the thick layers of rock that lay between them and the outside world.

The sweet smell of her hair settled around him, and he gently kissed her forehead.

"Thank you for letting me come with you," Mary whispered. She was nearly asleep, and he knew she would not hear his answer.

He had fought bringing her, did not want her to come, and had even begged God's forgiveness for endangering her this way. He was about to ask forgiveness one more time when a thought settled in his mind with such force that it stunned him.

She had to come.

But why? Why here? he asked himself.

His mind picked at it, but he was too exhausted, his eyes heavy and desperate for sleep. Tomorrow he would try to understand.

CHAPTER 13

Upon awakening, Joseph and Mary were surprised to find the entrance well lit by sunlight and knew they had overslept. Joseph quickly dressed and went outside, stretched in the bright morning sun, and took in his surroundings. The valley stretched for several miles east and west and was dotted with tall fir and cypress trees. The green grass looked well grazed, and most of the sheep foraged at the western end of the valley and along the rim of hills that surrounded it. A shepherd sat on a rock above his sheep playing his flute, and the music wafted across the valley, touching everything with its peaceful sound. Joseph listened for a moment before remembering his purpose and forcing himself to work his way along the hill to a stand of fir trees, where he broke off a dead limb and drug it back to the mouth of the cave. Snapping it into pieces, he used his knife to make shavings and kindling to start a fire. Mary was dressed and had mixed the last of their flour to make bread by the time he was finished, and he quickly retrieved their portable clay oven from where he had stacked their luggage.

After a breakfast of bread, olives, dried fish, and dates, Joseph removed Saul and the other donkey and cleaned out the cave, dispersing the saturated straw in a fallow field just below the cave. When finished, he led Saul up the steep, narrow path to the threshing floor for fresh straw. Finding Abel and some of the younger children winnowing barley, he said his good mornings, and Abel handed him a pot.

"Some goat's milk for Mary," Abel indicated.

Joseph thanked the old man and returned to the cave with a straw-laden Saul. He gave Abel's gift to Mary, who drank a bit, smiled with satisfaction, then found a cool place in the cave to put it while Joseph spread the straw and went for a second load. When he had finished, the room smelled much better. With daily removal of the donkey's waste, the cave would serve them quite well. Taking Saul and the other donkey to the valley floor, Joseph staked them where he and Mary could keep an eye on them. When he returned, he found Mary visiting with Adah, who had brought them more water. The two women were making plans to go to a secondary well near the synagogue to wash clothes.

"It will be crowded," Joseph said with concern. "And such work might rush the baby. Maybe . . ."

"I will do the work while Mary tells me about your journey and about Nazareth and Capernaum," Adah replied. "As for being busy, that is true enough, but it will only get worse as the day goes on. Better to do it now."

"If the baby comes, I want everything to be clean," Mary added.

Joseph shrugged a reluctant agreement and watched them go, then led Saul up the hill to help Abel harvest barley.

* * *

Mary and Adah worked at washing until mid-afternoon, then returned to the cave to put the clean clothes on large rocks to dry. In the hot sun, it did not take long, and soon the items were folded and put away.

"I must return to Grandmother's," Adah said. "She needs help with the cooking since there are so many of us. I will bring you something if you wish."

"No, no, you have done quite enough," Mary answered. "Go, I will be fine."

"I will come back later, and if the baby comes—"

"I will have Joseph come for you. Thank you, Adah. You have been wonderful."

Adah nodded, then ran up the trail and disappeared through the old wall.

Mary thought of her own diminished food supply and decided she must go back to the village and buy grain and a few other things. While she was there, she would try to find the midwife Abital.

Removing Joseph's purse from its hiding place inside a crack in the wall of the cave, she took a few coins, then hid the purse again. Taking a basket, she started up the hill to the village market. She felt a slight twinge of pain and hesitated. It was a strange pain, different than before but quickly gone, and she continued on her way.

The crowds were growing, the narrow streets filled with people, animals, noise, and dust. Mary covered her mouth and nose with the tail of her headscarf and wound her way through the streets until she found the market near the northwest gate.

With the abundance of guests in town, the food items had been picked over, and some vendors had sold everything and gone home, but Mary was able to purchase grain, cheese, and honey, along with several herbs, some beans, and a few early cucumbers. There was a lone pomegranate left on one vendor's cloth, and knowing how Joseph loved them, she longed to buy it. But having seen what was left in his purse and knowing that money might be scarce until Joseph actually found work, she forced herself to resist. It was then that another pain, stronger this time and deeper inside, forced her to stop and sit for a moment to catch her breath. Again, it was quite different from the previous pains. It hung on longer than the first, but soon left her. While catching her breath, she thought of returning to the cave, but she knew that if the time were drawing close for the birth, she must see the midwife and obtain her help.

Getting to her feet, Mary found the house of Abital, knocked, and was told by a young girl that the woman was busy delivering another baby in a nearby village and would not return until tomorrow. The news made Mary a bit nervous, but there was nothing to be done but leave a message with the girl to have Abital come to where they were staying as soon as possible.

As Mary walked slowly back through the village, she noticed a man struggling to fix a broken plow and stopped to watch. The arm of the plow had split in a bad place, and the farmer was obviously frustrated at his attempt to mend it. Mary had watched Joseph mend enough such plows over the last few months that she knew this man's efforts would prove fruitless. The man had wrapped a strip of water-soaked leather around the broken piece and then allowed it to dry, but the repair had not held up when he began plowing again. Mary knew that the dried leather remedy, though good for some things, was not strong enough to withstand the pressure of an animal pulling the plow through wet or rocky soil.

"It is a waste of time to try and mend such a break," she said. She felt a twinge of pain again and gritted her teeth against it, keeping her face clear of a reaction.

The farmer looked up, a bit annoyed, then turned back to his work. "You are a stranger here and a woman with no experience in such things, and yet you find it easy to interfere in a man's business."

Mary blushed. He was right, but she knew Joseph could fix the plow. She took a deep breath, glad that the pain had passed once more, and pressed her argument. "Only because I wish to save the man time and frustration."

The man stood, and Mary used the opportunity to grab the handle of the plow and push it right, then left, as she had seen Joseph do, looking it over carefully. "Here," she pointed. "Another crack in the handle. It also needs replacing." She searched each part. "The rest is sound. In three days, my husband can have it good as new."

"Your husband is a carpenter?"

"Yes."

"He must not do very well if his wife has to find him business."

She stiffened, angry at his words, but bit her tongue and spoke with her head instead of her heart. "Three days. If you don't like his work, you need not pay."

The man smiled. "I have no money."

"But you have grain." She looked past the house to a small grove of olive trees. It looked well kept, as did everything else. The man was a hard worker, a sign he could be trusted to pay a fair price. "And olives. My husband will trade."

"And where is your husband's shop?"

She thought to tell him of the cave, but for some reason decided differently. "Bring it to the house of Abel ben Bethuel. We arrived only yesterday."

He eyed her carefully, wiping his dirty hands on his already-stained robe. "Abel is a trustworthy man. Very well. Three days, no more. After that, I pay nothing. I will deliver it tonight."

She nodded and bowed slightly. "You will not regret it."

The man smiled. "But your husband might. I think his wife over-estimates his ability, and I will have a new plow without cost."

As Mary turned to leave, another pain struck, and she stopped, catching her breath before going on. This contraction was much harder and frightened her. She leaned against the wall, grimacing, and let it subside before struggling on. She was halfway across the village square when it struck again and nearly knocked her to her knees. The basket fell from her hand, and her vision seemed blurred.

"Here now, you'll lose your food," said a woman at her side. She was gathering Mary's things when she noticed the pain in Mary's eyes.

"The baby is coming, isn't it?" the woman asked gently.

Mary could only nod, sweat gathering on her face. She felt weak and needed to sit. The old woman helped her to a step nearby and sat her down, Mary's basket at her side. The pain began to subside but she knew it was far from over.

"Are you all right, dear?" the stranger asked.

Mary nodded again, forcing a smile. "I . . . I just need to catch my breath, that's all."

"Well then, I'll be on my way. We're leaving for Jerusalem in a few minutes. Are you sure you are all right?"

Mary nodded again as the woman touched her hand, said good-bye, and disappeared through the crowd. Mary felt awful, but the pain did subside after a few moments, and she caught her breath, struggled to her feet, and carefully headed down the street that led to the cave. She reached the old wall and was nearly past it when the pain hit her again, this time so hard it made her double over, drop her basket a second time, and fall to her knees. She gasped for breath, her head spinning, and she feared she would pass out and never reach the privacy of the cave. Her mind struggled to remember the instructions her mother had given her so many times about delivering a child.

"Joseph!" she called, but the words would hardly come, her mouth too dry, the pain too difficult. She felt blackness overcome her, and she thought she was surely dying. Then she felt someone's arms enclose her, lift her, hold her close. She heard his voice, knew it was Joseph and that she would be all right. She laid her head against his shoulder and held as tightly as she could to the arms that held her.

"He comes, Joseph," she whispered. "Our Messiah comes."

CHAPTER 14

Joseph laid Mary on the straw, quickly retrieved a vessel of water, dipped his fingers in it, and put some on her face and neck as she gritted her teeth against the pain.

"I must go for help."

She grabbed his arm. "There is no time. Build a birthing chair from the stones I found this morning. There, put it there." She pointed at a spot near the wall, then moaned loudly. "Hurry, Joseph! Hurry!"

He ran for the stones and quickly laid them out for her.

"Water! Get water from the pot over the fire. And rags from our bag." She gritted her teeth, beads of sweat gathering on her face. She pulled her headscarf free and tossed it aside. "Help me to the chair," she ordered, holding out a hand.

Joseph picked her up and hoisted her into place, sweat running down his face, and his heart aching for her. He had helped sheep give birth, and even Saul had been delivered at his hands, but he had never seen a child born! How could he possibly . . .

"Joseph, you can do this," Mary encouraged between contractions.

"But . . ."

She put a finger to his lips. "I will tell you what to do. You must. There is no more time."

He nodded even as she gritted her teeth and moaned so horribly that he thought his heart would burst with sorrow for her.

"Please help us, Father!" he said toward the heavens.

And then it began.

* * *

Joseph wrapped the baby in a blanket just as the infant found his lungs and began to cry. While Mary finished the birthing, Joseph tried to comfort the baby, but he did not mind the cries. The boy was healthy, strong, at least a cubit long, and of good weight.

When Mary had delivered the afterbirth and cared for her bleeding, she used a blanket to cover herself long enough to slip from her stained inner garment. With the blanket wrapped tightly around her, she took the baby and fed him while instructing Joseph to bring water from the covered jar near the entrance.

"Adah brought it from a spring. It is pure water, and I must wash both myself and Jesus."

Joseph brought the water and placed it within her reach. It was then that he felt the chill of the cave.

"I will start a fire. Do you need another blanket?"

She nodded affirmatively and asked that straw be placed behind her and against the wall so she could recline. Joseph quickly saw to it, then placed his own blanket over hers before scurrying from the cave to get rocks for a fire pit, wood to burn, and coals from the fire at the entrance to set the fire ablaze.

Once Joseph had built the fire near the crack in the stable's ceiling, the chill was replaced by both the warmth of the fire and the light it gave. Joseph returned to the ledge, where he found Mary just finishing feeding the baby.

"I will need clean clothes. The birthing seat . . . the wet straw . . . everything will need to be removed, but first help me wash the baby."

She laid the infant on some clean straw. "Open the blanket, and use the pure water to cleanse him." She laid her head against the wall and watched as Joseph began. Cries once more filled the room and Jesus' little legs and arms flailed about as Joseph washed him with the cool water.

"His voice does not lack for strength." Mary laughed softly.

Joseph chuckled. "And he will be good in a fight. Look at him. His arms move so quickly, one would have to be as fast as the wind to avoid his reach."

With the baby washed clean, Mary wrapped him in the swaddling clothes she had made in Nazareth. Warm and tired, the infant closed his eyes and slept.

"We must have a bed for him," Mary indicated. "The small manger that Saul was using for feed—it will do."

Joseph examined the manger, found it a bit soiled, and took it outside, where he cleaned it thoroughly with hot water from the pot over the fire, also rinsing off his hands and arms. When he returned, Mary had cleansed herself and was just slipping into fresh undergarments. He stepped back and waited before entering to find her remaking her bed, the baby asleep on a clean blanket.

As Mary lay down and pulled the covers over her, Joseph placed the manger nearby. He handed Mary the child, then put some clean straw into the trough and covered it with a folded blanket.

When he turned to take the baby, he saw that both mother and infant were asleep. Instead of disturbing them, he removed the blanket from the manger and covered them both.

Though Joseph was tired, the stones used as a birthing chair—and the straw around them—still needed to be removed. When he finished this duty, he used the last of the water to ritually purify himself of the blood on his hands and arms while saying a prayer of both cleansing and thanksgiving. Exhausted, he sat with his back against the wall and watched Mary and Jesus in quiet amazement. It had all happened so quickly and yet so wonderfully! And her strength! It humbled him to his center.

A few moments later, Mary opened her eyes and smiled weakly at her husband. "I have never felt so contented, so happy." Tears came to her eyes as she looked at the baby. "He is beautiful, isn't he?"

Joseph only nodded, his emotions in his throat.

She motioned for him to come closer. He stretched out on the straw, his head on his arm, the baby between them. Mary reached over the baby's head and stroked Joseph's hair tenderly. "You were wonderful."

He held her hand and kissed it softly. Her eyes closed, and she drifted back into sleep. He lay on his back, tears of joy cascading from his eyes and down the sides of his face into the straw. After a moment, he wiped them away while giving thanks to God once more. Then his eyes closed and he slipped into a peaceful sleep. The Messiah had come.

* * *

Joseph awakened to find a stranger standing in the entrance to the cave, a lamp in his hand. He blinked then rubbed his eyes as he sat up and squinted to be sure that he wasn't dreaming. It was then that he noticed there were other strangers sliding quietly in beside the first.

Suddenly very awake, Joseph sat bolt upright, putting himself between Mary and the uninvited guests.

"Wait," said the man. "We are only shepherds come to see the child."

Joseph wasn't sure he heard right, his mind still a bit of a haze. "But how could . . ."

He felt Mary's hand on his arm. "It is all right, Joseph. They won't harm us," she said softly.

Joseph turned to see that Mary had already placed Jesus in his bed, and he wondered how long she had been awake.

"Come," Mary invited the shepherds. "The baby is here."

They walked slowly across the lower portion of the cave until they reached the ledge. The smallest of the four, an older gentleman with a bit of bow to his back, craned his neck to see.

"Let me get him in my arms so you can see him better," Mary said with a smile. On her knees, she removed Jesus from the manger and held him close to her chest. The old shepherd climbed the steps, came close, and knelt down. The others, tall enough to see from where they stood, watched as the old man gently stroked Jesus' blanket, then gingerly touched the child's face.

"He is a beautiful baby," he whispered, "but he does not look different from any other."

Mary smiled broadly. "You expected something different."

They all nodded.

One of the men spoke for them. "We have been taught that he would be as the angels, with great power to perform miracles and return our people to this land, and yet he is just like one of our children."

Joseph, still confused by this sudden interruption, posed a question. "How did you know to come here?"

"We were told in a vision. Angels appeared to us."

Joseph leaned forward. "Angels?"

"A host of them," the old shepherd said matter-of-factly. "What is his name?" he asked Mary.

"It is to be Jesus," Mary replied.

"The one who saves. Yes, that is what we were told."

For the first time Joseph really looked at the four shepherds. They were dressed plainly, two with shepherds staves. Two were about his age, and one was probably close to Joachim's age. The old one, though carrying many years, seemed as strong as the others. Each shepherd's face was content in appearance, his eyes clear, and a humbling feeling of righteousness emanated from the small group.

"This is your family?" Joseph asked the old gentleman.

"My sons. We were in the fields watching over our sheep. It is the time of lambing, and we do not leave it to the children. Several sheep had given birth, and we had worked quite late, but we had lain down to sleep without even eating when the sky . . ." He cleared his throat, his emotions ready to overflow.

"It opened," finished one of the others, his voice filled with awe. "The heavens opened and the angel came. I was about to run, all of us were, when Father . . ." He looked reverently at the old shepherd. "When Father grabbed my arm and whispered to all of us that it was all right, that we would not be harmed."

"The angel that appeared first said he brought us good tidings of great joy," explained the third.

"And not just to us, but to all people," the second added excitedly. "Then he told us about your son."

"At first, we had a hard time finding you," declared the youngest. "The angel told us that he was born in Bethlehem and we would find him in a manger, nothing more. We asked at the houses of the midwives, at the kahns, but found no child."

"Then Father brought us here," the eldest son said.

The old shepherd shrugged. "Years ago, I took shelter in this cave myself. It was in winter and it saved my life from a storm. It came to mind tonight, and I knew if we came, we would find you."

"God led him," revealed the eldest son reverently.

"You said there were other angels," Joseph said in wonder.

"They joined the first and praised God. I have never heard such singing. The heavens seemed filled with the sound, their brightness and glory . . ." He shook his head as if still not sure it had all happened. "They were surely heard clear to Jerusalem!"

"And yet . . . And yet they didn't seem to be there . . . in the sky, but in a place separate. As if the very heavens had opened to show them to us."

"And their words?"

"Glory to God in the highest, and on earth peace, good will toward men," recited the old shepherd.

Mary only nodded, and Joseph could see relief in her eyes as he felt relief himself. Here were other witnesses. God had not left them to carry the burden, the wonder, all alone.

The old man leaned forward and gently kissed the baby on the cheek. "All my life, I have waited to see him. The last few years, as illness has come and I could no longer do the work I once did, I began to doubt that it would be my blessing. Now God has granted it to me. I praise Him . . ." He choked up, tears rolling off his cheeks.

The eldest son took the old man by the arm. "Come, Father, we must let them sleep."

He regained his composure. "Yes." He stroked Jesus' cheek. "You are right." Once more, the old man kissed Jesus reverently before crawling back toward the steps leading away from the cave.

The eldest son handed his father his walking staff while his brother spoke.

"Since the time we were old enough to listen, Father has taught us that the Messiah would come and that he would be born here. Out of Bethlehem-Ephrata he said, out of the city of David. All of us have grown up waiting, watching, wanting Father to be right. I still pinch myself, it seems such a dream, but it is not. He has come."

Joseph felt his heart stop. Of course! That was what had been eluding him! *But thou, Bethlehem Ephratah, though thou be little among the thousands of Judah, yet out of thee shall he come forth unto me that is to be ruler in Israel.* He smiled at the sudden remembrance. "The prophet Micah. I had forgotten."

"Come, Eliahu," his father said. "You were right, we must go." He turned to Joseph. "The child will be in danger if others know where he is. Though we will speak of his coming, no one shall know from us his true identity and where he sleeps."

Joseph nodded, then the old one hugged him tightly and stepped back and bowed, first to Joseph, then to Mary. "You are both God's chosen. We honor you as well as the child."

"Thank you," Mary replied quietly.

Each of the four shepherds faced Jesus, knelt on one knee, and bowed his head. Such humble men, so willing to accept a mere baby as their Messiah. No wonder God had sent His angels to them. As they left the cave, Joseph felt as if light left the room as well.

Mary held Jesus snugly, both she and Joseph thoughtful, wondering at it all.

* * *

"God brought us here," Joseph finally commented. "The census, even the gossips who made you feel so uncomfortable, were just part of getting us to see, to leave Nazareth and come here. I should have remembered sooner."

"It frightens me," Mary said.

Joseph was a bit shocked. "Frightens you?"

"That others know." Mary looked fearfully at her child's face. There was so much she did not understand and wasn't sure she would ever understand about her child. He was her flesh. He cried and hungered and suckled just as any other child born of a woman. She would change his loincloth, dust off his dirty hands, and walk with him through the fields as she would any other child. Joseph would teach him his trade, they would work side by side, and as the eldest of her womb, he would welcome and help raise his younger siblings. This Jesus she understood.

But inside him dwelt the very Son of God. It was this child that she could not understand, almost feared to touch. Even as he was born, she felt to gather him up, run, and hide him from the world. Only Joseph's presence and her absolute weariness kept her from it.

And now God was announcing it to the world. Shepherds had come to see, then bear witness. Surely his name, his very presence would be all over the village tomorrow. How could they possibly protect him? Mary shuddered, tears welling in her eyes, and she sobbed.

"Mary," Joseph said softly, putting his arms around her.

"No, Joseph." She pushed him away. "I . . . I am unclean. You shouldn't . . ." Then she melted into his arms, her tears a flood.

"Shh, it is all right. You heard the old one. They will never tell where he is. Never." He stroked her back, and Jesus snuggled between them, his warmth coursing through Mary like the sun, touching and warming her heart.

"Oh, Joseph, why am I so afraid for him? I know God will never let harm come to him at this young age and yet . . ."

"Because you are his mother. It is only natural. God would not send shepherds He could not trust with such news."

"But that is not my only worry. Don't you see? I worry that I might harm him in some way. That . . . that I might trip over a stone and drop him or . . . or . . ."

Joseph held her close again but did not say anything more, not knowing what to say. While he had his own fears about their ability to protect Jesus, Mary felt comfort and strength in his embrace.

She touched a tiny hand. "Will he bleed and bruise, Joseph? Will he feel pain like the rest of us?"

"Yes, mortality will be his to endure, but death will never come to him until God wills it. Of this I am certain. We must trust God." He laid his head next to her arm. "Now, what has happened to that woman with such great faith I have always loved? Where did she go?"

"She gave birth," Mary exclaimed with a tearful smile. Turning into him, she snuggled close. "Oh, Joseph, I am so thankful for you! I thought I was strong, but now it seems my heart will be crushed. Having him in my arms . . ." She bit her lip.

"All children should be so blessed as to have a place in your arms, Mary. You will be a wonderful mother, and when he is old and is our King, he will build you palaces and honor your name as no other."

"I do not wish for palaces, only for his happiness . . . and his safety."

"Then trust God, and you will have both."

He held her for long minutes until her tears dried and her fears eased.

"I suppose I am just tired."

"Yes, and a mother for the first time. Such emotions we have both seen in others. Do you remember my sister?" He chuckled. "For nearly a year, she would not let her firstborn out of her sight! Now, you must sleep." He took the sleeping baby and put him in the manger. "Lie down, Mary. Get your rest. God is watching over him. Nothing will do him any harm."

Mary slid under her blankets while drying the last of her tears. Joseph pulled his own bed next to hers and lay down beside her, wrapping his arms around her. She pulled him close, and they lay still until her breathing slowed in sleep.

CHAPTER 15

Joseph's eyes popped open at the sound of someone approaching the stable. He rose and quickly donned his robe, then turned to see Adah clambering across the straw with wide eyes. As Mary put the child in his new bed, Adah rapidly spewed forth enough questions to befuddle even a learned scribe. Mary gently calmed the young woman, then answered each question in turn. When asked how she had given birth alone, Mary informed Adah that she hadn't—Joseph had helped. A short gush of sympathy followed.

While Adah coddled Mary and cooed over the baby, Joseph busied himself refilling the lamps before going outside. He was startled to find it was late morning, and he squinted until his eyes adjusted to the light. Stretching, he once more took in the cool air and the smells of the valley and hills around him. *A man could learn to love it here,* he thought. *A good place to raise a son.*

First, he went to the small stream nearby and retrieved more water for purification, then cleansed himself as the law demanded. That done, he retrieved more firewood before reentering the cave to kindle the fading coals into a new blaze.

"Joseph, the basket of food I had with me when the baby came— we will need it," Mary said.

He nodded and left the cave to retrieve the basket he had left in his rush to get Mary inside the cave, the memory of finding her giving him chills.

Joseph had been impressed to leave Abel's threshing floor and return to the cave. When he ignored the impression, it came even harder—like a voice shouting in his head. Leaving Saul behind, he had rushed down the path in time to see Mary collapse at the head of the trail near the ancient wall. It had been a terrifying moment.

Now he heard the bray of a donkey and looked up to see Abel leading Saul down the trail toward him, a broken plow tied to the animal's work pack. They exchanged greetings, and Abel handed the lead rope to Joseph.

"We took him to pasture with the sheep. He is well fed and ready for work." Abel pointed at the plow. "As you see, you have your first job."

Joseph looked at the plow and saw the break. "It is yours?" he asked.

"A friend's. It seems your wife told him you could have it good as new in three days or he would get the labor free." He smiled.

"Mary often misjudges my skill."

"I think not. Anyway, he brought it to my house last night. He said Mary told him you would pick it up, but I thought since I was coming and your Saul is a strong animal, I would bring it along."

"Thank you," Joseph responded. He took Saul's lead rope and tied the animal to a nearby tree.

The sound of the baby crying brought a large grin to Abel's face. "Your child has come! So that is why you left the threshing floor so quickly! Has God blessed you with a son?"

"Yes, and as you can tell, he is very healthy." Joseph laughed.

"I must see him! I must tell my family! Congratulations, Papa!" He slapped Joseph on the back before heading for the cave entrance, meeting Adah as she came into the sunlight carrying Mary's blood-stained clothes.

She pushed her grandfather back. "Not now! She is feeding the child, and there is still some cleaning to do."

Abel's shoulders rose with indignant determination. "Then I will wait."

Adah shook her head. "I need milk, Grandfather. Go home, milk the goat, and tell Mother to bring the milk, along with some bread. Then find a midwife. Mary should be checked to be sure she will heal properly." She started pushing her grandfather toward the trail. "Go! You can see the child when you return."

Abel went, grumbling all the way.

"I see you found the food." Adah took the basket from Joseph. "You did very well for Mary. Few men would be of such help." She turned to go back inside. "You must remove your bed and put it somewhere else until the days of her purification are complete. Though the blood of the birth did not make you unclean, lying in the same bed with Mary will, at least until her cleansing in seven days." She started inside, then turned back. "We need more wood for the fire."

Joseph grunted in agreement and wanted to tell Adah it was too late, that he had already lain next to Mary, but he didn't bother, going for the wood instead, returning to find Adah holding Jesus and Mary asleep. Both mother and child looked like angels, and both, at least in Joseph's sight, were as clean as the deep winter snows of Mt. Hermon. And yet, at the moment, Mary was unclean according to the law.

Joseph pondered the contradiction. God had declared that due to blood loss, a woman was impure after childbirth, not through sin but because the loss of blood could lead to death. By giving the Israelites such laws, He put them in constant remembrance of the dangers of mortality and the need to rely on Him, while also reminding them about the greater death, the death from sin.

After seven days, Mary must bathe in pure water to become clean from this impurity, the simple act showing her faith in God. The water itself did little or nothing, but the spiritual determination to obey God was of great worth and would bring her closer to God.

But all was not finished with this first purification. According to the law, Mary remained spiritually impure for another thirty-three days. In a symbolic way, Mary's bleeding, or any other impurity in Israel, had touched the sanctuary of the temple and made it unclean as well. To remove this uncleanness, and to thus gain access to the temple once more, Mary would have to offer sacrifice at the temple they had symbolically defiled.

They would go to the temple and offer their burnt offerings and purification offerings to do their part in purifying Israel so that they would be worthy of the continued presence of God in His temple.

It was providing these sacrifices and the redemption money for his first-born that worried Joseph at the moment. The law of Moses said he would need a lamb and a pigeon or turtledove, or at the very least two pigeons or two turtledoves. Though he was not a poor man, like most men in Israel who had no sheep of their own, it would be difficult for him to raise the large sum of money required to purchase a lamb at the temple. But regardless of what he could afford, these sacrifices were a gift to God for the lives of both Mary and the baby; Joseph would make them if he had to sell himself into slavery to do it.

As he picked up the last piece of wood, the small bag of money hanging from a strap around his neck fell from its hiding place behind his tunic. He smiled. Joachim's gift. He had forgotten. There were at least five shekels in the bag. The offering for their firstborn son was thus provided for. The realization grew into gratitude as he considered what the money meant.

Under the law, all of the firstborn of Israel were dedicated to God, and though God had taken the Levites to fulfill this dedication, all other firstborn sons must be released from the oath by the payment of five shekels. Joseph was now grateful that his father-in-law had been adamant. Already having the redemption money would give Joseph a better chance of raising the money needed for the purification sacrifices.

When he took the wood inside the stable and built up the fire, Mary was slowly removing her bedding from the upper level. Adah stood by with fresh blankets. Though Adah could do it, and then go through a ritual cleansing of her own, they apparently had decided that Mary was strong enough to help. Once the bedding was washed it no longer could defile.

"We also need more water for heating. Mary will need to wash her hands often until the day of her first purification," Adah explained.

Joseph nodded. The law did not banish a woman to hiding during her impurity, nor did it keep her from touching or feeding her husband and children, but she must wash before doing any of these. Others could not sit or sleep where she did, or even touch the blanket that her continued issue might touch, but after washing, she could touch others. Thus Jesus would not become impure while she fed him, nor would Joseph become unclean by eating food she prepared, but she could not lay Jesus on her blanket, nor should Joseph have lain upon it last night while comforting her.

Joseph had known he would need to cleanse himself when he had lain next to Mary and comforted her. Thus he had gone to the spring to wash himself and became clean from what he saw as a necessary defilement but not a sin. Mary had needed comfort, and God expected him to give that comfort. Still, God would require a cleansing so that Joseph would be reminded to be careful about his purity, but He would not require a sin offering.

Joseph picked up his bed and clothes and left the cave, placing them out of the way near the entrance. He looked for the food bag. He must eat, build his strength, then get busy repairing the plow. He would be pushed to have it ready on time.

He found dates and cheese and ate his fill, washing the food down just in time to receive Adah's mother and three other women, two of whom he had seen at Abel's home the night they had arrived in Bethlehem and one who was introduced as the midwife Abital. They were excited to see the child, and they carried the goat's milk and bread Adah had requested, disappearing inside the cave with the sweet scent of bread following in the air. As Abel was not with them, Joseph assumed something important had come up.

Removing the plow from Saul's back, Joseph looked it over carefully. Mary was probably right. He could finish it in three days, but he would need a solid piece of seasoned hardwood to do it.

Knowing Mary was in good hands, he took his axe and led Saul down the hill and across the valley, then up the far side and along the rim until he found a small stand of dead and seasoned cypress and fir trees. He searched for just the right one, chopped it down and sized it, then stacked the extra pieces in a thicket of bushes, hoping he would have enough carpentry work that he would need them later.

Returning to the stable, he found the campfire hot but no one in sight. Assuming the women were still inside the cave, Joseph tied Saul up and went to the water jar sitting in the shade, dipped a wooden cup inside and drank, then poured the rest over his hands and washed before going inside. He was surprised to find Mary alone, sitting on a blanket near the fire, Jesus sleeping in her arms.

She looked relieved to see him. "Joseph!" She attempted to get up, but Joseph prevented it.

"No, no," he said, kneeling beside her. "And why are you out of bed? You should rest and . . . and where are Adah and the other women who were here?"

The smile left her, replaced by a look of concern. "They went back to the village." She looked down at Jesus, who fussed a little, smacked his lips as if hungry, then quieted. "The shepherds have done as they said. They have told others of their vision."

Joseph felt his stomach turn but calm came quickly. "God sent them to bear witness that the Messiah has come. They have no choice but to declare what they saw. God must prepare all Israel for the coming of His Son. We must trust in Him." He paused to smile. "And Adah and the others went to learn of this strange thing?"

She nodded.

"Obviously, the shepherds kept their word and did not reveal the location of the holy child. If they had shared that, I do not think we would be alone."

Mary nodded once more. "You should probably go and hear what is being said."

Joseph shook his head. "No, it is not necessary. And," he smiled, kissing her lightly on the cheek before standing, "thanks to my wife, I have a plow to repair."

Mary laughed. "Have I promised too much?"

"No, I think you judged the task very well. Have you eaten?"

"Yes, and Adah said she would return before the evening meal." Jesus whimpered, made a face, and tried to open his eyes while licking his lips. "He is hungry once more," she sighed.

Joseph turned to leave the cave and continue his work on the plow when he thought to say something. "Mary."

She looked up at him.

"Do not worry. We are safe. God watches over us."

She nodded and smiled. "I know, but thank you for saying it. Hearing it from you gives me even greater strength, Joseph. More than I can express. Especially now when my emotions seem so close to the surface that I want to cry all the time."

With a curious kind of pride mingled with greater confidence, Joseph went into the bright light of day and untied the wood from Saul's back. Then he prepared a work area near the entrance to the cave where he could hear Mary if she needed him. Retrieving his tools, he scraped the wood clean of dried bark and had begun the task of shaping the wood to the proper size when he heard the excited chatter of women. Adah, Abital, and one of Adah's cousins were coming down the trail.

"But they are so unclear," moaned Adah's cousin. "Angels announce the birth of a king, but they never say where he is born and to whom?" She rolled her eyes in disbelief.

"Surely King Herod could not father another child!" said Abital. "Though he has many wives, they say he has been too sick to even lie with one of them. I'm sure the lecherous old hypocrite would try if he could."

Adah was the only one who did not laugh.

"Our Messiah will not be of Herod," Adah retorted. "The old fool is not even a Jew, not by blood, and certainly not of the lineage of David as the prophets declare!"

"You take this too seriously, Adah," laughed her cousin.

"Old Benjamin and his sons are only shepherds," replied Abital. "Why would God send angels to them instead of to our rabbi or the high priest of the temple? If you ask me, the old man and his sons have lost their senses."

"But couldn't you *feel* what he was saying?" Adah asked. "Surely God is in it!"

"Adah, you must face reality. God would come to His temple, not to shepherds who are neither men of authority nor of the high priesthood."

"Benjamin is a righteous man, as are his sons," Adah said defensively. "I have known him since I was a child, and if any man were worthy of a vision, it would be Benjamin, priest or not. Besides, the temple is corrupt and so is the high priesthood. Why would God send witnesses to such men when they sin as they do? Even I, a woman, am more holy in God's sight than the high priest!"

The others grew serious. "You should not speak of God's high priest that way, Adah. The Lord will strike you dead for it!" Abital insisted.

Adah merely harrumphed, and Joseph could not help but chuckle.

The women saw him and sobered, dropped their conversation, and began gathering Mary's now-dry clothes and bedding. Adah walked to the fire and began poking the nearly cold embers into life with a vengeance that showed her mood.

"So what is the news from the village?" Joseph queried, his hands carefully rubbing the adze over the log.

"Shepherds. Visions. Announcements that the Messiah is born," Adah recounted with a fake smile. "The usual."

Joseph laughed. "And the mood of the villagers?"

The others kept busy but watched Adah.

"Amazed. They wonder, they discuss." She tossed the stick into the fire while glaring at the others. "Then they make fun and dismiss it as . . . as the ravings of lunatics."

The others stiffened, then whispered angrily to one another before one of them spoke. "We have to go back. Our men will need their dinner."

"Yes, yes, go then," Adah said with a wave of her hand.

They dropped the last of the clothes into a basket and scurried up the path.

"And thank you for your help," Joseph called sincerely. The women gave him forced smiles and disappeared. "You should treat them more kindly," he suggested to Adah.

"They are fools." She picked up the hand mill and began grinding grain on a flat stone.

Joseph pitied both grinder and grain but took several strokes with the shaping tool and let her calm down before he spoke. "Because others do not see what we see does not always make them fools, Adah, just momentarily blind."

"But you should hear Benjamin, Joseph," she complained. "He and his sons are so sure of what they saw, so powerful in their witness!" She paused, nearly despondent. "But even Uriah is unsure. I don't know what to think."

"Uriah?" Joseph asked.

Adah blushed. "Yes, Benjamin's grandson, the son of Shaphat. He . . . he is a friend."

"But he did not see this vision."

She shook her head. "No, it surprises even him."

"Does he believe the others?"

"I am not sure. I think he struggles with it. He is a good man, Joseph. If . . . if what his father and grandfather are saying is true, surely he will know it," she replied firmly.

Joseph shrugged. "All of us struggle with the visions of others, Adah. In time, if he is sincere and seeks to know, he will feel what you feel." Joseph scraped another piece of wood with the adze. "Is what Uriah thinks that important?"

Adah looked at him as if he had just walked over the tomb of Abraham. She acted like she was about to say something, then clamped her jaw shut.

"Ah, I see. You want him to be more than a friend," Joseph stated with a smile. "Let me put it another way. For you to believe, must Uriah also believe?"

"No, I suppose not, but it would make it easier, and all of us would find it easier to believe if the shepherds would just tell us where this newborn child is. Then we could all prove it for ourselves."

"And how would this prove anything to you? Do you expect him to be sitting on a throne, to have angels at his side? What if he were just another baby, born to a poor family or—"

"Like Jesus."

He gulped. "What?"

"You know, if he were like Jesus. Just a baby." She paused. "I suppose you are right. If he were just a baby like any other baby, it would be hard for others to believe, and it would be dangerous. If the Herods learned of it . . ."

Joseph started breathing again. "The point is that most people would not believe even if they did see, unless they also saw angels or had visions. Even when he is revealed, many will not believe, even if he comes with great power, and some will try to harm him to save themselves from having to bend their knee to him." Joseph blew thin shavings from his tool, then stroked the wood with the palm of a trained hand before applying the tool again. "You asked the other women if they felt something. Why?"

"That is what is so frustrating! I . . . I seem to be the only one who did."

"The shepherds are good men, and from what you said, many were amazed at their words and probably felt what you did; they just didn't say so." He stopped working. "I believe them, Adah, but it is not time for me to know everything. By the testimony of the past prophets, we know he will come. Now, humble shepherds, righteous men I would think, bear witness that he has been born somewhere. Shouldn't those of us who feel they are right do something about it?"

"Do something? But what?"

"Prepare and watch for the day when he will rise to power," Joseph declared.

She looked up from her grinding. "You really believe it, don't you?"

He stopped working and smiled down at her. "Yes, I believe. Like you, my heart tells me it is true."

"But Uriah—"

"Do not be critical of others who do not feel what you feel or who cannot see. We are all a bit deaf and blind sometimes. If he is a good man, when it is time, he will see."

Adah thought about that for a moment. It was obvious she had deep feelings for Uriah and was trying to reconcile this difference between them. After a moment, she shrugged. "Yes, I suppose you are right." The grinder she was using settled into a less-irritated movement, and Joseph went back to work on the plow with feelings of both wonder and gratitude. He marveled that someone like Adah could sit only a few cubits from the very Messiah she wanted so badly to come and not recognize him, yet Joseph was grateful it was so. It comforted him and he knew it would bring Mary peace as well. Their son was in no immediate danger simply because God, though announcing to His people that their Messiah was born, protected him from their seeing him before he could protect himself from his enemies.

Joseph's back ached and he stood to stretch, then left Adah preparing supper while he went inside the cave to tell Mary what had happened and that she did not need to worry. God truly was watching over them.

CHAPTER NOTE

1. By giving the Israelites laws dealing with purification and sacrifice, the Lord put them in constant remembrance of the dangers of mortality and the need to rely on Him, while also reminding them about the greater death, the death from sin. This reinforced the doctrine that only God could save his people from both mortal death and from the death of the spirit.

According to Jewish Law, those who had touched anything declared impure by God had to cleanse themselves. In a symbolic way, their impurity touched the sanctuary of the temple and made it unclean as well. Cleansing themselves and offering sacrifice symbolically cleansed the defiled temple as well. If a man or woman did not, the temple would remain defiled, and if many in Israel refused to come before God and remember Him in their sacrifices, soon God would no longer reside in His sanctuary because it was unclean. Israel would then be left with no God to hear their prayers and protect them. In this lay the sickness that could bring Israel's destruction, and Joseph, as one righteous in Israel, would have been determined that he and Mary not have their garments stained by disobedience.

CHAPTER 16

On the third day, Joseph went to the village, purchased parchment in the village square, and wrote a letter to Mary's parents telling them that Jesus had been born and that Joseph and Mary hoped they could visit soon. It also contained a reminder not to share the divine nature of the event.

He thought of writing to Matthias and Salome but decided against it, at least for now. They would want explanations, and he was not prepared to provide them.

Joseph sealed the letter and handed it to the scribe who owned the shop. "How much to see that it goes to Nazareth, a village a few miles from Sepphoris?" he asked.

The man indicated the price and Joseph paid it, then noticed a group of men laughing and joking loudly across the square. Among them was Adah's father, Reuben. They were discussing the vision of Benjamin and his sons, and Joseph listened to find most comments thoughtless and condescending, even derogatory toward the old shepherd and his kin. It saddened Joseph, but he also felt some relief. He did not relish his wife and son being the object of such derision, and if these men would not believe the shepherds, why would they believe him or Mary, strangers to their village? Once more, he thanked God for His wisdom and that Benjamin and his sons were keeping their word.

They must be special men, Joseph thought, *humble, willing to obey God no matter the personal cost.* But then, God would not have trusted them with such information if they were otherwise. Such greatness of spirit rarely existed among men and had certainly been recognized by the God of Heaven before He sent angels to witness of His Son. It saddened Joseph to see Reuben and the others treat such good men this way because of their own lack of spiritual understanding, but he supposed it had always been this way among men. Prophets were never accepted in their own country, among their own people.

Joseph went to the table of the Roman census and stood in a short line. While he waited, Abel entered the square and approached the group of which his son Reuben was a part. After hearing only a few seconds of the conversation, Abel walked away, shaking his head in disappointment. He was about to pass by Joseph when he lifted his chin and their eyes met. He visibly brightened.

"Ah, Joseph, how is that new son?"

"Very well, thank you," Joseph replied.

"I am sorry there is no better place than my stable for them," Abel said sincerely. "But soon the village will empty of Passover worshippers and we can find something more suitable."

"Is the land around the cave yours?" Joseph asked.

"Yes, and a rocky place it is. I tried to plant olive trees there, but the soil is so sparse and the stone so plentiful that the water could not feed the seeds, and they blew away in the wind."

"But a good foundation for a home," Joseph commented. "I can pay you very little, but I would like to build a place for Mary and the baby as soon as I can."

Abel rubbed his beard. "Yes, for a house . . . possibly . . . But I do not see how you can raise a garden. And I will need the cave in the fall . . ."

"The land atop the hill could serve as the courtyard to the house, and nearby is a small, fertile spot for a garden."

Once more Abel stroked his beard. "I will come at sunset. We will take a look at what you plan, and then we will see."

"I can only pay you with my hands," Joseph explained.

Abel smiled. "I could use a new plow and a sturdy table for my wife. You could help in the fields and with the sheep until the full price we decide on is reached. Yes, yes, we can find an agreeable solution."

More loud laughter came from the group of men, annoying Abel.

"What do you think of the old shepherd's story?" Joseph inquired.

"Benjamin and I have been friends for years. He is a righteous man and has never lied or deceived another. If he said he saw an angel, he saw an angel. But, as you see, for some it is hard to accept, even from Benjamin."

"But where could this Messiah be?" Joseph queried.

"Does it matter as long as he is safe? When the time is right, God will reveal him. Benjamin only informs us of what the prophets have been telling us for years. Watch and be ready. We will know him when he comes." Laughter interrupted him, and he glared at the men, his jaw hardening like stone. "Even if Benjamin has not seen angels, he does not deserve this kind of treatment. It disgusts me, and when we meet in synagogue on the Sabbath, I will show them in the scriptures that they have much need of repentance. Much need!" He took a deep breath and patted Joseph gently on the arm. "Take care of Mary and the baby. I will see you at sunset." He looked around. "Now I must hurry. I have a buyer for the small portion of my barley that the thieves of Rome and Herod did not steal from me with their unholy taxes!" With that he walked quickly away.

Joseph watched Abel disappear up the street, amazed at his elderly cousin's words. He of all men should be able to connect Benjamin's testimony to Jesus, and yet Abel could not see.

"Name."

Joseph snapped out of his thoughts, two Roman officials looking at him with some annoyance.

"What?" he said.

"Your name," repeated a soldier. "This is no line for daydreamers."

"And your connection to this village," said the other man with obviously bored disinterest. This one, a Jew, spoke in Hebrew, and was richly dressed, probably a representative of the Sanhedrin.

"Joseph, son of Jacob. My father and I are of the tribe of Judah and of Jesse, the father of David."

"Are you married?"

"Yes. My wife's name is Mary. She is also a descendant of David, and we have a newborn son."

The official made a notation, wrote something on a slip of paper, then waved his hand impatiently for Joseph to move on.

Joseph stepped aside, glad to have it finished.

Returning to the cave, he found Mary resting in the shade of several small fir trees, Adah squatting near the fire stirring something in a pot that smelled wonderfully like mutton. Joseph dismissed the thought; they had no sheep and certainly could not afford to slaughter one for soup if they did.

"Shalom, husband." Mary greeted him with a warm smile.

Joseph smiled a hello as the aroma drew him toward the fire, his mouth watering. "Surely my nose deceives me, but I could swear . . ." Then he saw the chunks of meat swimming in the broth and looked at Adah incredulously. "Where did you get meat?"

"Uriah, a friend of Adah's, brought it." Mary grinned. "A gift from Benjamin and his sons," she added.

"Ah, Uriah!" Joseph said, smiling at Adah.

Adah blushed a deep red, then regained her composure. Joseph saw a look of concern in her eyes.

"Why would they send you meat?" Adah asked.

Caught off guard, Joseph stammered. Mary came to his rescue.

"We are not sure, but I would guess it has something to do with Uriah wanting to see you. The meat was only an excuse."

Adah blushed again, and Joseph felt relief. "Whatever the reason, it smells wonderful," he commented.

"Sit, Joseph, and hold your son. He is quite awake now," Adah said, shoving aside her bothersome thoughts.

Mary washed her hands while Adah retrieved Jesus from his makeshift cradle and handed him to Joseph, who laid him on a blanket separate from Mary's and unwound his swaddling clothes. The babe immediately started moving his arms and legs rapidly, glad of this new freedom.

"He will grow up unruly and disobedient if left free too often," Mary declared in a partially scolding tone.

Joseph put a finger in Jesus' little hand while making a clicking sound with his tongue. The infant stared blankly in Joseph's general direction but did not react.

"He is only three days old, Joseph. He cannot even see you," Adah explained.

Joseph marveled at the perfectly formed tiny toes and fingers.

"His hair is just like mine," Mary said. "Dark, unruly, as if the wind were blowing through it all the time."

Joseph gently stroked the soft, thick, curly locks, and the flailing limbs stopped their motion.

"Your touch calms him," Mary said with a pleased smile. "Even when I stroke him, he is not so comforted. It is a good sign."

"I must go," Adah declared suddenly, setting the soup next to Mary's blanket where she could reach it. "Eat. Through you it will make the boy strong." She smiled genuinely at Jesus. Joseph could see the look of longing there, and for the first time he really saw Adah. She was a young woman, at least fourteen, and ready to think of her own children. No wonder she was so eager to help with Jesus, no wonder her blush at the thought of Uriah.

Falling to her knees next to Jesus, Adah leaned over and kissed him gently on the cheek. It was obvious that she had to force herself away from the child.

She was halfway up the path when she spoke. "I'll be back tonight." She quickly disappeared up the trail and past the old city wall.

Mary dished some of the soup into bowls, and she and Joseph ate. The food tasted wonderful, and Joseph quickly devoured his and cleaned out the bowl with bread before speaking. "Are she and Uriah betrothed?" he asked Mary as he laid his bowl aside.

"No, but there was some talk of it, and it is her wish." Mary finished her last piece of meat. "But now she thinks it impossible. Her father has a growing dislike for Uriah's family because of their insistence on seeing angels. She asked her father if he would still accept a proposal from Uriah, but Reuben said no, that his family would have nothing to do with such foolishness."

He sighed. "I saw Reuben at the village square. He and a few others seem determined to ruin Uriah's family. It would be hard for Reuben to betroth his daughter to a family he mocks and says has a devil."

"And was Abel among them?"

"No. He is disgusted with his son and what he says." He paused, his fingers gently touching Jesus' small foot. "It is wisdom in God that such men do not know of Jesus and of us. I am afraid I would not stand for their insults. I have broken men's noses for less."

Mary chuckled. "Then if they find out, we leave Bethlehem. You cannot break everyone's nose without getting your own bent, at least just a little, and I refuse to be seen with anyone other than the handsome man I married."

He laughed. "I thank the God of Israel for your obvious blindness. But you are right, having my nose bent would only make things worse. I will try to keep it out of trouble."

Mary smiled and then touched his cheek lightly. "You are handsome, Joseph, and a better man would be hard to find. God has truly blessed me." She wrapped her arms around him and put her head on his shoulder.

"I am the one blessed," Joseph said quietly. He gently kissed her hair, then pushed it back and smiled. "Now, let me tell you the good news." He told her of his discussion about the land with Abel.

"Oh, Joseph, that is wonderful!" she exclaimed, beaming.

Joseph wrapped Jesus in the swaddling clothes, and the baby began to fuss. "You know he hates these. They hinder him."

"I will not see him grow up with crooked bones and a wild spirit," Mary answered firmly.

Joseph handed the baby to her, and she tucked and smoothed the wraps with a loving hand. "When will we know how much Abel will want for his land?"

"He is coming tonight. Do not worry, Abel is a good man. He would not speak to me of such a possibility if he were not willing to give us good terms. He will help us, and God will bless him for it."

Mary stiffened as she remembered what else it might mean. "Oh, Joseph, but . . . but Nazareth!"

Joseph smiled. "Do not worry, Mary. We will return, but for now, this is to be our home, and when we leave, someone will surely pay us well for a sturdy house. It can only be a blessing."

Mary relaxed. "Yes, of course, you are right. Well then, if we are to live here for a while you do not want your wife's reputation soiled. You had better keep the promise she made and deliver that plow. It is the third day, you know."

"Yes, I know. You will be all right alone for a while?"

"Yes, fine. Help me to my feet."

"But—"

"I need to walk and move around, Joseph, or I will become a lazy wife and of little use. Help me up."

Getting to his feet, Joseph extended a hand to her. Mary grimaced slightly then gave him a smile and a peck on the cheek as she stood. "Now, off with you. I have things to do," she declared.

Joseph went to the nearly finished plow and drove in the last of the wooden pegs that attached the two armatures. Mary busied herself with the dishes, though at a slower pace than usual. When she was finished and tending a now-fussing Jesus, Joseph was loading the plow onto the donkey's back.

Walking back to his wife with a concerned look on his face, he asked, "Are you sure you will be all right?"

Mary smiled. "I will be fine. Off with you now. The sooner you go, the sooner you return."

Joseph stood, hesitated, then untied Saul. "Do you remember which house this man lived in?"

"Yes. It is just past Abel's home, five houses. Adah says his name is Haman."

Joseph bid Mary a reluctant good-bye and led Saul up the path, through the ruins, and into the village street that ran past Abel's house.

Finding the plow's owner in his olive grove tending his trees, Joseph gave the traditional greeting, and Haman looked over the plow with a critical eye, finally nodding his approval.

"Your wife was right. You are a good carpenter." He ran his hand over his beard, considering. "Such a plow is worth half a modius of grain . . ." He glanced at Joseph, who shook his head to indicate that it was not enough. "And half a modius of olives. When they are ripe, of course, but you must pick them yourself." He waited for Joseph's response. They bartered back and forth until they came to a fair price. Joseph would receive two-thirds a modius of grain and one-quarter saton of olive oil, pressed and ready for use. He had no oil press, and though Abel and his sons probably did, he did not wish to rely on their kindness more than needed, especially as he wished to deal with Abel for land.

"I will have my son bring the grain tomorrow. The oil will come when we are finished with the crop." The agreement was signed with a simple nod.

"I know a man looking for someone to build him a table. I will tell him about you," Haman said. "Also, Herod's soldiers look for a carpenter to repair the northwest gates of the town. If you do not mind working for Gentiles—"

"I prefer the table," Joseph answered. "I do not relish being around soldiers all day." He bowed slightly. "Thank you, and if you hear of others . . ."

"Of course, of course. Your wife was expecting. Has the child come yet?"

"Yes. It is a boy," he stated proudly.

"God grants you a great blessing then." He reached into a nearby sack and pulled out some nuts. "A gift for her." Joseph quickly removed a cloth and formed a pouch. Haman dropped the nuts in, then retrieved another small handful and did the same with them. "So she does not have to eat alone." He smiled. "Shalom."

Joseph thanked him several times before he began his walk back to the cave, where he found Mary grinding grain and Jesus asleep in his manger. Joseph breathed more easily when Mary smiled and quickly went to the fire to dish out the last of the lamb and pull a small cake from the clay oven they used for travel. He washed his hands, took the food, and squatted near the fire to eat.

"Feeding me so much, you will make me fat and lazy," Joseph commented. Then he remembered the gift and handed her the cloth filled with nuts. "A gift from Haman. He liked my work and will send a man who needs a table."

Delighted, Mary took the cloth but offered him first choice of the nuts. He declined, and she picked out a nut and put it in her mouth, then folded the cloth and put it in the pocket of her robe. Such a treasure should last a long time.

Joseph finished eating, set the dish aside, and sat back, noticing Mary looking at him with a critical eye. He rubbed around his mouth as if to find food there. "What?"

"If you were a sheep, it would be time for shearing."

He ruffled his hair, grinning. "Then you should shear me," he sighed.

"Sharpen your knife, and I will take care of you. With Jesus asleep, now is a good time."

He retrieved his shearing knife from their pack and pulled it from its old leather scabbard. It was his father's, and though the blade was somewhat thinner from use, it still sharpened to a fine edge. He used the hand stone to hone it still more, then gave it to Mary before sitting on the edge of his own blanket.

She washed her hands and dried them, then knelt behind her husband and deftly used the knife to cut some length from his hair.

Then he faced her so she could trim his beard. As she worked, they talked of the bargain Joseph had struck with Haman.

"You did well," Mary complimented.

"There is work enough to survive, and with a little extra effort, I can get enough to pay Abel for his land in two years' time."

"If he accepts your price."

"Yes."

"And what did the scribe say of our letter? How long will it be?"

"Many days, possibly a month." He shrugged.

Both of them knew that letters sometimes did not arrive at their appointed destinations. Because of this, she and Joseph would watch for someone going north and send word with them as well. People were good about delivering such messages at least as far as they could. Mary remembered being in the fish market in Capernaum when a man spoke up loudly saying he had a message for someone in Cana. Half a dozen people were either from there or going that way and said they would take the message. It was a message the man had received in Rome, and though it had been months since he had received it, he seemed to give it word for word.

"I wish to sleep outside now. Could you make us a shelter?" she asked.

"Of course," he said. He loved to sit under her hand, to feel her touch, her breath softly caressing his hair, and he hated it to end, but soon she finished and brushed the clipped hair from his robe, blowing it gently from his ears. Standing, he pulled her close and kissed her.

"My reward for missing your ears?" she smiled up at him.

He chuckled. "And for saving me a second portion of the lamb."

She laid her head on his shoulder, and he held her for a long time before Saul began to bray. "He hasn't been fed all day," Joseph exclaimed.

"Then a few more minutes won't hurt him," she answered, hanging on to her husband.

Then Jesus began to cry. "He hasn't been fed since you went to the village," Mary explained.

"Then a few more minutes won't hurt him," Joseph said.

Mary laughed. "No, I don't suppose it will . . . then again . . ."

They kissed one last time, then parted.

"I will talk to Saul about his timing if you will talk to Jesus," Joseph joked.

Mary laughed again as she lifted the baby and began rocking him. Joseph untied Saul and took him inside the cave and tied him before giving him a large portion of dried grass. Joseph then went into the woods with his axe and cut down a number of small trees for the construction of the shelter. Hauling them in, he decided to put the shelter near the cave entrance. Using leather straps he had brought from Nazareth, he connected the four posts to one another with crossbeams, then added others at angles to give the structure strength.

Sunset came, and Abel appeared as promised. Soon they had struck a deal for the land, and Abel left. Mary moved her bed and blankets under the shelter, and Joseph moved Jesus' crib just as they heard the daily call to synagogue. Joseph retrieved his prayer shawl and, after kissing both Mary and Jesus, went up the hill for prayer and discussion of the Torah. When he returned an hour later, both mother and son were asleep, the fire nothing but embers.

Wanting to collect his thoughts before he slept, Joseph walked along the edge of the hill and found a spot to sit. After several moments of just breathing deeply of the night air, he lay back on the grass of the slope and stared up at the heavens. He noticed a particularly bright star he could not recall seeing before, a star that hung over the eastern sky and outshone all others. Joseph wondered how he could have missed it. Though there had been other bright stars come and go from time to time, they were not nearly as large and bright as this one. Joseph remembered being at the temple a few years earlier and hearing a learned rabbi speak of such a star. What was the scripture? He searched his mind. "There shall come a Star out of Jacob, and a Sceptre shall rise out of Israel." The rabbi had said it would be a sign of the coming Messiah. Joseph smiled. Another witness! He wondered how many people would even take notice or remember that ancient declaration.

Getting to his knees, Joseph put on his prayer shawl and began his prayer. "Proclaim by Thy loud trumpet our deliverance, and raise up a banner to gather our dispersed, and gather us together from the four ends of the earth. Blessed be Thou, O Lord, who gatherest the outcasts of Thy people," he said more quietly, more reverently, than he had in the past. He found it nearly overwhelming that this prayer, one spoken by men of Israel all over the civilized world, could be answered now. Truly the dispersed of Israel could be gathered—an overpowering thought.

Joseph heard the baby cry and immediately stood and went back to their camp. He found Mary pacing. Jesus' cry was a different cry, a cry of anguish, a cry that made Joseph nervous.

"His stomach bothers him greatly," Mary explained in a worried tone. "I have herbs in our bag. Please boil some water."

Joseph searched for the bag, found it, and retrieved the herbs. Though Jesus was divine and his conception miraculous, Joseph knew that the baby was still of Mary's flesh and thus susceptible to the woes and pains of any other child. From the sound of the cry, it might be a sleepless night for all of them.

CHAPTER 17

The next morning, four days after the birth of Jesus, Joseph and Abel went to the synagogue to make arrangements for Jesus' circumcision.

The chief elder of the synagogue asked if they had a relative or a friend who might be a priest, someone they would prefer to do the circumcision. Joseph and Mary had considered Zacharias. He lived only a few miles from Bethlehem, at Juttah, but he would have been working in the temple during Passover and would still have duties there until the end of the month Nisan. Joseph asked the chief elder if there was a local priest not involved at the temple and therefore available to perform the rite. He mentioned an aged man, unable to go to Jerusalem as he used to, but quite strong enough to perform the circumcision for them. Arrangements completed, Joseph and Abel returned to their homes and went to work.

After helping Abel at the threshing floor much of the day, Joseph came down from the hill, and he and Mary carefully selected the spot for their new home. Naturally, the back side of the lower level would be the limestone wall of which the cave was a part. To make this wall straight, he would need to cut into the stone at least two cubits. He would use the rock as foundation stone for the rest of the house. Because the cave would be needed by Abel and his sons for their own animals, especially during the coming winter, this first floor would serve as their home until Joseph could finish the top floor. When that was done, their door would exit into a courtyard just outside the old city wall. Then this lower level would be used as a home for Saul and other animals they hoped to purchase.

The next morning, Joseph began drilling holes in the stone to carve out space for the first floor and also make the blocks he would need for the first few tiers of the three additional walls. It was hard work, but the limestone was soft compared to some rock he had worked; by the end of the day, he had a dozen holes drilled a cubit deep. Filling these with pieces of cypress wood barely smaller than the holes, he poured water in the remaining space and left them overnight, knowing that the water would force the wood to expand and crack the stone from hole to hole. He could then use his sledgehammer to break out the rock and size the pieces for foundation stone.

The next day was the Sabbath, and though Mary wished to go to the synagogue, the days of impurity were not finished, so she remained behind. Adah kept her company, and Joseph went alone, taking the shortest and most direct route to the village square so as not to walk more than needful on the Sabbath.

* * *

The synagogue was much less crowded now that the Day of Passover and the Feast of Unleavened Bread had passed. Furthermore, those who had come to register for the census had already completed this task and now traveled to their distant homes. Though other registrants would come, Joseph was glad to see the pace of the village quickly returning to normal.

He entered the men's section of the synagogue and found Abel sitting on a bench against the wall. Covering his head with his shawl, Joseph sat next to him with a greeting of *shalom* and received the same. Pleasantly surprised to hear no talk of Benjamin and his sons, he commented on it to Abel, who nodded and gave a satisfied grunt. "I visited with the elders," Abel said. "I told them it bordered on bearing false witness and that as such, God would consider it a sin." He grinned. "I also told them that if an angel *had* appeared to them and we made light of it, God would send another angel to our village—one of death like he sent to Egypt. As you see, they seem to have taken the words to heart. At least they do not make their jokes so openly."

Joseph only nodded as a priest brought out the Torah scroll, then one of the men quickly walked to the stand and found a verse to quote and comment on. For nearly two hours this continued, with the quoted verses ranging far and wide but most of them centered on the actions of the law with regard to treatment of others. The most pointed came from Deuteronomy. "If there be among you a poor man of one of thy brethren within any of thy gates in thy land which the Lord thy God giveth thee, thou shalt not harden thine heart, nor shut thine hand from thy poor brother: But thou shalt open thine hand wide unto him, and shalt surely lend him sufficient for his need, in that which he wanteth." The man's commentary then centered on the unjust treatment of Benjamin and his sons. Joseph watched as most of the men looked at their feet and fidgeted in their seats. Reuben and his friends, however, were not among these, their jaws hardened like stone at the obvious reprimand.

When the meeting was over, Joseph said to Abel, "You're right. Your discussion with the leading elders has had good effect."

"Too bad Benjamin and his sons are not hear to witness it," Abel replied.

Joseph hadn't noticed. "Where are they?"

"At the temple offering sacrifice. Benjamin said they must. God had given them something few men would ever know."

The two men sat quiet for a few moments before Joseph spoke. "I thank God today for your kindness to us, Abel. I don't know how to repay you for—"

"It is not necessary, Joseph," Abel answered, staring at Reuben sitting across the hall from them. "I only hope God will bless me by opening the eyes of my son to his pride!"

After leaving the synagogue, Joseph spent the rest of the day sitting across the shelter from Mary, trying to read Seth's scroll of Isaiah in Greek. As he was able, he spoke the words aloud so Mary could hear. It was a slow but gratifying process as over the next few hours he worked through the scroll, discussed the meaning of some of Isaiah's prophecies with Mary, finally settling on a few verses where Isaiah prophesied about the Messiah as the Stem of Jesse.

"But with righteousness shall he judge the poor, and reprove with equity for the meek of the earth: and he shall smite the earth with the rod of his mouth, and with the breath of his lips shall he slay the wicked," Joseph read. "Then a period of peace will follow in which he will gather home all Israel." He let the scroll roll itself together. "Can you imagine, Mary? The land filled with the descendants of Ephraim, Manasseh, Benjamin, and all the others as well as Judah? Lost for ages because of their wickedness, now to return, to build homes and raise families in peace. What a glorious day!"

Mary smiled at his exuberance, then looked at Jesus lying on the blanket in front of her, his eyes closed in sleep.

It was near sunset, and Joseph put away the scroll and watched the sky turn red. When it turned to dark blue, the Sabbath was over. Joseph quickly changed into work clothes, and by the light of several lamps he began his work again. He had removed nearly thirty blocks of stone and shaped half of those, but they would need twice that number, and he could not afford to waste any time.

* * *

Joseph continued working the next day, and at about noon, Mary alerted him to several men coming down the trail toward their camp, Abel leading the way. Each had tools in his hands.

"Joseph, these men all live in the village. They saw you at the synagogue on the Sabbath and asked about you. I told them you were from Nazareth but that you were building a home here and would be willing to trade work for their help. Each knows how to drill and work stone." He smiled while looking at the solid stone wall. "As you see, one cannot live in this village without such ability."

"Haman says you are a better carpenter than any other he has seen," commented one of the workers.

"Haman is kind," Joseph replied. "But I must warn you, until my own home is finished enough for winter storms and I have enough for the temple sacrifice for my wife and child, you will have to wait to be paid."

The four men looked at each other, then nodded agreement. Joseph put them to work, and by the end of the day, Mary rejoiced to see them carving off the last of the stone where the stable of her house would sit. As they said their good-byes and walked up the trail to the village, she quietly thanked God for opening such doors.

Several hours later, Joseph finished smoothing the surface with chisel and hammer and stood back to look over his work.

"It is good work," she called from the shelter.

Joseph nodded. "Tomorrow, after the circumcision of Jesus, I will hunt for more stone," he said happily.

"You mean that is not enough?" Mary asked, looking at the stack of finished and unfinished blocks.

"For the foundation and several tiers above it, but not all. We will need many more stones. Abel has offered his wagon, and though many fences have been built of stone around olive groves and houses, there is still much more stone to be had." He smiled. "Sometimes I wonder why this village was called the House of Bread instead of the House of Stone." He ran his hand over the wall. "Gomer, the thin one, is a good mason, and once I have the rocks gathered and shaped, he has offered to return. Between the two of us, the walls to this lower section will not take more than two weeks. Then I will have to go to the forest for trees for ceiling beams. By the time the early rains come, we should have them and the walls packed with mud and prepared for winter."

Mary nodded. They would need woven mats to cover the beams and hold the layer of clay mud. She would need to begin working on them immediately. "Does Abel have extra straw for the weaving of the mats?" she inquired.

"Yes." Joseph turned away from the wall and came to sit on his blanket in the shelter. "God has given us a good friend in Abel."

Mary agreed.

"I will not be able to finish all these things right away. I have a table promised to the friend of Haman, and we need the money, not only for food but for the sacrifices. The time of your purification at the temple is only thirty-three days away."

Mary had been thinking about the sacrifices a good deal lately and knew Joseph had not been given sufficient work to provide for them. She decided to broach a subject that had been on her mind. "Joseph, I wish to help raise the money."

Joseph had stretched out on his blanket to ease the ache in his back and raised his head to look at her, then laid it down again. "I will find the work, Mary."

"Still, I would like to help if I can."

He raised his head again. "How?" he asked sincerely.

"I am good at the potter's wheel, and I can weave baskets faster than anyone in Nazareth. I will make water jars and storage baskets and sell them in the square."

Joseph laid his head back, thinking. He did not know how she would find the time for these additional efforts, but he could see how much it mattered to her.

"Very well. I will help you find the clay for the pots, but you will have to gather your own material for weaving. I have seen no reeds here, but Adah may be able to help you find some."

"Thank you, Joseph." Mary spoke quietly. She paused, her heart beating even faster. "And Joseph," she started.

"Yes," he answered, the tiredness showing in his voice.

"Tomorrow I go to the mikveh."

"I know," he said softly.

"Will you place our bedding back in the cave in the morning?" Mary asked.

"Yes."

Mary lay down and covered herself again, and both of them tried to sleep but could not. After nearly an hour, she heard his breathing finally grow heavy and knew he was asleep. She slipped from her covers and without stepping on his blanket placed part of it over him, then gently touched his cheek. Oh, how she loved him! She knew before he ever approached her father that he would be kind and generous, a good provider, and a religious man dedicated to God. But since the night she walked into his home, she had come to know him more deeply and found him so much more than she had ever dreamed. His goodness ran deep, and her heart longed to love him, truly love him.

He stirred, then turned on his side. She stood and went back to her own blanket, an excited feeling mingled with apprehension in her stomach. She supposed this was what most women felt the night before the final wedding ceremony. She had experienced some of it at the feast celebrating their marriage, but this . . . this was different. She could not sleep, and when she was finally overcome by sheer weariness, Jesus awoke for feeding.

An hour later, the sun turned the sky to blue.

CHAPTER 18

Adah arrived early in the morning, and she and Mary left for the ritual bathing pool housed in an enclosure near the synagogue. Mary carried the new clothes she had brought from Nazareth and saved for this day, and Adah carried Jesus. When they entered the walled area surrounding the building, they waited in the tiny courtyard until another woman had finished using the pool. Mary went inside and put her new clothes on a stone shelf near the pool before removing her old clothes and lightly spattering them with water from the small pool to remove any ritual impurity. Later, she would wash them thoroughly, but her mother had taught her that, for now, this would keep any uncleanness from returning to her when she was finished bathing and had to carry them home.

She stood in the first pool, a small one holding pure water, to wash her hands and feet as required before entering the mikveh. To the side of the small pool was a large storage basin of spring or rainwater, also considered pure. Clay pipes connected the two so that the fresh, pure water of the basin was always refreshing the smaller washing pool in which she stood and the mikveh itself.

When she had washed her hands and feet thoroughly, she eased herself into the tepid waters of the mikveh, immersed herself to her neck, bowed her head, and began praying. She expressed her reliance on God for both physical and spiritual healing and thanked Him for such a blessing. She thanked Him for Jesus and the joy of his birth, and she prayed for the purity and strength to raise him as a righteous man. She hoped that what little she had offered would be acceptable to God. After thanking Him for Joseph, she immersed herself fully in the mikveh.

Mary had gone through purification many times since her first time of bleeding, and it always made her feel clean and that everything was right with the world. She expected nothing different this time, but as her head emerged and water flowed down her face, she was overwhelmed by a sudden, powerful warmth cascading through her like the heat of the sun, something so wonderful and peaceful that she felt she would be consumed.

Before me, you are holy.

She opened her eyes to see who had spoken, the depth of the voice and the warmth all around her bringing tears that fell gently into the water that covered her to the neck.

Then the power, the warmth, seemed to contract, leaving her toes and fingertips, traveling up her legs and arms, and coming to rest in her heart. She looked up to heaven, and for the first time she truly remembered that moment over nine months earlier when that same power had seemed to envelop her. She had received a child then, God's Son, the Messiah, and yet the power of this cleansing seemed just as wonderful! Her sacrifice, her willingness to obey, had truly been accepted. Mary was whole again, complete and virtuous, and she was Joseph's.

Hoping the feeling would never leave, Mary sat awhile, giving thanks for it and for her marvelous child.

Then an anxious knock on the door shook her out of her reverie.

"Mary, others wait. Are you nearly finished?" Adah asked gently but with some apprehension.

Mary did not want to speak, afraid the moment would flee, afraid she would never feel such love again, but when Adah rapped on the door again, she knew she had no choice.

"Yes," she said softly, "just a few minutes more."

Mary felt the warmth shrink to an even smaller place in her heart as she reluctantly stood and left the pool, praying the feeling would not entirely leave her. She dried with a cloth and dressed in new clothes, then knelt and once more thanked God.

The pounding on the door came again, and other voices, irritated and angry, drove the sublime feeling from the room. Picking up the basket with her old clothes, Mary opened the door to find several women waiting impatiently while Adah rocked a fussing Jesus. She made her sincere apologies, then took the baby in her free arm. They left the courtyard and entered the street, going immediately to the well, where Adah drew water and poured it into a trough used by the women for washing clothes. Mary fed Jesus, her mind relishing the wonder, the feeling that still lingered in her heart.

When the trough was full, Mary gave Jesus to Adah and washed her clothes thoroughly. She must not think upon the wonderful experience in the mikveh too long, but save it for times when she would need strength. Softly humming a hymn she had learned from childhood, Mary realized she had never felt so clean, so full of joy.

"I know this tune," commented a woman washing next to her.

"And I," another said. "My mother taught it to me, and her mother taught it to her."

"Psalm 111." Adah spoke. "A song of thanks for the Lord's compassion and mercy."

"And for His redemption," the first lady added. She looked over at Mary. "You are new among us."

"Yes," Mary replied softly. "But we hope to stay, at least for a while."

"My husband, Gomer, helped with your new house," the other woman explained.

"My husband—his name is Joseph—says Gomer is a fine mason," Mary responded.

"The child, is it a boy?" asked the first woman.

"Yes, this is the eighth day."

"Ah, the day of cleansing for you and of circumcision for him. A day of joy and of pain, at least for your son," she chuckled.

"You have been to the cleansing pool?" questioned the second. She eyed Mary's clothes lying close to her own.

"Yes," Mary answered, and the woman relaxed.

"They say your husband is a fine carpenter," the first woman stated.

"There is none more skilled than Joseph. If you need a table, cupboards . . . He has carved doors for the wealthy and helped build the synagogue at Capernaum," Mary reported with some pride.

"There is work here. If he is good, he will provide," said the first in a matter-of-fact tone.

"I wish to find clay for making pottery and sturdy material for weaving baskets to sell. Do you know—"

"We have a pit south of the village for our own pots, but if you are making them for sale, the best clay is found a few miles from here, to the east on the borders of the desert," the first answered.

Mary leaned back on her knees and began wringing out her clothes.

"We have no sedge or palm fronds, and reeds are not readily available, though Egyptian shipments of these pass through the village occasionally."

"They cost too much," retorted Adah. "Barley straw is the most available, Mary, and when you mix it with the stem of flax plants, they make a good basket. Grandfather has both and will let us take what you need." She leaned close. "I may be able to get reeds."

Mary nodded and smiled her thanks, finished wringing out her clothes, and placed them in the basket. "Come, Adah. We must go to the synagogue soon. Thank you for your help," she said to the others. "I hope to see you again."

"Oh, yes, you will see us! Between us, we have twelve children," the second woman said. "We spend our *lives* here!" Her voice was filled with the sound of a martyr, tinged with the pride of a woman highly favored, and Mary couldn't help smiling.

"I pray that I may be so blessed."

"You have made a good beginning," replied the woman. "But do not pray for too many. They make slaves of their mothers."

Mary and Adah returned to the cave to find Joseph dressed and ready for the cutting ceremony. Mary walked directly to him and held him close. With a blush and an envious grin, Adah turned aside and put Jesus in his bed.

"It is a wonderful day," Mary whispered to Joseph.

"The very best." Joseph smiled. She had never been so beautiful. She had always been lovely, the most beautiful woman he had ever seen, but today . . . today she looked radiant. "You . . . you look stunning this morning!" he stammered.

"Isn't it amazing what a bath can do?" Mary teased. She kissed him, then pulled away. "I must put these clothes out to dry, then we can go. Adah, will you give Joseph a clean set of swaddling clothes so that he can wash and dress Jesus? They are in the basket next to his crib." She turned to her husband. "And Joseph, use the water in the large jar, the one Adah brought this morning. It is from a spring and is pure." She was already removing the wet clothes and laying them out on the large rock face of the cave.

Joseph nodded as Adah handed him Jesus and the wrappings. He sat down and began unwinding the old ones to find them quite soiled, the pungent odor making him wrinkle his nose and turn away. Adah handed him a bowl of water and a rag for cleaning, an amused look on her face.

"Mary does well to let you share the joy of being a parent."

Joseph pulled the soiled wrappings away from the small body, then the soaked and stained loincloth that was tied around Jesus' middle. He soon had a new one in place and washed the old as clean of stains as he could. As he completed his task, he saw Abel and his wife coming down the trail.

Mary greeted them warmly, knowing they had come to walk with them to the synagogue. As Adah finished wrapping Jesus in his blankets and handed him to Mary, Abel pulled Joseph aside to talk with him briefly. Overhearing part of the conversation, Mary knew Abel was instructing Joseph on the circumcision ceremony.

"The priest will do the actual cutting. You will hold the child and offer the prayer in which he is named."

Joseph nodded and Mary grimaced. She had seen circumcisions, and this time it was her own son who would suffer.

"Abel, I don't want the priest saying anything about this freeing Jesus from sin," Joseph declared. "Though I know many in Israel believe that it does, it is not in Torah or in the prophets."

"No, he will not say it. Though some believe this way, it is not part of our ceremony," Abel answered.

Mary had never been able to understand the teachings of some of the Pharisees who thought children were somehow unholy at birth and that circumcision restored their holiness. She supposed that it had come from some perverted idea that the blood of the woman somehow made the child unclean, but that was never spoken of by Moses or any of the prophets. If one knew the law, he would be a fool to believe such a thing. The cutting, the bleeding, and the pain were all part of coming under the covenant made with Abraham, nothing more, nothing less.

Joseph's arm slipped around Mary and pulled her close. "We should go," he said.

She nodded, and they started up the trail in the bright sunshine of a clear morning that seemed lovelier than any other. She noticed flowers where there had been none before. The scents of olive and pomegranate, fresh-cut barley, and cooking fires were stronger, more pleasing than she could remember.

The rabbi, the chief elders, and a man dressed in white priestly robes welcomed them warmly and then brought them to a room where a silver basin sat atop a small altar, the sharp knife of circumcision lying at its side.

Mary hesitantly placed Jesus in Joseph's hands, then stepped back so that the priest could take his proper place. She watched nervously as Joseph unwrapped her child and the priest said a prayer of benediction, then quickly made the cut.

Jesus' anguished cry filled the room and forced a rush of tears down Mary's cheeks. She took a step forward to take the child, but Joseph shook his head in gentle reprimand. She watched as Joseph stroked Jesus' hair and then his arms and torso, gently and lovingly settling Jesus' cry into a sorrowful whimper.

Then Joseph prayed.

"Father, by this act revealed to Abraham and all our fathers, we bind your son to you. May he honor you and all of us forever. Let him be known to his family and friends as Jesus, the son of Joseph and Mary. Rejoice in him, as I rejoice in him, and as his mother rejoices in him. Jesus, I say unto you, as it is written in Proverbs, 'Thy father and thy mother shall be glad, and she that bare thee shall rejoice.'"

A pause brought Mary's head up, and she blinked and wiped her tears away. There was more to the prayer; she had heard it many times. Ezekiel, Psalms, Genesis should all be quoted. Had he forgotten?

The priest leaned toward Joseph and whispered something, but Joseph did not respond until after another moment, then he was able to collect his emotions, stammer through the rest of the words, and close the prayer.

There was a deep, united sigh, then the whispered chatter of congratulations as Joseph added the salve to Jesus' wound and redressed and wrapped him in his blankets. Mary stepped between the chief elder and the priest to receive her son, and she and Joseph thanked the priest for his help and the elders for their kindness. Finally Joseph and Mary embraced Abel, his wife, and Adah and received their congratulations before leaving the room and entering the street.

Abel and his wife accompanied Joseph, Mary, and the baby as far as their own home. Adah went with them back to their cave, helped Mary prepare a simple meal, then excused herself to see to her duties at home. By the time she disappeared up the trail, Joseph had already changed into his work clothes and had begun shaping the stone.

Mary took him food, and he quickly ate and drank. The stone seemed especially malleable to his touch today, and while she made several trips to the threshing floor for straw, selecting those stems she would use for weaving, he trimmed and stacked nearly a dozen blocks. Jesus fussed occasionally, and Mary tried to keep his loincloth dry and the ointment on his wound thick.

At about the ninth hour, she was feeding Jesus in the semi-privacy of their shelter when a stranger came down the trail and greeted them, asking if he could speak to Joseph. Joseph stepped away and they talked. Though Mary could not hear the conversation, she saw Joseph shake his head in a fashion she had seen before. Thank you, but no thank you, was its meaning. The stranger seemed to appeal to Joseph a second time, but the result was the same, and the visitor departed down the hill and across the valley toward Jerusalem.

Joseph came to the jar for water and sat down in the shade of the shelter to drink and watch Mary weave.

"He asked that I come to Jerusalem. They need more carpenters. It seems Herod is getting impatient about the completion of the temple."

"They say his illness worsens. I'm sure he would like to see his greatest work finished before he dies," Mary stated.

"Finishing God's house will not undo his evil," Joseph replied.

"I am glad you declined," Mary said.

He shrugged. "Abel was right, they do not pay enough." He finished the last of the water. "But he may return. If he does, the request will come directly from Herod's chief steward. I cannot turn it down without trouble."

She nodded. "Joseph, are we going to stay here?"

"For a while, yes. I am not sure why, but I think it is best."

She nodded again. "I miss Nazareth already."

"I do as well. We will return, Mary, but for now—"

"I trust you, Joseph. We'll go when God says."

Both went back to their labors. The afternoon crept toward evening, and Mary hated to see the day end. It seemed an especially comfortable one accompanied by a feeling of contentment that she did not want to lose. She knew it stemmed from the wondrous experience at the mikveh and also from the contentment of having Jesus under the covenant and the excitement of seeing Joseph build their home, envisioning their new future in Bethlehem.

Mary finished the second basket before Adah appeared lugging a load of reeds she could hardly handle. Overjoyed, Mary stood and clasped a hand over her mouth. The reeds would add strength and quality to each basket, resulting in a better price.

She thanked Adah, then silently thanked God for Adah's friendship. Everything would have been so much harder without her.

While Adah held a waking Jesus, Mary worked to prepare the reeds for drying.

"Where on earth did you get these?" she asked Adah.

"The Pools of Solomon," Adah replied. "Uriah told me he saw some there."

Mary's eyebrows lifted at the mention of the boy's name, but she kept her eyes on her work.

"But that is the water supply for Jerusalem. It must be watched."

"It gives water to Bethlehem as well," Adah explained. "They do not care if someone takes the reeds if you bring them some cheese or bread."

Mary looked up. "I do not want you endangering yourself—"

"Oh, I did not pick them. Uriah did!"

Mary grinned. "You have seen Uriah again?"

Adah blushed. "This morning, after I left here. His sheep graze south of the village, near the pools, and I told him we needed some reeds."

"He must have spent his whole day . . . Thank him for me, Adah."

"Uriah is no ordinary shepherd, Mary," Adah declared with pride. "His family provides many of the lambs for the temple."

"Has your father changed his mind? Surely he does not believe that Uriah is somehow tainted by the vision of his father and grandfather, even if it were a lie, which it surely is not."

Adah looked forlorn, tears gathering in her eyes. "No," she answered softly. "He has not changed his mind."

"Tell Uriah to go and make a proposal," Mary stated firmly.

"My father would not listen. It would be humiliating for everyone."

Mary patted Adah's hand, then smiled. "If Uriah's family has many flocks and Uriah could offer a goodly number to your father and make him a rich man, I think his pride would blow away on the wind."

Adah licked her lips as she mulled it over. "No." She shook her head adamantly. "Father has too much pride. He could never eat his words."

They sat silently, each in her own thoughts. "God will help you, Adah. I'm sure of it," Mary affirmed with a reassuring smile. "But you are still young and—"

Adah guffawed. "I am nearly *sixteen,* Mary! All of my friends are married or at least betrothed and . . ." The tears began to break again, and she bit them off with a set to her jaw that showed her bitterness.

My age? Mary thought. She looked at Adah more carefully. She was small, and her womanly features were only now beginning to mature. There were some blemishes in her face, but these were clearing up nicely and would cause no deep scarring or loss of beauty. Apparently Uriah was already seeing Adah as a woman who could grace his home, and others would as well, but Mary would not have guessed she was almost sixteen. "You will make Uriah or any man a wonderful wife. Can he provide a good bride price?"

"Father was never concerned about getting a good price from them before. Now he says they could never pay enough for one of his daughters."

"And you would have a house?"

"Not at first, but Uriah's father has a house south of here, near where the aqueduct loses water and men bathe. Uriah is his only child, and there are enough rooms. I love his mother and would be happy there."

Pleased with Adah's words, Mary pushed aside the basket she was weaving. "It is late. Off with you. You have duties at home, I am sure. Trust in God a little longer, Adah—He will provide you a good husband."

Adah beamed at the compliment, put the baby in the crib, and hugged Mary before nearly bounding up the hillside, passing Joseph as she went.

Joseph wiped blood from his hand. Even callouses wore out after a while. He wrapped the wound in a rag as he scooped water out of a jar. "She seemed especially happy," he said to himself as he wiped the sweat from his forehead with the rag bandage.

"Joseph, you have accomplished a lot today!" Mary called up the hill to Joseph. "The sun is nearly set, and you should stop soon and have something to eat."

"When you have it ready, I will stop," he called back, but he ambled down the hill anyway.

As he stepped toward her, she wrinkled her nose and put a hand between them. "Time to bathe, my love."

"That bad, huh?"

"I am told that there is a place where men go, under the aqueduct south of the city. It is only a mile and . . ." She stepped closer. "And I have a favor to ask."

"A favor?" His brow wrinkled. "Does this have anything to do with Adah's sudden happiness?"

She looked surprised. "How did you know?"

He smiled. "I have big ears."

"Will you find Uriah's father and grandfather and talk to them? It is near the place where men bathe."

"And what am I to ask, exactly?" he wondered.

"I think Adah will make a fine wife for Uriah. Find out how much they can give for a bride price."

"And if they don't want Adah?"

"It will break her heart," Mary explained.

"And yours, I can see."

"She deserves to be happy. If Uriah no longer wants her, it is better to know now. If he does, maybe . . ."

"Maybe? Mary, this is meddling. Besides, do not forget that Reuben is not a man about to eat his words or change his heart." He sighed. "But I do agree, Adah and Uriah would make a good match. What if Uriah and his family have decided on another?"

"Change his mind," she commanded only half teasingly.

Joseph chuckled. "I have never seen you like this. You are meddling, Mary. Just like your mother and—"

"Never you mind," Mary retorted. "Besides, this is different. Adah is a fine girl and needs our help, that is all."

"Just this once?"

"Of course."

"No more meddling?"

"No more," she acquiesced. "Now be gone, and don't forget your bath! I refuse to sleep next to a man who smells like a camel."

Joseph's eyes widened, and he quickly put down the bowl and walked from the shelter, a grin on his face.

* * *

Fifteen minutes later, Joseph reached the pond fed by a leak in the aqueduct. Hidden in a stand of rocks and trees, he could hear voices, and stopped long enough to make sure they were all male, then entered by a well-trodden path. The sky now dark blue, he could only dimly see two men washing near the shore while two others swam in deeper water. Joseph immediately recognized two of the voices.

He slipped from his clothes and walked into the water.

"Benjamin," Joseph greeted the old shepherd.

"Who is it?" Benjamin asked, squinting through the near darkness.

"Joseph, the carpenter of Nazareth."

"Ahh, welcome, welcome! And how is the child?"

"It is the eighth day. He is nursing a wound, but well otherwise."

Benjamin nodded agreeably. "He comes under the law, as he should."

"I thank you for the gift of meat. It was very delicious."

"For such a child, I will give more. When we shear the sheep, you shall have wool enough for clothes."

Joseph knew these were not rich men as to things of the world, but they would be rich toward God no matter what it took. It was in their hearts.

"You are kind, but I will repay you. I am a skilled carpenter—"

"We shall see when the time comes," Benjamin replied.

"I am also grateful that you and your sons did not say more than you did."

"Some things are for God alone to tell."

As Joseph went deeper into the water, he could see that two of the other men looked familiar. He assumed that the fourth, floating on his back and somewhat separated from them, was Benjamin's grandson Uriah. Things were working out very well.

Benjamin and his two sons followed Joseph into the water, and one of them handed Joseph some soap made of the ashes of Borith. He introduced himself as Shaphat and his brother as Eleazar. "The boy is my son, Uriah," said Shaphat.

"Ah, the one Adah speaks of often," Joseph said loudly enough to carry across the water.

Uriah seemed to suddenly lose his ability to float and splashed around as he tried to find the bottom of the shallow pond. He sputtered, wiped his face free of water, and came closer. "You are the man who has a new son. I brought meat to your wife."

At an age near Joseph's, Uriah was strong through the shoulders and chest, of a good countenance, and had the calloused hands of a worker, though to Joseph he seemed a bit prideful.

"He is fond of Adah. A marriage proposal was . . ." Shaphat cleared his throat. "Her father no longer finds my son an appealing match."

"That is too bad. She would make a wonderful wife."

"We had settled on a price, but now Uriah fears making a proposal, and rightly so. In the last few days, Reuben has made it well known what he thinks of our family," Eleazar stated stiffly.

"You cannot blame him, Uncle!" Uriah exclaimed. "Your vision . . ." He turned and started for shore, obviously upset.

"He still struggles with what we saw."

Joseph suddenly realized that he understood Uriah's disappointment. The young man's chance to marry the woman he wanted had been dashed by something he could not understand. Joseph had nearly given up Mary due to his own unbelief. The situation might take a little more meddling than Joseph had thought. "Assuming

Reuben could be convinced to let them marry, how much could Uriah pay?" Joseph asked.

Uriah stopped in the water. The others looked hard at Joseph.

"How much?" Joseph asked.

Benjamin stroked his beard. "Twenty sheep and ten lambs, unblemished."

Joseph chuckled as Uriah slapped the water and continued toward shore. "He will never get our sheep! He is wicked for his treatment of you, even if you did not see angels!"

"Then you will never marry his daughter," Benjamin declared.

Uriah hesitated, then continued toward shore, but at a slower pace.

"It is a price that would have him eating his words," Joseph stated.

"Now there is a pleasant thought," Shaphat said sarcastically.

Benjamin chuckled. "And to get a granddaughter of such quality in the bargain . . . It would be worth twice the sheep and lambs, but, alas, we are not wealthy men."

"We could go ten more lambs, Father," Eleazar suggested. "God has already blessed our flocks this season."

Uriah turned back. "He would never accept even double the sheep and ten times the lambs, and we would look like fools for offering!"

"He could not resist, and if he does, he will look the fool, not us. Who but a fool would turn down twenty sheep and twenty lambs for a daughter past her age and still unbetrothed?" His uncle regretted the words the moment he finished them. "Sorry, Uriah, it isn't that she is not beautiful. I . . ."

Even in the darkness Joseph could see the hot glare in Uriah's eyes. "She is worth it and more, believe me," Joseph retorted. Then he added with a wink: "If Jesus were old enough, I would betroth them!"

"Joseph is right, Uriah," Benjamin affirmed. "Her father doesn't deserve such a daughter, but you deserve such a wife. Will you make the proposal?"

Uriah moved his hand through the water, obviously thinking hard.

Benjamin spoke firmly. "You do not have to like her father. She will move to our family and become my daughter and your wife. That is why you pay in sheep. If you do not see the bargain, you are the fool, not Reuben."

Uriah raised his head. "But twenty sheep and twenty lambs, Grandfather? That is one-tenth our herd! Only the twenty sheep and ten lambs. Though she is worth more, Reuben will have no more than this!"

"A good bargain!" Benjamin exclaimed exuberantly. "Tomorrow, then."

"Tomorrow," agreed Uriah's father and uncle in unison.

"Very well," answered Uriah, his chin up. "Tomorrow, but he will turn us away, I know it."

"You let me work on Reuben," Joseph said.

"You know him?" Uriah asked.

"Unfortunately, I must claim him as kin, but that is not what will change his mind." Joseph smiled. "We will use a stronger weapon against Reuben. We will use his pride."

CHAPTER 19

Joseph awoke to only a dim light coming through the entrance to the cave, felt Mary's warmth, and immediately fought an inner battle of whether or not to do as he'd promised.

"Go," she said gently.

They had talked of Joseph's plan on his return from the aqueduct, and Mary had been delightedly agreeable.

He sighed, kissed her softly on the cheek, then slipped from under the covers, dressed, and grabbed a few dates on his way out of the cave. He was waiting at the threshing floor when Abel, Reuben, and a half dozen men from the village, one of them Reuben's youngest son, came to begin the day's work. The boy and two other men led donkeys pulling carts. Joseph recognized Gomer, the mason who had helped with the cutting of the stone for Mary's new house.

Shocked to see Joseph, Abel said, "You have a house to build."

"And a debt to pay. I will work when I can, and this is one of those times. What is the task?"

Reuben quickly spoke. "We have fences to rebuild around our olive trees. One of them was damaged in a storm, and another wall was taken by Herod to build roads."

"A strange tax, but a tax just the same," Joseph muttered.

Reuben grunted agreement, and the others nodded.

"Gomer, good to see you again," Joseph said.

"And you, Joseph." Gomer quickly introduced Joseph to the rest of the men, most of whom Joseph had seen at the synagogue on the Sabbath. Joseph could not have asked for a better audience.

The group walked the mile to the place where most villagers maintained and cared for their small olive groves. In the distance,

Joseph could see a large herd of sheep, as well as the aqueduct winding its way toward the Pools of Solomon.

"A rich man's flocks," he commented. "A man could do well with a tenth of what that one owns."

In response, Reuben nodded but said nothing.

The men removed their outer robes to work in their tunics, then spread out in groups of three to collect rocks and put them in carts. As they did so, they spoke of their families, the Romans, the Passover, and the temple hierarchy. Joseph found them to be an interesting lot, willing to speak their minds and enjoy one another's company. Even Reuben was well liked, although when he said too much or tried to steer the conversation to unpleasant talk about others, including Benjamin, the men either did not respond or quickly changed the subject. For Joseph, things looked better all the time.

They had all come together to stack their loads and build a wall when Joseph decided to broach his topic.

"You have a fine daughter, Reuben. She has been a great help to Mary and to the baby, as well as to me. As strangers in a new town, we appreciate her kindness and yours."

"She is a valuable girl, a good worker. We miss her at our house, but I know my duty under the law," Reuben answered stiffly.

"You are right, Joseph," Gomer added. "She is a fine girl, and if I had a son old enough to betroth, I would make the offer myself."

"You mean Adah is not betrothed?" Joseph asked in mock surprise. "I thought . . . A girl of her quality . . ."

Reuben's son chuckled, but straightened his face quickly after a glare from his father.

"No proposals have been made," Reuben explained stiffly, "but I am sure they will be forthcoming. Soon." He looked at one of the other men, who seemed to blush and busied himself straightening the stones stacked next to his feet.

Another man changed the subject, and Joseph realized this subject was uncomfortable for that man as well. He guessed that their sons were of marriageable age and they had not responded in the affirmative to Reuben's desire that his daughter marry one of their sons. Initially amazed that they did not see quality in Adah, Joseph realized that their sons were probably interested in other girls.

Whatever the reason, he was glad of it. It would only make his little ploy work better.

After a second load of stones was stacked and the men took turns guzzling water from sheepskins, Joseph broached the subject again.

"And if a man knew someone . . . someone who would be good to your daughter and make a good husband . . . What would you expect as a bride price?" Joseph asked, glancing around the group. The men who had seemed so nervous before were now paying very close attention to Joseph. A new suitor would obviously be a relief to them.

Reuben stopped drinking so quickly that the water slopped down his chest, drenching the front of his loincloth, but he hardly noticed. "You . . . you know someone?"

Even Abel seemed shocked. And Joseph understood why. If Joseph knew a suitor, why hadn't he mentioned the fact sooner? He hoped Abel would not ask that question, not now at least.

Joseph shrugged. "It is possible."

"And this family, do they have . . ." Reuben swallowed. "Well, Adah is worth a good deal. As you said, she is a hard worker and would be sorely missed in our home. She would be a great loss financially."

Several of the others rolled their eyes, making Joseph smile inwardly. Mary had judged Reuben correctly. Joseph was really beginning to enjoy this and immediately felt both guilt and satisfaction for it.

"They are considered rich by some," he answered. "But compared to the king," he added, shaking his head, "they are but poor peasants."

"And do they live nearby?" Reuben said.

The others stepped a bit closer, enraptured. Joseph smiled, his eyes wandering toward the distant city of Jerusalem. "Close enough that they can deal with the priests of the temple on a regular basis." He shook his head. "But I can make no promises. The boy has a mind of his own, and the father, well, he has his pride. Marrying the daughter of a farmer when he is—"

Reuben broke in. "Remind him that you and I are of the same family, the lineage of David through Jesse. All Bethlehem looks up to us, and we hold prominence in the synagogue and influence with the priests that surround our village. We are men of consequence and . . . and we are not poor, either. Half these olive trees belong to my father and me."

Some nodded agreement, but there were shrugs as well. Gomer rolled his eyes again.

"Yes, yes, I will tell him, but you have not stated your bride price. It is this he will want to know," Joseph said, feigning impatience.

The others leaned forward.

"Of course, of course." Reuben paced a bit, seemingly struggling with how he should respond. He glanced at Joseph as if measuring him and by doing so measuring the man he seemed to represent.

Finally he stood straight. "Adah is worth many cattle and sheep. I must have at least . . . at least fifteen." He seemed determined, as if it was his final position.

Joseph acted shocked. "What? For Adah? You must be joking. Surely . . ."

"Yes, yes, it is too much! You are right. I—" Reuben replied, humiliated.

"Too much?" Joseph exclaimed, shaking his head. "Too much?" He smiled and put an arm around Reuben as if dealing with a child. "Reuben! Reuben! Adah is worth twice that. And if you ask so little, what is my friend to think of Adah's value?" he asked.

The man who seemed so concerned gulped. Joseph wasn't sure why but thought it might be because the man suddenly realized he might be losing a valuable bride for his son. The others were all nodding agreement while Reuben swallowed hard, his eyes wide. "Twice as much?" he said softly. "You think your friend . . ." He swallowed. "Would he pay twice as much?"

"We won't know until I ask, but remember, I know Adah. I know her quality, her beauty, and I will speak of these things to him." He changed his grin to a concerned frown. "But we cannot play games here! This is a man of some reputation. To turn away his offer . . ." He shook his head.

"No, no, if you can bring an offer of anything more than twenty cows or sheep or both together, or the equivalent in money, of course, I will accept it!"

Joseph looked at the others. The trap had been sprung—now Joseph must make sure Reuben was firmly in its grip. "I have your word on this? After all, it is no small blow to a man's reputation to break his word."

"I swear . . ." He paused. "I swear on—"

Joseph cringed. He hated such oaths and quickly put a hand on Reuben's shoulder. "I do not need an oath, Reuben. You stand among friends. Your word to them and to me is good enough."

They all nodded, but it was Gomer who spoke. "We'll hold him to his word, Joseph. All of us."

"Then it is done," Abel said with a wide grin.

"And when will you . . . When will a proposal . . ."

"Within the day," Joseph replied. "In fact," he looked at the group, "if all of you will be at Reuben's house two hours before the setting of the sun today, you can witness a betrothal."

They all clapped Reuben on the back or by the hand, except the two men who seemed to have suddenly realized a loss. Joseph thought it appropriate and relished the moment. When everyone was finished congratulating Reuben, he approached. Now came the hard part.

"You and I must go and visit with the father of your daughter's possible suitor."

Reuben looked a bit puzzled. "Now?"

"Yes, now."

Abel smiled. "Go, Reuben. We will finish here."

Reuben nodded and put on his outer robe, and the two of them walked back toward the village. When at a good distance and out of view of the others, Joseph pulled Reuben aside and told him to sit down.

Even more confused, Reuben hesitated. "What is it, Joseph? Have you changed your mind? Is it too much?"

"No, no, Adah is worth more." He sighed. "I have trapped you, Reuben, and you have to decide how you are going to deal with it."

Reuben leaned against a large rock, a fearful smile breaching his lips. "Trapped me? What do you mean? I—"

"In front of friends, you have given your word to accept the proposal of marriage for your daughter. They will not let you break your word without some humiliation. You should know now that the groom will be Uriah, grandson of the shepherd Benjamin."

Reuben went pale, then his face turned to stone. "No! I will never allow this . . . this . . . shepherd boy to marry my daughter. Never."

"Then your word will be broken. No one will trust you again, and your daughter, who loves Uriah, will be humiliated."

Reuben made an attempt to stiffen his neck. "Never." The word was used less forcefully this time.

"Benjamin will pay you twenty sheep and ten lambs. The lambs will be unblemished and bring a high price in Jerusalem. This bargain will make you a rich man," Joseph declared.

Reuben swallowed hard. "But Adah is not—"

"She is worth that and more, and you have been acting differently too long."

Reuben felt humbled by these words, and his shoulders slumped. "In this, you may be right, but there is nothing I can do. I have said too much. I will look like a fool if I take back my words. Even this price cannot change that."

"No, it cannot, but you were wrong in what you did, Reuben, and it requires a payment. But this I promise you, if you do as I say, your daughter will forgive you any ill thoughts of her, and good men will respect you. The rest do not matter." Joseph gripped his shoulder and smiled. "You will also be rich."

* * *

News traveled fast in the small village, and when Joseph, Mary, and Jesus arrived at Reuben's house just outside the dilapidated old village walls, the entire village's population stood in the open space before it.

"You are sure this is going to work?" Mary asked. "He could turn the coward and ruin your little scheme."

"No second thoughts allowed," Joseph answered. "And don't forget, it was your scheme before it was mine."

She laughed. "I would never have thought of such a devious plot, and we both know it."

"Yes, well, you inspired me."

Abel stood near the gate watching the crowd when he saw Joseph and Mary. He pushed through the crowd and greeted them with a warm welcome, but in his eyes there was a troubled look.

He spoke quietly. "I don't know what is happening, Joseph, but Reuben has spoken to no one since he returned from the fields with you. And Adah . . ." He rolled his eyes. "She is beside herself." He sighed. "She wanted another and now this. Whoever it is . . ." He shook his head. "She will call you an enemy for this."

Joseph and Mary smiled at each other.

"We'll see. Where is Reuben?" Joseph asked.

"In his prayer chamber," Abel said with some frustration. "Reuben seldom prays, except at synagogue when it is only to be seen praying. His wife thinks that you have sold their daughter to the devil himself." He swallowed hard. "I must say that even I am very concerned, Joseph. Surely you can put this to rest if—"

Joseph laughed, then touched Abel's arm. "Do not worry, my friend. You will see the answer soon, and I don't think you will be disappointed."

The back of the crowd grew quiet first, then began to part. Joseph saw Benjamin's tall sons coming through, Benjamin and Uriah just in front of them. The murmur of voices reverberated around them.

Abel saw them but was speechless until they stood directly in front of him. The crowd grew very still.

"Benjamin? What are you doing? You know Reuben . . . You know he would not like you here. As much as I love you, old friend . . ." Then it struck him. He looked at Uriah standing next to Benjamin, dressed in his finest clothes, then at Benjamin again, then at Joseph, a smile growing on his face as he looked back at Benjamin. "It . . . it is your . . . your grandson? You are the ones?"

Benjamin nodded and a murmur erupted through the crowd. Abel put up a hand for silence. "You are welcome, my friend. Very welcome." He turned to Joseph. "You are a shrewd one." Then the smile left him. "I hope we are not all disappointed. Reuben's pride is a powerful thing."

Benjamin bowed slightly. "Is he at home? After all, we have come to offer a proposal."

Abel stepped to one side and pushed open the door to the inner courtyard. Benjamin and the others went in, and Abel grabbed Joseph by the arm and nodded for him to follow.

"Both of you," Benjamin said to Mary. "My guess is this is a woman's work."

Mary and Joseph smiled at each other as they went through the gate into the courtyard. The crowd pushed through until the forepart of the courtyard was filled to a respectable distance from the house. The rest of the crowd remained in the street trying to hear, whispers coursing through them. It took little imagination to know what was being said.

Joseph watched Adah and her mother as they first saw Benjamin and Uriah. The mother went weak in the knees and Adah had to prop her up. Adah, however, had a wide smile and aimed it directly at Uriah, who blushed. Then Reuben appeared.

He held onto the side of the door for a moment as if collecting his strength before stepping outside and bowing slightly.

Joseph held his breath.

"Benjamin," Reuben said with no smile and a sad look in his eye. He pointed at some carpets to the right and indicated that Benjamin and his family should sit. Then Reuben joined them and asked Abel and Joseph to sit at his side. Mary slipped into the house to find Adah tending to her mother, who had melted to the floor in a half-conscious state.

Mary picked up the bowl by the water jar and filled it before handing it to Adah. Wanting to listen at the window, Adah simply dumped the water on her mother's face before deserting her to flutter back to the door.

"We have come to make a proposal of marriage for your daughter, Adah," Benjamin began.

Reuben nodded, and the crowd began to murmur again. When they quieted, Benjamin spoke. "Twenty sheep and ten unblemished lambs—"

"*Twenty?*" Abel parroted. "And . . . and ten . . ."

Reuben grabbed his father's arm to silence him. Joseph was gaining a new respect for Abel's son as he watched him handle what Joseph knew was a complete swallowing of his pride.

"Shaphat will also provide a place for her in his own large house until we can build one for them, and for five years, we will give you a homer of wool for cloth."

Abel had a hard time getting his chin off his chest as Reuben spoke. "I am sorry, I cannot accept your offer."

The glint in the eyes of Benjamin and his sons disappeared, Abel stiffened, and Joseph heard a loud gasp from inside the house.

Reuben steadied his father while continuing to speak. "I have offended your family by what I have said about your . . . your vision. Today, I looked at what I have done from your eyes and"—he glanced at Joseph—"from the eyes of God. I was wrong to attack you for something you believe. Because of this, I have sinned and cannot take any sheep or lambs."

He stood to a loud murmur through the crowd and raised his hands for silence before turning to the house and calling for Adah.

A moment later, Adah appeared at the door, Mary at her side, cradling Jesus in one arm and holding Adah up with the other. The girl seemed near tears, but nodded when Mary whispered in her ear.

"Come here, Adah," Reuben called softly.

The crowd went silent, and Joseph smiled. Reuben was doing wonderfully.

"Adah, I owe you an apology. You are worth much more than many sheep or lambs, but . . . but I could never see it until"—he looked at Joseph, then back at Adah—"until it was pointed out to me. Forgive me." He hugged her tightly, then turned back to Uriah. "Please, take my daughter as your wife. Your bride price is only that you be good to her and give her many sons."

Uriah stood and took Adah's hand. The crowd erupted, and the celebration was on. Joseph stood and put an arm around Mary, and they watched as Benjamin and Reuben shook hands and became friends once more. Abel was still on the ground, shaking his head in disbelief, and Joseph reached down and pulled him to his feet.

"Twenty sheep and . . . and . . ."

"Ten lambs, unblemished," Joseph finished. "And don't forget the five years of wool."

"And he gave it all up for his daughter's happiness," Mary gushed. "You should be proud of your son."

Abel walked away shaking his head, mumbling, "Yes, yes, of course. Proud."

Joseph did not say anything. Eventually, Abel would figure it out himself. Benjamin would still give Reuben the sheep, and the village would know of Adah's worth. One did not take a daughter into his house without giving something to the family, especially with a daughter so valuable that her father would suffer the swallowing of his considerable pride through public apology. Though Joseph had worried about how sincere Reuben would be, the man had proven to be of quality. For this alone, he deserved the sheep.

"You have worked a miracle," Mary whispered.

"It was your idea, my love, and a very good one." He smiled. "You should meddle more often."

"Take me home," she suddenly demanded.

"You do not want food and wine?"

Mary smiled, already pulling on his arm. "I want only to be with my husband."

Joseph grinned and let himself be led away.

CHAPTER 20

Adah did not come as often. She was preparing for her own marriage, and there was much to be done. Even Mary spent time at Adah's house, weaving cloth and making clothes. Mary gathered friends quickly, and soon women were coming to the cave to learn her method of basket making and to visit while working to prepare Adah. Mary loved the women, though she often moved their conversations from gossip to more productive thoughts.

As one of the newest infants in town, and in Mary's eyes the most beautiful, Jesus drew many of the younger women to their home, especially those yet to be betrothed or waiting for their final marriage ceremonies. Mary was continually astonished how they were drawn to him yet failed to connect him to the shepherds' vision.

On occasion, Mary longed for Nazareth, for family and friends and the security of home. She heard nothing from her parents, and she worried, especially about Josiah. News passed on by travelers going south revealing that a rebellion was coming in Galilee added to her worry, and she asked Joseph to send another message. Though they could not afford another letter, he did send word with a traveler going from Egypt to Damascus. She hoped they would hear something soon, but she kept busy, thus distracting her mind.

Joseph received more orders for tables, plows, and other items; the funds from these were gratefully received as Mary mostly shared her talent for weaving and pot making but made little money. Bethlehem was a poor village, and most women made their own baskets and pots, and travelers usually made their purchases in Jerusalem. Mary was disappointed at only adding a few coins to their purse, not nearly enough for the sacrifices required for her final cleansing, but Joseph seemed grateful and, in humor, pointed out that they would have plenty of pots and baskets for themselves.

In the long evenings of a hot, early summer, Joseph and Gomer finished the walls to the first level of Joseph and Mary's home. Mary had begun weaving mats for the roof, which would not be finished until after their trip to the temple when Joseph would cut and haul the beams. For now, they continued to use their shelter and the cave, both of which were quite serviceable for summer weather.

All in all, they were quite contented, though Joseph did worry about work to carry them through the winter. Without the ability to raise their own food and animals, his work had to provide everything they needed. As fall and winter drew closer, the villagers would think less of a new table or chairs and more of holding onto the food or money these would cost. Mary knew he could always go to Jerusalem, but the wages there were poor, and she disliked the thought of having him working so far away.

The month Nisan had passed, and the new moon of the month Iyyar was nearly full when they awoke and prepared to travel to Jerusalem for Mary's purification. It was hard for her to believe that the required forty days of waiting had passed and it was now time to offer their sacrifice. Though disappointed that they could not offer a lamb, they also knew they had done all within their power to try to do so and that God would accept the offering of two turtledoves instead. A man's whole heart was what God wanted, and Mary knew that in this they were not lacking.

On the night before their day's journey, Mary washed all their clothing and packed some food. She and Joseph left their nearly finished home three hours before sunup to begin the long walk. They did not bring Saul on this trip. Mary felt fully recovered and quite strong enough, and the donkey would be hard to keep safe while they were in the temple, at least without extra expense.

Carrying a large oil lamp to light their way, they reached the top of the mountain just south of the city as the sky in the east turned a dark blue. As they rested, Mary fed Jesus and changed his loincloth. When she was ready, Joseph snuffed out the lamp's wick, the dim light of predawn now enough to show the way.

Descending the steep slope to the city, they could see the temple already coming to life, the lighting of torches allowing the priests to begin their early cleansing and preparations for the day's sacrifice.

Mary had always admired the look of the sanctuary as the light of torches and lamps reflected off the golden surface of its walls and towers, but it seemed especially beautiful this day, and it caused a swelling of joy in her bosom that threatened to bring tears to her eyes.

"How wonderful!" she exclaimed. She and Joseph stood on the side of the slope, taking it all in before finally forcing themselves to continue their journey.

"Herod may be an evil man, but he has certainly built a most beautiful building," Joseph remarked.

Mary felt her stomach churn a bit but quickly put it to rest. She had worried about coming to Herod's city from the moment Jesus was born. No one would be of greater threat to her son than Israel's paranoid king, but Joseph had told her that short of a revelation, there was no way Herod could know that Jesus was at his doorstep. She should not worry; Herod was not worthy of such revelations.

She knew it to be true, but the knot in her stomach was not so easy to untie.

They descended the last of the hill and passed the pool where they had stopped for water nearly a month and a half earlier while on their way to Bethlehem. She had given birth to Jesus the next day. It seemed so long ago.

Roughly half of the thousands of tents they had seen then still remained. Some pilgrims came from thousands of miles, not only for Passover but for the Feast of Pentecost, which followed fifty days later. That feast was now only a few days away, and though people in the camps were still mostly asleep, a smattering of lamps and fires spread across the hillside, and a few men were already walking to the city gates to attend the morning sacrifice.

Mary and Joseph arrived at Gennath Gate just as it was being opened. Passing by sleepy guards without incident, they entered the street known as Kings Street. The dividing wall that separated the upper city from the business district to the north was on their left, and high walls with intermittent gates leading to the homes and palaces of the rich were on their right. Ornate gates leading to Herod's palace were the first and by far the largest they passed. Mary reached for Joseph's arm and held tight while gripping Jesus more firmly with her other arm. Joseph patted her hand softly, but both quickened their pace until free of the shadow of the king's palace.

Foot traffic was still scarce but growing, the time for the temple opening drawing nigh. All would try to reach the Court of the Women before the morning sacrifice was actually offered. There they would wait for the opening of the Nicanor Gate, which would give them entrance into the Court of the Israelites, where they could see the sanctuary itself. Mary had seen the service on several occasions and never tired of it. The singing, the lighting of incense, the prayer, and the sacrifice itself all held great promise for Israel. But today, the day of her purification, would make it even more wonderful.

Just beyond what they both knew was the Hasmonean Palace of past dynasties, a wide bridge spanned the Tyropoeon Valley and led directly to the temple. There were no purification pools at this entrance, and Mary and Joseph veered south and wound their way through narrow streets until they were at the base of the western wall of the temple complex. Shops lined this street, and food and a hundred other items were sold here, mostly to visitors. Some of the shopkeepers were beginning to open their doors, but Joseph and Mary hardly noticed, their eyes on the large set of stairs that bridged the street and climbed the southwest corner of the temple entrance high above them. Mary always felt overwhelmed by the sheer size of the walls, stairs, and porticoes of the temple complex, and this trip was no exception. Even now, she could not help but stop and gaze up with admiration. Torches burned at intervals along the top of the high walls, illuminating pillars and stones, making all look to Mary like a part of heaven.

"Come." Joseph put a gentle arm around her waist. "We must hurry." He said it with reverent awe, his own eyes on the porticoes high above them, then tugged her forward along the street.

Passing under the staircase at the southwest corner of the temple, they entered the broad southern courtyard outside the complex. Pools for washing and cleansing lay here, some for men, some for women.

Carefully, Joseph took Jesus from Mary's arms. "I will hold him while you cleanse and dress. Then I will go into the pool for men."

Mary took her bag and hastened through the door to the pools. Several women were already bathing, and she entered a small room to undress and go through a ritual similar to what she had done on her eighth day. This time, she felt rushed, and with other women present, she hurried to wash then immerse before putting on her clean white tunic and robe. A sudden wave of emotion overcame Mary as she remembered when her mother had given her the robe. Made of tightly woven yarn, it had taken a good deal of time and extra wool, and her mother had sacrificed a new robe of her own to create it. Oh, how she wished her parents were here!

She forced herself to hurry. Though they could do this ceremony at any time, and another day—or even another month—would not really matter, she felt a strong desire to move forward, to give thanks to God for so many things and to be obedient.

Mary found Joseph in a growing crowd and took a sleeping Jesus from him, then waited while he went through a washing similar to Mary's in preparation to enter God's house.

More and more people flooded into the courtyard and entered the buildings for cleansing or, already cleansed in their own pools or other pools around the city, approached the Hulda Gate and awaited its opening. The city was coming alive all around Mary, and she could hear the noise, smell the odors, see the activity. She watched as small groups and families found places together and ate while they visited or sang and even danced, as men in dress both familiar and unfamiliar conversed in various languages, and as children played and mothers fed and cared for crying babies. A teacher near the steps, his students gathered around him, asked questions and quoted Torah. All these people waited eagerly for the gates to open. Mary felt her heart pound with the excitement of it all and did a little dance of her own, Jesus snuggled against her breast, as a nearby group played music on flute and lyre.

Joseph returned, and they walked to the gate as quickly as they could through the crowd.

"Do you have the shekels?" Mary asked as they approached the Hulda Gate.

Joseph nodded.

"And the price for—" she caught herself. "I'm sorry, dearest. I know you would not forget."

They waited, the smell of burning lamps mingling with the fresh scents of morning and the sounds of celebrants and activity all around them. Quickly, the sky turned a lighter blue and dawn neared. Then the gates opened and people moved forward in a remarkably orderly fashion. The music and laughter stopped suddenly, the mood quickly becoming one of reverence and awe.

The throngs of temple visitors walked through a short tunnel with stone floors and finely carved columns to a set of stairs leading up to the Court of the Gentiles. A few turned left to the area where sacrificial animals were sold, but most kept going north to the east gate of the Court of the Women. Mary handed Jesus to Joseph and received her husband's purse in which the money for her sacrifice and for Jesus' redemption price was placed. Then Joseph went back the way they had come.

Inside the temple, the morning sacrifice had been slain and the priests had entered the temple to burn the incense. She knew this was finished when the Gate of the Firstborn opened and she and several others covered their faces, climbed the steps, and entered through the gate. Walking along a corridor a short distance, they came into the open on the highest step before the Nicanor Gate, which led into the Court of the Priests. To the east and behind them was the Court of the Women, and though the crowd was large, she saw that Joseph had worked his way past most of them and stood holding Jesus only a dozen cubits beyond the bottom step. She looked at them nervously but was forced to turn away as the gates were opened so that those offering individual sacrifices could present them to the priests inside the sanctuary.

Mary's breath caught in her chest as the beautiful gates swung open to reveal the sanctuary. Though she had seen it, or at least portions of it, from the floor of the Court of the Women, she had never been this close, never seen it so clearly. It towered above her, the first rays of the morning sun glinting off its gold-covered columns and facade to cascade over everything inside the Court of the Priests. Surely there was never a building so magnificent!

She watched as the lamb's blood was splashed upon the altar and the daily sacrifice completed with the singing of the last of the Hallel. Mary was still taking it all in when a priest approached her and bowed.

Taking a deep breath to get her wits about her, Mary handed him the money with a slight bow before requesting that two turtledoves be offered for her purification. He nodded, bowed again, then went to the place of sacrifice and purchased the turtledoves for her and took them to another priest, who quickly cut them and sent what was needed to the altar in a silver bowl before giving a small portion of the blood to the priest. He approached Mary, who knelt and prayed, thanking God for her son, for His trust of her, and for her purification. The priest then sprinkled some of the blood of the doves lightly over her, declaring her cleansed before bowing and stepping away to wait for the five shekels.

While still kneeling, Mary removed the coins from the leather pouch and handed them to the priest.

"As it is written in the law of the Lord, every male that openeth the womb shall be called holy to the Lord," she recited.

The priest then offered two benedictions, one for God's blessing them with a firstborn son and one for the law of redemption.

"Your offering is accepted of the Lord, and your son is free," declared the priest.

Mary felt a wave of satisfaction and whispered a thank you to the priest as she bowed. He bowed in return and started back the way he had come. Then he turned and looked back at Mary. "You're welcome," he said with a smile.

Mary rose to her feet, once more feeling that warm, powerful glow of comfort in her heart. She was clean, her blood no longer stained the sanctuary, and she knew that God was pleased with her. Since her purification in the mikveh she had nearly forgotten how this warm glow had felt. Now she realized again that He was watching out for His Son and for her, and that He had given them both Joseph to care for them. Mary felt wonderfully blessed and at peace.

She delayed a moment, letting the feeling wash over her while her eyes feasted upon the beauty of the sanctuary before her. She would come to this place of purification again, hopefully several times as she gave birth to other children, but the significance of this birth, the wonderful feelings in her heart, made it difficult to pull away.

Finally, she turned back to the Court of the Women and descended the steps to Joseph, who put an arm around her and pulled her close. She laid her head against his chest and felt the warm, steady beat of his heart.

"God is surely in His house today," Joseph said.

"Excuse me," called someone behind them.

Mary turned to see an old gentleman dressed in a white tunic and robe with a white prayer shawl covering his head and draped loosely across his shoulders.

"Yes?" Joseph answered.

The old gentleman bowed. "I am Simeon," he said in a wavering voice. "I am old and cannot come to the temple as often as I like, but . . . but today I felt I must come. It was God's will." He glanced at Jesus. "May I hold him?"

Simeon looked at Mary with clear, deep brown eyes, and she thought surely he could see into the very depths of her soul. And yet his look warmed her, like God's Spirit warmed her, and the love in his gentle voice testified that this was truly a devout, even a holy man. She nodded. "Yes, of course."

Joseph did not hesitate to let Simeon take Jesus from his arms. Tenderly, the old man pulled back the blanket that shielded the baby's face from the sun, and a sweet smile creased his cracked lips. "Yes, it is him." He turned his eyes to heaven and spoke quietly. "Lord, now lettest thou thy servant depart in peace, according to thy word: for mine eyes have seen thy salvation, which thou hast prepared before the face of all people; a light to lighten the Gentiles, and the glory of thy people Israel." Tears wet his eyes and cascaded down his face, and he gently kissed Jesus on the forehead and hugged him close before handing him to Mary, his eyes fixed on hers.

"Behold, this child is set for the fall and rising again of many in Israel; and for a sign which shall be spoken against; that the thoughts of many hearts may be revealed."

His eyes suddenly darkened, a sadness creeping into them that made Mary feel weak. "And yea, a sword shall pierce through thy own soul also." He squeezed her hand comfortingly, and the fear flowing into her heart suddenly fled. She did not want Simeon to let go of her hand, but he bowed and pulled away, and she reluctantly let his aged hand slip from hers and watched him walk haltingly toward the east gate. Without even looking at him, the crowd seemed to sense his presence and make way, then close behind him until he disappeared from Mary's view.

* * *

Mary still pondered Simeon's words as they left the Court of the Women and walked into the Court of the Gentiles and to Solomon's Porch. Suddenly she felt a tug on her sleeve, and she turned to face a small woman, bent with age. Mary knew her immediately—she had seen her at the temple every year that she had come with her parents.

Like Mary's mother, this woman's name was Anna, and for more than eighty years she had spent her days at the temple, praying, fasting, serving God through acts of kindness she did for others, from giving them her last mite to washing their feet and putting ointment on them. Women gathered around Anna when visiting the temple, listening to her words of wisdom, and went away refreshed and filled with a new love for God and a desire to serve more willingly. Even rabbis and other learned teachers respected Anna's teachings, and when she prophesied, all appreciated her words, whether poor or rich.

"May I hold the child?" she asked in a clear voice.

Mary smiled. "The child and I would be honored if you did."

Anna looked at Jesus for a long moment, her tender eyes searching his. Then she lifted him to her lips and whispered in his ear so that only Jesus and Mary could hear. "It is you," she said. "At last, you have come."

Once more, Mary felt her spine tingle at the words, and she looked deeply into Anna's gray eyes. "You know as well?"

Anna smiled but did not answer immediately, as the followers who always trailed her pressed in on them, trying to hear, drawing close to see what the old prophetess was doing. Finally, Anna handed Jesus back and leaned close to Mary. "I give thanks to God for this child and for you. Truly, blessed are you among women." Her sallow, wrinkled cheeks were wet with tears as she kissed Mary lightly on the cheek before caressing it with her aged finger. "Go now. Take care of him." She gave a nod of respect to Joseph then walked gracefully toward the place where she often sat to teach.

"What is it, Anna?" asked one woman. "Who is that child?"

Anna did not respond until she was in the shade of the small south portico of the Court of the Women. She glanced back toward Mary, gave her a loving smile, then spoke.

"All who look for redemption in Israel, bless this day," she declared with full voice.

The crowd around her grew silent, then there were whispers as those who did not know Anna were informed of who she was. With the news, all seemed to press in so they could see and hear, blocking Mary's view.

"Come, Mary," Joseph said. "It is better if we are not here."

Mary too felt the urgency and let herself be led away, hearing only the first words in which Anna declared that redemption was at hand, even at the doors. Then she lost the words in the murmur of the crowd, the rush of people trying to get closer to the aged prophetess, and their own hurried retreat out of the temple and into the Court of the Gentiles.

They crossed the marbled floors to the steps, then went down and through the tunnel and out the southern gate. Joseph did not run—he was not fleeing in panic—but he did not slow his pace until they were moving rapidly downhill through the streets of the old City of David.

"Are you tired?" he finally asked Mary.

She smiled and shook her head in the negative, but they continued on at a more leisurely pace until they reached the gate that led out of the old city and directly into the courtyard surrounding the Pool of Siloam.

"We'll rest here," Joseph stated.

The pool was about fifty cubits wide at its closest end with steps leading into it. The tunnel built by the ancient King Hezekiah to feed the pool with water from Gihon Spring entered its northern side, but the steps lay on the east. Just to the south of the steps, Mary and Joseph sat in the shade of a portico built by Herodian workmen. Since the pool was one of the water sources considered pure, men and women stood or sat on the steps to wash their hands and feet in a partial cleansing before entering Jerusalem, and women filled jars to take to their homes for daily purifying. It was from this pool that water was drawn by the priests for the water-drawing ceremony during the Feast of Tabernacles.

Mary covered herself with her headscarf and fed Jesus while Joseph removed the food she had prepared for them. While watching people come and go, they shared dates, cheese, small cakes, and a pomegranate.

With Jesus asleep in his blanket, Joseph and Mary leaned back against the wall, and she laid her head on his shoulder and closed her eyes. She was contented and happy but wondering at the events in the temple: why had Anna and Simeon been shown Jesus' identity, and, especially, what had Simeon meant?

"This child is set for the fall and rising again of many in Israel; and for a sign which shall be spoken against; that the thoughts of many hearts may be revealed," she repeated. "What does it mean, Joseph?"

Joseph did not answer immediately, gathering his own thoughts before finally speaking.

"Jesus will judge Israel, Mary, but not before he shows them he has the right. He will give them a sign, an undeniable one, maybe more than one. Unfortunately, even then many will refuse to believe. When they do, they will leave themselves open to be judged of him, and he will reveal their hearts before the world."

"And the other part, the part he spoke to me?" Mary said tremulously.

"Did it frighten you?"

"At first, then the fear went away with his touch." She paused. "Ever since my first cleansing, I have felt this warmth in my heart. It brightened when his hand touched me . . . It took my fear."

He pulled her tighter to him. "Your love for Jesus will cause you grief when he is rejected. It will hurt you deeply, but as now, God will give you comfort."

"Do you have these feelings, this warmth?"

"Yes. I've had them ever since the dream of the angel. God is with us. We have but to listen to Him and everything will be as it should be."

Mary lay against him, her eyes suddenly heavy. They had arisen early, and she and Joseph were weary.

They awoke at midday to find a teacher gathering his students around him for a lesson, while others continued to come and go from the pool. There was no washing of clothes here, no bathing with soap, no swimming. Considered one of Jerusalem's holiest places, it was approached with reverence.

Joseph and Mary gathered their things, made sure they left nothing unclean, and went back through the gate in the wall, turning right and down the slope to the Water Gate. They followed the road directly south, circumventing the Valley Hinnom, considered unclean because of an evil past in which children had been sacrificed there. Turning west, they crossed under the aqueduct that fed Jerusalem from the Pools of Solomon south of Bethlehem and finally caught the road that would take them home. Picking up their pace but resting several times along the way, they did not get back to their cave until dark.

* * *

"It was a wonderful day, Joseph. Thank you," Mary said. He was lying with his back against a log, her head on his shoulder. With his arm tucked around her, he rubbed her back lightly with his fingers while thinking of what he had seen and felt as he watched Mary first become clean from any impurity, then buy Jesus' redemption. He had pondered many things all the way back to Bethlehem.

Mary snuggled into his arm, and he looked down to find her asleep. Carefully, he slid out from under her, then lifted her easily into his arms and carried her to her blankets. Placing one over her, he returned for Jesus, who still lay sleeping. Wrapping his prayer shawl around his own neck, he picked Jesus up and cradled him in the crook of his arm before taking him along the side of the hill where he came often to pray and to think.

It was a beautiful, clear night, and the new star he had seen shortly after Jesus' birth seemed to be closer, to shine even brighter.

There had been a time when Joseph had wondered if he could ever love Jesus as his own, but that moment had come and gone as he brought the baby from Mary's womb, giving him life. He loved this baby, almost as deeply as he loved Mary. How could a man not love such a child? His nose, his chin, his eyes were all like any other child's, but knowing who he really was and what he would do for all mankind made Joseph love him so deeply it sometimes made him ache.

Using his free hand, he put his prayer shawl over his head and draped one corner over Jesus' body. Each day, he gained more knowledge, more understanding of him, and this day was no exception. Each day he had come here to pray and give thanks, and this day would be no exception either.

As he bowed his head, he thought of Simeon and Anna. How long they had waited! How at peace they must be this night!

After the Shema and the usual benedictions, Joseph gave thanks that God had let him be a part of this day. Certainly he did not fully understand what it all meant, but he would cherish these moments more than most.

He removed his shawl and went back to the cave, putting Jesus in his manger bed, noticing that it would soon be too small. Joseph must make something larger before the Sabbath. He blew out all but one lamp, which he filled to the brim with oil before removing his outer robe and crawling under the blankets next to Mary. She backed against him for warmth, and he closed his eyes in contentment. Of all God's creations he surely must be the most blessed.

PART TWO
FLIGHT INTO EGYPT

CHAPTER 21

The storm had dumped rain intermittently all morning, finally becoming so furious that the workers could not stay on the bridge any longer and deserted it for the shelter of the temple. Joseph sat down near one of the pools and pulled off his drenched headscarf and wrung it out. At this rate, they would never get the work done by the deadline. To him, it did not matter; it was his last day anyway.

Though work in Bethlehem had been steady enough to get Joseph, Mary, and the baby through the first fall, the winter had not offered the same blessing. The harvest had been poor, and few people had extra goods or money for new doors, tables, and shutters for their houses or plows and carts to work their fields. To keep his family from going hungry, Joseph had been forced to work in Jerusalem.

Upon arriving in the city, he had been immediately hired to repair the bridge that led from the east gate of the temple across the Kidron Valley to the Mount of Olives. From this gate and by this bridge, the red heifer was brought from the temple to the mount for burning. The ashes were then used for the purification of those made unclean by the death of others. The bridge was also used to send the scapegoat into the wilderness on the Day of Atonement after the priest placed the people's sins on it. From the east side of the bridge, the goat was taken into the desert, a symbol for the uninhabitable place where all sins dwelt until their final cleansing by Jehovah. How this goat took their sins was something Joseph had never understood, but he was sure that, like the lamb, it was a symbol of the Messiah. He just wasn't sure how their Messiah could be the scapegoat and then survive to lead them to a better world.

Work had been steady, paying enough to keep them in food and allow them to save a little. Joseph was grateful, but much more so now that for him, the work was coming to an end.

It was time for planting, and men preparing to enter their fields needed plows and other tools either repaired or replaced. Tomorrow Joseph would work in his own shop again.

Gomer sat beside him and leaned forward, putting his elbows on his knees. "I spoke to the steward. They still want it done in time for Passover."

Joseph shrugged. "It will be nearly impossible. It only gives you twenty days to do two months' work."

"Then you are not coming back," Gomer stated rather than asked.

"No, not until I have finished the work needed in Bethlehem." Joseph looked up at the top of the temple, which was now crowned with a heavy cloud. Except for its dark gray color, Joseph thought it must look like the cloud of God that hung over Mount Sinai in Moses' day. Except this one had no divine presence in it, only rain.

Gomer shrugged. "I wish I could be so lucky." He paused to cough. "They're adding workers. They want it done."

"Then tell the high priest and the king to appeal to God for less rain and more sun," Joseph suggested.

Gomer chuckled. "That would be like the devil appealing to God for a kingdom." He stood. "I am going to pray. My sick son . . ."

"I will go with you," Joseph declared. Gomer's son had become ill more than a week ago and was not getting well. It had been a very wet winter and spring, and the constant dampness had caused considerable sickness. Even Jesus had caught a fever that he was just getting over, and Mary had one earlier that prevented Joseph from coming to work for more than a week, and even then it was another two weeks before she fully recovered.

Under the roof of the east portico known as Solomon's Porch, Joseph and Gomer decided to make their move, dashing across the Court of the Gentiles and into the Court of the Women. Here they found cover near the Nicanor Gate, not far from where Joseph and Mary had met Simeon and Anna nearly a year earlier. Several priests had also taken shelter there and sat listening to a rabbi teach his students. Joseph and Gomer had faced the temple and begun praying when Joseph heard a familiar, booming voice. He lifted his head and his wet shawl to see a large young man striding across the Court of the Women toward him.

"Matthias?"

"May God be praised," Matthias exclaimed loudly. "I have found you!" He grinned, then wrapped his arms around Joseph and lifted him off the ground with one of those embraces that cracked bones and took a man's breath away. When he put Joseph down, Gomer and everyone else within earshot were staring at them, some curious, some angry, some amused. As they were in the house of God, Joseph lowered his own voice, hoping Matthias would do the same.

"Matthias. How good to see you! You remember Gomer," Joseph said. He saw that most of the men around them lost interest and went back to their own business.

"Yes, yes, of course. The stone mason who helped us finish your house when we came for the Feast of Tabernacles." Matthias smiled while extending a hand and arm for greeting.

Matthias and Salome had traveled to Bethlehem along with Mary's family nearly six months earlier, arriving at Joseph and Mary's a week before the feast. They stayed a week afterward, helping Joseph complete the house by hauling timbers for the roof from the forests south of the village. Salome had given birth to a son only weeks earlier but had made the journey anyway. The boy was of ruddy complexion and large stature with thick, dark hair and the round face of his father. They had named him Simon, after his grandfather. "How is everyone in Nazareth?" Joseph asked.

"Well. Though Mary's family could not come this time, they send their love."

It was unusual for Joachim to miss one of the required feast days, especially Passover. "Josiah has not become sick again, I hope," Joseph said.

"No, no, Joachim has taken on work for one of the rich of the Jezreel Valley. With last year's poor crop, he needs to raise money for his taxes. We will make sacrifice for him and for the family," Matthias replied.

"And where are Salome, Mara, and little Simon?" Joseph asked.

"In Bethlehem. When I found you were here, I returned to see if you have lost your touch with the hammer and chisel." Matthias grinned.

"It is not I who may have lost his touch, fisherman," Joseph quipped.

Matthias laughed heartily. "Yes, well, I brought my tools. We will see who can skin a rock of its rough edges the quickest." He paused. "Mary says you work on the bridge. Do they need more hands?"

"Many more. They want to finish for Passover," Gomer explained.

"And your opinion?" Matthias asked Joseph.

"It can't be done," Joseph answered. "Even with a hundred more men. It isn't numbers we need but skilled workers in stone. Herod has most of them working on his lower palace and does not free them for this work."

"But surely I and my skills must change your opinion." Matthias smiled. "I do the work of five men!"

Joseph laughed and clapped his friend on the back. "It is good to see you again, my friend. We were about to pray for Gomer's sick child. Will you join us? Then," Joseph paused to look up at the dark skies, "if the God of Heaven will stop the flood, I will present you to the overseer and show you our task."

By the time they finished praying for Gomer's son, the rain had stopped and the sun peeked through the clouds. As they returned to their work, warm rays of sunlight cascaded over the temple and the bridge, causing water puddles on the stone floor to steam. Joseph and Gomer found the overseer rounding up his workers in Solomon's Porch, and Joseph presented Matthias to him. The foreman looked at Matthias, blinked, and mumbled something about Matthias being a large one. Then he muttered, "Our oxen should be so big. Maybe we would get some stone hauled around here if they were." Then he hired him.

The sun grew bolder as the day wore on, drying the stone and allowing the laborers to hasten their work. Joseph had nearly forgotten how strong his friend was and how skilled with the heavy hammer. The three of them worked twice as fast as other teams, and Joseph was enjoying being around his friend again. Matthias was an ox, though a gentle one, and with him and another five like him, they might finish by Passover.

But that was not Joseph's worry anymore. His shop would be his only concern now, and he looked forward to it.

They took a break for water and sat along the wall of the bridge, their legs dangling over its edge. The Kidron Valley was deep here, and the road that ran beneath the bridge looked small. Years later, the Mount of Olives had been stripped of its wealth of fifty kinds of timber, but olive groves had been planted in their place and nearly covered the entire mount. One fairly young grove sat directly north of them and was especially well kept with a high stone fence and gates alongside the road leading east to Jericho. Just as Joseph suggested that they go back to work, a large caravan appeared at the top of the hill.

"Foreigners," he warned, pointing at the caravan. Several armed men led the caravan, and a dozen more followed it. Noblemen rode sturdy camels in between, with servants leading half a dozen more camels loaded with the supplies needed for a long journey.

Matthias nodded. "Parthians, from the look of them." He squinted. "Priests and nobles come to see our king."

The Parthian empire stood to the east of Arabia and had been in conflict with Rome for several decades. As a country caught between two world powers, Palestine had belonged to each over the last hundred years, and both Herod and his father Antipater had suffered defeat at the hand of the Parthians. Only with the sending of thousands of troops by Rome, which needed Palestine for military and economic purposes, were the Herods able to run the Parthians out of Palestine and continue to keep them at bay.

"It is men like these that make or break kings," Matthias remarked.

"What do you mean?" Gomer wondered.

"They are magi, the priests of the eastern religions. They have great influence with their king and their people, and enough power to cause war or bring peace. If they have come to see Herod, it is to bring a message of great importance from their God or their government. Herod's treatment of them will be very important for him and for all of us."

"There have been no rumors of such a visit," Joseph added.

"Then Herod will need to be even more careful. The purpose of this visit could be to make demands that, if not dealt with carefully, will precipitate war." He shrugged. "If the Parthians come, the rebels of this country will join them. Out of it may come great changes in Israel."

"You mean the Herods would be gone," Gomer stated.

"And Rome."

"The Parthians are not strong enough to defeat Rome. No one is," Joseph declared.

"With our rebels, who knows?" Matthias said.

The long caravan disappeared along the road directly north of the wall of the city even as a trumpet sounded from the Antonia fortress.

"Herod's soldiers know they are here. They call the troops to their posts," Matthias explained.

"But surely they do not fear such a small group," Gomer replied.

"No, but they fear offending them. It will be an honor guard, not a fighting one."

"Come, let's get back to work. I told the foreman we deserved to leave early if we finished the extension to the east abutment. He did not think it could be done," Joseph said.

"But did you get an oath out of him?" Gomer asked. "He promised to let us go early if—"

"He promised, but only because he does not believe we can shape and lay that much stone, even with Matthias," Joseph clarified.

"Then we will show him he is a poor judge of us." Matthias grinned as he picked up one large stone and put it in place, then another. He was right. The foreman had misjudged them.

* * *

When the caravan approached the city, Marcus was dining with several men of Jerusalem. He was particularly interested in the talk of one Seth, son of Aristamaeus of Athens, whose daughter had been introduced earlier along with others of the aristocratic families. Marcus had never seen such a beautiful woman and was anxious to learn more of her. Suddenly, his second in command, Banat, came through the doors and quickly to Marcus's side, breaking into his thoughts. After whispering into Marcus's ear, Banat stood at attention while Marcus stood, bowed, and excused himself, leaving with Banat.

As they walked from the room and down the long corridor to the outside, Marcus spoke to Banat. "What do you know of them?"

"They are from Parthia. Priests, from the looks of them."

"You have called the guard to the walls," Marcus stated.

"Yes, sire. They are ready for your command."

Along with a dozen of his personal guard, Marcus and Banat mounted their horses and rode briskly to the northern gate as guards climbed to the walls of the Antonia fortress and the city. There had been no announcement of any embassy from the East, and it concerned Marcus that the caravan had gotten all the way to Jerusalem without his being notified. But that did not matter now; they were here and it was his situation to handle. It would not be easy if unrest broke out. The Passover was near, and the crowds were growing.

Marcus and his soldiers reached the gate to find the magi already off their camels, speaking with the captain of the guard for the northern gate. Halting his men and signaling them to stay ready, Marcus dismounted and walked forward. The captain and his men saluted and came to attention. "Sir," said the captain in Greek.

The apparent leader of the magi stood a little forward of the others, armed guards on both sides and to the rear. Servants, at least a dozen that Marcus could see, stood by the camels but were not unarmed. Marcus had seen Parthian soldiers before, and these were neither armed nor clothed like Parthians. He suspected that they were personal guards brought along to protect against bandits and robbers during a long journey and were not meant for war or intimidation. This was a special embassy come in peace, and though he was curious about their message, Marcus did not feel threatened by their presence.

He thought of dismissing the men along the walls but still felt uneasy and decided to hear the magi first. He bowed slightly to the eldest, then spoke. "Marcus Vitellius, a Roman centurion attached to King Herod's army. I command the first cohort of his troops and am responsible for the defense of the city. Can I be of service to you?"

This elicited a bow from the magi before the eldest spoke.

"Where is he that is born King of the Jews? For we have seen his star in the East, and are come to worship him."

Marcus heard murmurs and whispering from both his soldiers and the gathering crowd. It was justified. For an embassy from another government to ignore Herod and request knowledge of a different king showed that they no longer considered Herod sovereign of Palestine. Saying that a star had appeared announcing the arrival of this new king gave God's sanction to the newcomer while rejecting Herod. Herod would not like being snubbed, but he would like even less the announcement that, in the eyes of these magi at least, his reign had ended and a new king was coming to power. Had they heard of the recent attempt by one of Herod's sons to have him killed? Had they been part of the plot and not heard that it had failed? Marcus eyed them carefully. No, these were not conspirators of low means and few brains.

As the murmuring grew and more citizens ran to encircle the new arrivals, Marcus was glad he had not dismissed the guard so quickly. These men offered no threat to him or his men, but their message would concern the citizenry and word would spread quickly. Coupled with rumors of Herod's serious illness, the words of the magi might give some the impression that he was already dead or that there had been a coup. The king's enemies might want to take advantage of such rumors and confusion, and at Passover, it would be easy to start a riot.

"We have only one king in Palestine. He is Herod, son of Antipater and friend to Augustus Caesar. If you wish to counsel with him, my men and I will take you to his palace. But there are no other kings in Palestine."

The eldest smiled and bowed. "Thank you. Lead and we will follow. It would be an honor to meet your king in his palace. After all, isn't that where a new one would be born?"

Marcus felt the calming of the crowd and admired the leader of the magi for understanding the gravity of the situation. His last words had settled things a bit.

Marcus ordered his Thracian troops to form up and clear the road to the Gennath Gate. As he returned to his horse, soldiers bustled into position while the guards of the magi escorted their masters to their camels.

While they mounted, Marcus gave orders to his second in command. "Banat, dismiss the men along the walls and make the city aware that there is no need for alarm. Then go to Jecundus, commander of the king's personal guard, and let him know we are coming. He will notify the king. If Herod has not completely lost his mind, he will treat these men like royalty and give them rooms in the lower palace."

Banat saluted and had turned his horse to leave when Marcus spoke again.

"And Banat, in an hour, I want men in the streets, especially around the temple. A show of presence, that is all. No action is to be taken without my order."

Banat saluted once more and gave the order, which was quickly passed up to the walls by a set signal. A trumpet was blown and the gates thrown open again as he and two other soldiers galloped their horses into the city.

The eastern priests mounted, and the animals regained their feet. Marcus and his men led out, and the road was quickly lined with people eager to see the escort and to discover the identities of these honored visitors.

Giving Banat opportunity to deliver his message, Marcus took his time leading the entourage to the Gennath Gate. Jecundus would not be pleased at this sudden appearance of an embassy he knew nothing about. The man was nearly as paranoid about Herod's safety as was Herod himself.

The responsibilities of Marcus and Jecundus often overlapped, and it had not taken long for Marcus to learn that his authority never superceded that of Herod's commander of personal security. The latest example was when Herod had discovered that his son Antipater had planned to kill him with the help of Herod's brother Pheroras. When Herod lured Antipater back from Rome, it had been Marcus's responsibility to arrest and imprison him for trial in the Antonia. However, Jecundus convinced Herod that he should take no chances and forced Marcus to give up Antipater to be taken to the palace and imprisoned there. Marcus did not care where the king's son rotted while he waited for the death he obviously deserved, but Jecundus had slurred Marcus's name by telling Herod that he and his men were not to be trusted and could be easily bribed by Antipater's friends. It hadn't been the first time Jecundus had insulted him, and Marcus knew it would not be the last, but he was sure there would come a time when their swords would cross simply because their ideas of justice were so far apart.

As they approached the three towers of Herod's palace, Marcus did not need to wonder if Banat had been delayed or whether Jecundus had received the news. Guards were already pouring onto the walls of the king's palace.

CHAPTER 22

When Joseph, Matthias, and Gomer finished their task, the sun was still an hour away from setting and the foreman could do nothing but let them go. He gave them their wages and was still shaking his head, his eyes on their work. "Are you sure you will not return?" he asked Joseph.

"I am sure, but thank you for the work. It kept my family from going hungry this winter."

"And you." The foreman grinned at Matthias. "We could use you for a few days at least."

"Maybe; we will see. I love the work and . . . well, I need another fishing boat. I could use the money."

The three men walked through the temple and once outside, they purchased hot bread for their journey. Joseph and Gomer had found routes through the city that cut nearly an hour off the trip home, and a few hours after sunset, Joseph and Matthias were saying good-bye to Gomer and walking down the street that led to Joseph's house.

As they passed the well, Joseph saw Adah and Uriah and waved to them. Their marriage had been completed only six months after their betrothal and, if her sickness was any indication, she was already carrying their first child.

"The shepherd boy," Matthias remarked. "The one who gave you a sheep on the day we finished your house. No small gift for a matchmaker."

Joseph had told Matthias the story but left out the details of Benjamin's vision and its connection to Jesus. When they had first spoken during their visit six months before, it had been obvious that Jesus was older than he should be, but Matthias and Salome had said nothing, apparently content that Joseph and Mary were happy, no matter what had happened to give them a son so soon. Joseph hoped that someday he could help Matthias understand, but even now he did not feel an inclination to do so.

Matthias and Joseph entered Joseph's house to find the women preparing food, and Jesus and Simon playing in the middle of the floor. Mara, quickly becoming a young woman, was sitting on one of Joseph's new chairs.

The house had turned out nicely, with a living area and two rooms for sleeping. One stairway, on the exterior of the eastern end, ran up to the roof, while one on the west went down to the lower level where the donkey, the sheep given to them by Uriah, and their two lambs now resided. One of the lambs was without blemish and would provide them with a sacrifice this Passover.

Mary looked especially radiant, beaming when she saw Joseph enter. Salome grinned at Matthias as well, and Joseph was glad to see that their love hadn't waned.

"You are home early," Mary exclaimed.

"Matthias was a big help."

"I can imagine."

"I told the foreman I would not be back, for now at least."

She beamed. "It will be good to have you close again."

Matthias kissed Salome and tweaked at her headscarf, pulling it askance. She gave him a hard look but obviously relished the show of love. He then picked up Jesus and swung him onto a shoulder and danced around with him. Just under a year old, Jesus loved it and giggled and laughed, even reaching with one hand to try to touch the ceiling.

Though just recently walking, Jesus was into everything inside and out. He had grown particularly infatuated with Saul, and they took constant care that the child didn't get under the donkey's hooves. Jesus loved the wooden toys Joseph made for him in his shop and played under Joseph's feet much of the time.

Joseph lifted Simon to get a good look at him. Of solid and round build, the baby was as heavy as Jesus, even though half his age. "He is . . . growing."

"Even now he eats more fish than I can catch!" Matthias declared proudly.

"He is after Jesus all the time," Mary pointed out. "Simon loves to hold onto him."

"And Jesus' reaction?" Joseph queried.

"He has learned to keep his distance."

They chatted, catching up on one another's news and what was happening in Galilee, Matthias deftly avoiding questions about Judas ben Hezekiah and his rebels. Joseph was pleased to hear—and see—that Salome was expecting again.

"Four months and he will join us," Matthias explained proudly.

"Another boy? God has given you a dream to know this?"

Matthias grinned. "He kicks his mother to bruises just as Simon did. It must be another boy."

"That is a sign you can rely on," Mary agreed. "I still have bruises from Jesus."

Joseph saw the sadness in her eyes. They desired a second child but no such blessing had come.

Mary turned to Joseph. "It is hot in here. See if the weather is clear and the roof dry. If it is warm enough, we can eat there."

Joseph went outside to find the air was cool but pleasant enough. Matthias joined him, and they both went up the steps to the roof. The roof drains let the water cascade away from the house, and most of the surface was dry enough to be comfortable.

"Still magnificent!" Matthias remarked, his eyes on the heavens.

Joseph looked up. "A new star. I saw it when we first moved here, and it seems to grow bigger and brighter every night. But this is far beyond its past brilliance." The star looked as if it hung directly over Jerusalem, though they both knew it to be high in the heavens.

"We have seen it for months as well," Matthias replied. "But you are right—it has never been so clear, so bold. The storm I suppose." He turned to face Joseph. "You have heard of the prophecy of Balaam."

Joseph nodded. "You've been studying your scriptures."

"You said I should read, and I have done so."

"'There shall come a Star out of Jacob, and a Sceptre shall rise out of Israel.'" Joseph smiled. "Yes, I know it."

"Then you also know it is of the Messiah." He paused. "Some say it is a sign meant for Judas ben Hezekiah."

Joseph frowned. "I told you, Judas is nothing but a robber. This is not a sign of him, and those who think it is will be sorely disappointed."

"You said that the night before you left Nazareth to come here. You also said I should trust you and read God's revelations and I would understand. Well, I am no closer to understanding than I was then. The Romans and the Herods continue to steal from me and from our people, and Judas wants to do something about it. My patience is wearing thin, Joseph. I am ready to join his fight."

Joseph held back his response. He wanted to tell Matthias everything, had wanted to tell him the last time Matthias and Salome had come to Bethlehem, but always he could not speak. He loved Matthias and wanted to share this knowledge with him, but for some reason, God forbade it.

He put a hand on his friend's shoulder. "Please, Matthias . . . Listen—"

"To what, Joseph? You tell me nothing to listen to." He sighed. "You are a mystery, my friend, but I must have an answer before I leave for Capernaum, one that is very convincing. Judas ben Hezekiah has already contacted Salome's father, and even he has decided to fight. He asks that I go with him."

Joseph only nodded, and a hard silence fell between them. Finally, Joseph spoke of other things. "Come, we must gather rugs and cushions. Our wives will be ready with supper." He turned to Matthias. "The Messiah is coming, Matthias. You will see his face, and it is not the face of Judas ben Hezekiah. Wait."

Though the cloud of their conversation hung over them both, they tried to make it a pleasant evening. It was difficult. Both Mary and Salome noticed something wrong between the men, but neither mentioned it, and everyone went to bed uncomfortable.

After two hours of sleeplessness, Joseph wrapped himself in his blanket and returned to the roof to say his nearly forgotten prayers. As always, he began with the Shema, but this night he said only a single benediction before his thoughts returned to Matthias. His final prayer was to understand why his friend could not be told. No answer came, but he still knew he could not speak of Jesus to Matthias. Not yet.

This caused Joseph deep concern. Matthias would not speak of joining Judas if he did not mean it, and if Joseph did not find a way of convincing him to stay clear of the robber, Matthias might lose his life fighting a battle he and his rebel friends could never win. Worse, if killed or sent to the galleys to die a slow death in captivity, as would likely happen, Matthias would leave Salome alone with three children to raise. This troubled Joseph more than anything else.

He stretched out on the floor and stared up at the heavens. The star seemed to fill his vision, making the others look pale. Matthias was right, it was Balaam's sign, and if it continued to dwell in the heavens as it did, even Herod's inept scholars and supposed priests would eventually stumble onto its meaning and tell the paranoid Herod and . . .

Turning to his side, Joseph shoved the thought away, reminding himself that God knew what He was doing and had His purposes. For another hour, he mulled over possible things to say to Matthias, then slowly drifted off to sleep.

* * *

Joseph was awakened by the sun just beginning to rise above the horizon and looked up to find the star but did not see it. He searched the sky and thought he found it, still directly above Jerusalem but much dimmer because of the rising sun.

By watching it, he had become intrigued with it, then with all of the stars. He wondered how far away they were, what they were made of, why some were different colors than others, why this one seemed to move about more dramatically than the rest. God created the heavens and the earth! How magnificent a God He must be!

After stretching, Joseph went downstairs to find Matthias, Salome, and their children gone. Mary explained that Matthias had decided to work on the temple, and Salome wanted to visit a cousin in the city. They had left quite early but would return in two days' time. Joseph felt both relief and guilt.

He ate breakfast then went to his shop, where he began sharpening his tools in preparation for the day. Two broken plows were delivered by the time he finished his last tool, and he went to work on the repairs.

* * *

The day flew by. Mary visited several times, bringing Joseph water, food, and conversation, and Jesus crawled underfoot, his curiosity insatiable. At about the time he heard the distant cry of the rabbi for prayer at the synagogue, Joseph noticed that the baby was gone and found him asleep under Saul's belly, the donkey standing over Jesus. Joseph felt instant panic as he carefully approached the old donkey to remove his son, immediately awakening him. He cried at being suddenly startled, and Joseph held him close and rocked him, apologizing for his panic but grateful the baby was unharmed.

After returning from the synagogue and eating supper, Joseph worked a while longer before having his personal prayer and going to bed. He had spent a wonderful, comfortable day doing what he loved most while being near his family. As he drifted off to sleep, he could not see how life could be better. On occasion, he had thought of returning to Nazareth, but now he wondered why. Everything he and Mary and Jesus needed was here. They were settled, comfortable. Joseph placed an arm over Mary, felt her snuggle next to him, and drifted into a pleasant sleep.

It was the middle of the night when Joseph was shaken to full consciousness. Mary was already sitting up. Jesus, with his head in her lap, was sleepily sucking his thumb.

"Look," Mary said almost reverently as Joseph sat up, blinking away the fog of sleep. Light was streaming in through the window, and he put his hand up to block it. Had night passed so quickly? He realized immediately that it was not the light of the sun at all, but a different light, one he had seen only in his dreams, the light that enveloped the angel who had come to him before their marriage. He was suddenly very awake.

"Someone is here, Joseph."

There was no fear in her voice, and Joseph realized that he was not afraid either, the light itself calming him. Even Jesus was now taking it in, a slight smile on his lips as if it brought him joy.

Getting to his feet, Joseph stepped to the window, where he once more shaded his eyes against the intense light. He could make out shadowy figures on the far side of the yard near the road, the light cascading over and around them. He could not make out their features clearly but knew they were strangers, though he felt no fear of them—no fear of anything, the light reaching deep into him.

As he looked up, he could see that the light was already dissipating. It was as if it was pulling heavenward until finally the light was no different from any other star. Joseph blinked as his eyes adjusted then refocused on the dark shadows across the yard. Flames were ignited and torches were lifted, revealing the strangers more clearly. Joseph had seen them before.

"Foreigners, from the East," he explained. "I saw them come to Jerusalem yesterday."

Mary joined him at the window, Jesus in her arms. "They were led here by the star, Joseph. I know it. They have come to see Jesus."

Joseph only nodded. "Stay here," he said softly, "and light the lamps."

He stepped outside. The place seemed enveloped in an unearthly quiet, and he looked around to see if any villagers had seen and come in wonder. There was no one but the men standing in front of him, light from the torches spreading around them. It seemed almost a dream.

Around the fringes of the magi stood at least twenty men, some armed, some holding either torches or the ropes of many camels, obviously well cared for and well equipped. These were wealthy and powerful men.

One of them spoke in a foreign tongue, and all of them bowed deeply at the waist. When they had lifted their heads again, the first spoke a second time but in concise Hebrew. "You have a child here, born no more than two years ago. We have come to honor him."

Joseph felt a sudden wave of awe and humility. He could not speak. Instead, he simply unlatched the door and pushed it open. Their guests walked across the hard-packed earth of the courtyard and entered. When Joseph followed, he found Mary sitting on a chair, Jesus in her lap. The child looked up as their guests knelt before him, heads bowed. Joseph shut the door, skirted them, and stood just behind Mary.

"Please, you need not bow. Sit, rest yourselves," Mary said. "You are not of our country and must have traveled far."

The eldest raised his head to speak, but all remained on their knees. "We are men from the East, students of the scripture and writings of ancient peoples, including our own." His beard was white as the snows of Mount Hermon, as was the hair that showed just above his ears and below his turban. But it was his face and eyes that were remarkable. Lined with the years of life and experience, they radiated a warmth and tenderness that few men ever attained in a lifetime. And there was even more to this man: a deep love of God and an insatiable desire to serve Him and others. A feeling of awe swept through Mary, both for the magi and for their coming to worship a small child they already accepted as Israel's future King. As the elderly man looked at Jesus and tears sprang to his eyes, Mary felt her own trickle down her cheeks.

"Forgive me," the man implored. "My heart is full to overflowing. God has been good to us, patient with our impatience and misunderstanding. We nearly lost our way in Jerusalem, relying on our own judgment to discover your son. But now, in the brightness of God's star, He gives us absolute surety."

Another spoke, a younger man. "The star is to be a sign to all people. Since the time of its appearing, it has grown in brightness and moved through the heavens to witness to us and all men that your son is to be the Messiah, Lord of the whole earth." They bowed together.

"It is a sign worthy of such a King and one that can leave little doubt of God's choice," added another. "The oracles we study say it will appear to many nations as well as to ours and to you. Though some will ignore it, many will record the day it appeared and testify of it as the sign of the Lord's birth. When these testimonies are read together, it will leave all men without excuse to accept our King."

"We have brought gifts," one indicated.

They bowed slightly again, and the old one was the first to lift a square box sitting next to him and extend it to Mary. Jesus immediately wanted to play with it, and before she could stop him, he had flipped open the lid and spilled the contents.

Both Joseph and Mary gasped at the sight of the bright gold coins that jingled into her lap. Jesus picked up one and immediately began sucking on it, found it not to his liking, and dropped it back in the pile with a clink. Liking the sound, he jumbled the coins about with his hand while making happy noises.

The old man grinned. "A gift that brings such joy is a gift well chosen."

Four jars carved from stone and about a span high each were handed forward and placed in front of the little family. Mary opened the first to find a sweet smelling ointment. "Myrrh and frankincense," she exclaimed. "But these are very costly and—"

Jesus stuck his hand into the opened jar, and Mary immediately clasped his little hand in hers, cleaned off his fingers, and closed the lid before handing the jar to Joseph.

"They are hardly worthy of so great a King as your son will be," said the young magi. "But they are freely given and can be sold when money is needed. Use them as you see fit to protect and prepare him."

The old one removed a small leather pouch from his pocket, opened it, and removed a piece of honey candy. Jesus spotted the candy, climbed down from Mary's lap, and crawled the short distance to sit in front of the magi. He did not grab for the candy—Mary had taught him differently—but a grin showed his few small teeth. The old man pushed the candy gently into the boy's mouth, then sat with his legs crossed and the leather bag in his hand. Jesus crawled into his new friend's lap, his mouth working over the sweet delicacy.

"As you see," Joseph remarked, "he is no different from any other boy his age. Sweets dim even the glitter of pure gold."

Mary used the opportunity to gather up the coins and put them in the box while the other visitors changed their position to sitting, their legs crossed.

"I don't know what to say," Joseph said. "Such gifts . . . Thank you. We will use them wisely."

"I will prepare something to eat," Mary stated. She arose, but the old man placed a gentle hand on her arm.

"Thank you, but it is late, and sleep is what we need. He is a beautiful child." He looked at one of the younger magi, apparently his own son. "Very much like you when at this age. I remember wondering at times if you would survive your curiosity." He smiled and looked again at Mary. "He is your son as well as God's Messiah. For now, enjoy him. When it is time, God will visit him and begin preparations for a work none of us can begin to understand. In generations to come, men will look back and marvel at the life he led, the power he used, and the future he gave through his sacrifice. And then he will come again."

Mary wondered at the words. She wished to ask, but the old one was already being helped to his feet, Jesus still in his arms. He lifted him overhead and looked into his eyes. "At last, God is with us." He lowered Jesus, kissed him on the head, and held him close. Jesus put his arms around the magi's neck and hugged him tightly, bringing tears to his aged eyes once more. Jesus leaned back a little and touched the flow, then kissed the cheek. The old one handed him to Mary and wiped his own tears.

"Other than the village well, is there a spot where we can lay our beds and find water?" his son asked.

"Yes, near the aqueduct," Joseph answered, giving them directions. "Will you come again before you leave? We have so many questions."

The old one bowed slightly. "It would be an honor."

Each of the others held Jesus for a moment. He pulled on the graying beard of the first, curiously eyed an amulet around the neck of the second, and gave a loving squeeze to the others before the last man handed the child back to Mary. Then the old one took Mary's hand and kissed it lightly. "You are blessed among women."

She bowed graciously and thanked him and then all of them for making such a long journey. He smiled. "One does not get to see the King of all the earth very often. The journey was small compared to its reward." He touched Jesus' foot reverently once more then left the house, the others behind him. His son was the last to go and shook Joseph's hand, bowing slightly.

"Tomorrow then," he said almost reverently.

"You will be most welcome," Joseph replied.

Then he and Mary stepped outside to watch their unexpected guests mount their camels and disappear into the darkness. They stayed until the noise faded to silence.

"Will others come?" Mary asked. "Is this the announcement to all that he is here?"

Joseph smiled. "No, they may be the only ones. Look around you. None from the village are here. No one heard the caravan, no one saw the glory of the star though it was like the sun at noonday. Would they believe if they had seen? They did not believe the shepherds. If they had, maybe God would have shown them this sign as well."

"And when they visit tomorrow, what will our neighbors think then?"

Joseph chuckled. "That we have rich relatives from the East."

They went inside, and while Mary laid Jesus down for sleep, Joseph carefully placed the gifts in a vault he had made in the floor where they kept what little money they could save.

Lying down, Mary snuggled into Joseph's chest. They said nothing, their hearts full of wonder and gratitude as slowly they drifted back to sleep.

CHAPTER 23

Joseph awoke before dawn, refreshed and eager to converse further with their new guests. He fed the animals, ate bread and drank the goat's milk that Mary gave him, then rushed to check on the magi at their new camp. He found them gone.

Disappointed, he returned and told Mary. They discussed the possible reasons for the magi's departure but decided it was for the best. If God had wanted such men to be announced, surely He would have sent them in the day or at least made their presence known by waking up the village at the time the star shone so brightly. Apparently this visit was solely for the magi.

However, Joseph felt uneasy most of the day, as if there was something he should know but was simply missing. For some reason, he felt his family was in danger.

He searched his memory of the magi's visit for clues as to why he felt tense, then searched his heart and feelings but found nothing concrete. That evening after work, Joseph went to the roof for his personal prayers and noticed that the star was no longer in sight—another marvel that he could neither explain nor understand fully. The star had brought them the magi. That was enough.

By the end of the day, Joseph felt a bit more peaceful, but an uncommon weariness overtook both him and Mary. They went to bed earlier than usual, falling asleep almost immediately.

* * *

Joseph awoke with a start, shook Mary, then jumped to his feet and peered out the window. It was still dark, with not even the hint of sun. How long had he slept? Why had the angel come now? He didn't know, but they must go!

"What is it, Joseph?" Mary asked wearily.

"We have to leave!" Joseph declared.

"What?" Mary answered.

He knelt in front of her and took her hands. "The angel came to me, Mary. We have to leave. Jesus is in danger."

"Tonight?"

"Now."

Mary threw off her covers, and the two of them began filling baskets with clothing, food, and other items.

"Where do we go, Joseph?" Mary asked fearfully, her hands shaking, hardly able to grasp anything.

"Egypt. He said we must go to Egypt."

"Egypt, but why? It is—"

"Herod has no authority there. He cannot reach us."

"Herod?"

"Yes, he is seeking Jesus. He will destroy him unless we leave."

Mary began to cry, and Joseph stopped what he was doing and wrapped his arms around her.

"I need you to be strong, Mary. We *must* go." He held her tight again. "I will get Saul. Take only what we will absolutely need, and don't forget the gifts in the vault."

When Joseph returned from preparing the donkey, he found everything Mary had packed sitting by the door ready for loading.

"How could Herod have found out about Jesus?" Mary wondered anxiously.

"I don't know. But he knows, and we must leave and do it quickly!"

Mary seemed to stop midstride. "That is why the magi were sent!" She began working feverishly again.

"What?" Joseph questioned.

"Don't you see? They were not sent just to bring gifts to us, even to see their King. It would be foolish to have them come so far just for that. They were sent as witnesses."

Joseph stopped. "Witnesses? Gentile priests?"

"Herod understands and accepts their gods more than he does our own. To have them witness what our own prophets say leaves him no choice but to see that the Messiah has come!" She paused. "God is truly gracious, Joseph. Even a wicked man like Herod is given a chance to choose to repent and stand blameless before Him."

"If that is true, God is now showing us that Herod has chosen poorly! Now hurry, we must go!" Joseph picked up the first of the baskets and tied it shut with a rope, then the second and the third until all were secured and ready for Saul's back. "I will pack these, and we will go."

Joseph felt an increased urgency as the full weight of Mary's words sunk in. Herod had been given a chance, and in his greed for power he would slay even Jesus! And he would not wait! Had they delayed too long? No. The angel would have come sooner if that were true, but they must leave quickly.

Joseph picked up the second basket.

"Joseph, surely we can say good-bye to Abel, Adah, and the others. We have so many friends . . ."

He stopped and turned back. "No, Mary, we can't. They will ask questions. We cannot tell them where we are going. Fleeing before Herod only to leave word of where he can find us would be foolish, don't you think?"

"Yes, you are right," she answered, handing him a basket. "Give me a minute. I will change Jesus' loincloth, and we can go.

Joseph kissed her on the cheek. This was hard for both of them. Why, after all their work, after just starting a new life . . . But he already knew the answer. God commanded it. It was their task to obey, no matter the loss or the difficulty. After all, better to lose this house than put God's Son in danger because of doubt.

"It will be all right, Mary. God will help us and strengthen us. Egypt holds no fear for me as long as God goes with us. And as long as you have faith in me."

She leaned against him. "I have faith in you, Joseph. And in God."

He kissed her on the forehead, then pulled away and took the last of the baskets to load.

Mary went to Jesus and woke him, changed his loincloth, and wrapped him in his warmest blanket. The night was chilly, but tomorrow . . . Tomorrow would be very warm.

When would they return? How long would it be before they saw her parents again? Before they saw Matthias and Salome? Oh how her heart ached that they had gone to Jerusalem to stay! If she could at least say good-bye to them!

Tears came to Mary's eyes, and she cried quietly, then prayed fervently for the strength to do what she must.

"Ready?" Joseph asked softly.

Mary turned her head slightly and quickly choked back the tears, wiped them away, and picked up Jesus and went to the door. Joseph blew out the last lamp, dumped the oil into a lidded jar, and placed the lamp and jar in his pocket. They stood for a moment, looking around the room, then Mary turned and stepped away into the dark and Joseph closed the door behind them.

Mary strapped Jesus into a nest of blankets amid the baskets, and they started their journey. She turned back once, tears flowing down her cheeks, looking longingly at the place they had called home.

CHAPTER 24

Matthias did not go to work that morning. Since the magi had come looking for a new king, the city was in turmoil and the temple closed. Jerusalem's entire population rumbled with rumors about the death of Herod and about war with Parthia. The crowds gathering for Passover reeled with unrest, spiced with stories of rebels marching to join the Parthian hordes in the Jordan Valley before attacking Jerusalem, and of Roman soldiers coming from Caesarea by the hundreds to stop them.

The rumors had all started with the arrival of the caravan Matthias and Joseph had seen from the bridge two days earlier. Some said they were from Parthia, emissaries to make demands and set terms. Others said the visitors had declared Herod an illegitimate king, and that a child, born King of the Jews, would replace him. The Messiah had come, said others; at last God would overthrow Roman rule. Like dense smoke, a hundred rumors filled every corner and blinded every eye. Soldiers patrolled the streets by the dozens, and the entire city and surrounding camps were under careful watch by fresh troops recently arrived from Sebaste and Jericho.

Most of the time, Matthias had stayed in his house in Jerusalem and kept his family close to him. He left on two occasions simply because he couldn't sit still any longer, but only for short periods to hear news and stretch his nervous legs. The day passed without any great upset, though he had been uneasy as he heard various rumors. Finally, after sending the children to bed, he and Salome had gone to bed more exhausted from the tension than any day of work had ever made them.

And yet Matthias had not been able to sleep. He had seen the star himself. Could it be? Was God about to pour down judgment on Jerusalem's wicked and free the righteous from oppression?

As much as he wished for it, he knew it was unlikely. There was no man strong enough to stand against Rome. As much as he might delude himself into thinking Judas ben Hezekiah might someday be that man, Joseph was right—the time simply was not yet.

But something was happening, something dangerous. Matthias could feel it clear to his toes. Before dawn, he woke Salome. "We have to leave the city."

"Where are we going?" she asked.

"Bethlehem. We promised Joseph and Mary we would return."

She did not question him further, and they rose and quickly packed their things and woke the children. By daybreak, they were headed south out of the city. Three hours later, as they marched up the last stretch of path that led to Joseph's house, Salome pulled on Matthias's arm.

"Something is wrong!" she exclaimed.

Matthias stopped, and Mara immediately ceased teasing Simon. They stood very quiet, listening.

"Did you hear that? Someone screamed," Salome breathed as she gripped her husband's arm more tightly.

"There is another," Mara added nervously.

Even Simon began to fuss, his voice especially shrill against the oppressive quiet. Mara immediately shushed him, but Salome picked him up to quiet him.

Matthias felt the hair on his neck rise. These were not ordinary cries of pain. He had heard them before—they had haunted his dreams since the destruction of his home in his childhood.

"There, in the trees. Hide until I return," Matthias directed quietly but firmly. "And keep the donkey and Simon quiet." He pulled his knife from his belt and handed it to Salome without needing to explain. She led the children into the shadows as Matthias warily climbed toward Joseph's home.

The cries were getting louder but were obviously not coming from Joseph and Mary's house. Seeing no one in the stable or shop, he searched them. Saul was gone, as were the packsaddle and Joseph's tools, but the lamb and other animals were still in their pens. What was happening?

Running outside, he cautiously climbed the stairs and peered across the courtyard toward the village. He could see no one, but there were trees, and stones from the old fallen wall lay scattered around. Someone could be hiding there.

He heard the shouts of several men, anguished pleading, more shouting; the sound of horses' hooves, more screaming; a crying baby whose voice was suddenly ended, more cries of agony. Surely the plague in Egypt could not have been worse!

Were they being attacked? Had the Parthians come? If not . . .

He looked again, saw no one, and pulled back, catching his breath. He must get back to his family, get them out of here, but first he must check the house for Joseph and Mary. Wiping the sweat from his brow and taking a deep breath, he jumped from the steps and ran to the door, then inside, fearful of what he might see. A few things were scattered around, but generally speaking the interior of the home appeared as he remembered. Then he saw the open lid to the money vault and searched to find no food in the kitchen. He realized that his friends had fled, and relief filled his soul.

As another scream rang out nearby, Matthias tensed. Carefully peering around the edge of the door, he saw a woman stumbling toward the house, carrying a small, crying bundle. She stumbled, then fell, trying to get to her feet as a horseman came around the ancient wall, bearing down on her.

Matthias reacted instinctively, running and reaching her with the horseman still fifty feet away, charging at them at an incredible pace. Matthias quickly pushed the woman to the side and faced the soldier, stunned to see that he wore the uniform of the palace guards. At the last second, Matthias threw himself out of the way of the rampaging horse and ducked under the slice of the soldier's sword. The soldier pulled up quickly to avoid a collision with the house, then executed a labored turn. Matthias used the moment to get to his feet and charge the animal and its rider. Using the bench in the courtyard, he leaped and thrust his weight into the soldier's back, knocking him from the animal. The soldier struggled to stand and grab his fallen sword, but Matthias got there first and used its hilt to pummel the assailant in the back of the neck. Though the man went instantly limp, Matthias clutched the sword until he was sure. Out of breath, he got to his feet and was about to toss the sword away when he heard footsteps and turned to fight. It was Salome, and he tossed the weapon aside. She looked at the soldier, then at Matthias, and finally at the woman lying nearby, a baby at her side. Salome froze.

"Where are the children?" Matthias asked urgently.

She didn't answer.

"Salome," Matthias said firmly. "Palace guards are attacking the village. Where are the children?"

She seemed to awaken, even greater fear in her eyes, and dashed down the steps as Mara met her carrying little Simon. She took the whimpering baby and tried to quiet him. As she turned back, Matthias was already at the side of the fallen woman.

He turned her over, and she blinked several times though her eyes were blank, her life oozing from the wound near her stomach.

"Easy," Matthias soothed. He quickly looked around them, knowing other soldiers would surely follow; they didn't have much time.

"Take my . . . my child . . . Don't let them . . . They are . . . are killing the children. Don't . . ." She tried to move her arm to the baby, then she went limp. "Go . . ." The breath left her, and her dark, frightened eyes stared blankly.

Matthias was no stranger to death and knew it had come. He stood, unwrapped the blanket to try to quiet the baby, his eyes again searching for assassins. Salome joined him, giving Simon to Mara and taking the crying baby, rocking and holding him close.

"Come. We have to go, now!" Matthias ordered.

Salome and Mara, each carrying a baby, stumbled after him while looking back at the woman, at the walls all around them, fearful and wary.

Matthias cornered the sweating horse and quickly helped Salome into the saddle, the infant still in her arms. He then put Mara behind her and lifted little Simon onto his own shoulders.

"What about the donkey?" Mara asked.

"I will come back if I can." They started out at a brisk trot, Matthias running alongside the horse, and quickly entered the trees, then hurried over the hill and down into the valley. The sounds of horror soon faded, but they went another mile before crossing the valley into thicker brush and trees. Finally, Matthias had to rest, the rush of battle and shock taking its toll.

Sitting Simon down, Matthias helped Mara and Salome from the horse before tying the animal's reins firmly to a tree. Then he sat beside his family, his head bowed in exhaustion. Simon crawled between his legs, and Matthias pulled him into his lap.

"Why, Matthias? Why?" Salome moaned, tears dripping from her eyes.

"I don't know," he replied softly.

"Joseph and Mary, Jesus . . ." Mara said almost in a whisper. She was pale, and Matthias put an arm around her and held her to him.

"They weren't there." He took a deep breath. "The place was stripped of everything, as if they had been warned and fled. But I'm not sure." He shook his head. "I'm just not sure."

"Will they hunt us too?" Mara asked.

He rubbed her back. "I won't let anything happen to you. I promise."

Mara cried softly, and Matthias held her tighter, tears of shock, fear, and exhaustion coming to his own eyes. He blinked them back as Salome leaned into him, trying to be strong but feeling so cold and fearful. He closed his eyes tight, took a deep breath, and prayed for strength.

"You can't go back there," Salome entreated. "The soldier will have regained consciousness by now and they will be looking for you."

He nodded, trying to think if the donkey they had abandoned was carrying anything that might lead them to him. No, there was nothing. He had left his tools with Salome's cousin.

"We have to go."

"Where?" Salome wondered.

"Home to Capernaum."

They each got up, and Matthias untied the horse and whacked him hard on the rear. The animal tore through the trees heading northwest, toward Jerusalem.

"But Father . . ."

"If we are caught with him, they will know we were in Bethlehem," Matthias pointed out. No further explanation was needed, and he picked up Simon and they continued walking north. It was nearly noon. In another two hours, they could be at Bethany. He would find them an inn, recover his senses, and buy what they needed for the journey. He touched the small purse hanging around his neck by a leather cord, glad that the temple had paid wages daily.

"What of Joseph and Mary?" Mara asked.

"If they can, they will come to Nazareth," Matthias answered.

There was no further talk. Matthias felt helpless, frustrated, and angry. Where were Joseph and Mary? Had they escaped? Why had the soldiers attacked in the first place? What had the villagers done to warrant such brutality?

Salome clasped his hand. "They are all right, Matthias, I know it," she said softly. "I know it."

Matthias only nodded. Yes, they had to be. Joseph was smart, shrewd. They had escaped and they would survive. They would come to Nazareth—somehow they would come to Nazareth.

Matthias and his family continued walking, a prayer in their hearts for their friends. There was nothing else they could do.

PART THREE
RETURN FROM EGYPT

CHAPTER 25

Mary adjusted her position to catch more of the shade cast by the stately set of palm trees near the spring. She watched Jesus playing with several of the other children in their caravan while rubbing her tight stomach. Her son was lithe and handsome, his dark hair even curlier than when he was a baby and his dark eyes filled with both curiosity and a strange sort of maturity. Only three years of age, he had already learned how to read and write the Egyptian and Hebrew alphabets and was beginning to use the megillah, a small scroll on which passages of the Torah were copied. Using these, he was learning to read, a near miracle in the eyes of most, for a child so young. But his endless questions nearly exhausted both Joseph and Mary.

Though most children did not join the bet sefer, the "house of the book," until they were six or seven years old, one of the sages of the synagogue in Alexandria had told Joseph that unless something changed dramatically in Jesus' ability to learn, he would probably be ready by age five. The sage had written a letter to that effect that they could give to the leading elder in Bethlehem. Mary was both proud of and humbled by her son's special gift for learning—proud because his ability was known to others, and humbled because she knew where the gift had come from. For God's Son and the Messiah of Israel, such a gift would be natural, even needed.

She touched her stomach. She now carried her and Joseph's first child together, though he had raised Jesus as his own. She estimated this baby would be born in another two or three months. Though with Jesus she had learned to hate the sickness announcing the coming of a child, she had been grateful when the nausea finally hit her this time. She had feared that God would grant her one child only, but now she and Joseph would have one together.

Another miracle. There had been so many.

Keeping Jesus in sight, Mary walked a short distance to a small hill and looked east and north. She could see the green of the mountains of Judea, their rolling hills beckoning. The day they had walked away from them and into the desert of Sinai, she had never been so afraid. When leaving Nazareth for Bethlehem, her sorrow had centered on leaving the home of her childhood, her parents and family, but she did not fear where they were going. Bethlehem, Jerusalem, and the land in general were all familiar to her. Other than the words of a few travelers, she had known nothing about the Sinai, about Egypt. She remembered the moment she and Joseph had stood atop a hill south of Bersabe and looked into the vast expanse of endless stone and desert to the south. Even with Joseph at her side, Jesus in her arms, and God in His heaven, she had never felt so alone and at risk. As Joseph had pulled on the donkey's lead rope, Mary wanted to stop him, to find some other way. Surely they could go back to Nazareth, to anywhere but the wasteland before them!

But she knew there was no choice. The angel had not commanded them to go back to Galilee; he had directed them to flee to Egypt. She hadn't been sure why, and only her faith had forced her to put one foot in front of the other and follow Joseph that day. Only later would she understand why it had to be Egypt.

Fearing that Herod still searched for Jesus, they had avoided the highways, making their journey even more difficult. Though the head of a desert tribe had given them directions to a less-traveled route, they had still found themselves lost. Joseph had walked to a high hill one night and prayed, not returning until morning. There was no vision, no dream, but he knew the way. After only a few hours' travel, they came upon the well-worn trail that led them south to the Red Sea. How refreshing its salty waters had been. Traveling west along the seashore, both Mary and Joseph marvelling at the sea's expanse, they beheld a great ship, its sail filled with air and its oars plying the surface. They watched in amazement until it disappeared to the south.

That night, they sat atop a large rock and watched the setting sun glisten off the surface of the sea while they discussed how the great miracle of Israel's deliverance from Pharaoh's army might have happened. They wondered exactly where the children of Israel might have crossed the Red Sea, what it must have been like to walk through such a sea with waves taller than mountains on both sides, held there only by the hand of God. It was truly the greatest of miracles, and yet their ancestors had been so quick to forget!

Joseph, Mary, and Jesus arrived in the land of Egypt the next day and proceeded along the green fields of the Nile delta for another day. They slept in the cubicle of a small inn a few miles from Alexandria that night and rose early to finish their journey. Mary marveled at the green fields and the endless fingers of the Nile River that fed them. Palm trees, villages, and farmers' houses dotted the landscape, and the roads of hard-packed earth teemed with humanity going to and from the great city. Men and women worked the fields, and there were nearly as many camels laden with people and goods as there were donkeys and mules.

When they had entered the city of Alexandria, Mary remembered the conversation she and Joseph had had with Seth, the Greek traveler on the road to Jerusalem more than a year earlier. He had been correct—it was a magnificent city, but Mary immediately began longing for home.

How strange she felt as they entered the city with the small mud huts of the peasants dwarfed by the stone palaces and houses of the rich. Greek was the primary language of the people, and Mary wondered if she would ever be able to speak to those around her, but when they arrived in the Jewish Quarter, she was relieved to once more hear Hebrew and Aramaic used freely.

The people in the Quarter had made Joseph and Mary feel welcome. Soon they located a small synagogue near one of the Nile's many outlets, finding the rabbi cordial and helpful. He directed them to a woman whose son and his family were out of the country on business and who would allow them to stay with her until Joseph could find something more permanent. They accepted the offer and soon found a small, one-room house in desperate need of repair to its roof and walls. Joseph immediately set out to make it livable, finishing two months later.

It was about that time that they heard the news of Herod's death. News from Palestine came regularly via travelers and businessmen who bought and sold at Jerusalem. According to their report, the king had died a horrible death from some curious disease for which there seemed to be no cure. Of course, when the news first arrived, Mary expected a celebration. Among some groups this occurred, but most Jews in Alexandria expressed concern. Herod had expanded commerce and had given the Jews a temple to be proud of. Those who lived outside Herod's direct rule and oppressive taxation worried that his son Archelaus, whom Herod had apparently designated his successor, would not be strong enough to keep the country's enemies at bay or shrewd enough to continue the relationship with the Romans wherein the temple and its sacrifices were free from interference. Joseph and Mary understood their concerns but were relieved that the man who had sought to kill them—more particularly their son—was no longer alive.

After news of Herod's death, they waited in eager anticipation for some sign from the angel that they could return, but it did not come. At first, Joseph thought he was unworthy, that he had offended God in some way, but after days of supplication and prayer, he received reassurance that God was not displeased with him, but that it simply wasn't safe to return yet.

Shortly thereafter, news of rebellions breaking out all over Israel, of men trying to overthrow Herod's family and assume power, flowed into Egypt and particularly the Jewish Quarter, causing great sorrow. Joseph and Mary feared for their friends and for God's house while realizing why God's angel had warned them to leave the country. Innocent men, women, and children were all caught in a war they could neither prevent nor escape. Had they not heeded the warning, they would still be in danger, even if they had escaped the initial slaying of infants in Bethlehem.

But the revolt that had most concerned Mary and Joseph was the one reported to have sprung up in Galilee under the leadership of Judas ben Hezekiah. Emboldened by events in Jerusalem, Judas and his followers had attacked the city of Sepphoris, seizing it and its armory. Using the weapons captured, they armed still more men, and Judas's following grew larger than that of any other rebel in the country. With Sepphoris as the center of their rebellion, his men began raiding estates, villages, and even cities where Herod's family and supporters lived.

Mary and Joseph had worried about Nazareth, about their families, about Matthias and Salome, about friends and neighbors, and prayed that somehow they would all be spared.

After a time, reports had begun speaking of Judas ben Hezekiah as the Messiah who had come to fight the last great war of liberation and return Israel to the glory days of David. But Mary and Joseph knew the truth and feared the Roman retribution that would surely come. The angry Romans would leave horrible destruction in their wake.

Through all of the wondering and waiting, Mary and Joseph had been sobered. Was this what their son's life would be like? One filled with the violence of war? She returned to the shade to sit near Jesus where he was playing in the sand with the other children. As Mary watched him and tried to envision it, she could not. Her mind simply refused to deal with the horror of those possibilities for her son.

These thoughts reminded her yet again of all those who were even now suffering from the fighting that had ravaged Palestine. Amidst rumors of the successes of Judas ben Hezekiah's rebel forces, Roman legions had entered Palestine under the harsh and cruel leadership of Varus, head of the Roman army for all Syria. With thousands of professional soldiers now prepared, they had begun the painful eradication of the rebellion.

Entire families were wiped out or imprisoned, and a stupor of anxiety and depression fell over the Jewish Quarter of Alexandria just as it must have fallen over Palestine. Each day, they waited for reports of villages attacked and families affected, but word was sketchy and inconclusive. One day Joseph would hear that Nazareth had not been touched, but on another day word would come that it was gone, burned to the ground, every soul butchered. Finally, he used some of the money from the magi to send a letter to Mary's parents, but it would be days or even months before they could expect to hear something, and if the worst was true they would never hear.

As word of the destruction and slaughter in Israel filtered into Alexandria, Mary and Joseph understood even more fully why the angel had told them to flee to Egypt. It would not have been enough to leave Bethlehem and go to Nazareth or Capernaum or anywhere else in Palestine. Instead, God sent His Son to a place of complete safety. With this knowledge, the harshness of the journey had been washed away by the tears of what might have happened had they stayed in Palestine.

Only after the Romans had quashed the rebellion had the angel returned, telling Joseph that those who sought Jesus' life were dead and that they must return—not that they *could,* but that they *must.* Once more Mary had cried. Tears of joy, tears of sorrow at what they might find, tears of gratitude that they could finally go home, that they had been spared.

"They say we should begin if we want to reach Gaza before night-fall. How do you feel?"

Mary looked up to see Joseph smiling down at her. She touched her stomach. This journey seemed to take more out of her than had the one from Nazareth to Bethlehem nearly four years earlier.

"Thank you, husband, I am quite rested." She extended a hand, and he pulled her to her feet.

"Will you ride or walk?" Joseph asked.

"Walk, for a while at least." She pointed at Jesus who was just about to rub a second handful of mud over his bare chest. Joseph immediately grabbed him by the arms and lifted him from the mud before washing him clean. He then helped the boy into his tunic and robe before plopping him atop Saul.

"How far is it, Father?"

"To Hebron, ten miles. After that, Bethlehem is a day's journey," Joseph answered happily.

"Will our home still be there?" Jesus asked.

"We hope so, son, but if not, you can help me build another."

"Really, a whole house?" Jesus said with wide eyes.

"Yes, a whole house." Joseph ruffled Jesus' hair with a smile, then picked up Saul's lead rope and that of the second donkey, which Jesus had dubbed Alexander after the city they had lived in.

The caravan—composed of Jews going to Jerusalem—began moving, and they made good time. The Day of Atonement and Feast of Tabernacles neared, and this was a pilgrimage for some—a first-time visit to the temple for many. Joseph and those who had been to the Holy City spent evenings telling the others of the temple and its magnificence, how the sacrifice would be performed, and of the grand but simple symbols they would see all around them. Even Jesus sat in rapt attention at the descriptions of God's house.

Nevertheless, those planning to visit Jerusalem were also nervous. There had been war in Palestine, and the temple had been directly affected. How much had been destroyed, and were they in danger if they went there? With the sons of Herod still in Rome fighting over their father's will, the Romans were running things, and that made the pilgrims apprehensive, even a bit frightened.

Because of these concerns, some Jews who lived in Egypt had stayed away from the feast this year. For most, however, there were questions to be answered about family, friends, and the future of the country; business arrangements to be renewed or completed; and above all, the continuing need to sacrifice at the temple. A letter from the high priest Eleazar, son of Boethus, to all the dispersed communities of Israel announced that all was well and safe, pushing most Jews in the direction of Jerusalem.

Jesus asked for the lead rope and guided Saul while asking Joseph to sit two of his friends behind him on the animal. His request was granted, and in their childlike way they chattered about what they would do once in Jerusalem, about the temple, and about a hundred other things from the color of a bird flying above them to what the sea really tasted like. It kept Mary and Joseph smiling clear to Hebron, where they made camp just outside the town.

* * *

Several locals came into camp after supper, selling their wares and bringing news, joining in dancing and singing.

Mary watched from the door of her tent, Jesus asleep beside her. Joseph seemed to be in a serious but friendly discussion with several men, and she knew he was gleaning information he would share with her later. Few men included their wives the way Joseph did her; it was one more thing she admired in him.

There were so many qualities Mary saw and appreciated in her husband. One of the most important was his thirst for knowledge. He studied, asked questions, and forced even the most learned sages of Alexandria to back up their statements with passages from the Torah. They had even spent some of Jesus' money buying scrolls to add to that which Seth had given them, scrolls that would someday belong to Jesus and from which he would learn the law by his own reading.

In Alexandria, study and discussion of the Torah by ordinary men was not frowned upon as it might be in Jerusalem or even in the synagogue at Nazareth, but Joseph's thirst had only been partially quenched, even though he seemed to be as learned as any rabbi Mary knew. He continued to study for understanding and to discover the principles behind the law, with good reason—he must teach Jesus, prepare him for what lay ahead. To do so, Joseph must know for certain *what* to teach him. His search had given him depth, humility, and peace, and it had deepened Mary's love for him.

Jesus stirred, then rose and laid his head on his mother's lap and watched the dancers and musicians around the fire. She pushed the curls off his forehead. An obedient son, Jesus never gave his parents a moment's worry, but he did seem more aloof than the other children, as if he were always thinking, working things out in his mind. Even now, when the other children were active and playful, he was quite comfortable simply watching.

"Are you tired?" she asked.

He shook his head lightly.

"You didn't eat much at supper. Would you like something now?"

Another shake of the head.

"You are not ill, are you?" she queried. "Jonathan is ill tonight, and you were playing with him today."

He raised his head and got to his feet. "I am not sick, but I will go and see him. He must be lonely." He stood.

"He may be asleep, and his illness—"

"It is all right, Mother. I won't get too close." His skinny legs trotted him off toward Jonathan's family's tent. She watched the boy until he disappeared—it was not easy to let him out of her sight. It had never been easy, even after Joseph had told her to have a little more faith in God, that He would warn her if Jesus were in any danger. She knew that was true; in fact, she had received such warnings.

She felt the baby kick and adjusted her position as Joseph left the group of men and came toward her. Half a dozen others stopped him for brief conversations before he sat down by Mary, stretched out, and crossed his legs, a worried furrow to his brow.

"What do you hear?" Mary asked.

"Bethlehem has changed." He leaned forward and took a date from the wooden plate between them, turning it over in his hand. "You remember there were a small number of Herod's soldiers stationed in Bethlehem at the time of the census?"

"Yes, but they left the village after the census was finished."

"Well, they are back with even more men."

"The rebellion?"

He nodded. Even before Herod died, there had been an attempt to rein in the bandits raiding caravans between Bethlehem and Gaza. After such an uprising, it seemed only natural for more soldiers to be spread about. Whatever the reason, it made Joseph's stomach churn.

"But if the rebellion is under control, why so many soldiers?"

"To *keep* things under control, to show strength, to get their men into the field quicker." Joseph shrugged again. "It is hard to say." He sat up. "I asked about Abel and Reuben, and Benjamin and his family. They are all gone."

"Gone . . . but where?" Mary questioned in surprise.

He shrugged. "No one knows. The rebellion sent many people to far-off places. Nothing will be the same." He poked at a clump of dry grass in front of him. "There is news of the Herods."

"At last," Mary replied cynically.

"Archelaus will be ethnarch of Judea and Samaria, and Antipas will be tetrarch of Galilee and Peraea. Phillip is tetrarch of Batanea in the north."

"Then Archelaus will still rule Bethlehem," Mary deduced disappointedly. "I was hoping that Antipas . . ." She paused. "For a man of only nineteen years, Archelaus matches his father's brutality unbelievably well. I do not relish living where he rules."

"Antipas is only seventeen and already wine is his master, but I suppose a drunk is better than a butcher."

Mary smiled wryly. "Doesn't he have a wife to sweeten his life so that the aged grape of the vine is not so appealing?"

Joseph chuckled. "Not one as beautiful as you." He grinned. "Antipas married for purposes of an alliance. She has little influence on him." He turned on his side and put a hand under his head to prop it up.

"You do not think we should go to Bethlehem, do you?" she asked.

"I don't know what to think. Bethlehem seemed the right place for us. We had friends there, work that was readily available, and a good house. Now the friends are gone, and I am sure others have taken the house."

"But work is still available," Mary stated.

"Yes, and if we live in Jerusalem, we will be closer to the temple, and schools for Jesus will be led by some of the great sages of Israel. If we go to Nazareth, work would be more difficult to find. To provide for a growing family, I will have to go to other cities, and the journey each day will detract from the time I can spend with you and the children, not to mention make it more difficult to protect Jesus if the need arises. And the synagogue school there would never be able to teach him what . . ."

"The sages of Jerusalem can?" she said with a smile. "Joseph, I have seen you grow in knowledge and understanding to where even many of the sages of Alexandria admire you. The law of the Lord is in your heart, and this will teach Jesus more about what is important than anything the learned men of Israel or Alexandria can give him. I do not fear for Jesus' learning, no matter where we live." She reached out and touched his leg. "Nor do I fear you will be missing when Jesus needs you. God has always shown you the way. This time will be no different." She adjusted her position, her hand on her stomach. "What does your heart tell you we should do, Joseph?"

He didn't answer immediately. "I have been having dreams of Nazareth, Mary. I see our home, the village. Even Matthias and Salome and their children are there, working and playing under a bright sun and blue skies. It is green and lush and beautiful, and I always hate to wake up. Every night since leaving Egypt, the same dream."

"But you think it just a dream, a longing for home and things as they once were," Mary remarked.

"It isn't like the other dreams. There is no angel warning me to save Jesus from a king or telling me that I have been stupid and shouldn't put away the greatest blessing of my entire life, as he has in the past."

She smiled at him. "Don't you see, Joseph? God is telling you again and again to go to Nazareth, that everything you seek can be found there, not in Bethlehem." She touched his leg again. "Maybe it isn't as critical as when we fled Bethlehem—maybe it is just best."

Jesus came running across the camp just as an adult came out of a tent. They collided, and Jesus went down. He scrambled to his feet before the man could give him a hand, bowed and apologized, then continued his hurried journey. He dropped into Joseph's lap with tears in his eyes.

"Are you hurt?" Joseph asked.

Jesus nodded. "My knee."

Mary held up a small hand lamp, and they looked at the knee to see a scrape and bump but little bleeding. Mary took one of the jars from the magi out of the bag next to her and opened it.

"How is Jonathan?" she asked.

"Better. I told him a story."

"Which one?" Joseph queried.

Jesus glanced at Mary. "The one Mother told me today."

"You mean the one about Zacharias at the temple?" Mary wondered. She looked at Joseph, a bit concerned.

Joseph posed a question. "Were Jonathan's parents there?"

"Yes. His father said he remembered hearing something about it but couldn't remember everything, so I helped him. Ouch," he said as Mary rubbed on the ointment.

Joseph nodded. They had been surprised at how many had heard the story, even in Egypt. Of course, there were several versions, but all of them were of a miraculous visitation to a priest who couldn't have children but was promised a son. Mary and Joseph knew that Zacharias had told no one any details, and yet all the essentials of the story were there, proving it was hard to hide some things, especially when the result was a child nearly as miraculous as Jesus. It was another testament to God's wisdom in keeping Jesus' identity a complete secret. She could only imagine what rumors would have sprung up about a miraculous birth in the line of David—and how fearful their lives would have been because of it.

"Where is Zacharias, Mother?" Jesus asked.

"They live in Juttah," Mary explained. "It is a village west and north of Bethlehem. We will try to see them sometime. Now, it is late. Off to prayers with your father." Mary and Joseph had taken the short journey to Juttah once before fleeing Bethlehem. Elisabeth had looked quite well, even younger than she had before John's birth, and so had Zacharias. The boy was a round, pudgy toddler then, and he and Jesus had rolled around on the floor with one another most of the afternoon. After they had fled, Mary had regretted only visiting them the one time and had thought about them often.

Jesus scrambled into the tent and retrieved both his and Joseph's prayer shawls, and Joseph stood and took his hand.

"Joseph," Mary called as they began to walk away. "This time you must *feel* what God is telling you. He will not send an angel."

Joseph nodded, and he and Jesus walked into the darkness outside the camp. Facing the temple, Joseph recited the Shema and Jesus repeated it. Jesus knew it by heart, along with the benedictions and other segments of the rote prayers, but Joseph had also taught him to talk to God as a part of their prayer time. For this portion of their prayer together, they prayed silently so they did not disrupt one another, and because Joseph thought it unwise to let others know what was in their hearts.

"Father," Jesus said when they had finished praying and dropped their shawls to their shoulders.

"Yes."

"What did Mother mean?"

Joseph sat down and pulled Jesus into his lap. "You mean about the angel?"

"No, about feeling what God tells you."

Joseph hesitated, trying to find words that would explain such a thing to a boy so young. Before Joseph could put it into words, Jesus spoke again.

"I feel Him sometimes," Jesus said.

"You do?"

Jesus nodded. "Do other people feel Him?"

"Yes, but some feel Him more than others."

"Why?"

"Because they obey the law."

"How does He do it when He lives so far away?"

Joseph thought a moment. He didn't have an answer, and it bothered him that he didn't. The boy's body was three years old, but in his mind and heart, he was much older and ready to learn. Surely God was speeding up his education, quickening his mind, but it was hastening Jesus to questions beyond Joseph's ability to answer. And he was only three. What would he be like at twelve or twenty?

"I'm not sure."

"Torah does not tell us?"

"Torah does not have the answer to every question."

Jesus thought about it a moment. "Then we must listen to God. He knows."

Joseph chuckled, "Yes, He does."

"Father."

"Yes?"

"I'm tired. Let's go back to the tent."

"Good idea."

Once they stood, Jesus took Joseph's hand, then lifted his face toward the heavens one last time. The moonlight shone in the boy's eyes, and Joseph once more saw the man inside the boy's body. He was hearing God already, feeling Him close, learning from Him in little ways, but learning from Him just the same. Already Jesus was becoming the teacher.

"I should listen more closely, shouldn't I?" Joseph asked as they walked back to camp. In the moonlight, Joseph saw the nod of his son's head, but there were no words. *Out of the mouth of babes and sucklings hast thou ordained strength.* The Psalmist must have had Jesus in mind when he spoke those words!

Joseph and Jesus walked back to the tent. Since Mary was saying her prayers, Joseph put Jesus to bed before taking off his robe and sandals and washing his feet and hands. He blew out the lamps and slipped under the covers, and soon Mary cuddled up next to him. They kissed several times before she turned over and curled up with her back against him, said she loved him, and went to sleep.

Joseph lay awake, troubled by his own blindness. God had shown him the correct path in the repeated dream, but Joseph had wanted more. He had wanted the angel, a clear, definite voice of decision, when he should not have needed one. The feelings and the spirit of the dreams—and their regularity and sameness—should have been sufficient. Joseph sighed heavily, disappointed in himself.

He turned on his side and closed his eyes when a thought came to him. God was not displeased with him, but He would have been if

Joseph hadn't listened to Mary or had been upset with Jesus for pointing out his earthly protector's imperfection. Joseph suddenly realized that God hated pride, not those who couldn't always see what God wanted of them.

He thanked God for his family, for Mary and Jesus, and for the little one yet unborn. Tomorrow the family would say good-bye to the caravan and go to Nazareth. Moments after finally deciding this, Joseph fell into a deep and dreamless sleep.

* * *

Mary rubbed her nose against the itch, then opened her eyes to find the sun streaming through the tent door. Jesus sat beside her with the leaf of a small plant in his hand, a leaf he had obviously used to tickle her. He grinned and darted away as she tried to grab him. As his mother crawled after him, he danced around the tent, giggling until she grasped his ankle and pulled him down to tickle his belly.

"Where is your father?" she asked.

"Saying good-bye to the others," Jesus responded.

Mary smiled. "Then we are not going to Bethlehem."

Jesus shook his head, a smile on his face. "To see Grandmother and Grandfather in Nazareth, but . . ." He hesitated.

"But you are sad to leave your friends."

He nodded again.

Mary smiled. "Then we had better say good-bye to them." She sat up, quickly got to her feet, and pulled on her outer robe before pushing aside the covering of the door and stepping into the early-morning sun. She shaded her eyes and saw Joseph standing a few feet away talking with several of the men. Some of the women were looking in her direction, bewilderment on their faces. She had become friends with several, and she quickly strode to them and gave each a hug and bid them good-bye. When she was finished, Mary noticed Jesus standing at the feet of one of the donkeys, on which sat the best of his friends. Mary picked Jesus up and sat him on the donkey facing Jonathan, then stepped back and let them talk while she said a few more good-byes. When she turned back to get Jesus, he was already gone, and she went to the tent to find him. He lay on his bed, tears rolling down his cheeks. She sat beside him and ran her fingers through his long curls.

"Are you sad?" she asked.

He nodded. "My chest hurts."

"Mine too. It's hard to say good-bye to those we love, isn't it?"

Another nod. "I never want to say good-bye to you, Mother. Or to Father. It would hurt too much."

Love for her son made her heart ache, and she turned him over and pulled him into her lap and held him close. "I never want to say good-bye to you either, my love. It would break my heart."

She kissed him. "But don't be too sad. We will see your grandparents and your aunts and uncle. You will make many new friends in Nazareth. It is a beautiful place." The words seemed to cheer Jesus some.

Mary and Jesus listened as the animals and then the children grew very noisy. The caravan was leaving. They went outside, but Jesus suddenly thought of something. He struggled to be let down and disappeared inside the tent. Seconds later, he bolted from it and ran as fast as his tiny legs would carry him until he reached Jonathan's already-moving donkey. Mary saw him extend his arm and hand his friend something small and shiny, then wave good-bye. Jonathan waved back, a very large smile on his face. Jesus kept waving until the dust and the other animals blocked his view of his friend.

Joseph came to her side and watched as Jesus walked toward them. "What was that all about?" he asked.

"Well, do you remember telling Jesus that the money in the fine wooden box belonged to him as much as it did to us?"

Joseph nodded.

"Jesus took it to heart."

Joseph chuckled. "Well, I hope Jonathan's father believes his son when he tells him where the gold piece came from." As Jesus took his mother's hand, they went back to the tent and began to pack.

"I would like to go to Juttah on the way. Is that possible?" Mary asked.

"Yes, of course. I would love to see Elisabeth and Zacharias as well, and their son. Then we go to Jerusalem. I wish to make a sacrifice before we go on to Nazareth. It has been a long time."

An hour later they were on the road. All three walked until they stopped for water, then Jesus and Mary each rode one of the animals. They passed through Hebron about the middle of the day and approached Juttah close to the ninth hour. When they reached the village well, Mary asked to be helped from the donkey. She quickly washed Jesus and then herself while Joseph tended to his own washing. Then they walked rapidly down the road to the house where Mary had spent four happy months.

They found it empty.

* * *

Joseph looked around the place but saw no sign of life, and it didn't look like it had been used recently. Weeds grew in the paths, and there were no animal droppings in the small stable.

"I don't understand," Mary exclaimed worriedly. "Try the door, Joseph!"

He did, and it opened. Mary went inside to find it neat but dusty. There was no food, no wood for a fire, no bedding or mats, no clothing.

"They left over two years ago."

The three of them turned to see a man standing in the doorway. Mary immediately recognized him and bowed slightly, then gave a wide smile. "Jeremiah! How good to see you."

Mary introduced him to Joseph and Jesus. "This is Zacharias's best friend and fellow priest," she told Jesus.

"He is a handsome boy," Jeremiah said, looking at Jesus, then he sighed. "But, I do not understand this tradition you have of naming your children. First Zacharias, now you. Does anyone in your entire family name their firstborn son after his father?" He smiled.

"Where are they, Jeremiah? What has happened?"

Jeremiah's face sagged from sadness. "I don't know. We haven't heard from them since the day they left."

"But why did they leave? This is their home. Zacharias was very pleased that he had a son to whom he could give this house."

"I don't know that either." He moved to a chair, dusted it off, then sat, leaning on his walking stick. "More than two years ago, he and I were working our regular course at the temple. He was very dutiful that morning, but he seemed agitated. Finally, when he had time, he said he was going into the Hall of Hewn Stone for prayer. He did not come out for some time, so I went to see if he was all right, and he was gone. My son and I searched everywhere for him and only stopped looking when a message arrived from him saying he had to go home. It was a long note and very strange, filled with gratitude for our friendship and asking me to forgive him for leaving this way. When I came home at the end of our week of service and found him gone, I was even more mystified." His face hardened. "Then the soldiers came. They asked questions, searched everywhere, and even whipped several of us trying to get information we did not have. Then I was thankful he was gone. They would have killed him."

"Can you remember when this happened? Was there anything strange, any reason he would just up and leave?" Joseph questioned.

Jeremiah began nodding even before Joseph finished. "Yes, yes, there were visitors to the city, mysterious men from the East, priests of some foreign religion or something. It caused quite a stir in the city."

Joseph glanced at Mary, whose eyes were wide with understanding. "Then they fled when we left . . ." she began.

"Thank you, Jeremiah," Joseph said, interrupting his wife. "We must get to Jerusalem by nightfall if we can." He picked up Jesus and put a hand on Mary's arm, moving her toward the door. Mary hugged Jeremiah as she passed and thanked him again.

"I'm sure he will contact you when he can," she stated.

"I hope so. He was not well at the time, and . . . and we are all very worried about him and Elisabeth and John. Such a smart little boy, and his birth . . . miraculous. I'm sure this all has something do with the vision Zacharias had, but he never did tell me what it was all about. I don't suppose you—"

"I'm sorry, Jeremiah, but we have to go," Joseph replied.

Jeremiah sighed and nodded again. "I have kept the house for them, but there is no need. I don't suppose . . ."

"They would want it lived in, but make arrangements with those who use it, in case they return," Mary instructed.

"Of course, of course. Good-bye," Jeremiah said, then meandered toward his own house.

After Joseph had put Jesus on one of the donkeys and they had walked a short distance from the house, Mary waved to Jeremiah one last time, then spoke to Joseph.

"Do you think John was in danger as well?" she asked.

"Rumors of Zacharias's vision were talked of even in Egypt. Surely they would have reached the ears of Herod or his supporters at the temple. When the magi came and announced the birth of a new king, the talk of Zacharias must have become more significant, and they sent soldiers to find the child."

Saul nudged the other donkey in the side, and they nipped at each other until Jesus grabbed Alexander's ear and gave a firm command for both animals to stop their foolishness.

"Then they thought John might be the Messiah?" Mary queried.

Joseph nodded, the hair on the back of his neck standing on end. "They must have searched every village in the area." It made him sick to think what the result might have been, how many innocent children might have been harmed.

"But it is safe now," Mary affirmed. "The angel told you that they who wished to kill Jesus were dead."

Joseph nodded, but was beginning to see why he had such feelings of fear about their return to Bethlehem. Archelaus, a butcher like his father and just as jealous of power, would be watchful. If somehow their presence were discovered, he would be just as brutal as Herod in finding and dealing with them. Nazareth, far removed from the past and its rumors or events, would be safer. Joseph felt strangely comforted by coming to Juttah. On one hand, what they had learned disturbed him deeply, while on the other he was reassured that they should move on to Nazareth.

"Where was Elisabeth from?" Joseph asked.

"Hebron, but after her parents died there was no one left there."

"Any other family she might go to?"

"There was a brother, also a priest, but he moved to a different village when he married. He lives in the wilderness of Bethabara, near Jericho."

Joseph nodded. Of the twenty-four courses of priests, twelve resided in the Jordan Valley near Jericho, but there were priestly villages all over Judea as well and a few in Galilee. Any of them would welcome Zacharias and Elisabeth.

"I was there when Zacharias prophesied great things of his son. He will be a prophet and prepare the way for Jesus. One thing is certain: God will hide him as He has hidden Jesus."

Joseph remembered Mary telling him about Zacharias's miraculous vision and the instant recovery of his hearing and voice upon naming the child John. She remembered clearly every word Zacharias had spoken, both about Jesus and about John. Her recollections had given Joseph a deeper understanding of Jesus' need for spiritual preparation, and of John's. As a rightful heir to the priesthood of Aaron, he would prepare the spiritual way for the greater kingdom Jesus would bring. It had given rise to many questions in Joseph's mind, questions he simply had not been able to answer at first. But slowly through his studies, he was beginning to see things more clearly. Jesus' kingdom was going to be much more than a political one.

They traveled nearly a mile before Mary spoke again. "It is still dangerous, isn't it?"

Joseph stopped walking and faced Mary, putting his hands on her shoulders. "If Jesus' presence becomes known, a new generation of murderers will seek his life, Mary. It will always be dangerous." He saw that Jesus was nodding off to sleep and helped him settle into the nest of blankets on Alexander's back before putting an arm around Mary and moving forward. "Come, we will skip Jerusalem this time. I am eager to see Nazareth."

Mary put her arm through his and leaned against him. Five days to Nazareth. It seemed like an eternity.

CHAPTER 26

Anna sat down. Normally a strong woman, the last few months had taken a horrible toll on her. "Dinah, please finish grinding the wheat," she said weakly.

Dinah stared off toward the fields, a worried crease in the usually smooth skin of her forehead. Her father should be coming soon, but if he did not, she would send Ruth after him. Their mother seemed worse each moment, her skin sapped of its color, and it worried Dinah. Over the past week, she had become much more ill.

After looking one last time, Dinah returned to her seat next to the heating oven and began grinding the grain while watching her mother out of the corner of her eye. The war had done it, at least it seemed so to Dinah. It had aged both her parents, that and the sudden disappearance of Mary and Joseph.

Though Sepphoris was five miles distant, they had all watched the city fall to the rebels from the protection of rocks at the top of a hill a mile away. It had been strange to see forces approach the walls on three sides, like waves of water flooding toward them. Dinah had seen their ladders against the walls, seen the ladders topple, seen them put up again. She had watched the smoke billow from the gate and then, like ants to honey, the masses outside the walls break through the first gate, then a second and third, and take the city. Her brother, Josiah, had gloried in it while her father had become worried, even frightened.

Suddenly, the village had become two different worlds—some anxious and ready to join the fight, others counseling against it. Her brother and her father were on opposite sides. The argument went on for days, the whole village divided over it. *Judas is the Messiah! Judas is a liar! Judas, Judas, Judas!* It had split families, and the synagogue was nothing but a place to fight and argue. Dinah had hated it.

Along with many others, Josiah had decided to leave, to join the rebels. Rumors of victory, bounty, and future riches as the new ruling class drew them away even faster than did Judas being hailed as the new Messiah. The night before Josiah was to leave, Joachim called his family together. He told them that he *knew* that Judas ben Hezekiah was not the Messiah, that this war would only lead to a bitter end, that the village would be attacked by the Romans for their complicity when they put down the rebellion. Josiah fumed and demanded how his father could know such a thing. Joachim had seemed on the verge of answering when their mother had told him to keep quiet. She turned to Josiah and simply said, "Tell me, Josiah, other than the fact that he has a sword in his fist, what tells you that Judas ben Hezekiah *is* the Messiah? Is he a son of David? A worthy man, who can lead spiritually as well as fight a battle? Have you searched the scriptures as your father has? Do you even have any idea of what the Messiah will truly be?"

Josiah had been about to respond, but he clamped his mouth shut when she raised a hand and said she was not finished. "Your father knows, and I know, but we are not at liberty to tell you how. Our word should be enough for you, but I will tell you this. If you leave Nazareth, you will not find things as you think among those bandits. You will see death like you have never seen it. And when it is finished, you will either be dead or a slave. Now listen to your father."

She had been right. Josiah had ignored their advice and had not come back; none of the fighters had. The Romans had driven them into Sepphoris then attacked with huge war machines that allowed them to breach the walls and lay waste to the city, killing or taking into slavery everyone who remained.

And Nazareth did not escape the Romans' fury.

Dinah gave gratitude to God every day for her father. He had known the Romans would come and convinced most of the others that they should leave. They did not go together, or to the same place, but spread out across the land, hiding here and there, living with relatives in places they did not think the Romans would come, taking their animals and essential provisions but leaving everything else behind. Dinah, Ruth, and their parents had gone into hiding on the far shores of the Sea of Galilee until the cloud of Roman destruction had passed to the south. When the villagers returned, they found no food, their fields of grain trampled or burned, and their homes badly damaged by the theft and vandalism of the Roman forces.

The marauding soldiers had passed by the groves of olives and fruit, probably because they might need them later, but they had not passed by those who remained in the village. The bodies were still rotting in the sun when the first villagers returned. A half dozen families had perished, among them two of Dinah's best friends.

The villagers mourned for weeks, and they were still mourning, at least inside. Each day they had risen to the tasks of finding nourishment and rebuilding their homes and lives. A stern and hardworking lot, Joachim and his family had soon cleaned up and begun repairs. Along with several others, their home still lacked a roof, so they were staying in Joseph and Mary's house, but the fields were plowed and ready for seed, and olives were maturing in their groves. One could not survive on olives and the oil squeezed from them, but it was a beginning, and though they ached for their loved ones and friends, they would find a way through the coming winter. They would endure.

Except for Anna. She still mourned Josiah and worried about Mary, but it was more than that, something deeper, a physical illness that had cut her weight in half. She could not eat, and when she did the food went through her like water. Dinah did not know what to do for her mother, how to make her well. No one did. Her father prayed for her three times a day at the synagogue, but God seemed to have His ears closed. But then He seemed to have His ears closed to a lot of things these days. And His eyes. Could He not see and hear the pain and sorrows of His people? Could He not hear Dinah's prayers and the prayers of her parents? If He did, why did He take Mary and Josiah? Why did He not protect them?

Bitterly, Dinah finished grinding the allotment of grain for the day. When they fled the village, everyone had taken the grain that remained from the previous year's harvest. It hadn't been much then and dwindled daily. Her father had gone to harvest a small patch of wheat that had survived the Romans. They would need every kernel they could get.

"Mother, Father will be home soon. He will need bread. The oven is heated, the kneading trough ready, but your mix is so much better than mine. Could you . . ."

Anna only nodded, a distant look in her eyes. She did not move.

Dinah felt her heart breaking, and tears came to her eyes and flowed down her cheeks. She set the hand grinder aside and wrapped her arms around her mother's legs. Her mother made no movement of recognition, but Dinah didn't care. She wanted her mother back— the woman who yelled at her for her laziness, the mother who scowled with her lips but had the smile of pride in her dark brown eyes, the wife who scolded her husband playfully, the woman who could make Dinah feel all right about God.

Ruth came through the gate at a run. "Father is coming! He has a chicken!"

Dinah wiped away her tears and got to her feet. "What? A chicken, but where—"

"From the market. He walked clear to Sepphoris to get it! It is a wonderful chicken, Dinah. Fat as a gentile pig!" Her eyes were wide. They hadn't had such a feast in months. They'd had only a few chickens when they fled Nazareth and had used them for food in the two months they were away. They did not dare eat their sheep or goats—they needed the animals for wool and milk. And there was no money for such things. How on earth . . .

Dinah went to the gate and gazed up the street. Her father was coming, and he did have something hanging from his hand! She squinted. Her eyes did not always focus just right, and it was hard to see at this distance. It *was* a chicken!

"Quick, Ruth, bring more wood for the oven."

Ruth was grinning as she darted around the side of the house. Dinah went to her mother and bent over to grasp her hand. Her mother looked up at her with sad, confused eyes.

"Mother, Father has brought dinner. A chicken, and you know I can't roast it to his liking. Won't you fix it for him?"

With effort, she forced a smile and squeezed Dinah's hand. "Yes, dear," she replied softly. "In a moment. I just need to catch my breath."

Dinah felt the weak squeeze of her mother's hand go right to her heart. It was worse today, much worse.

Her father came through the gate smiling, the chicken raised for all to see. "God has sent a fine chicken to grace our table. Mother, prepare the oven to welcome him!"

Dinah saw the smile leave his face when he saw Anna. He handed Dinah the chicken. "She's worse, isn't she?" he queried. He stepped past a nodding Dinah and sat on the bench next to Anna. "You should rest in your bed, wife," he suggested gently.

Anna attempted to smile at him. "There is so much to do. I—"

"Come, lie down. Dinah and Ruth will fix you some nice chicken broth." He stood and tried to get her to stand, but she couldn't. He bent over and picked her up in his arms. At about half her normal weight, she was not hard to lift.

Dinah felt so sad inside, so frightened. How would they ever get along without Mother? *No, no,* she said to herself. *She is only ill. She will get better. She has to get better!*

Ruth came around the corner with the wood, and Dinah took it and put some in the bottom of the oven. Then she sent Ruth for water.

"But the cistern pots are nearly empty!" Ruth moaned.

Dinah wanted to yell at her younger sister but bit her tongue. The pots buried in the ground were made of clay and were filled from the village well. They had needed replenishing for days, but there just hadn't been time. "Ruth, please, go to the well and get fresh water. I need to clean the chicken and soak it in salt before we cook it. You know that." She said it as gently as she could, but it still came out too harsh, and Ruth's lip quivered. Dinah knelt in front of her while holding back her own tears. "I'm sorry, Ruth. Please, forgive me."

Ruth nodded. "Is Mother going to die?"

"No, no, she is just ill, but she needs soup. It will help. Won't you go and get some water?"

Ruth nodded again, picked up the pot near the door, and left the courtyard.

Dinah looked at the forlorn chicken. It wasn't a chicken at all, but a sage grouse. Her father had been hunting and had gotten lucky. She was grateful, but it wasn't much.

As she started pulling the last of the feathers from its skin, she heard someone on the path behind her and turned to see Jerusha, a neighbor and good friend of her mother's, at the open gate to the courtyard. She carried a small loaf of sweet bread and extended it toward Dinah. "How is your mother?" she asked.

Dinah thanked her for the bread, knowing it was a sacrifice. Jerusha had even less grain than they did, and like others she would have to try to purchase something to get her family through the winter. But even if they had the money, there was so little food to purchase! Everywhere around them it was the same. People mourning for lost loved ones, scavenging for food, even stealing from one another, desperate to live. The village elders had even built a watchtower in the olive grove to keep thieves out. All were desperate, and it was a horrible time of hunger, making the small loaf even more precious.

"Father has put her to bed," Dinah answered. "I don't know what to do for her."

Jerusha put a comforting arm around Dinah. She had seen this sickness before—sometimes called consumption. Few survived its ravaging effects on the body. It brought tears to her eyes to think of her friend losing such a horrible battle. She had been such a strong woman! Even when they had returned to their ruined village, Anna and Joachim had been the ones to push everyone forward, to keep despondency at bay. So strong, and yet the first to suffer so horribly.

Jerusha shuddered. She knew there would be others. Though young when Parthia battled with Rome for Palestine and Herod was catapulted to power with Roman conquest, she remembered the hardships, the destruction and death. She bit her lip against the fear and worry, praying that God would somehow soften the blow, that the increase in heartfelt prayers at the synagogue would bring forgiveness for whatever they had done to deserve this beating and would save them from worse.

Joachim came through the door, his face ashen. "She . . . she went to sleep . . ." He paused. "It . . . it is different. I can't wake her." He fell onto the bench, his head in his hands.

Jerusha quickly stepped across the threshold and rushed into the bedroom to kneel beside Anna's low bed. Dinah entered behind her, standing near the door, her lips quivering with fear.

Jerusha put a hand to Anna's lips and felt the air. "She is breathing, but barely. Heat water, Dinah, and go for the—"

"Father, what is it, what is wrong?"

Dinah heard the voice outside and stiffened. She turned about and stared into the courtyard. It could not be!

Mary was kneeling in front of Joachim, Joseph near the gate holding a child. It was a dream. Dinah was dreaming! She had to be dreaming!

Joachim had lifted his head and was staring blankly at the apparition in front of him. Dinah watched wide-eyed as he reached a shaking hand to touch the angel face that watched him with great concern.

"Mary?" he cried softly.

Dinah jumped from the door and danced by the side of her father as he took Mary into his arms and hugged her so tightly it surely would break her bones. She wrapped her arms around them both as Ruth came through the gate with the jar of water. Her eyes went wide, and she dropped the jug, spilling the water onto the hard earth.

"Mary!" she screamed, running toward them.

Mary turned and stooped to catch her little sister in her arms and hug her tightly. "Ruth! My, how you have grown!"

Mary quickly hugged each family member again, the two girls' shouts of joy and happiness mingling with their tears. Joachim sobbed as he stared in relief at his eldest daughter. Then he saw Joseph and Jesus, and he quickly separated from the girls and stepped to them. He embraced Joseph warmly, Jesus snuggled between them. "Thank the Lord of heaven and earth and all the angels! You are safe!" He stepped back and looked at the young boy, whose eyes were wide with a curious sort of apprehension. Then a shy smile came to the boy's face and he reached out to Joachim. "Grandfather."

Joachim lifted the child and swung him round and round overhead to see a larger smile form on his little lips.

"Jerusha!" Mary exclaimed. Jerusha had stepped from the house, a relieved but sober look on her face. Mary threw her arms around her and gave her a hug. "Where is Mother?" she asked.

"Inside, Mary," Jerusha replied, motioning. "She is quite ill." She stepped back, and Mary quickly went past her and into the bedroom, knelt, and took her mother's thin hand in hers. She bent her face to the frail, limp fingers and kissed them gently. She had never seen her mother so thin, so sickly, and it was a shock.

"She is breathing," Jerusha said explained, "but—"

"Mother? It is I, Mary," she said softly.

The others pressed into the room, Joseph the last, holding Jesus. They stood quiet, watching. When Anna did not respond, Mary squeezed her hand tighter. "Mother, I am home. Please don't leave me now. I have so much to tell you! Please . . ." she bit her lip against the anguish and could not speak any more words.

Suddenly Mary seemed to snap out of her sorrow and stood. "Dinah, heat water. Quickly now!" She smiled at Dinah, who was relieved to have Mary take charge. Dinah pushed past Joseph and into the courtyard, grabbed the jar, and ran for the well.

"Father, go to the synagogue, bring the rabbi and any others who will pray for her."

Joachim was staring humbly at his wife and did not move.

"Father," Mary said firmly. "Go, get the rabbi. Bring him here. Bring as many as will come."

Joachim started out of his stupor and, nodding, retreated through the door. Joseph set Jesus down and spoke to Ruth, who was standing with her back against the wall, her wide, frightened eyes on her mother. "Ruth, Jesus' toys are in a bag on one of the donkeys. Get them for him, will you? You can play with him in the courtyard."

Ruth nodded. She took Jesus by the hand and led him outside. Joseph closed the door behind them, then found several lamps and lit them.

Mary was already stroking her mother's forehead. Her flesh was clammy, cold.

"We'll need blankets."

* * *

Joseph left the room and went into the courtyard. The oven was heating, but the wood stove, a separate unit, was cold. He picked it up and took it inside, then took several of the flaming sticks from under the oven and put them in the bottom of the stove and added others. The house seemed chilly, and they would need hot water.

Going back into the courtyard, Joseph saw the wild hen lying in a bowl next to the oven. God must have truly blessed Joachim. There were so few sage grouse in the hills of Galilee before the invasion, and with so many hungry, there would be even fewer now. He took the bird inside and prepared it for the pot. Anna would need broth.

As they came north, they had seen the destruction left by the Romans. Though most of Samaria had been spared, the Jezreel Valley had been laid waste. Where herds of sheep had wandered, not even a stray now fed; where crops were usually stored, granaries were empty, fields trampled and burned. Sepphoris had been put to flame, and though there was talk that Antipas would soon rebuild it, promises would not give the people food.

When Dinah returned with water, Joseph had a fire going, and it quickly heated the cold room. She poured water into the cooking pot, and Joseph used his knife to cut the chicken into pieces, dropping them in the water before placing the pot over the hot coals.

As he wiped his hands clean and washed them, he noticed Dinah sitting on the stool nearby watching him. Her eyes were filled with sadness, and he opened his arms. She ran into them to have a good cry.

"We . . . we thought you were dead," she groaned through her sobs.

"We sent letters, but with things the way they are . . . Anyway, we are quite alive and are here to stay." He looked into her eyes. "You have grown up since we last saw you."

She nodded, sniffing and wiping away the tears. "I am so glad you're here. Everything is so bad, and we have no food, and . . . and I thought God had forgotten us."

"Shh, God has not forgotten. He will provide; you'll see. You had to go to the well for water. Are the pots empty?"

She nodded.

"Then you must fill them, okay?"

Another nod.

With his rough fingers, he wiped away a tear from Dinah's cheek, and she stiffened her back, then picked up the jar and left. Joseph went back in the bedroom and knelt beside Mary. Putting an arm around her shoulder, he looked at Anna. If he had seen her on the street, he would never have recognized her. So thin, with dark circles under her eyes and her hair now thin and covered in strips of gray.

"Where is Josiah?" he asked.

Jerusha told them the sad story: the rebellion, the feelings that led many to join, the destruction that followed. Mary and Joseph both ached inside, and Mary gripped his hands tightly against her tears.

"He may still be alive," Mary stated. "They take slaves . . ." She bit her lip, the horror of what even slavery might mean refusing to let her finish.

"Matthias and Salome, have you heard anything about them?" Joseph asked.

"They were living in Capernaum. I . . . I don't know their fates," Jerusha answered. "There are many families missing. My sister and brother . . . We haven't heard."

"Go, Joseph, pray for Mother. Pray for all of them," Mary pleaded. "I must wash her and dress her in warmer clothes."

Joseph kissed Mary lovingly on her head, then stood and left the house. As he breathed in the fresh air, he realized how much the room had smelled of death.

Men knelt in the courtyard, their shawls in place, their prayers going to heaven. This was not what Joseph had seen in his dream, not what he expected to find. Had he deceived himself because of his love for this place? The answer came immediately. No, more than ever he saw that they had been meant to come here. They were needed more than he had ever thought possible.

Faces turned up and smiled, happy to see him, but the men went immediately back to praying as he went to his donkeys and retrieved his own shawl. He saw Ruth playing with Jesus, but when the boy saw Joseph put his shawl over his shoulders, he immediately stopped his play and came running. Joseph found Jesus' small shawl and handed it to his son. Kneeling beside Joachim with Jesus just in front of them, Joseph began to pray. Joachim was crying, and Joseph put an arm around him.

Yes, they had come just in time.

CHAPTER 27

Four days later, Anna was mourned and buried. She never regained consciousness and probably never knew that Mary sat by her bed with little rest until death closed the door between them.

The time of mourning lasted seven days, and because their house had been defiled by a corpse, Mary and Joseph could not immediately return there. Instead, they slept in Joachim's roofless house. It was just as well. Joachim needed Mary, and he needed Jesus.

After Anna's death, the immediate family could not work, so Joseph, Jerusha, and others did most of the water-carrying and other chores. Mourners dropped by Joachim's house, bringing what little food they could and expressing their sorrow.

On the third day, the family went to Joseph and Mary's home for the cleansing ritual. They met the eldest of the village priests there, and he began the process.

Every few years, a red heifer was to be sacrificed at Jerusalem and its ashes distributed to priests both in Palestine and abroad. When defilement from a corpse took place, the ashes would be mixed with water and then, using hyssop, the mixture would be sprinkled over everything and everyone who had come in contact with the body. This would return ritual purity to all concerned and to the village.

This ceremony had been done often lately in Nazareth, and the priest, who lived near Joseph, had commented that he would have to go to Jerusalem on the next Day of Atonement to receive more ashes, his usually ample supply running low.

Like all sacrifices, the ashes had no ability to purify of themselves. The ashes, like the blood of lambs and doves, were a symbol of Him

who removed sin or gave life after the grave. The ashes were a remembrance that God would not allow death to keep Mary's mother from
them. For Joseph, the most important ceremony after losing a loved
one was to have the priest sprinkle them with this symbol, as it
brought him comfort and peace.

The ceremony completed, they returned to Joachim's home, and
Joseph removed the burned roof timbers and other debris and
repaired the walls of Joachim's house while Dinah and Ruth watched
Jesus. Mary slept—their second child would be coming soon, and she
was exhausted.

As was the custom, Joachim sat on the ground in the courtyard
under the shade of the tree and entertained mourners who came by
the house. Between visits, he talked with Joseph while he worked,
mostly speaking of Anna. Joseph did not truly know his mother-in-
law until now, nor had he known how much Joachim loved her.
Joachim had lost a part of himself, and Joseph knew the pain would
last a long time.

Stopping for water and rest, Joseph sat down on the bench next to
Joachim. It was comfortable in the shade of the tree, and they visited
more about Anna. After a long silence, Joachim spoke softly. "She
believed Mary without question."

"Yes, I know. You and I were a bit dimwitted in comparison,
weren't we?" Joseph replied.

Joachim chuckled, then sighed. "Oh, how I wish she could be
here to see him reach his destiny." He was looking at Jesus, who was
playing with Ruth near the stable. "I wanted her to see him become
what she knew he would become! Why, why couldn't God let her
stay, Joseph? Why?"

Joseph laid his head back and closed his eyes, praying for the right
words. He wanted to comfort Joachim, but how could he when so
little was known about God's purpose? Sages shoved such questions
aside with statements like, "It is God's will," but *why* was it His will?
What good did it do to suffer unless there was something more, some
reason for it that made sense? Did one just live and die for nothing?
In Joseph's mind, only a cruel God would put His children into such
an existence. In his studies, he had come to find there was a purpose
and that God was not cruel.

After Jesus' birth he had become obsessed with what the child's life would mean. He knew he would be King of Kings. He had found dozens of scriptures in the Torah and the prophets and in the words of the sages that attested to and prophesied of that. It was what Israel dreamed of and prayed for. Most thought of it only as an earthly kingdom, one in which, as Isaiah said, salvation would reach the ends of the earth, even among the nations of the Gentiles. But Joseph had come to believe it was much more. Isaiah also said that the Messiah would raise up the tribes of Jacob and restore the preserved of Israel. For Joseph, the first referred to the dead, the second to the living. Jesus would be the Savior of both. In some way Joseph did not fully understand yet, Jesus would begin the resurrection, and those lifted from the prison of the grave would live with him during his endless reign. Salvation through the Messiah must come to all, both living and dead, or else the great prophets Moses, Jacob, Abraham, Adam, and so many more had lived in vain.

It had been a wonderful revelation for Joseph, but one he could not share with others. How could a child, one who looked no different from any other child, bring about such a thing? Joseph was not sure, but he did know Jesus was God's own Son and that because he was, he would accomplish it. The power was in him or would be given him, or both, but that was his purpose for being here. Joseph knew it as he knew little else.

He patted Joachim's leg. "She is not gone forever, Joachim. She is in a good place, and you will see her again." He looked at Jesus. "And she will see him one day. In some way that I cannot explain, he will bring her back to you." Joseph hoped it would be enough. Joachim believed in an afterlife. For now Joseph hoped his father-in-law would feel comfort in that knowledge.

He went back to work as Mary came from the back room of the house and stretched.

"You slept well?" Joseph asked.

"Yes, very well, thank you." She saw Jesus and gathered him up. "Jesus and the girls will go with me to check on the sheep," she explained.

"Micah's son is watching over them. You know the law. You shouldn't help bring them home, not yet," Joseph stated.

"Just for the walk. We will be back in time for the final cleansing of the house." They left the courtyard, and Joseph could hear the echo of their voices in the street. A few minutes later, he saw them climbing the hill outside the village.

He worried about bandits and other hungry survivors. Lawlessness was still the rule in Galilee, and a woman . . .

Joseph took a deep breath. His own fears were speaking. The sheep were just beyond the top of the hill, well within hearing distance. Getting back to work, his mind turned to what lay ahead. There was much work to be done on this house and on a number of others. Part of the roof and walls of Matthias's home were missing, and he intended to repair those as well.

He was on the top of the wall and stood straight, arching his aching back while picking out Matthias's house where it sat near his own. He passed it several times each day and could not help but wonder what had happened to his friend. Joachim had told him that they had gone to Capernaum in hopes of staying with Matthias and Salome, but found their house empty and cold, the town nearly deserted. They had then gone into hiding on the far shores of the Sea of Galilee and never discovered the fate of Matthias's family. Joseph feared the worst. He did not think Matthias could stay out of such a battle and thought he had probably taken Salome into the camps of the rebels. When the Romans arrived, they, like all the others, were probably killed or imprisoned. Such thoughts made Joseph's heart ache with guilt. If he had just told Matthias *why* he shouldn't fight with the fool Judas ben Hezekiah!

Then he shook his head. No, he had felt strongly that he should not tell Matthias, and he knew the warning was of God. Now he must trust that God had warned Matthias about Judas.

He worked for another hour before the position of the sun told him the time was nearing for the final cleansing of their home, and he was relieved to see Mary and the children coming over the rise in the hill above the house.

While waiting, Joseph surveyed his work. The burned logs had been removed, the cracked stone replaced, and everything prepared for new logs, mats, and packed earth. Getting down from the wall, he washed, finishing just as Mary and the children entered the courtyard.

Joachim was entertaining other mourners, and Dinah said she would stay behind and look after him and the little bit of food the visitors brought while they saw to the final cleansing.

* * *

They arrived at the house at the same time as the priest, the rabbi, and several of the city elders, and the ceremony was quickly completed. When he heard the last part of the prayer, Jesus looked excitedly at Joseph and received a smile and permission to go ahead. He ran inside, touching the mezuzah as he passed through the door, while Mary and Joseph went to the shop and began taking the furniture and other items inside the house.

"Where is Grandmother?" Jesus asked as Mary entered.

Mary felt a tear coming and had to choke it back. "She went to the tomb, remember?"

"That was her body, Mother. Where is the rest of her?"

"With God," was all Mary could think to say.

"Then she is not far away!" He ran out of the house and went to the shop to retrieve some of his things.

"I suppose he is right," Joseph said. "She isn't far away."

Mary stood still. "Yes, I can still feel part of her in this room."

Joseph stopped what he was doing. There was something different, something peaceful, about the house. He had been around places where people died before—his father, mother, neighbors—but he had never felt this. Had something changed? Had his learning changed his very ability to feel things he had simply brushed aside before?

There was a knock on the doorpost, and Joseph turned to see the rabbi standing just outside. He would not enter for at least another seven days. A meticulous keeper of the law, he often extended its requirements beyond those of either the Torah or the sages, especially as it applied to him and his family. Joseph knew his custom and went outside to greet him. They bowed slightly. Because Joseph had touched the bier, the rabbi would treat him as he had the house.

"The elders have met. As you know, we're desperate for grain, both for seeding the fields and for food. There will be a special day of prayer and fasting tomorrow, and we would ask that all people, both men and women, join in."

"Of course," Joseph responded.

The rabbi bowed again and left the courtyard to go to the next house. The entire village would be notified door-to-door.

"We have the gold coins, and the remaining ointment could be sold," Mary suggested. They agreed that if no other solution presented itself, the coins would be used.

The next day as Joseph, Joachim, and the rest of the villagers continued to repair homes around the village, one of the shepherds came running from the flocks screaming that soldiers were coming. Joseph took Mary and Jesus to the synagogue and arrived just as Joachim brought Dinah and Ruth. They, with all the other women and children, were locked inside, and to defend their families, the men armed themselves with farm tools and the few available swords. Joseph saw the fear in their eyes. The Roman legions were still ravaging the land to the south. Had they returned to do more damage?

There was a united sigh of relief when only one Roman and five men wearing the uniform of Herodian soldiers appeared. Still, the villagers held their place, afraid others might follow.

Armed with only the standard short sword but without the shields or spears common to battle, the soldiers walked their horses down the slope and into the square. Joseph lowered his weapon.

"They are not here to fight," Joseph reported. "Put down your weapons."

The few swords were quickly hidden, and the scythes, forks, shovels, hammers, and other tools were set aside to show they would not be a threat. Word had reached the women inside the synagogue, and they and the children reappeared to join their husbands and fathers. Mary, Jesus in her arms, slipped between Joseph and Joachim along with Dinah and Ruth. Ruth stayed half hidden behind Joseph, clinging to his leg. He patted her head gently.

The Roman pulled up his horse and dismounted, removing his helmet. Once more Joseph was pleased to see Marcus Vitellius, the man who had protected Mary so long ago and who had come just in time to keep him from being entangled in the judgment of a thief when they were passing through Jerusalem.

Marcus handed the rabbi a papyrus scroll with a smile. "We are not here to harm you," he said. "The time for such things is passed." He looked around the group, saw Joseph and Mary, then gave them a smile and tipped his head slightly in recognition before speaking to everyone.

"Antipas, son of Herod, has become tetrarch of all Galilee and Perea. He knows what the legions of Rome were forced to do here and has sent food, purchased from Egypt at great expense to him, to get his people through the winter."

Looks of skepticism greeted the remarks, but Joseph could see the flicker of hope in the eyes of many and heard someone whisper that God had honored their fasting and prayers and that he would never doubt again.

"Herod's army has been split into parts," Marcus went on. "I and my men were at Jerusalem, but we come here now to protect the domain assigned his son Antipas by the Emperor. The Romans will support our numbers until peace is restored, then they will go back to Syria. As commander of the tetrarch's troops for this region, I promise you there will be no more attacks on villages or cities unless it is known that you harbor rebels or thieves and refuse to give them up."

This time there were sounds of approval from the villagers. Lying in bed at night wondering if they would live until morning, having to watch over their flocks and children for fear they would be killed or kidnapped, held no joy. However, for Joseph it was the sign that little had changed. Lives had been sacrificed, friends and family had died, but their oppressors were still with them. Since the time of his first dream, Joseph had contemplated how Jesus would defeat the Romans, the Parthians, and endless other troops of evil kings. In his natural mind, he had pictured an army of such strength that none of these could withstand, but as they had traveled north and seen the devastation of only a few Roman legions, he realized it would take a greater power than the sword. Jesus would have to be given the very power God gave Moses.

"The tetrarch has decided to rebuild Sepphoris," Marcus continued. "All artisans and workers will be paid fair wages; the rest of you can work for food for your families and will be dealt with according to your ability and the time you can spend away from your fields." He looked around the village. "You have damage to your homes and need timbers. The army left war machines behind. There is much wood in them, and you and other villagers are free to take what you need for repairs to houses and barns. Better it be used than left to rot."

Suddenly, wagons appeared at the top of the hill, soldiers surrounding them. Several of the wagons held sacks of grain, but one held a cage with prisoners inside. The crowd immediately identified several faces, and astonished fathers and mothers pressed forward, calling out the names of their sons. Then the entire village rushed toward the descending wagons, cries of joy and amazement filling the air. Thin, bruised, wounded, and filthy hands were extended through the wooden bars and were immediately grasped by family members shedding tears of joy. Joachim, Mary, Dinah, Ruth, Joseph, and even Jesus all looked desperately at the fearful faces of the captured.

"Do you see him?" Joachim cried out. "Do you see Josiah?"

They looked desperately, but Josiah's face did not appear, and Joseph put a strong arm around the sagging shoulders of his father-in-law.

"As a show of good will, Antipas will release these prisoners to your care. If there are others still missing, we will do our best to tell you their fate, but I will tell you now that many died in this foolish rebellion and, as in the case of other villages, some of your sons will never return to you." He signaled to the wagoneer who stood near the locked door of the cage, and he turned the key. The prisoners, emaciated and injured, crawled out and into the arms of waiting family.

"My son!" Joachim exclaimed. He broke away from Joseph's grip and pushed through the crowd toward the back of the wagon.

Joseph and Mary looked over and around heads, desperate to see what Joachim could see. "It is! It's Josiah!" Mary cried. She handed Jesus to Joseph and tried to catch Joachim, with Dinah and Ruth eagerly following in her wake. Josiah, lying at the bottom of the wagon, was wounded and hardly able to lift his head. His wide eyes, filled with anguish, searched the crowd from between bars, anxiously looking for his family. They filled with relief as he saw his father pushing past the last of the crowd to grab his hand.

"Father," he said with weak relief. "Father." Then he saw Mary, and tears sprang to his eyes. "Oh, Mary!" he cried. He broke into uncontrollable sobs as Mary threw herself into the cage and wrapped her arms around his frail shoulders.

Weak, emaciated, and with a filthy rag stained with dried blood and infection wrapped around his arm, Josiah was too weak to stand on his own, so Mary tried to lift him out of the cage.

Joseph quickly handed Jesus to Dinah, reached inside the cage, and lifted the suffering boy into his arms. He would never forget the look of relief in Josiah's eyes as he laid his head on Joseph's shoulder.

"Is it a dream, Joseph? Have I died and gone to heaven?"

"No, Josiah, it isn't a dream." With tears flowing, they started up the hill, Dinah and Ruth clinging with relief to their father's hands, and Mary carrying Jesus while still trying to console Josiah with the gentle touch of her free hand.

"He's home, Papa," Ruth sighed. "He's home."

"Mother, where is Mother?" Josiah asked.

Joseph glanced at Mary, whose lip quivered at the sound of her brother's words. She could not speak, her emotions making her whole body quake.

"Oh, no. Not Mother." Josiah wept, his whole body racked with sobs.

When they reached Joachim's house, Joseph laid Josiah under the makeshift roof he had put up for the girls, and Mary immediately began unwrapping the wound. She caught her breath as she saw the extent of the damage and immediately covered the arm again so the others could not see.

"What is it, Mary?" Dinah asked. "Is . . . is it very bad?"

"Yes. We'll need hot water and bandages. Ruth, go to my house. You will find jars of ointment in the cupboard Joseph built. Bring the one with the broken seal. Quickly!"

Dinah and Ruth rushed out, and Mary returned to kneel beside Josiah. With Joseph's help, she carefully inspected the mangled arm.

"How bad?" Joachim stood at the foot of the bed, concern on his face.

Mary did not answer.

"I missed you." Josiah smiled up at her with sad eyes.

Mary smiled. "And I missed you."

Dinah brought the water, and Mary cleaned the wound as best she could while Joseph tried to hold the arm stable. Badly broken, the bone still protruded through the skin, but it was the rotting flesh around the wound that gave Mary the most concern.

Dinah handed her a cup of wine for Josiah, and Mary lifted his head slightly and gave him a drink. With his good arm, he pushed against the cup wanting more. Soon it would take the edge off the pain.

"Dinah, take Jesus outside and when Ruth comes back, keep her out as well," Mary said firmly. "Joseph and I will have to set this bone. It will not be pleasant."

They shuffled from the room, and Joseph closed the door, then went to Mary's side. She folded a piece of cloth and placed it between Josiah's teeth. She saw the fear in his eyes and gently stroked his forehead while speaking comforting words, beads of perspiration on her own brow. Yet she seemed calm and self-assured.

"I will have to pull the bone into place as best I can. You must not fight what I do, Josiah. Do you understand?"

Josiah gave a fearful nod, his body tensing.

"Joseph, you will have to hold his upper arm steady," Mary said.

"I must help," Joachim moaned. "What can I—"

"Pray for him, Father. Pray for us."

Joseph positioned himself and nodded when he was ready.

She took a deep breath. Josiah closed his eyes tightly and bit down on the cloth, and Mary pulled.

* * *

Josiah lay unconscious from the pain as Mary and Dinah finished cleansing and wrapping the wound. A bit lightheaded himself, Joseph stepped out to get some fresh air. Joachim was in fervent prayer, and to avoid disturbing him, Joseph left the courtyard and wandered toward the main square. Mary had astounded him once again—her strength, her ability to know what to do. There was no other quite like her.

"We meet again, Joseph of Nazareth."

Joseph was jerked from his thoughts to see Marcus Vitellius standing a few feet away, his horse and others being watered at the well. He pointed at two large sacks of grain. "I saw you leave with the boy and had them put aside."

"It will keep the winter from killing us. Thank you," Joseph said.

"Your gratitude is undeserved. Antipas needs workers, and dead men cannot work, nor can they pay taxes." He finished drinking from a cup, then put it in a bag hanging from a strap attached to his saddle. "The boy is of your family."

"My wife's brother."

"He was captured when Sepphoris fell and was held at Aochis. We kept only those strong enough to work. The rest are being returned to their parents and families."

"An honorable thing to do, I suppose," Joseph replied.

"Again, you mistake the facts. Antipas can ill afford the loss of your young men if he wants to build a kingdom here. It is a matter of necessity with him, not a matter of honor."

"You sound as if you do not like him any more than the rest of us."

"He purchases my sword, not my soul."

"How can he purchase one without the other?"

There was silence between them for a moment.

"I have fought with the sword all my adult days. I know no other life." The reins of his horse were handed to him, and he took them. "Do not misunderstand my frankness. My duty is to the king. If your village fights against him or harbors rebels, I will act without mercy. There will be peace in this part of Galilee, by force or by agreement, but I will see to it." He mounted his horse.

"I consider you a fair man, Marcus Vitellius, and as long as that remains, there will be none in this village who will raise the sword against you."

"Then you will be left in peace." His horse danced a bit, and he had to turn it back to face Joseph. "There are those of your neighbors who think you are the best carpenter in the region. You will be paid well if you come to Sepphoris."

Joseph only nodded, and Marcus reined his horse up the street, his soldiers following him out of the village.

CHAPTER 28

Joseph and a dozen other men left the village before sunup the next morning. With them were the village's ten oxen, which would drag logs from the siege towers used to conquer Sepphoris, and a large wagon pulled by six donkeys. It would be used to haul any loose planks gleaned from the towers.

They reached the burned-out city of Sepphoris just after the third hour, approaching along the aqueduct. The Romans had removed part of it to stop the water from reaching the city when they put it under siege, and water gushed from the opening, creating a small lake. Slaves were working to make repairs, and soldiers pushed them to their work.

As they neared the eastern gate, the road widened into a vast plaza where local farmers had once sold their goods. With food sparse and repair work taking place, the market had disappeared.

The two towers on each side of the gate still stood, but the gate itself was burned, its melted, twisted hinges hanging empty. Soldiers stood atop the walls and watched them and other men who had come to garner wood from the two war machines placed against the wall on either side of the gate.

Looking up at the closest tower, Joseph marveled at its size. Taller than the wall itself, its timbers were covered with planks and the skins of animals to prevent the wood from catching on fire. Inside, rough-hewn stairs led up to a box-like room with a ramp that lowered when the machine was pulled into place against the wall. When Joseph climbed these, he found the ramp still lying on top of the wall. Dark bloodstains bore stark witness of the fight that had taken place when the Romans had forced their way into the city.

Joseph studied the structure to determine how to dismantle it, then retraced his steps and shared his plan with those who had gathered from several villages to glean their share of the wood. They agreed and elected Joseph overseer, then started the work, pulling both planks and logs apart from the top down. By the eighth hour it was dismantled.

Joseph worked with other village carpenters to divide the spoils before helping his own men tie two logs behind each ox. The logs would be dragged back to Nazareth. They then filled the cart with planks, and all but he and Jerusha's husband, Micah, began the journey.

After seeing them on their way, Joseph and Micah passed into the city to the sound of whips and the shouts of slave drivers as charred roofs and heat-cracked stone were removed from the burned-out city. The wide, paved street that led to the acropolis had already been cleared, and the sound of chisel and hammer, saw and pulley echoed off the walls as hundreds of men worked to rebuild the tetrarch's Galilean capital.

Joseph kept an eye out for Matthias as he dodged animals, carts, and workers. Entering the large plaza outside the theater, he recognized an overseer he had worked for on other projects and approached him immediately.

"Joseph, good to see you! And you, Micah!" He extended a hand and arm for the usual shake.

"Ananel. Nice to see you survived the fighting."

"A fool's errand. I stayed out." He looked at the buildings around them. "As you see, we have much work here. Nearly every piece of wood in the city is ashes, and much of the stone is cracked from heat and needs replacing. The tetrarch also wants a new arch here, and his palace will be nearly as large as that of his father in Jerusalem. It will take years to build."

Joseph named some of the men he knew and asked if they were still around. Ananel responded solemnly. "Half of them were killed in the rebellion. Some of the others are here, but as prisoners, not freemen." He paused. "One doesn't work as hard when he knows it will only lead to his death. I need you both. You are the only real artisans I have seen all week."

"Have you seen Matthias ben Levi?"

"The giant? No, but I could use him. I have never seen a man who could work stone like him, but I heard he took to fishing and building boats in Capernaum."

"He did, but I have word he left during the rebellion."

"I remember he talked of joining them." Ananel shrugged. "If he was captured, he is either here or will be soon. There are still some prisoners at Aochis."

"How many prisoners work here?"

"Nearly five hundred. Another hundred are on the way. Once the streets are cleared and the heavy work done, the force will be culled and the strong sent to mines or galleys. They belong to the Romans, not to Antipas."

"The governor's mansion. Matthias and I worked on the pillars there—"

"The pillars are burned or scarred and will need to be replaced. It will be the palace of Antipas now, with much larger—better materials from what I hear. You are good at carving, and all the doors and shutters will need to be replaced, not to mention the capitals of the columns. You can make good wages here, Joseph."

"I will come as soon as I can. We have some roofs to repair at Nazareth before the winter rains."

"I will put you both to work on the gates you saw burned to ashes. In one week, then." He smiled and turned to someone asking for his attention.

"Do you think Matthias is here?" asked Micah as they walked west past the theater.

"If he is, we'll find him." They looked through the city for another two hours. It was filled with dust and the smells of ashes, limestone, sweat, and fresh-cut wood. Joseph thought he saw Matthias once, but when he approached and the man faced him, he could see he was wrong.

After an exhaustive search, they stopped and asked a guard if there were others working in quarries or forests.

"Except for the fifty just put to work on the aqueduct, what you see is what we're going to get," came the answer.

"How long ago were the fifty put to work?"

"They just arrived. Fighters headed for the galleys eventually, but for now they work for us."

Joseph felt hope but quashed it for fear of disappointment. If Matthias had been captured, he would be a candidate for the Roman galleys.

They left the city through the east gate and approached the aqueduct.

"Look," Micah said, pointing.

Matthias appeared from behind one of the piers that held up the aqueduct, a large stone in his arms. Joseph shouted his name. Matthias looked up and saw him, but looked away. Joseph tried to get close, but guards prevented it.

"Matthias," he yelled again. "Matthias, it's me, Joseph!"

Matthias dropped the stone at its appointed place and went for another, ignoring Joseph's plea. Joseph could see now that his eyes were swollen nearly shut and his lip had a large cut on it. He refused to look at Joseph, his entire body saying, *Leave me.*

Joseph tried again to get closer, to talk to his friend, but was prevented once more. "Matthias, where is Salome? Where are the children?"

A jerk of Matthias's shoulders signaled he had heard, but he still did not turn around.

Frustrated and fearful, Joseph looked around desperately for the head guard. Instead, he saw Marcus riding toward them on the road that led east. Joseph thought to intercept him just before he reached the aqueduct, but two of Marcus's men saw Joseph running frantically toward their leader and immediately cut him off with their horses. One came so hard that his animal hit into Joseph and knocked him to the ground. Before Joseph could catch his breath and get to his feet, the soldier was off his horse and had a sword at his throat.

Marcus looked down, recognized Joseph, and gave him a broad smile. "Leave him be," he commanded. The soldier backed away and sheathed his sword as Joseph got to his feet.

"Don't be so foolish as to approach me or any of my men that way again. This is still a lawless place, and there are those who wish to continue the fight."

Joseph apologized, then declared, "I have a request."

Marcus dismounted and handed the reins to one of his men as he looked up, apparently inspecting the aqueduct. "Speak your mind."

"There is a prisoner, one who can be put to better use. He works stone faster than any man alive and is a fine artisan. He and I did the work on the columns in the governor's house."

"And you wish him freed. I am sorry, but that is not possible. All these men were part of the rebellion. They will die as slaves."

"I wish only to have him work with me while he is here. I will guarantee he will not try to escape."

Marcus eyed Joseph carefully. "And if he does?"

"I will pay five gold pieces as payment for the loss."

Marcus's smile showed his disbelief. "Five gold pieces? But you do not make that much money in years of work."

"I can pay and will put the money in your care at once. If this man escapes, the money belongs to Rome."

Marcus considered a moment. "Which one is he?"

"There." Joseph pointed. "The big one."

Marcus turned to those guarding the slaves and asked a question in Greek, receiving an answer before turning back to Joseph. "Your artisan tried to escape today. You see the result."

"Were any Romans harmed in the escape?"

Marcus asked the guard before answering. "None."

"Then he did not try."

Marcus looked at Joseph again. "This man means a lot to you."

"He is like a brother."

Marcus called to the guard and instructed that he bring Matthias to them, then instructed several others to be ready if the prisoner tried anything foolish.

Matthias was brought forward, his hands and legs chained. He stared into the distance, refusing to look at Joseph.

"He does not seem to recognize you," Marcus stated.

"He is afraid that if he does, you will imprison me as well, aren't you, Matthias?"

Matthias looked at Joseph, his eyes filled with a mixture of relief and fear.

Joseph spoke to Marcus. "Tell him I am not in danger."

Marcus had a wry smile on his face and looked hard at Joseph. "Did you fight with the rebels?"

"I did not lie to you yesterday. I was in Egypt and returned only a few days ago."

Marcus had become good at reading men and had liked this Joseph from the first time they met. There was something about him . . . something good and honest. He would not lie; in fact Marcus wondered if he could lie. He looked at Matthias. "Your friend is in no danger from us. He wants you to work with him as an artisan, but I am reluctant. He has pledged five gold pieces as security. Are you willing?"

Matthias looked at Joseph in disbelief. "Five gold pieces? Joseph, where will you get—"

"Never mind, Matthias. I have it. God has been good to us. Will you promise not to try to escape if they let you work with me?"

Matthias blinked several times as if he might be dreaming. "Yes, you have my word." Then he looked at Marcus with cold eyes. "But if any more of your soldiers try to beat me, I will fight. I have had enough."

"It was reported you tried to escape," Marcus pointed out.

"My wife and children appeared along the march. I tried only to talk to them."

"I will look into it. For now, you have my word that unless you start something, my men will not harm you."

"Then Salome and the children are alive," Joseph said excitedly.

"Yes, I told them to go to Capernaum. Our friends . . ." He glanced at Marcus, realizing he may be endangering his family. "I am only a fisherman. Other fisherman will take care of them."

"Then you were there when the Roman legions came from the north. Did you fight with the resistance?" Marcus asked.

Matthias stiffened. "I did not, at least not until your men attacked my family. We fled, but your armies don't seem to care if a man carries weapons or not. They attacked us. I protected my family and helped them escape, but I was captured." Matthias looked at Joseph. "Find Salome. Take her with you. The boy is ill and needs care."

"Simon?"

"No, another son. Salome will explain." He looked at Marcus. "I accept the terms. I will not try to escape and will remain your slave as long as I am alive. Only the word of Rome will free me from this oath."

Marcus nodded, satisfied.

"I will return as soon as I can," Joseph indicated. "Until then, the overseer Ananel could use him."

Marcus nodded and ordered two of his men to have the irons removed by an ironworker and then take Matthias to Ananel. The two men looked skeptical, even fearful of the assignment, and one attempted to draw his sword.

Matthias smiled at him. "I have given my word."

The guard looked embarrassed and slipped the sword back into its sheath before taking Matthias by the arm and directing him toward the gate. Matthias looked over his shoulder and smiled at Joseph with tears in his eyes. Joseph nodded a reply.

"I will bring you the five gold pieces when I return," Joseph explained to Marcus.

Marcus nodded but said nothing. Joseph walked away, and Micah quickly joined him. They cut across the country to the stone highway that led from Sepphoris to Capernaum. Looking back toward the city, they did not see Salome, so Joseph began walking quickly to the east. They found her resting by the roadside, a child lying in her lap wrapped in a blanket. Mara sat next to her holding a baby, and Simon lay on the ground in front of them, sucking his thumb. Joseph had never seen a woman who looked as weary and despondent as did Salome.

As Joseph and Micah approached, she looked up, but it was Mara who first recognized Joseph and scrambled to her feet crying his name and wiping her tears. He stooped down and took her and the infant into his arms as Micah picked up a now-crying Simon. Joseph looked over Mara's shoulder at Salome and the child in her lap. He seemed asleep but pale. Salome tried to smile, but when she looked down at the child, her sobs prevented any happiness at their reunion.

It was then that Joseph realized the child was dead.

CHAPTER 29

Joseph wrapped the dead baby in the blanket, covering his face. He could not be much more than three years old. Salome had stopped crying and was feeding the infant Mara had been holding.

"Whose child is it?" Joseph asked about the baby in his hands.

"We don't know." Salome told him what had happened when they had gone back to Bethlehem. "We thought of going back, but with the rebellion, it hasn't been possible. Then we . . . we fell in love with him and . . . when we fled Capernaum, we escaped the Romans but it was cold at night. He has been sick . . ." Salome forced the tears back but could not finish.

Joseph felt sick to his stomach, the knowledge of what must have happened in Bethlehem hitting him as he stared at the lifeless bundle. He closed his eyes against the pain, then asked the obvious question. "Has there ever been any word of how many died at Bethlehem?"

"No." Salome looked at Joseph. "No one is even sure what happened or why. God blessed you to escape."

"Yes," Joseph softly answered. The soldiers had come looking for Jesus, apparently slaying every male infant they could find. The woman had saved her son; now he was gone as well.

"Matthias. They beat him when we tried to talk. Is he hurt badly?"

"No. Bruised, but well enough."

"When you did not come to Nazareth, he thought you might have died at Bethlehem, but he never gave up hope. Something inside told him you were all right and that you would not forgive him if he fought with Judas. He stopped my father from fighting as well, but

Father refused to leave Capernaum. The Romans came and we . . . we fled. I don't know what happened to Father." She took a deep breath. "What will happen to Matthias, Joseph?"

Joseph told her what he had arranged.

"Oh, Joseph, thank you! But . . . but where can you find five gold pieces?"

"Do not worry, Salome; I have it. Come, we should go. Your home waits for you in Nazareth. The houses in our part of the village were not damaged as badly, and though part of your roof is gone, it can be repaired easily. Until Matthias is free, we will see to your needs."

They began the walk, turning off the main road and climbing to Nazareth. When they walked through the gate of Joseph's courtyard, Mary was ecstatic.

Then she saw the bundle Joseph carried, and concern replaced the joy in her eyes.

* * *

Before allowing the dead child or anyone who had touched it entrance into Salome and Matthias's house, Mary and other women cleared it of all the unnecessary furniture, pots and jars, cushions, and other items so that they would not become unclean. Once again, it was a sober reminder of how death touched everyone and everything and how much they relied on God to live again.

While Salome and Mary cleaned the body with oil then bathed it, villagers again gathered and, as the pipers played, discussed the situation. Of course, when they learned that it was an infant son, there was even greater sorrow than usual, but few were as vocal as they might have been under different circumstances. All were exhausted from weeks of mourning.

The pipers played, and several friends quoted scriptures learned from childhood that they felt fit this unfortunate death.

Mary and Salome wrapped the small form in the burial shroud, the final step before the procession would begin. Salome kissed the tiny face one last time before lovingly putting the face napkin in place and completing the wrapping. Joseph felt the weight of this burial more profoundly than he had even that of Mary's mother or his own parents, the vision of other children dying in Bethlehem and needing a similar burial haunting him. So much sorrow! Surely God would have a great blessing in store for those who died in place of His own Son.

Joseph quickly wiped away the tears as Mary came over to him. "She asks that you carry the body to the tomb," she explained softly. Joseph put an arm around her, noticing that she looked as tired as he felt. Did she know? Had Salome told her about the child's mother? About Bethlehem?

"She also wants you to say something at the tomb," Mary whispered. Her lower lip quivered. "They died when Herod's soldiers tried to find Jesus, didn't they?"

Joseph squeezed her tighter. "She told you."

Mary could only nod before going back to Salome, leaving Joseph to his thoughts. What could he say of a child who had tasted so little of life? He had heard many eulogies, had even participated in those of his father and mother, but this time Joseph lacked words, and he prayed that God would help him.

The rabbi signaled that it was time, and everyone stood. Joseph entered and lifted the little wrapped body from the table, and the procession began. He was tired of death, tired of these marches up the hill to the place of so much pain. He felt numb to his toes and prayed for strength. There were no stops for eulogies or mourning—after all, what could be said of a child who had died so soon—and it wasn't long before they stood outside Matthias's mother's tomb.

Micah and several others stepped forward and shoved the hewn stone from the entrance. Joseph knew the bed for the deceased would be empty, ready for the child. Tombs were family burial places. When one died, the body was placed inside, and after sufficient time for the flesh to return to dust, someone would return and place the remaining bones in an ossuary that would be placed on a carved-out shelf in the back of the tomb, thus making the burial bed available to others. Matthias had returned some time ago and interred his mother's remains in a box he had carved from limestone.

Salome stood next to Joseph, Mary supporting her. Jesus looked over the crowd once more, but this time it was from the arms of his grandfather, who stood with the others, the pain of his own loss still written in the emptiness of his eyes and the deep creases of his face.

The boy laid his head on his grandfather's shoulder and patted his back as if to comfort him. Joseph felt a sudden thought take his breath away. Someday Jesus would make all this pain go away. The Messiah had come. He would save them from such woes and mourning! Peace came to Joseph's soul, and he bowed his head in thanks. Soon all these wounds would be healed. This child, and all of them, would live again.

Joseph took a deep breath. "How does one speak of the good of a life ended so quickly? He had no time to perform acts of bravery or kindness or to even leave posterity. He was here but a moment, and now he is gone."

He looked over the crowd. "Some among our people would say this child has no hope because he had no good deeds. Some would say that with his death he ends, that there is nothing more. But I say unto you, he lives, reunited with his mother who now holds him in her arms." He paused, words flowing into his mind. He had never felt so strongly about what he must say.

"But that is a spiritual life. There is more." He looked at Jesus. "Our Messiah will come and make it so. He will bring this child and his mother a new life. That is the greatness and glory of his work. It is not the sword that will make him King of all people, it is the new life he will give. It is the resurrection."

The chief elder's eyebrows lifted, as did those of several others, but Joseph ignored them, stepping to Salome and looking into her eyes before touching her arm gently and leaning closer so that only she and Mary could hear him. "Be at peace, Salome. Both God and this boy's mother love you for your tender care of this child while he was here. He and many other children that died will receive a glorious resurrection. I know this as surely as I live."

Salome put her arms around Joseph and thanked him, and Mary wiped away her own tears. She glanced around at those who had come—there were nodding heads of approval and agreement by most, but the elders of the synagogue and a few others appeared concerned and were murmuring to one another. For some, it would always be hard to hear words in conflict with their traditions.

"Go, place his body in the grave," Joseph said tenderly.

Carrying the small body, Salome went to the tomb's entrance, stooped, and entered. A moment later, she came out and several of the men rolled the heavy stone back in place.

It was then that Joseph noticed the hush among the attendees, the usual vocal mourning gone. In its place was a soft, peaceful, sacred feeling. Mary took Salome in her arms, and the rest of the villagers lined up to speak to her, Mara, and even Simon, in quiet reverence. Many went out of their way to pass by Joseph and thank him for his words, saying that they had never received such comfort.

* * *

After everyone was gone, Joseph sat by the grave to give thanks to God and to mourn all those other children who surely had died at Bethlehem. They were martyrs, all of them, both the children and the parents who had died trying to protect them. Someday he would tell Jesus of their sacrifice and how they had died while he lived.

After nearly another hour Joseph got to his feet and walked home slowly. He felt the cool night air and the calm that had overcome the village. Would they remember, or would the words, the ideas, leave them like dew in the morning sun? He had never seen the villagers so humble, but he feared that it was temporary, that things would return to normal far too quickly, that they would forget.

As he reached the gate of the courtyard, Mary was sitting on the bench waiting for him, her hands busy weaving a basket, a large oil lamp in the niche above her right shoulder.

The gate was open, and she did not see him at first so he had time to look more closely. She was crying. He knew the reason and, taking a deep breath, he stepped through the gate, closed it, and locked it for the night. She had already gotten to her feet and was standing behind him when he turned. He took her in his arms and let her cry.

In their house, the children of Bethlehem would be thought of often.

CHAPTER 30

Excluding the Sabbath, the next week was spent putting logs over the houses without roofs, including Joachim's, then placing planks, woven mats, earth, and finally plaster on top of them. Joseph checked on Salome each day of the initial seven days of mourning, and Mary and the other villagers brought her and the children food and other necessities and visited with them, but there was little talk of death and little of sadness to haunt them. Joseph's words were discussed often, receiving praise from all but the village elders, who seemed to grow more determined to reject his words as each day passed. Micah reported to Joseph that a number of them would be visiting him to ask questions, and on the fourth day after the death, they appeared while Joseph and Joachim were working on the last section of Joachim's roof.

The two of them came down and joined the elders in the shade of Joachim's tree. Joseph listened to their questions and answered those he could before the chief elder declared that Joseph's doctrine was not supported by the voice of the Torah and the sages and should not be taught. Joseph gave them a tolerant smile and kindly reaffirmed his position. He quoted the Torah, the prophets, the sages of Alexandria, the Psalms of Solomon, and the writings of Enoch to support both his teaching of the Messiah as the sacrificial lamb as well as King, and of the reality of the physical resurrection he would initiate. The elders seemed a bit astounded by Joseph's understanding and said they would consult further and let him know their determination. They did not visit again, and little was said to Joseph after that, but the confrontation chilled the air between him and them—a chill Joseph knew would last a long time.

After the days of cleansing, Joseph said good-bye to Mary, kissed a still-sleeping Jesus, and met Micah in the square to take their journey to Sepphoris. Though there was still much to do in the village, Joseph knew that he must tell Matthias about the death of the boy. He approached Sepphoris with dread and waited nervously as Matthias was brought to the front gate where they were to work. Of course, Matthias immediately asked about Salome and the children, and Joseph gave him both the good and bad news.

Matthias took the death of the boy hard, rending his clothes as was customary and going into loud mourning. This unnerved the soldiers assigned to watch him, and they quickly ordered the metal worker to stop taking off the shackles he wore every night.

Joseph calmed them, asking that he and Matthias be given some time, that one of his children had died. The soldiers, still apprehensive, finally agreed as Matthias gained control of himself. Joseph took Matthias aside and sat him down. Matthias was filled with anguish, even angry, but Joseph demanded he listen, then told him everything he had said at the entombing. By the time he finished, Matthias was listening carefully.

"I have never heard this before."

"You are not alone," Joseph replied.

"But you believe it?" Matthias asked fervently.

"Yes, it is the truth."

"Then I believe it as well." There was a long silence before Matthias spoke again. "You told me not to fight with Judas, that he was not the Messiah. You were right, and though we lost the boy, I am glad I trusted you. You also told me I would see the Messiah if I waited. Do you still say so?"

"Yes. The prophets tell of our day, of his being born now, and of his being raised up among our people."

"And you believe he will show himself in our lifetime."

"Yes, I know it. You will see him perform his work."

"Then he had best come soon. We were told that in two months' time our usefulness here will come to an end and we go to the galleys."

Joseph put a hand on his friend's arm. "You will not be a slave, Matthias. I promise you."

Matthias looked at the shackles on his feet and wrists. "A bold promise for a carpenter."

Joseph put an arm around his shoulder. "Just the same, I know you will be free. God has shown it to me in a dream."

Matthias blinked. "A dream?"

"You will be free, Matthias," Joseph repeated, clasping a hand on his shoulder. "Now, you are an artisan. You must prove you are more valuable here than behind the oar of a galley ship. Are you ready to begin, or do you wish to fulfill the days of mourning for your adopted son?"

Matthias got up. "If he lives in a better place, why should I mourn? Let us begin."

Joseph put him and Micah to work obtaining the last of the lumber from the siege tower, while he measured and prepared drawings for new gates. He also noticed that the heat from the fire had cracked some of the stones; they would need to disassemble part of the wall to repair them. Joseph told Ananel that he would need laborers, and a dozen men were provided. Matthias took the workers in hand and began the removal, while Joseph and Micah continued to lay out plans for the gates.

It was mid-afternoon, and they had stopped for something to eat and drink when Marcus found them. As he dismounted, Joseph pulled the small leather purse containing the five gold coins from the pocket of his robe and held them out to him. Marcus refused to take them.

"It would look like a bribe, but I will join you for food and some of that wine." He smiled. "Hang on to your coins, Joseph. I still think you are wrong about your friend, and your promise to pay will require those coins."

Both Jew and Gentile turned to see what Joseph would do. Joseph ignored them and pointed to the line of shade along the wall, and he and Marcus went there and sat down to the accompaniment of muffled gossip. Joseph knew he would hear about this indiscretion from his Jewish brothers later, but he did not care. How one dealt with Gentiles was a matter of choice in most cases, not a matter of law.

They sat with their backs against the wall a few cubits away from the others. Joseph handed him the wineskin, and Marcus drank.

"Your friends do not approve of you eating with a Gentile, especially one who keeps them in shackles," he commented, wiping his mouth with the back of his hand.

Joseph broke off some of the bread Mary had sent with him and handed it to Marcus, then drank from the wineskin. "God told Moses to beware of those not of our faith, lest they lead us astray and we go after other gods, but He also tells us we should not vex the stranger nor oppress him, but that he be unto us as one of our own kind. Some have forgotten this part of the law."

"And yet all Jews say that I cannot enter their temple because I am unclean."

"You are not of our faith; that makes you unprepared to enter. If you join our faith, you can be taught and prepared. By joining, you show your willingness to abide by the laws you find in God's house and that you are ready to make a covenant with the Lord. Then you are prepared and worthy. As some would say, at the point of covenant, you are no longer unclean."

"And yet even your friend scowls at you for this indiscretion," Marcus stated, looking at Matthias.

"He thinks of you as his enemy. By eating with you, I do not agree with him. That is why he scowls. He does not know you as I do."

Marcus looked up. "How can you know me? We have hardly seen one another."

"But each time I have seen you, I see good in you. Even my wife thinks you have a good heart." He bit off a piece of bread. "But I also wonder about you. If you are good, why do you hire yourself to evil men?"

Marcus chuckled. "Why do you work as a carpenter? Build homes for Antipas and his governor?"

"It is my trade, but—"

"Being a soldier is mine. I was raised with a sword in my hand just as you were with the hammer in yours. I am not of nobility, and my father is not rich, so there is no other life left to me."

"But that does not explain your path to Herod's army."

"I served under Mark Antony. When Augustus won the battle for power and Antony took his own life, I, like many other regular soldiers of middle rank, returned to Rome. Herod was there begging forgiveness, and so was I. Both of us received what we asked for, but I was not popular with Augustus's army—few men who sided with Antony were. Herod invited me to come and train his troops for him, and I told him that if the emperor Augustus agreed to it, I would come. The move probably saved my life. Most of Antony's soldiers, even those who were forgiven, were put on the northern frontier where they would die either at war or of old age."

"Then the forgiveness of Rome is false and not worth having," Joseph declared.

"All Romans, like all Jews, do not act the same."

"You are married?" Joseph asked.

"No, and my prospects are not favorable here. Most Jewish fathers see me as—how did you say it?—unprepared. They do not seem to want a Gentile for a son-in-law and, like your friend, are especially adverse to one who is a soldier."

"There are gentile women in Sebaste and Caesarea on the Sea."

"Yes, and I have met some of them. None seem as interested in me as they are in my position." He shrugged. "Maybe my luck will change." He did not speak, and Joseph could see he was thinking of something or someone.

"Who is she?" Joseph queried.

Marcus smiled. "You are perceptive. A woman in Rome. I only met her once or twice, but she is quite beautiful."

"Then you should pursue her."

"Would you give such advice if she were a Jew?"

Joseph stopped chewing. "Is she?"

"Yes, and her father is quite religious."

"Then find another woman. She cannot be yours."

"Your view of my blood quickly changes."

"It is not your blood but your religion. If he is a religious man, her father will never consent."

They dropped the subject and finished their bread and wine. "I like you, Joseph, but I think even your motives for sharing your food with me are tainted. You wish your friend's freedom, and you think I can get it for you. It is not possible."

Joseph smiled slightly. "You are right. If Matthias is to be free, you will play a part, but in the end, it will be gold and good work that will free Matthias, not friendship."

Marcus chuckled. "Yes, I suppose that is true."

Joseph drank from the wineskin as Marcus rode away.

"You should not eat with him," Matthias said. "He has the blood of Jews on his hands."

"Eating with him may save your life, Matthias. As to the blood on his hands, it was shed in time of war. Many died, but this man did not kill anyone who did not know they might die trying to kill him." He stood and handed the wineskin to Matthias, who hesitated only a moment before handing it back, wiping his hand on his tunic. "I won't drink from the same vessel as my enemy."

Joseph watched him go back to his work. He was bitter and angry, filled with hate. Joseph could only wonder if anything could change him.

* * *

For the next month, Joseph and his men worked on the gates, which were built of solid hardwood nearly eight inches thick and heavily reinforced with strips of the same wood inside and out. Their weight required that they be lifted into place by use of a derrick with ropes the size of Joseph's forearm and handled by nearly fifty men. As they were about to hoist the first into place and hinge it, Marcus and the chief architect rode up and dismounted, joining Joseph next to the derrick.

The chief architect complimented Joseph on the work. "But the king wants more. He wants them carved and covered in sheets of brass," the architect explained.

Joseph understood the difficulty of such a project but also knew the reason. Brass would not catch fire as easily as plain wood, nor would it splinter as fast, but he also knew it could benefit his pursuit of Matthias's freedom. "It will take time."

"You have a month to carve the exterior of the gates and prepare them to be raised. You can apply the sheets of brass after that time."

"I have only three men who have the skill necessary to please the tetrarch. To do it in a month, I need at least three more. And the application of the brass takes even more skill. Only I and the prisoner Matthias ben Levi know the art. With his help, it will take six months to finish the task. Fifteen months if I do it alone."

The meaning was clear to the architect. Matthias was needed. "He can stay for the carving. After that, we will see."

Joseph nodded, forcing back a grin. Matthias would not be taken to the galleys with the others. It was a small victory, but a victory just the same.

"Thank you," Joseph said.

"Do not thank me just yet," replied the architect. "There are no other carvers, and if these doors are not finished on time, your friend goes to the galleys and that will be the end of him."

Joseph nodded again. It was a tough assignment, but if they worked long hours and did not go to Nazareth every day for sleep, it could be done. "Agreed," he stated. "But I will not carve the images of men or beasts. Our law—"

"There will be no images." The architect smiled. "Just a relief of some kind, a pattern, but he intends this to be the main gate of the city and wants it impressive."

Matthias stood nearby and stepped closer. "Do you remember the doors we carved for the home of the rich man in Jericho?" he asked Joseph.

"Yes, something similar would look good here."

The architect and Marcus looked inquisitively at them.

"Fruit, grapes with vines, pomegranates. The symbolism is of a fruitful city."

"A fruitful city, one born to give sustenance and life. Yes, that would be a good symbol, one the tetrarch would like."

"It will be a good symbol only if the tetrarch makes it so," Joseph declared.

The architect frowned a bit. "I will expect a beautiful gate. If you do not provide it, there is no future for you in this city." He took the reins of his horse and mounted. "If you do, the tetrarch's palace will need doors and shutters, and your friend here might have a future, at least until the city is finished." He spurred his horse and rode back the way he had come.

Joseph told Matthias to position the doors for carving and send the workers to Ananel for other assignments along with the derrick. After eating, they would create a design and begin work. Then he turned to Marcus. "I have not seen you for more than a week. My meal is not nearly as interesting when you do not share it."

Marcus had come to break bread with Joseph at least every other day since their first meal. They had talked of many things, and Joseph's words were sincere. On several occasions Matthias had even joined them, though he said little and did not drink from the same wineskin.

"I have been to Jerusalem." He removed a food bag and a sealed jar from his saddle pack and lifted them. "Figs from Jericho, dried fish from Galilee, oil with seasoning from Arabia, wine from the hills of Italy, and fresh bread baked only an hour ago. We eat like kings."

"You have something to celebrate then," Joseph remarked.

"Ahh, does it show? I never was very good at keeping a secret."

They went to their usual place in the shade of the wall and sat to eat. Marcus poured oil into a small plate he had brought along, then sprinkled the spices over it. He handed the bread to Joseph, who said a quick prayer then broke off a piece and dipped it in the oil before placing it in his mouth.

"The food of the gods, no?" Marcus quipped.

"No, but the one God would be pleased," Joseph answered.

Marcus laughed and ate a piece of his own.

"Now, what is it we celebrate?" Joseph asked.

"You remember me telling you about the Jewish woman, Joseph?"

"Yes, and I remember telling you to find another."

"I have decided to marry this one."

Joseph smiled disbelievingly. "And this woman and her father, they are of the same mind?"

"Give me time, my friend." He removed cups and poured wine from the jar. Joseph took his and sipped. It was very good and very fresh for coming all the way from Italy. He drank another mouthful.

"Her father is a merchant from Greece now living in Jerusalem and a confidant of our new tetrarch. They intend to move here and help restore commerce to the region. When one of the chief stewards of Antipas comes to check on the progress, they will come with him. It is then I will propose marriage."

"Ah, so that is why the gates must be ready to raise in a month," Joseph said.

"Yes, and the streets must be clean and a residence provided. The architect is under a lot of pressure." After drinking some of his wine, he spoke again. "She is beautiful. Not as beautiful as your Mary, but beautiful just the same. Her hair is dark brown, her skin fair as the milk of goats, and her eyes the deep blue of the Sea of Galilee."

Joseph chuckled as he removed one of the figs from its wrapping. "You are either quickly drunk or you are in love, Marcus. Which is it?"

"The wine is strong, but not that strong!"

Joseph grew serious. "You are in for a disappointment, Marcus. You told me before that this Jew is a religious man. He will not allow you to marry his daughter on that count alone. Now you tell me he is a noble. You are not."

"Thanks for reminding me." He paused. "There is some hope."

"What do you mean?"

"I have mentioned my wish to the steward I spoke of. He is a greedy man, anxious to make alliances that will help him, and for my friendship he was willing to make inquiry for me. Her father is open to the idea."

Joseph shook his head. "The steward is playing with you. A noble, a Jew—"

"My blood concerns him less than it does even you. He was a sailor and given a ship after saving the owner of a fleet from drowning in the sea. Using this single ship he has turned it into a fleet unmatched in the Mediterranean, thus becoming rich and welcome in places most commoners will never see. But he still understands his roots and does not look for breeding as much as for ability."

"A good sign for you, but there is still his religion."

"That is why I wish to become Jewish."

Joseph nearly choked on his wine. Marcus slapped him on the back to help him catch his breath, and everyone within a hundred feet watched with amusement.

"Jewish? You?" Joseph croaked.

Marcus nodded, smiling. "It cannot be so difficult. Besides, I will relish only answering to one God after having to answer to so many. Do you realize how many—"

"Yes, yes, I've heard," Joseph interrupted impatiently. "But none of yours are nearly as demanding as ours. There are endless rules to be learned and—"

"And sacrifices to be made. I have lived in Jerusalem, Joseph. I know most of it."

"And you would still do it to win the heart of this woman, even the cutting?"

"Yes—" He looked up. "Cutting, what cutting?"

"Circumcision, the sign of the covenant. It is what makes you of our faith."

Marcus winced. He thought a moment, chewing on a fig. "Yes, she is worth it."

"No, you cannot do it for a woman. Such proselytes do not last. There has to be understanding and a change of heart about one God versus many. It takes a long time to reach this understanding."

"Then you are afraid I will remain an idolater even though I convert."

"Or that you will bring your idolatry with you and convert others away from the God who can give salvation, thus destroying their souls."

Marcus's face turned serious. "I have studied your religion a little and believe it more than I believe in the gods of Rome. I am ready to learn more. Isn't that enough to be given a chance?"

"But you did not want this before you thought there was a chance to marry this woman," Joseph commented.

Marcus smiled. "Some men need a little more motivation for the cutting than others."

"And this will not hurt your position as commander of the northern army of Antipas?" Joseph asked.

"In the sight of Antipas, it will help. With my men, my religion does not matter. Some of them worship gods foreign to me, some worship no gods at all, others are God-fearers of your religion, and several are proselytes. No, it will not hurt my position. And I am not sure I would care if it did." He paused, setting aside his food and leaning back on one elbow. "Look at me, Joseph. I am nearly thirty-eight years old and have no children to carry my name. What of value does a man leave behind but that of his loins? A family is where joy and happiness are found. With this woman, I can have happiness." He sat forward. "Will you help me?"

"Again you speak of conversion so that you can have the woman. I cannot help on that basis, but I will teach you and question you until two days before she comes. If I think you are sincere, I will speak to the elders of my synagogue."

"Thank you," Marcus said.

"Do not thank me until you receive baptism. Neither I nor the elders will let you enter the waters of purification or perform the cutting unless we are sure you are converted to God and His commandments. You will have a great deal to learn in a very short period, and I will have little time to spend with you unless we do it as we work."

"I will come when you work," Marcus agreed.

"Then I will ask you your first question. Are you willing to give up all gods but the God of Israel, to never rely on them, think of them, pray to them, or honor them, even with a stone placed on Merkulis along roads and highways? Are you prepared never again to eat of the feast offered to idols on their so-called holy days?"

Marcus did not have to think long, though he did have to think. "None of the gods of Rome mean anything to me. I will have no trouble leaving them for the God of the Jews."

Joseph smiled. "I am glad you have no feelings for the gods of Rome, but do not be too quick to believe it will be no trouble going after the God of the Jews." He paused. "Are you a moral man? Have you ever lain with a woman who was not your wife?"

Marcus gulped, and his face went a bit pale. "I cannot say that I am clean from this sin, no, but—"

"If you become a proselyte, you cannot do these things, ever, but through your immersion and sacrifice, God will consider your past atoned for. You will be clean again."

Marcus looked into the distance, then down at the ground. "It will be nice to be clean again."

Joseph was pleased with the answer. "Can you obtain scrolls of Torah, particularly Genesis and Deuteronomy?"

"Yes, the architect has copies of all five books."

"He is Jewish?"

"A God-fearer, I think."

"Read them and prepare questions. I will try to help you with answers."

They both stood, and Marcus left the food and wine and mounted his horse. "Thank you Joseph. I promise you, I will not ask for immersion and certainly not the cutting unless I am sure I can be obedient to your law."

"It is a promise I will hold you to. Now, what is this woman's name, and who is her father?"

"Her name is Serah, and her father's name is Seth." Marcus turned the horse and walked it to the gate, waving as he passed out of sight.

Joseph had not been able to speak. Seth. Could it be? He thought of that night on the road to Bethlehem, of Seth's words about moving to Jerusalem and eventually to Sepphoris. It must be the same man!

"What is it, Joseph?" Matthias asked as Joseph approached him.

"What? Oh, nothing."

"What of the rest of the food?" Matthias asked.

"Eat what you like, and give the remainder to Micah and the others."

"Did he drink from this?" Matthias asked, staring at the wine flask.

"No, but in a few weeks it may no longer matter whether he has or hasn't. His wish is to become a Jew."

Matthias's jaw dropped a bit in disbelief, Micah nearly choked on his fig, and others nearby stopped to listen. Matthias's jaw closed, then hardened.

"No Jew in his right mind would baptize him," he muttered.

"Ah, salvation is just for Jews, eh, Matthias?"

"Well, it isn't for men who kill Jews."

"Then God is a liar," Joseph declared.

Matthias was shocked at the response. "I did not mean—"

"God says that if a man is truly repentant, then circumcision, baptism, and the offering of the sacrifice bring His forgiveness, no matter the past and no matter the person. If the blood of the Lamb does not clean everyone, it cleans no one."

Matthias handed Joseph the wine, his eyes cold and hard. "He is both an idolater and a murderer. You and even God may forgive such men, but I will not." He went about his work.

Joseph glanced around him. It was obvious that Matthias's viewpoint was held by the majority of the laborers.

CHAPTER 31

The next several weeks were spent working from first light to last, and Joseph spent most nights at Sepphoris. He had gone home the first night and explained everything to Mary, who had given quick approval with two conditions. First, he must arrange for them to be present for the final hanging of the gates, and second, he must get permission for Salome and the children to spend a night with Matthias, alone and without interference. Joseph was not sure about either but promised he would try.

Marcus had been quick to grant the first and said he would send a special wagon to bring them to the city the morning of the final viewing of the gates. But he did not grant the second immediately, telling Joseph that he would have to get permission from the Roman responsible for the slaves, and that Joseph should say nothing to Matthias so that there would be no disappointment if it was not decided in his favor.

More than a week had passed with Joseph, Micah, and a few others bedding down outside the city gates and Matthias being taken back to his fortified camp, when Matthias arrived late one morning, a wide grin on his face. Matthias hadn't shown a smile since Marcus's decision to become a proselyte, so Joseph asked why he wore one now. In response, the giant gave him a grateful look and an embrace Joseph thought would surely break his ribs.

After getting his breath back, he asked what the hug was for.

A wagon was just coming out of the city, and Matthias pointed, then waved. Salome and the children waved back. "For them!" he said. "They came last night, and we were given the comfort of a house! Do you hear? How did you do it, Joseph? How? Tell us all!" he said loudly.

Joseph looked around him, the men eager to hear his response. "I am gratified by your appreciation of such a difficult task being done for you, and I would certainly like to take the credit, but I cannot. Though Mary was the one who asked that I request such a meeting for you and your family, I have not the power to make such a blessing come to pass. You know that."

The smile disappeared from Matthias's face as he realized there was only one man who could have done it. "Marcus," he said, his jaw hardening. "This changes nothing. He is still an idolater, and I will have nothing to do with him." He picked up his tools.

"And you are a proud fool who cannot see the goodness in a man because of your own blind hate," Joseph retorted angrily. "And if you do not thank the man, I will send you back to your prison and the galleys, glad to be rid of you!"

Matthias stiffened as Joseph picked up his tools and the two turned to their work.

"The rest of you, have you nothing better to do than listen to things that are none of your concern? Get to work!" Joseph ordered.

That afternoon, Marcus came to the worksite at the usual time. He said nothing of what he had done and did not even look at Matthias. Instead, he had more than his usual number of questions about Judaism, about the law. Some of his questions had been hard for Joseph to answer, and this day would be no exception.

Marcus was reading the Exodus scroll and had become enamored with Moses as the Egyptian prince turned convert. "See, even your greatest prophet is a proselyte! Well, sort of. He was of your blood but raised an Egyptian warrior, had even led armies and taken life, and God forgave him, then made him His spokesman."

"The word is prophet, not spokesman," Joseph corrected.

"As you wish, but isn't it a story of hope, especially for a man like me?" Marcus wondered.

"A man like you?"

Joseph glanced at Matthias and could tell from his posture that he was paying more attention to Marcus and Joseph's conversation than to his work.

"A soldier, one who has to take life because of his orders."

"Do you think of your killing as murder?"

Marcus hesitated before answering. "Not until now."

"And why do you think so now? After all, God has sanctioned war, has even commanded it."

"Because God does not command Roman troops." He shook his head slowly. "What we have done has been for power and glory, nothing more. That makes it murder."

"But you did not know it was murder until now. God will not hold you accountable for something you did not know to be wrong."

"Then He forgives ignorant sin, even murder?" Marcus asked.

"Yes, but there are steps to arriving at that forgiveness. Even though you sinned in ignorance, you still sinned. That must be cleansed and atoned for. That is why purification and the offering of sacrifice are so important. You will be clean from the blood of others and worthy of God's Spirit and blessings."

Marcus seemed to be thinking. "It will be nice to feel clean, but it is hard to understand how water and the blood of lambs and goats can take away the stain of a man's blood."

"They can't. They are symbols, nothing more." He finished the part of the carving he was working on and told one of the men to polish it. "Israel's greatest sin is to have lost sight of those symbols, to believe lambs and goats can atone for us. Only one can make that atonement. Only his blood can wash away our sins, and only if we accept his sacrifice."

"You speak as if an actual being will pay for sin," Marcus stated.

"The Messiah, the very Son of God, he will pay," Joseph answered. "In some way I do not fully understand, he will be bruised and killed for us before his final reign." Joseph felt the weight of it once more, the picture of a small boy roaming the hills around Nazareth filling his head. He did not relish these thoughts and even wondered at times if it was all just the dream of a deluded mind. It was the *how* that eluded him, and he had come to wonder if it was even meant to be understood by men. All he knew was that it would be, and though the suffering it would cause their son oppressed Joseph, he knew it was essential. It was something he seldom shared with others, both because they would not understand and because it pained him. He had not shared it with Mary, though he felt she knew at least some of it. Now, while Jesus was still young and far removed from any such mission, was not the time to face or think of such a thing.

Shoving the thoughts of the boy aside, Joseph continued. "When you are immersed, you will be immersed in his blood; when you see the lamb slain, you will be watching his death. Give thanks, Marcus. Give thanks that he will die to make us all clean and trust that it will be enough. When you do, God will assure you that your sin will be removed by the holy acts of the Messiah."

Marcus sat silent for a long time before speaking. Even Matthias and Micah and others who listened seemed contemplative, wondering at the words and how they could be true.

"And if I am forced to kill again?" Marcus asked.

"Killing to protect others is the will of God; killing for power is murder. Let that be your guide."

Marcus only nodded, got to his feet, and untied his horse. He was about to mount when Matthias stood, wiping his sweating hands on his tunic. "Marcus Vitellius, my wife and children—"

"No thanks are necessary, Matthias," Marcus interrupted. "I wish only that I could do more." With that he rode back into the city.

After that day, Matthias quit brooding and listened more carefully to Joseph's teaching of Marcus, as did others. The workers soon were spending lunchtime sitting around Joseph and Marcus, listening and asking questions. Even the guards seemed enthralled with Marcus's retelling of what he was reading and the questions it elicited. They were days Joseph would not soon forget, and when he and Marcus rode to Nazareth the night before the gates were to be hung, he knew Marcus was ready.

* * *

The horses stood on the side of the hill that led to Nazareth, and Marcus released the plug on the waterskin he was carrying. He did not speak until he had finished drinking and handed the skin to Joseph.

"Do you think I am ready?" Marcus asked.

"As ready as anyone. You have read Torah, studied it, discussed it, even memorized much of the law. More important, your heart has changed, Marcus. God's Spirit is with you."

"I cannot argue that I feel different, but I am also frightened."

"Frightened?"

"I have been a man of blood all my life. I have taken lives I should not have taken. It was done in the heat of battle, and it is only a matter of time before that heat will be thrust on me again. I fear that the man I was will rule the man I want to be, and in the moment I strike down another in my anger or my lust for blood, I will lose my soul."

Joseph reached over and gripped Marcus's shoulder. "You must trust that God will help you."

"I trust that He will warn me, but I fear I may ignore Him, like so many I read of in Torah."

They started up the road again and soon arrived in the village.

Mary did not recognize Marcus at first as he was dressed in a white tunic and brown robe fashioned after the manner of the Jews. As she watched the two men lead the horses into the courtyard, Jesus ran to Joseph, who immediately took him into his arms and then gave in to his pleas for a horseback ride up the hill. Marcus and Mary watched them go, then Mary invited Marcus up to the roof to watch father and son trot the beautiful animal along the rim of the hill above the village.

"You do not seem as afraid of me as you were the day we first met," Marcus commented.

Mary remembered. "Joseph has taught me many things since then. A Gentile does not seem so fearsome as he once did."

"Nor so unclean?"

Mary chuckled. "That too, but I see something different in you now, Marcus. You have changed."

Marcus blushed. "Thank you. It pleases me that you would see such a thing in a man like me." He looked over the village. "I see little of the damage done by the war."

"Most of the injury that remains is in the hearts of the people. Many have found peace because of the words Joseph spoke at the funeral of the young child cared for by Salome and Matthias. He continues to speak of these things at the synagogue, and his under-standing of death and resurrection gives strength to all of us."

"Your husband puts many learned men to shame, Mary. Has he always been like this?"

Mary smiled. "He has always been a good man and one who has tried to study, understand, and obey the law, but since our marriage, his thirst for this is unquenchable. It has led him into new paths of thinking, paths that are not always in agreement with others."

"He is a master teacher. Who could resist his words?"

"Some of the elders of Nazareth and a few others," Mary sighed. "Tradition is a hard schoolmaster, Marcus. Most of these men are followers of men like the sage Shammai, who is very strict in his interpretation of the law. They will not be quick to accept a Gentile as a full proselyte. They think you are natural idolaters and will return to it when the newness of our beliefs wears away or when it is no longer advantageous to believe. In their way of thinking, your very creation as a Gentile makes you less in the sight of God. You can never be equal to a Jew and thus never receive God's full blessings. Your idol-atry attests to this and makes you unclean. To touch you or anything you have touched makes others unclean. To even speak to you as I am makes me unclean in their eyes. It is these teachings that made me afraid of you the first time we met, and they have been taught in this village all my life and even during the life of my father. It is not easy to change them."

"And yet Joseph never seems to have believed them," Marcus pointed out.

"He did, a long time ago, but his father died when he was young, and he had to leave the village to find work to support his mother and sister. He has heard the teachings of others, such as Rabbi Hillel, who takes a different view. He formed a different opinion about many things, but God has continued to school him, most recently while we were in Egypt. His teaching is correct, and unless they are very prideful, people see his wisdom. Unfortunately, pride has always been a weakness in Israel."

"And what does he think of a man like me?"

Mary looked at him. "You already know the answer to that, Marcus, or you would not be here, but I will tell you this: he hates your idols and would rather see you dead than have you return to them."

The horse came into the courtyard, and Jesus looked confidently at Mary and Marcus. "Look, Mother. I am guiding the horse."

"I see that. You are a very big boy," Mary called. She was already halfway down the steps, Marcus just behind her.

"I will wash and change into clean clothes, then we will go," Joseph stated. He slipped from the horse, ready to lift Jesus down, when Marcus spoke.

"Leave him be. I will care for the horses. He can help me. You probably have things to discuss with Mary," Marcus said.

"There is dry grass in the manger, and you can put them in the stable. It is small, but strong," Joseph explained.

Marcus led the two horses toward the stable, Jesus still riding one.

"I think he is ready," Mary declared happily.

"Let's hope the elders agree." He put his arms around her and gave her a long kiss. She laid her head on his shoulder.

He stepped back and looked at her growing abdomen. "How much longer?"

"Not long. Will you be disappointed if I do not go with you tomorrow?"

"Not if it might endanger the child. Do you want me to wait? Matthias and the others can raise the gate."

"No, I will send for you when it is time." They went inside the house where Mary already had hot water waiting for Joseph to clean himself.

"How are Josiah and your father?" Joseph asked. Josiah's arm had healed, but he had limited use of it and was relearning many things.

"Josiah gets better use of it every day, but he is still hurting inside because of his stupid actions and the grief they have caused. Perhaps you could talk to him again."

"When the gates are hung, I will be here a week without interruption." He scrubbed his hands, arms, and face, turning the water brown.

"Father is fine. He finished sowing the grain this morning and tends the sheep this afternoon. Dinah cares for Ruth and helps Josiah as well."

"And Salome?"

"Wonderful." She has never been the same since that night she and the children spent with Matthias. She has great hope, Joseph, but I fear it will be dashed to pieces by Roman pride."

"I told you when you made the request it might end this way, Mary. Do you remember your reply?"

"To have had hope, even for a short time, is better than to have had none at all."

"And so it is," Joseph responded.

He finished washing, dressed, and went outside to find Marcus and Jesus still caring for the horses. Marcus was lifting a hoof, explaining its shape and how it must be kept trimmed in order for the animal not to acquire an injury.

"Where did you get them?" Jesus asked.

"This one," he pointed to the brown horse Jesus and Joseph had been riding, "belongs to my second in command. He is a horse from Italy, strong, but not very fast. This one," he petted the neck of the black, "is an Arabian, given to me as a gift. Very swift, but he takes a firm hand."

"It is a wonderful gift," Jesus said. "I was given gifts once, by men from—"

"Jesus, it is time to feed the lambs. Will you take care of it quickly, please?" Mary interrupted suddenly.

"Are you ready?" Joseph added Marcus.

"I suppose so."

"You will return for food and a night's sleep," Mary said matter-of-factly.

"You are kind, but I must return tonight. Our guests arrive early tomorrow, and I must make sure everything is ready. Will you come?"

Mary touched her bulging stomach. "I think not, but Salome and the children will, I am sure. And Marcus, thank you very much for arranging for them to see Matthias. It has given her great hope."

"I pray that she will not be disappointed," Marcus replied.

They went into the street and walked to the town square, entering the synagogue. The elders were sitting along one wall and immediately arose and bowed slightly, one pointing at a bench they had drawn to within a half dozen feet of them.

The questions began; they were grueling, and Marcus could not answer all of them. Sweat broke out on his forehead and remained for the two hours they were there, but in general, Joseph thought his friend did very well. Finally, the elders looked at one another, nodded, and the final questions came.

"Do you do this for marriage or for political advantage?"

Marcus looked down. "It started out because of a woman, but it is not that way now. Joseph has made me see that his religion and his God are a way of life, one that brings peace and happiness and one that I want to live all my days." He took a deep breath. "As for political advantage, I will also be honest. I weighed the issue and saw no disadvantage. But as I have studied and weighed it more carefully, I find that to live this religion will require some change that may be looked upon with distaste by my fellow soldiers and those in authority over me. It may require that I retire from my profession."

The elders looked at one another a bit surprised. "This is easy to say," one responded. "But when their livelihood, their position, even their relationship with family are actually in danger we find that most Gentiles cannot give up what they have gained."

Marcus looked at him carefully before answering. "No one, especially Joseph, has ever said it would be easy." He looked at Joseph. "But I trust that God will give me strength."

"And you will give yourself to circumcision?"

"And purchase a heifer for the sacrifice, yes. I will do everything that is needed. Until I do, I cannot be clean of my sins, and the cutting is a small price to pay for such freedom."

There was the usual stroking of gray beards accompanied by wrinkled brows and whispering. Joseph felt especially anxious at the plodding pace of the ceremony, though he knew it would take at least this long and maybe days more. He knew Marcus's heart. Marcus was ready, and to see the elders delay was painful for Joseph. How could they refuse Marcus? And yet Joseph knew there was still that chance. These were exceptionally conservative men, and their nitpicking ways could not be changed even when faced with an obviously good man.

After a few more minutes of deliberations, one of them stood and cleared his throat. "You have studied much, and we feel you are as prepared as any Gentile who has come to us asking for admittance into the faith of Israel. But you are still a Gentile, and our experience tells us that you need more time to think upon your decision. We declare a one-year period of trial as a God-fearer. Then we will meet again." He bowed slightly as if nothing further was needed, and Joseph found himself on his feet, objecting.

"I see no precedent in the law for such a decision," he declared.

They all looked at Joseph in surprise. The spokesman smiled condescendingly. "The law is subject to our interpretation, Joseph. You know that. And we have decided—"

"Your interpretation goes contrary to established law and is therefore of no effect," Joseph replied.

Marcus wasn't sure this was a good time to argue with such men and was about to object, when Joseph spoke. "You have one question to ask that you have not. On this question you must base your decision."

"But we have asked all the questions we intend to ask," retorted the elder.

Joseph bowed slightly. "Then you have erred and must reconsider." He turned to Marcus, saying, "Do you know that this is a time of affliction in Israel? That they are distressed and suffer?"

Marcus looked at Joseph, then at the floor. "Yes, I know, and I am unworthy to stand in their presence because of it. I can only hope to help heal their wounds."

Joseph turned to elders. "This is a repentant man who seeks salvation through God and His law. To delay him may bring condemnation, both upon him and upon us. This is neither wise nor lawful. God said through Moses, 'And if a stranger sojourn with thee in your land, ye shall not vex him. But the stranger that dwelleth with you shall be unto you as one born among you, and thou shalt love him as thyself; for ye were strangers in the land of Egypt: I am the Lord your God. Ye shall do no unrighteousness in judgment.'"

The spokesman's face blushed scarlet, and Marcus thought surely he would raise his staff and strike Joseph for his affront, but he did not. Instead, the others tugged him farther to the back of the room and they counseled again. It was more heated this time, and Marcus overheard snippets of the conversation. At least two of them were now more against his entrance than before, but there did seem to be some support. Finally, the elders faced Joseph and another spoke, the first obviously too angry to do so.

"The sages tell us that it is on account of the Gentile's natural depravity that we should be cautious. But we see you have good feelings toward this man, and as friend of a proselyte you are loved by God. However, if this man betrays Israel and turns away from our God, his sins will be upon your head, Joseph ben Jacob. They will not be upon ours." He looked at Marcus. "If you are ready to accept our fate, to die for us as we die for one another and for God, you may prepare for the cutting of the flesh."

Marcus stood, his mouth dry, a sudden doubt flitting through his head at the word *cutting*. He licked his lips and stiffened his back, then replied, "I am ready."

* * *

Joseph helped Marcus onto his horse. They had returned to the house, and Mary had given them some ointment for his wound. Marcus had applied it in private and nearly fainted at the pain. Only the actual cutting had been worse. But finally the sting had worn away, the ointment deadening the pain, and Marcus felt enough relief to ride.

"Will you be all right?" Joseph asked.

Marcus handed him a small purse. "I have been cut and immersed in your baths. If I die in anguish on the way to Sepphoris, purchase my heifer and offer it for my sins. I would not want this horror to be in vain."

Joseph chuckled and took the money. "Now you see why we do it while our sons are still young."

He took Joseph's hand in a shake of friendship. "Is God pleased, Joseph?"

"He is pleased, Marcus, and He notes your sacrifice. Remember this pain. It is only a small part of what our Messiah will suffer for you someday. Sleep well tonight, my friend, sleep well."

Unable to speak, Marcus gave him a smile and tighter grip of the hand, then turned his horse up the road and disappeared into the darkness.

Mary stepped to Joseph's side. "I went to the well for water. Some say you berated the elders."

"Already the rumors begin."

"Others say you were right to do so." She put her arm around his waist, and they went back into the courtyard. He locked the gate while she waited near the steps that led to the roof, then they went up. There was a full moon, and they could see the dark shadow of Marcus and his horse walk the rim of the hill and disappear.

"The elders and I have had our disagreements, but tonight enemies were made," Joseph reported.

"Unless God was one of them, they are of little consequence." She turned into him and laid her head against his shoulder. "You did the right thing, and I love you for it, Joseph. Jesus has a good example to guide him. Because of you, many in the village see things differently. Except for a few whose pride stiffens with age, there is great peace here. God's wrath has humbled them." She pulled at his hand. "Come, time for bed. You must rise early." They went down the steps and into the house, closing the door behind them.

"Have you decided on a name for our newborn?" She laid a hand on her stomach as they passed into the sleeping room.

"Jacob, or James, as Marcus would say." He sat down on the bed to remove his sandals.

"The patriarch of Israel. It is a good choice. And if it is a girl?" She had removed her robe and lay down next to him.

"She will be named after you," Joseph answered. "But it is a boy."

"Another angel has told you this?"

He laid his ear against her stomach. "No, he speaks to me. Can't you hear it? 'Hello, Father, this is your son speaking. Call me James.'"

She laughed. "You have very good hearing. I carry him, and I have never heard such a voice."

"We men understand one another." He kissed her lightly. "He will be a good son, a righteous man, and a support to his elder brother." He lay flat on his back, and Mary ran her fingers through his hair.

"Do you think it will be easy for them, being the brother or sister of such a child?" Mary asked.

"No, it will not be easy." He yawned. "But they will not see him for who he is, Mary. Not right away. God will show them when they are ready." Joseph's eyelids closed.

"They will be very intelligent and strong, just like their father. If they are girls, they will have your charm and, hopefully," she added slyly, "my beauty." Mary expected some kind of answer but received none. She looked down at him, his mouth already falling open. He was sound asleep. She removed his robe and covered him with a blanket. He would not be happy with himself for missing his prayers, but Mary was sure God would understand.

She felt the pain in her lower abdomen and grimaced, lying back and waiting. The pains had been regular occurrences this day, and she was sure the baby was not far away from delivery. She remembered Jesus' birth and glanced at Joseph. She was afraid he would not be here for this one. His work in Sepphoris was providing grain for more than just the three of them. Even though the tetrarch was sending more supplies from Jerusalem and Caesarea, they were not free, and there were many in the village who would starve if the few who could find work did not provide for them. Already Joseph's wages had bought fruit and other items needed for survival.

Mary felt as big as a house, her abdomen stretched far beyond the size of her pregnancy with Jesus. Either this was a very big child or she was carrying twins. She was sure she was overdue now and that if she did not have this child soon, it would become difficult and even dangerous for both of them. She had begun praying that God might soon help her push the child into the world.

When the early contraction ended, Mary struggled to her feet and went into the main room to check on Jesus. She was not completely surprised to see him lying awake, staring at the ceiling. She sat down on the edge of the bed and ran her fingers through his dark, curly hair. She had found him like this a lot lately. It didn't seem to affect his health or the level of his energy; he just didn't seem to need as much sleep.

"Can't you sleep again?"

He shook his head.

She kissed him on the forehead.

"Sing me one of the psalms, Mother."

"Which one would you like?"

"Israel and the Shepherd."

Mary hummed the tune to warm her voice then began, her soft soprano filling the room. "Give ear, O Shepherd of Israel, thou that leadest Joseph like a flock; thou that dwellest between the cherubims, shine forth. Before Ephraim and Benjamin and Manasseh stir up thy strength, and come and save us."

She hummed softly again, stroking Jesus' hair, noticing his eyes getting heavy. She skipped many of the verses, going to those she knew he enjoyed most. "Return, we beseech thee, O God of hosts: look down from heaven, and behold, and visit this vine; And the vineyard which thy right hand hath planted, and the branch that thou madest strong for thyself. It is burned with fire, it is cut down: they perish at the rebuke of thy countenance. Let thy hand be upon the man of thy right hand, upon the son of man whom thou madest strong for thyself. So will not we go back from thee: quicken us, and we will call upon thy name. Turn us again, O Lord God of hosts, cause thy face to shine; and we shall be saved."

Jesus' eyes were closed and his face relaxed. Mary adjusted the blanket to cover his feet, then kissed his ear lightly and told him she loved him before standing and looking down upon him, wondering if he knew that the psalm was about him. *No,* she thought, *he is surely too young.*

She blew out all the lamps except the small one in the niche near their bedroom door. Entering her room but leaving the door open, she readied herself for bed, had her prayers, then slipped in next to Joseph and closed her eyes.

* * *

Mary did not wake until Joseph stirred next to her, slipped from bed, and dressed. She could not believe it was morning already and had to force her feet from underneath warm covers to the rug covering the cold floor. There was a definite chill this morning, and she thought she could hear water dripping from the roof. She went into the living area, where Joseph was starting a fire in the clay stove.

"It is raining." She yawned.

"Yes, but there are stars as well. It should not last." The kindling leaped into flame, and Joseph signaled for her to come closer and get warm.

He put his arms around her from behind and nuzzled her neck. "I will return tonight and will not leave for a week. I have work helping people here prepare their houses for winter, and I have a wagon to repair for hauling wood for the village, and—"

"And a son to welcome into the world. He will come soon, I know it."

"Good." He kissed her on the neck, and she turned into his arms.

"Be careful, Joseph. The roads will be muddy and slippery, and the horse could easily fall, and—"

He kissed her. "I will be fine." He turned and was gone.

When she heard the horse's hooves on the stones of the courtyard, she opened the door only to have Jesus suddenly appear, duck under her, and step outside, his eyes still filled with sleep but eager to say good-bye. He stepped into the rain without thinking, and Mary pulled him back to the shelter of the door. Joseph saw him and came close enough to take Jesus in his arms and give him a hug, the horse just behind him. Jesus reached out and petted the already damp hair of the gelding's face. Joseph gave Jesus to Mary and mounted, waved, and disappeared out the gate.

Mary shut the door and put Jesus down. He ran back to his bed and snuggled beneath the covers. She was tempted to do the same but resisted. There was much to do.

CHAPTER 32

The morning dawned a bit bleak, the clouds of winter finally beginning to arrive, but by the time Joseph arrived at the worksite, the rain had stopped. As the sun peeked over the hills and under the clouds to the east, Joseph, Matthias, and a dozen others worked feverishly to wipe away the water from the oiled surface of the wooden gates and move them into place for raising by the crane.

"The work is exquisite," Micah remarked. "The architect says it is the finest he has seen."

They heard the hooves of Marcus's horse before they saw him come through the gate. He rode slower this morning, obviously uncomfortable in the saddle, then dismounted carefully before approaching a grinning Joseph.

"I see God has kept His promise," Joseph quipped.

"Promise?" Marcus asked, his face slightly contorted.

"That the Gentile will suffer as the Jew." He chuckled. "Has the lady of your dreams arrived?"

Marcus's countenance brightened. "The entire party is at the home of the chief architect. I will bring them here shortly. This afternoon, I meet with her father."

"Does he know of your conversion?" Joseph queried.

"The steward of Antipas will tell him this morning. He goes out of his way to help me reach my goal." He paused. "Of course, there will be favors asked in return. There always are." He looked at the gates. "The quality of your work has pleased the chief architect. If everything goes well this morning, I think he will support your effort to keep Matthias here."

"What about the Romans?"

"With the need of slaves in the galley ships, the price will be high." He looked at the towers and walls to be sure his guards were getting in place.

"How much, Marcus?"

"Ten pieces of gold."

"Ten?" Joseph sighed in disbelief. "But I cannot—"

Marcus smiled. "Do not worry, the support of the steward will reduce the price. God will provide." He looked at the gates. "I have never seen such fine work, not even in Rome. You are a master carpenter, Joseph."

With care, Marcus mounted his horse, "Get your men in place. I go to bring them. "

Joseph gave the orders, and everyone scurried about, finishing just as the procession came through the gates. Marcus and his men were out in force, but the steward had a personal guard of a dozen men as well, surrounding their charge as if he were the king's gold. Joseph could not see the steward clearly, his view blocked by Seth of Athens and his wife, their fair-haired daughter Serah behind them. Joseph smiled with satisfaction, both at seeing Seth again and at seeing that Marcus rode at Serah's side.

The group rode along the wall, and as they came to a halt, the soldiers positioned themselves around the charges. It was then that Joseph saw the steward.

He leaned over to speak to Matthias but was too late.

Matthias spoke first. "Crispus. Well, well, it seems my old friend has made his place in the world."

Joseph felt sick. "Matthias, do you want your freedom?"

"Yes, of course, but—"

"You must keep still, do you hear me? Not a sound unless he speaks first, and then you do it with respect! Do you understand?"

Matthias gave a wry smile but said nothing, leaving Joseph in fear. "If this goes well, you may get your freedom. If it does not, you will go to the galleys. I swear if you so much as smile crooked at him, I will hit you with my hammer."

Matthias seemed stunned, but the smile disappeared, and he looked confused but nodded. "I . . . I don't know what to say. My freedom? But how can this be?"

"This is not the time for questions. Just do as I say."

"Yes, yes, I'll keep quiet. I will beg if I need to. Freedom? Is this possible?" he questioned eagerly.

The dignitaries had all dismounted and were inspecting the panels, admiring the work without noticing Joseph and Matthias; Joseph hoped it would remain so.

The architect gave the order to put the panels in place.

"Keep your head down and stay on the scaffolding unless you are forced to come down," Joseph said to Matthias.

Matthias nodded, and they both went to work. Joseph checked everything one last time, signaled, and the slaves began pulling. The first panel lifted and was slowly swung into place. Matthias had climbed the scaffolding and was standing near the top hinge directing the panel until it was positioned. There were two parts to the hinge, one attached to the gate, the other to the stone wall. These had to be carefully matched so that heavy steel pins could be driven through both parts, attaching them. Metal workers would then heat and bend the pin so that it could not slide free or be removed.

Joseph watched as both gates were soon in place. The sun peeked through the clouds at the opportune moment and glistened off the oiled wood design, accentuating the patterns repeated over and over in the smaller panels within each gate. It was impressive, and the loud gasp by those who had come to see indicated their great pleasure.

Joseph stood near the gate as the steward approached to congratulate him for his work, the architect and Seth of Athens behind him. Marcus stood to the side, Serah at his arm.

"Well done!" exclaimed the steward. "Antipas will be very pleased." Then he stopped, a curious look to his face. "I know you, don't I?"

Joseph bowed slightly. "I worked in this same city before its destruction."

"Ahh, well, it doesn't matter." He turned to the architect. "I am told there were others who should be congratulated. Who are they? Bring them forward," he insisted, enjoying his moment of condescension.

Joseph signaled for Micah to come forward. Unaware of any problem, Micah looked up at the scaffold and called out the name that made Joseph cringe.

"Matthias, come down."

"Matthias?" the steward said. His eyes narrowed. "Ahh, now I remember. You worked with Matthias ben Levi on the governor's mansion. The columns." He smiled evilly. "Yes, I remember." He looked up at the scaffolding. "The big one fastening the hinges. I should have recognized him sooner, but the garb of a slave . . . Tut, tut. What has the man come to? Come down, Matthias. Let us congratulate you! Come down, come down!"

Matthias appeared and quickly slithered down the framework, brushing off his hands when he stood in front of Crispus. "Crispus, nice to see you again."

Crispus turned to the architect and Marcus, who stood a few feet behind him. "*This* is the man you wish to free?"

The architect looked stunned at the tone, but if Marcus had any reaction, he did not show it. Seth, his wife, and his daughter all looked confused, unsure of what was happening. Marcus looked at Joseph more carefully, then nodded recognition and shrugged as if to ask for some explanation. Joseph could do nothing now but ignore him.

The architect answered, "As you can see, his work—"

"This man is an enemy to the state and should be sent to the galleys immediately!"

"He is not the only one who knows your past." Joseph said it quietly enough that the architect, standing a few feet behind Crispus could not hear.

Crispus looked down his nose at Joseph. "No, he is not. Antipas is not as particular as his father about a man's past, especially when he sees the value a man like I can bring to him. I have told him about my family, and he does not care. So, you see, your blackmail will no longer work." He sneered, then turned haughtily away, speaking to the guards. "Put him back in chains and add his friend to the lot. They are both criminals."

Seth was about to step forward but was preempted by Marcus, who stood close enough to hear the conversation and no longer held back. "I will vouch for both these men. Neither are criminals, and both are needed on this project."

"If he is not a criminal, why is he a slave?" Crispus asked with obvious disdain.

"Because he fought Roman soldiers trying to harm his wife and family. They were fleeing at the time," Marcus said.

"That is what he told you? And the soldiers . . . How many of them lived to agree with this . . . this monster?"

"I do not need his verification. He has been vouched for, and I believe him."

Crispus stepped closer to Marcus. "Your newfound religion biases you, centurion. I want these men in chains! Do it or Antipas will learn—"

Joseph watched as Marcus's face hardened and his eyes turned cold, but he did not speak. There was confusion in his eyes, a struggle. Standing next to him, Serah watched, her eyes curious, obviously wondering what he would do. Even Seth did not act, waiting to see how this man who seemed to love his daughter might act.

Marcus lifted his shoulders. "I believe Antipas would be most unhappy if artisans such as these were sent to the galleys, especially when he sees their work and knows their next assignment will be his own palace."

Crispus had only grown in pride since their last meeting, and Joseph could see it rise through his neck and into his ears. "You dare question me?"

"I do. You are one of the king's stewards, but I am the commander of his northern forces. I know who his enemies are and who they are not. Do not come here and try to force your personal wishes on us or these people."

Crispus became nervous. He was thinking, wondering if his position was secure enough to counter the request of the tetrarch's hand-picked commander for Galilee. He seemed to decide, his chin lifting. He turned to Marcus, his eyes flaring. "He is to remain a prisoner until Antipas comes. If you do not have the stomach for it, my men will see that his chains are put in place!" He signaled to his guard, and they dismounted. Marcus gave a quick nod to his second in command and his soldiers immediately reacted and cut off the steward's guards.

"You have no authority over such matters," Marcus said coldly, stepping to within easy reach of Crispus, his hand on his sword. "Tell your men to step back or I will have your head in my hand before the first draws his weapon."

Crispus stiffened with angry pride, but the fear in his eyes showed that he was once more defeated. He wanted vengeance, but he wanted life more.

"Very well, centurion." He waved with his hand, and his men stepped back. With a sneer, he then turned to the nobleman and bowed. "I was wrong about this man. His protection of this assassin is indefensible and will be brought before Antipas. He is no friend of our tetrarch or of Rome. He is not worthy of your daughter, no matter his . . . his religion." He walked past Seth to his horse.

Seth and his wife looked at Marcus for a few seconds, then waved for their daughter to join them. The light went out of her eyes, and she hesitated. He waved again, a kind but curious look to his face, and she complied. He took his wife and daughter to their horses and helped them mount. There were whispered words before he removed items from a bag and returned to Marcus.

"How much to buy this man's freedom?" Seth asked.

Joseph could not believe his ears and had to close his mouth when it fell open in disbelief.

"Ten gold coins," Marcus answered.

"A fair price for such a man." He pulled a small tablet from his pocket and quickly pressed writing into the wax surface with a stylus, then struck it with his ring. Withdrawing a purse, he tossed it to Marcus. "There is more than enough. I authorize you to make the purchase and set him free."

Marcus blinked several times as Seth stepped to Matthias and handed him the tablet. "Your freedom. All I ask in return is that you and Joseph of Nazareth work for me. I have a house to build and want it done as well as these gates." He winked at Joseph.

Matthias felt his legs give way and fell to his knees in tears. Seth pulled him up. "No, no. Such thanks is for God alone." He smiled and leaned closer. "Crispus is a thief and a fool, like his master. If he had liked you more, I would have liked you less. It is worth every coin to ruin him."

"Thank you," Joseph managed. "Your money is well spent." He nodded toward Crispus, now mounted on his horse and fuming.

Seth chuckled. "It will get worse for him. I intend to tell Antipas I will have no dealings with this steward." He went to Marcus. "You will be welcome at our table this night. You are a friend of the people, and that is what matters. Such a quality is hard to find in Rome these days." He turned to Joseph. "Please, come with him. It will be good to talk about what has happened since we last met."

Joseph smiled at the confused look on the faces of Marcus, Matthias, and Seth's wife and daughter. "I am honored, but Mary is expecting another child, and he will come anytime. I must go back to Nazareth immediately."

"Then another time, and wish her well," Seth replied. He turned and went back to his wife as Crispus rode away in a huff.

As Seth mounted, the word of what had happened spread through the crowd. Shouts and cheers reverberated off the walls and new gates as Matthias hugged Marcus, then kissed him on both cheeks. "I was wrong. You will make a fine Jew." He slapped him on the back and then turned into the welcoming crowd.

"I think you have won a wife this day," Joseph remarked.

Marcus was stunned, able only to nod, his eyes on the woman as her horse walked toward their gate. She turned and gave him a smile that nearly melted his heart. "I thought for a moment . . ."

"If she had shunned you, God would have provided another."

Marcus gave a wry smile. "I suppose you mean that to be comforting, but for a moment, I nearly had you both thrown in irons, and I was trying to figure out the best way to beg forgiveness of Crispus."

Joseph laughed until he saw that Marcus did not. He cleared his throat. "Then I thank God for giving you strength."

"As well you should," Marcus declared.

They laughed together, as Matthias lifted the tablet into the air for all to cheer his newfound freedom. Tonight he would sleep in Nazareth.

CHAPTER 33

After Joseph left that morning, Joachim came to the house to get Jesus. He was going to watch the sheep today and wanted company. By afternoon, Mary's back ached, and she was tired of bending, standing, bending, standing, over and over again, so she took a walk. She left Dinah and Ruth at the house, cooking bread and grinding wheat, and walked out of the village to where the flocks grazed. She saw her father and waved, and he returned the greeting. Jesus came running and met her before she could go much farther. Mary stooped to give him a hug, then he was off again, scampering toward some rock cliffs, then up them like a spider. His grandfather, very protective of him, grew anxious and scolded him a bit.

"Father, you worry about him too much," Mary indicated.

"He will kill himself at an early age if I don't! You should worry about him more than you do. Especially in a place like this," he said impatiently.

Mary was both stunned and hurt at the accusation but tried not to show it. With others who did not know her, she might have been successful in hiding her feelings, but with her father she was not.

"I'm sorry, Mary. I was wrong to say such a thing. You are a good mother, chosen by God for His Son. I had no right to condemn you."

She put her arm through his. "You are forgiven, and I do worry, but I am not afraid, Father. God watches over him as well as Joseph and me."

Joachim bid Jesus to come down but in softer tones this time, then offered Jesus a hand, though he obviously didn't need it.

Jesus covered his disappointment, and Mary knelt down in front of him and brushed some dried grass from his tunic, sticky from the rain. "Grandfather is just worried. You frighten him with your climbing."

"Please, be careful, Jesus, and don't play in such dangerous places," Joachim begged.

Being young and thus quick to forgive and forget, Jesus stooped down to look at a bug hanging precariously from the leaf of a bush, and Joachim seemed to breathe easier, though the grandfather squinted at the bug to make sure it was not the biting kind.

They walked a short distance without talking, and Mary could tell her father was working up the courage to say something. She remained silent, giving him time.

"Mary, do you ever wonder why you had such a miraculous conception? Why he could not be Joseph's son and have his lineage and God's power bring him to the throne?"

Mary sensed some frustration. "Yes, Father, Joseph and I have both wondered." Mary sat on a rock, the length of the walk tiring her. It was warm, the clouds having dispersed across the heavens, giving the sun room to shed its light and take the chill off the day.

"And do you have an answer?" he asked.

"Not a complete one, no. In time, I suppose God will show us. But Jesus' nature is to learn much more quickly than others. Already he has learned to read and knows the alphabet in Aramaic, Hebrew, and Greek. He writes the alphabets as well. And he sees things. Not visions, I suppose, but pictures of the past, a view of the stories we have told him." She looked at her son, chasing some kind of flying thing through the wet grass, soaked to his shoulders. "But even then I see another side to him. Knowledge is easy, but it is not what he loves the most. He would rather be sitting in Salome's lap making her happy than reading. He knows when people need cheering and desires to comfort them. Because of this, people are drawn to him and feel better when he is with them. He loves everything, everyone. Have you noticed he is never one to take toys from other children or be demanding or hurtful, even when they hurt him? When he plays with them, they all just seem to want to be kind to each other. There is something deep in him, Father, as if there is a much older person inside his little body."

Both of them looked at Jesus, who now had the bug in the palm of his hand. He threw it upward and watched it fly away, then ran to see where it would land.

"But, maybe all of these things are not uncommon to other children, even though I do not see them in most."

She paused a moment, picking a lily and smelling it. "You are right about one thing. He did not need to be born as he was to have some of the power he will need. That will come later, a gift from God. Power like that of Moses, used to part the Red Sea. When wars are to be won, this will win them. These did not come with him at birth any more than they came with Moses at birth." She felt a slight jab deep in her abdomen and winced a bit, took a deep breath, then continued.

"Jesus is God's Son because he needs something even greater than these—a power so simple that Joseph and I looked past it." She stood and put an arm around her father's waist and started following Jesus. "The reason Jesus had to be the Son of God is so that he could have a power that can come only that way—the power over his own death."

Joachim was startled by the words, his own ideas of mortality and death getting in the way. "But that cannot be. All men—"

"Joseph and I didn't see it at first either, mainly because God hid him from men and warned us to flee Palestine to protect him. If he has power over death, why must we flee Herod or fear any man? One answer is obvious—we were in danger as well as Jesus. It is also obvious that he was a baby and even now is just a child and does not understand this power within him and how to use it. He needed to be fed, nurtured, and raised up to manhood like any other child. When he is ready, God will tell him about this great power and tell him what must be done with it." She hesitated, trying to think of how to say what she had learned. "Somehow, God placed a part of Himself inside my womb and gave Jesus a part of who He is, a part of immortality. That is the miraculous part of Jesus' birth."

Joachim looked at his daughter through the haze of his own understanding and the teachings of sages and even the scriptures.

"But he bleeds and bruises, Mary. Surely he can die as well."

"Bleed, yes, and bruise and die until he is taught how to prevent it. That is why no one is to know who he is until the time of his instruction by God. Then he alone can set aside his immortality. Even the scriptures say that he will do that someday, but not until he has finished his mission. It is this . . . this mission that I do not fully understand, but I know now that he has the ability and will receive the power to do what God asks, and that no man will prevent him." She looked at Jesus playing in a small pool of water in the cavity of a large stone. "You are right to watch him. I watch him as well. He needs our protection, our teaching, and our love just as other children. He does bleed and bruise and hurt, and none of us wants that for any child, but we do not need to fear that he will die before his time. God will watch over him and has already done so by warning us to flee Israel and go to Egypt, then to come here. Even you have experienced God's protection of him."

"When He kept me from revealing that you carried him in your womb at the synagogue before you left Nazareth to go to Bethlehem. I remember," Joachim said. He shook his head lightly. "Still, God . . . God is something far beyond man and unknowable, a mystery. How can a part of Him come to earth?"

"That *is* the mystery," Mary replied. She had never remembered what had happened and knew she probably never would. All she knew was that God had given her Jesus and that he was God's Son. "But remember, Father, with God nothing is impossible."

Joachim sighed. "It strains my faith at times."

"Faith is believing that which you cannot see or touch, Father. It is believing in things you cannot fully understand," Mary moved him along to keep up with a scurrying Jesus, who disappeared just over the lip of a small rise in the side of the slope. "For now, we have many wonderful years ahead with Jesus, and sooner than we think, he will be teaching us things we never understood or thought possible. Over time, we will see him use his power and fulfill his mission. Even the words of the prophets will be made clear, but many things will come as a surprise, and we will be amazed and wonder but also be frightened for him. When those times come, we must remember who he is and trust what we do know of him."

Once more, Joachim looked at Jesus and tried to see what he would become, what the scriptures said of him. He could not. He never could. He sighed again. "God give me faith . . . and patience."

Mary chuckled, and both of them looked up to see Jesus standing on the top of the rock wall again, a wide grin on his face. Joachim was about to scold him, then clamped his jaw shut. The boy was so proud of his accomplishment, and though Joachim's heart thumped for Jesus as he stood near the edge, he controlled the desire to pull him down and lock him in the house.

"Jesus, please be careful," Mary beseeched nervously. She chuckled again. "See, even knowing what I know, I fear for him. I suppose that is natural to all of us for our children and grandchildren."

"Look at me, Mother," Jesus said, his hand raised above his head. "I'm on top of the world. I can see everything from here!"

Mary smiled nervously. "Come down now," Mary said after a few moments. "We have to go back. Your father will be coming soon, and there is much to do. Ohh," she said, wincing with pain. She touched her stomach and bent slightly against the pain. She had felt this before, on the path to the cave at Bethlehem. "We must go back, Father. Quickly!"

Joachim's smile left, and he took her arm. Jesus had scrambled down from the rocks and was now by her side and looked up at his mother with concerned but excited eyes. "Is he coming, Mother?"

Mary forced a smile. "Yes, I think he is. I need you to go and bring Salome. You must be my big boy now. Can I depend on you?"

Jesus was already running across the slope, darting around small bushes, his legs churning as fast as they could.

"Careful now!" she called after him. "Ohhhh," she moaned. "They are hard and fast, Father."

Joachim swept Mary into his arms and hurried as fast as his legs could carry him. He would have to send someone for Joseph. Mary groaned deeply, and he felt her stiffen against the pain. He would have to send someone immediately.

PART FOUR
THE AGE OF A MAN

CHAPTER 34

Joseph watched as Jesus put the final touches on the stone box. The carved relief of flowers in full bloom on the front, sides, and lid was as beautiful as any he had ever seen, and the lid fit so snugly, it would take little wax or gum to seal it. The customer would be well pleased.

"Well done, Jesus," Joseph stated proudly.

"Thank you, Father." Jesus looked up and smiled, showing slight dimples in his cheeks. At twelve, his hair was still dark, curly, and thick, barely touched his ears, and was cropped short at the back. As was the custom, it had been allowed to grow a little longer at the sides, and a single curl hung in front of each ear. His dark eyes were set in semi-deep sockets, his nose aquiline, and his lips full and constantly turned up at the corners in a pleasant smile.

"We'll deliver it on our way to Jerusalem," Joseph said.

Jesus nodded and returned to his work as his younger brother James stepped through the shop door and set the shaved length of cut log against the wall, then wiped his hands on his worker's apron.

"Finished?" Joseph asked.

"Finished," James answered.

"Then you and I can cut it into slabs while Jesus completes the stone box. The pieces can dry while we are in the Holy City."

James nodded, his eyes on Jesus' work. "That's the best I've seen you do, brother."

Jesus gave him a smile. "Your idea for measuring the design worked very well, don't you think?"

"Perfect." At nine, James was nearly a foot shorter than Jesus, but then Jesus was nearly an inch taller than Joseph and big for his age. With a round face like his father's, James's hair fell long and straight and was tied in a tail at the back, his sidelocks falling nearly to his chin. Though different in appearance, both boys were quite mature for their age. Joseph and Mary supposed that much of it was because of Jesus. They seldom left each other's side, and Jesus' natural gifts and uncommon maturity seemed to be clinging to his younger brother.

"Where is Jude?" Joseph asked.

"Watching little Anna. Mother has gone to the house of Matthias to help deliver Mara's baby."

"Then it is time." Joseph smiled. Matthias was about to be a grandfather. Mara had been married only a year earlier to the son of a family friend from Capernaum. They lived in the fishing village, but Mara had come home for the delivery of the baby.

Matthias had lost his ships during the rebellion, the tax collector confiscating them when he found out that Matthias was a prisoner of Rome. He had taken the house as well. When Matthias had been freed, he and Joseph had gone to the fishing town to check on the house and fishing boats and had discovered the theft. For the first time in his life, Joseph had seen Matthias control his temper. Instead of beating the tax collector, he had gone to the governor and filed a complaint. When no satisfaction had been forthcoming, they had returned home, then to Sepphoris to continue their work. He mentioned it in passing to Marcus, and a week later, a worthy amount of money was delivered from the governor's house at Capernaum. Matthias had used it to buy a donkey, new tools, and several sheep and chickens.

Joseph, Matthias, and Micah had continued to work at Sepphoris until Seth's house was completed and the doors and shutters in place. Their services were now in such demand that they could work from their shops in Nazareth. Micah and his eldest son built the framework of the doors and window shutters, and Joseph and Matthias did the carving and finishing work. They also built plows, carts, furniture, and doors for villagers and helped add on to the synagogue as the village continued to slowly grow. They were not rich, but they were comfortable, and with both their families growing, they praised God for their good fortune.

Jude appeared at the door, the hand of his little sister in his. At six, Jude was cut from the same mold as James, and four-year-old Anna looked like a miniature Mary.

"Father, Anna ate a bug."

Joseph looked up from his work, as did James and Jesus.

"What kind?" Jesus asked.

"A grasshopper, but a large one. She nearly choked," Jude answered.

The three of them smiled at the look on Anna's face. Apparently it had not been a pleasant experience.

"Did you give her a drink of water?" Joseph queried.

Jude nodded.

"Then she will be fine. Will you do me a favor?" Joseph asked.

Jude nodded.

Joseph picked up Anna and put her on the workbench, handing her a toy before turning to Jude and bending over. "Go to the sheep and find Joses. Help him bring them home for the night."

Jude's eyes lit up, and he turned and ran for the gate, afraid his father would change his mind.

"No wandering, Jude," Joseph called after him. "It is going to rain, so go straight to the sheep and remember what I told you—take your time and watch what you are doing."

"Yes, Father," Jude yelled back from the street.

Jesus chuckled. "Mother will have you by the beard," he said.

"And make you sleep on the roof," James added with a grin.

Joseph chuckled as well. Mary did not like the younger boys sent on such errands, but he felt they needed to be given responsibility as early as possible "She will be at Salome's most of the night, and unless one of you tells her . . ."

"Us?" Jesus said, glancing at James. "Not us."

They all laughed and went back to work.

* * *

Jesus finished the box and went for a drink, taking a restless Anna with him. He dipped the cup into the water jar, then handed it to her. She managed to spill half the water down her front, then gasped as she came up for air and handed the cup to Jesus with a brilliant smile. He sat on the bench and pulled her onto his lap. She lay against his chest and put her thumb in her mouth, contented.

"What is J'ushalem like?" she asked, her face turned up to his.

"Big, noisy, beautiful, and ugly all at the same time." Little Anna had been to Jerusalem as a baby but did not remember. Since then the illness of one of the family or the delivery of a child for their aunt Dinah had kept Mary and the little ones at home.

"Does it scare you?" she asked.

"It makes me sad, but it does not scare me."

"Sad?"

"Yes, sad." He did not explain.

He felt a drop of rain and looked up. Dark clouds hung above them and were settling in. The clouds suddenly burst, and Jesus quickly stood and took Anna back to the shop, shielding her face with his hand. His father and James were just finishing splitting the log into planks, and all of them watched out the door as the rain spilled over them.

"It is God's blessing," Joseph said. "The crops will mature well with their thirst quenched." Wrinkles of concern developed in his forehead, and he grimaced as lightning struck in the Valley of Jezreel. "Jude and Joses are out in this. Go and find them."

James nodded, and Jesus handed Anna to her father. The two boys ran with shoulders hunched out the gate and up the narrow street toward the hill. Water was already flowing heavily, making the dirt slick, and James went down. Jesus helped him up, and he shook the mud from his hands as they struggled to the grass for better footing. They were soaked to the skin when they reached the top and started down the back side toward Cana. Jesus found the shelter of a tree so they could catch their breath, his eyes on the dark sky.

"The sun will set soon and make things worse," he indicated.

"We should have seen them by now," James answered.

"Look." Jesus pointed.

James saw a herd of sheep moving toward home, their shepherd leading them at a quick pace. They ran to meet them and saw that it was not Joses or Jude but another of the village boys.

"Do you know where Joses is?" James asked.

The boy pointed to the east. "He took them to new pasture. I passed Jude an hour ago. He couldn't find him either.

Jesus looked at James as the shepherd continued on.

"What do you think?" James asked.

Jesus didn't answer immediately, his eyes on the clouds. James had seen this before, and because he had, he said nothing. Jesus did not act irrationally or without serious thought, ever, and James had learned to respect it. He took a deep breath and ignored his desire to run in every direction.

"We go north," Jesus said.

James nodded, and the two boys started off at a lope, the sheets of water pummeling them as they went. They walked and ran for nearly a mile with no sign of either brother before James asked to stop.

"They aren't here, Jesus. We should try east."

"No, they're here."

James wiped away the water from his eyes and nose with a frustrated swipe. "They can't be. We've come—"

Jesus put a gentle hand on his brother's arm. "Listen." He then walked through the grass to the west and came over the brow of the hill to look down into a depression with a few trees at its center. He pointed. "There."

James came to his side and saw the sheep huddled around something as if protecting it. They ran and slid down the slight grade to find their two younger brothers huddled together in the center of the flock. Joses saw them first and got to his feet, a relieved look on his face. Jude lay still, blood mingled with water flowing down his forehead.

"He fell and bumped his head on a rock. I carried him this far, but I . . . I didn't know what to do to get him to wake up."

"You did well, little brother," Jesus commented. He picked Jude up, cradled him in his arms, and started home. The boy was warm, but his breathing was shallow. The sheep followed, and James took Joses's hand more for comfort than support.

The rain let up, and the clouds drifted northeast until the sun peeked through just as it set into the sea to the west. Joseph saw them coming from the top of the street, and Jesus showed him the bump on the boy's head.

"He is pale," Joseph said. "James, go find your mother, and bring her home if you can. Joses, put the sheep in the stable and then get out of those drenched clothes."

James disappeared at the bottom of the street as they turned into the courtyard. Jesus carried Jude into the house and put him in his parents' bed. Joseph had sat Anna down on a chair, then used a cloth to wipe away the water and blood from the boy's scalp, finding a nasty gash there. As Jesus finished pulling Jude's clothes off and wrapping him in warm blankets, his mother came through the bedroom door and knelt by Jude, asking what happened.

"I sent him to help Joses. He got caught in the storm and fell on slick rocks, bumping his head," Joseph replied.

She looked at the gash as James joined them, then she asked him to bring the container of ointment from the cupboard. James retrieved the stone jar gingerly, knowing it had sacred significance to his parents but never really knowing why. He took it to the bedroom and handed it to his mother, who had already retrieved a needle and thread and was preparing to sew the cut shut, her eyes on Jude.

She stopped what she was doing, and a gasp came from her throat. "He is not breathing! Joseph, he is not breathing!"

Joseph looked at the boy and felt for breath but found none. He was about to shake the child's shoulder when Jesus stepped in and grasped Joseph's hand, making him look up.

"He is not dead, Father. He just sleeps." Jesus touched the boy's forehead and stroked his hair gently.

There was a sudden, shallow movement in Jude's chest.

Mary sewed the wound, then applied the ointment. It was nearly all gone—only one jar remained. Joses had joined them, and Joseph called them all around for prayer. Then they waited.

Jude awoke near midnight, hungry. They woke Anna with their celebration, then ate the meal none of them had seemed to have an appetite for earlier.

Mary and Joseph went outside. Jesus watched when they came in and smiled at the humble look on his father's face. He would not send Jude to the fields without supervision again.

* * *

Mary kept a close eye on Jude for the next week. She would not take him to Jerusalem for Passover unless she knew he was not experiencing pain or difficulty. Joses caught a cold but not a serious one, and James and Jesus took turns watching over the sheep while they grazed.

Mara had difficulty giving birth to her child. He was very small and had a hard time breathing, and Matthias and Salome decided they could not make the trip to Jerusalem this year. Mary's father was not feeling well either, and her brother Josiah, who had never married, said he would stay behind and care for their father. The day before their journey to Jerusalem, Mary went to spend time with both of them and came home several hours later quite encouraged. She had debated whether or not she should stay behind this trip and now felt comfortable about going ahead with her plans.

They started for Jerusalem the next day. The caravan was entirely from the village and numbered at least a hundred neighbors and friends. Each day, they would make camp two hours before sundown, prepare their meal, then join others at the center of the camp for play and talk, dancing and singing. On the eve of arriving at Jerusalem, Mary sat by her tent door with Anna in her lap and watched her husband and sons. Jude was back to tripping and falling over things, but Mary found herself glad that his head injury had not slowed him down. Joses and James were playing games with the older boys, but eventually James slipped away to sit next to Jesus, who sat just behind their father in the half circle of men outside Azariah's tent door. It was the tradition that men gather there, around the new rabbi.

Even from her position less than half a dozen cubits away, Mary could not hear the discussion because of the music and singing. But she knew, as always, that Joseph would share with her later.

These discussions would be particularly lively, as would the ones on the return trip. Jerusalem was the great center of learning, with several schools of thought vying for the hearts of men. Sides were being taken, positions clarified and challenged. On the return, new interpretations or other discoveries would be discussed and some-times bring changes to the village concerning day-to-day life. Much to the consternation of some, especially Azariah, Joseph had become a particularly important part of these decisions, his knowledge and ability giving his words weight. There was even discussion of making him one of the community elders, but since becoming rabbi, Azariah had tried to squelch the idea. But, whether Azariah liked it or not—and whether Joseph liked it or not—her husband's opinions were held in esteem by many, and an appointment could be forced on the village council regardless of the opposition of the new rabbi.

Mary knew of Azariah's dislike for them and of his attempts to discredit them by claiming Jesus was illegitimate. Few believed him. In fact, his words had hurt his own reputation with many, but he persisted, his jealousy of Joseph stronger than his good sense. Mary shoved these thoughts aside. Eventually such talk would go away. For now, people did not care.

She watched the sudden firm, almost angry motions of one of the men in the circle and knew the discussion was getting heated. She was grateful to see that he was shaking his finger at someone other than Joseph, but noticed that Jesus and James were both upset by whatever was being said.

Joseph made a rather long comment that, as usual, brought both nods of approval and disagreement, and another quickly spoke to share a different opinion. She watched James lean forward as if to say something, but Jesus put a light hand on his brother's leg as a signal. This was not the time or place for a nine-year-old, no matter his degree of learning, to speak. James relaxed but was disgruntled. A few moments later, Joseph got up and came to sit with Mary, but the boys remained, James quickly filling in the spot his father vacated only to be asked to move by one of the older men who had been standing. James was respectful and begged an apology but was visibly disappointed.

Joseph sat down and stretched out. Anna immediately climbed over him, and he turned on his stomach so she could sit on his back.

"Your comment?" Mary asked.

"Azariah believes fasting should be public, a kind of humiliation that is good for the soul."

"And your opinion?"

"To do something to be seen of men denies the blessing for what you do. You have your reward when you do it in public. Men grant you piety. How can God grant you a blessing when you have already received what you really want?"

She watched Jesus while Anna bounced up and down on her father's back.

"Do you think it is time to tell him?" Joseph asked. He carefully turned onto his back so that Anna could straddle him.

Mary didn't answer for a moment. "It is best that God tells him, but I thank Him every day that He delays."

"It has been nearly thirteen years, Mary. He cannot delay much longer. There is much to make ready, learning we are probably not even aware of, powers, abilities to be gained . . . skills of war. Surely these will take time," Joseph declared.

"Yes, I know, but I dread the day when he will leave. I know what the end will be."

"The end is a freedom from sin, a new kingdom, and the glorious return of our people. Don't dwell on what must happen to bring it about."

Mary blinked several times, holding back the tears. "It is getting harder, Joseph. I used to be rather calm about what lay ahead, but that was when he was small and I knew God was not ready for him. Now my fear grows. He is nearly thirteen. Thirteen, Joseph, the age when Israel says a boy is a man. God might take him at any time, and I will lose him to what I know must follow. We all will." Her lip quivered, and a tear rolled down her cheek. "I can't bear it, Joseph. I can't." The tears flowed, and she got up and went inside the tent. Joseph followed, sat Anna down with a doll made of rags, and put his arms around his wife, but there was really nothing more he could say. They had discussed many times all that the prophets said the Messiah would do. There was death, but there was so much more. Even so, Mary had become more and more discomfited about the end.

She finally gained control and wiped away her tears before giving Joseph a smile. "Even this helps. Thank you."

Anna crawled into her father's lap and grasped his calloused finger in her chubby ones when James suddenly appeared at the tent door. He plopped himself down rather hard, his face a sheet of anger, and was obviously unaware of Mary wiping away the last of her tears.

"Shammai, Shammai. Does Azariah not know the name of any other sage?"

Joseph chuckled. "Shammai has a strong following in our village, that is true." Anna stood against his chest and began playing with his beard.

"But he is so strict."

"Being strict is not always bad," Mary replied.

"It is when the purpose is just to declare you live the law in exactness. There is no feeling in it! Hillel has a heart at least!"

"You said once that you wanted to be a learned man, to attend one of the schools in Jerusalem or Alexandria. Apparently that will be the school of Hillel, not Shammai." Joseph grinned.

James didn't answer immediately. "Jesus is material for a sage, Father, not I."

"What Jesus is should not affect what you wish to be. Do you think we would be displeased with *two* men who knew Torah and gave it proper interpretation? Those who understand the law are needed now more than ever, James." He glanced at Mary. "When the Messiah comes, he will need learned men, but righteous ones, willing to listen. He will add to the law, even change it, and many will falter. A leader, a sage, who understands their concerns but who is willing to give himself to the new order of things will be a great help in Israel and keep many from falling to their everlasting destruction."

James looked at Joseph. Anna had crawled to the tent door and was staring at the dancers. "The Messiah will not come in my lifetime, Father."

Joseph looked at Mary again, then back at James. "He will come, and Israel will need to change before he does, or they might turn away."

"Turn away? Never!"

Joseph chuckled. "Matthias said that to me once, and others believe it as well, but it will happen, James, unless good men teach and help them understand who it is we really look for." From where he sat, he could see Jesus.

"But the scriptures tell us what to look for. A King . . . a man of power. How could we turn away from such a man?"

"He will be a Son of David, that is true, and he will come with power, and he will rule and reign over Israel when the time for the end comes, but there are other things, things that puzzle me and probably will you." Joseph leaned forward. "But you will *see*, James, you will see them clearly when he shows our people who he is. I promise."

James blinked several times. "Who he is? Then you think he is already among us?"

Joseph smiled. "See how hard it is to accept? How could he be here? Wouldn't we surely know him? Wouldn't he reveal himself? You doubt, because you have listened to our tradition and can see only one Messiah. Read your scrolls more carefully, James, and you will find another, closer than you think."

James shook his head. "Maybe."

"He tells you the truth," Mary added softly. "Listen to him, James, and study about your King. Only then will you know when you see him, and even then it will be hard. Very hard."

James pondered for a moment then got up. "I am going for a walk along the river and a bath. Jesus and I are sleeping under the stars tonight, so we will see you before sunrise." He had been sitting on the ground and dusted off his backside before picking up his bedding and travel sack and strutting off into the darkness.

"For his age, he thinks too much," Mary said.

Joseph chuckled. "He is mature in some things, but a child in others. He will understand someday."

* * *

There was a bright half moon, and James could see there were already a few people in the river. He listened to the voices of boys playing at some game in the water. Staying clear of them, he meandered downstream until he was sure he was alone, took off his clothes, and slid into the water. It was cold but refreshing, and he swam from bank to bank twice before floating on his back, looking up at the stars. How beautiful were God's creations! He felt himself begin to sink and put his feet down. He was surprised that there was no bottom and was not prepared. Water entered his mouth and nose, and he struggled to get back to the surface. Spluttering and treading water, he tried to get closer to shore, finally finding a place he could stand.

Once clearing his nostrils, he swam again, reaching the near shore to find Jesus stooped on its bank watching him.

"How is the water?" Jesus asked.

"Wonderful, and even if it weren't, you should come in." He pinched his nose between his finger and thumb. "You need a bath."

Jesus chuckled and quickly stripped and waded in. They swam and splashed water on each other, then raced to the far side and back. James won but knew Jesus let him.

"It isn't always a good thing to be kind," James said. "Sometimes it makes the other person feel like a beggar."

Jesus smiled. "I used to let you win, but not anymore. You're a good swimmer, James. You have power in your arms you did not have even a year ago."

James smiled at the praise. It was genuine—it could be nothing else. Jesus did not play with lies, even to make others feel good. If he could not speak honestly, he did not speak. James supposed that was what made his brother's praise precious to him, something to be treasured.

James retrieved his soap and scrubbed before throwing it to Jesus, who did not see it in the dark and took it in the head.

"Sorry," James called. "But you are not hurt. Soap against stone." He grinned.

Jesus rubbed the bump and then dove after James and dunked him. They scuffled playfully then washed and got out and put on clean clothes before taking their bedding and finding a place to sleep.

"We'll be in Jerusalem tomorrow," Jesus reminded as he rolled out his bedding.

"And at the temple the next morning," James answered. He sat down on his blankets and dried his hair with a rag. "Father thinks I should go to a school in Jerusalem or Alexandria, that I should study and become a sage or a scribe."

"You would be good at both," Jesus agreed.

"But I am just a carpenter's son, and from Nazareth, a village most Jews don't know exists. The sages would not accept me into their schools."

Jesus looked at James in the darkness, then put a hand on his shoulder. "James, God sent you here for a purpose. I think Father has told you what that purpose is, so why do you argue with it?"

James blinked at the rebuke, even though it was a gentle one. Jesus did not speak so directly very often and never unless he felt his words necessary to opening another's eyes to that person's own weakness.

But this was not so easy for James to face. He felt inadequate and feared rejection by the sages, but how could he say that to a brother who had such strength and had probably never felt inadequate a day in his life?

"Your fear of rejection is unfounded, James. They will take you the minute you answer their first question," Jesus said, then he smiled. "It is that booming bass voice. You sound like God Himself."

James's voice was far from booming; in fact, it continued to crack at the worst possible times. He hit Jesus on the arm at the wisecrack.

Jesus chuckled, then became serious. "Father knows that God needs you to prepare for something you cannot begin to understand today—it will be a great service for God's kingdom. You will change hearts and bear witness of events you never dreamed possible. But you are not ready. You must do as Father says. You must learn the law." Jesus stood. "I should bring the donkeys here. The grass is better, and we should have them where we can see them."

James couldn't speak, Jesus' words making his heart race and his palms sweat. He watched Jesus disappear around a stand of shrubs and blinked several times. What was he talking about? How could he say such a thing? And yet . . . it was true, all of it, and James knew it.

He heard the donkeys and quickly got to his feet and helped Jesus run rope from tree to bush and bush to tree to make an effective pen for the two animals. They washed before retrieving their prayer shawls, and James began with recitation of the Shema. When he was finished, Jesus recited another prayer for their safety before they put away their prayer shawls and slipped into bed.

"I will study then," James stated, looking blankly at the stars.

"Good."

There was a long pause between them before Jesus spoke again.

"I love you, James," he declared softly.

"And I love you," James answered.

CHAPTER 35

Mary watched her husband and two eldest sons disappear through the melee of tents and down the hill toward the city. It was the day of Passover, and though they had already been in the city for three days and visited the temple on each of those days, they had not made sacrifice. Today Jesus would offer his first.

She gathered the remaining three children and left for the city. Joseph had made arrangements for others to watch their tent and belongings and to feed the donkeys. Tonight they would eat the Passover at the home of Marcus and Serah. It would be good to see them again.

Marcus had soured on military work and had accepted an offer from Seth to run parts of his business. It required a move from Sepphoris to Jerusalem, and there had been some pain in no longer being among friends, but overall it had been a good move for Marcus and his family. Jerusalem was the hub of commerce in Palestine, and his business prospered.

They had two children now, one boy and one girl. Serah had trouble with pregnancy, and had lost another child while nearly losing her own life. She was doing much better now, and they were hopeful that at least one more child would come to them.

Mary and the children entered by Gennath Gate and walked into the upper city. Asking a man on the street where the house of Marcus Vitellius was, Mary received immediate directions and a side glance filled with disdain. Mary immediately felt that her own robes were rags and that they were surely out of place.

"Why did that man look at us funny?" asked Joses.

"I suppose he has never seen such handsome children and wanted to be sure his eyes were not deceiving him," Mary said with a smile. "Come along, we must hurry."

The great carved gate bearing the name of Marcus Vitellius made the courtyard door look like the door to someone's house.

"Wow, this place must be huge!" Jude exclaimed. "Is Marcus rich, Mother?"

Mary looked at him a bit annoyed and immediately scolded herself for it. "Yes, Jude, Marcus is rich, but unlike some rich men, he gives much of it away and doesn't let it change how he treats people."

"Good, 'cause I'm hungry, really hungry."

Mary chuckled again as she knocked and the gate was opened, a servant greeting them joyously and calling to the other servants that their guests had arrived. Serah immediately appeared from an open archway to the left and ran to meet Mary and hug Anna and then each of the boys, who squirmed at the attention.

"Ah, little men are we?" Serah said. "Not given to such affectionate coddling. Go on with you, then! The servants will show you where the horses are stabled. They are ready for you to ride—"

The boys' eyes grew big, and they dashed away, Serah instructing a male servant, "Only in the back courtyard near the stable."

Serah and Mary had become good friends. She and her family had proven unpretentious despite their wealth, and she and Mary had spent many hours together. Mary always felt comfortable around Serah and was glad to be off the street and in her home.

Mark and Miriam appeared on the balcony to the right and jumped up and down gleefully before Mark came down the steps two at a time to join them. Miriam, at age three, was more careful but finally reached the bottom and ran to Mary, who swept her up and gave her a big hug. Miriam had never seen Anna before and immediately wanted to lift her. Anna, enthralled by this precocious child who had appeared with such a flurry, let herself be manhandled, and much to the delight of Miriam, responded with a hug.

Mark was six, the same age as Jude, and along with Joses, they had played together a good deal before Marcus and Serah had moved to Jerusalem. Since then, contact had been relegated to a few visits, but the boys were still good friends.

"Where are Joses and Jude?" Mark asked excitedly.

"Where do you think?" Serah responded with a grin.

Mark ran for the stables as Mary helped Miriam move Anna inside the large living area of marble floors covered with handsome rugs and tables and comfortable sitting places. Mary and Serah chatted, fed the children after their horseback riding, and put Anna down for a nap, then conversed some more. Before Mary knew it, it was nearly time to leave.

Several servants were given direct charge of the children, and Mary and Serah covered their heads with their scarves, wrapping the tail of one end over the lower portion of their faces.

Though Marcus was wealthy, Serah had not let fashion and the clothes she could buy affect her. She dressed after the manner of Jewish women and acted like them as well. Mary appreciated the effort it would take to remain untouched by wealth in a city that seemed more and more consumed by it all the time, and she knew Serah was of special quality. God had truly blessed Mary and her family with Serah and Marcus's friendship.

They went up the western ramp and passed through the gate into the Court of the Gentiles. The place was packed with worshippers waiting for the special Passover sacrifice to begin. It was noisy with joyous talk and greeting, as it should be. Passover was designed by God as a time of joy; after all, they were celebrating their freedom from Egypt's tyranny and false gods.

But it was also a time of sober reflection as they thought upon how they had become captives again, this time to the Romans, and they prayed for their Messiah to come.

They went directly to the prearranged place of meeting but did not see their husbands or the boys and knew they must be a bit early.

"They are probably delayed purchasing the lamb," Serah suggested.

"If they can even find one," Mary replied. "Look at this place. I have never seen it so packed."

Joseph would not purchase the lamb on the temple mount where prices were exorbitant and the sacrifice often blemished. He would go to several markets within the city and pick only the very best one.

"I am sorry Matthias and Salome could not come," Serah remarked.

"Another purpose for our prayers today."

The people quieted as a priest appeared on the southwest corner of the outer wall, shofar horn in hand. When he lifted this to his lips and blew three times, it would signal the moving of the first of three courses into the Court of the Women for the sacrifice of their lambs. From the look of their position among the thousands present, they would enter with the first course, unless Joseph and Marcus were late.

A man passed, a loudly bleating lamb flung over his shoulders. Mary forced a smile as the man apologized for the noise and moved on. Over the years, Mary had come to understand the sacrifice as something quite different from what she had once imagined. The discovery had been both sweet and bitter. Sweet because of the knowledge of salvation that would come to all God created, and bitter because it forced her to face what lay ahead for her eldest son. The latter was the main reason she would not actually watch the shedding of the lambs' blood this day or any other day. She thought of Jesus' future often enough without being reminded so starkly by the ritual of blood sacrifice.

"It is good to be here, to be reminded," Serah spoke reverently.

Mary saw Joseph but did not recognize Marcus at first. "Oh, your husband is letting his beard grow! It is nearly as fine as Joseph's!"

"And a nuisance when we kiss." Serah smiled. "I will never get used to the irritation."

The first blast of the shofar horn sounded like thunder across the crowd, and all looked up, excited, ready, as two more blasts reverberated off the walls and columns of the temple. It was a unique and powerful sound that thrilled Mary from head to foot. How many times had she heard it, and yet it still held a thrill for her. It was as if God was speaking, calling all within the sound of His voice to enter His presence. She often thought it must have been similar to the voice her forefathers had heard while standing at the foot of Mount Sinai, a sound that had both frightened and awed them.

The crowd turned toward the gates and began moving.

"Just in time," Marcus said with a grin. "Hello, Mary." He smiled. "You are as beautiful as ever."

"And you are a wonderful storyteller, but I thank you for it." She pulled on his beard. "Finally becoming a Jew, are we?"

Marcus chuckled. "I never was very good at growing a beard, but this one is doing fairly well." He glanced at Serah. "I think I will keep it."

Serah gave him a scowl.

"I think not." Mary laughed. She was relishing Joseph's hand that had slipped into hers as she spoke, and she squeezed it. "Joseph did not have one at first, not a real one, like this."

Joseph stroked his chin. "More like what you would find on the chin of a goat."

"Then he was a boy; now he is a man," she said teasingly.

They were getting close to the steps, and Marcus turned to Jesus, who cradled the lamb in his arms, its feet dangling and its head tucked into the crook of his arm. "Only those who make the sacrifice can go beyond the outer gates, so we must wait here." He handed Jesus a shekel, which immediately brought a question into his eyes. "I know you are only twelve, but you are nearly thirteen, and this is your first sacrifice, so I wish to give you a gift. For a thank offering." He beamed as he drew in his breath. "I have a speech. We have watched you grow to manhood, Jesus, and we wish to thank God for the blessing you are to your family and to ours. May the God of Israel bless you this day, and may He know of our gratitude for you as a true son of Israel."

Cradling the lamb in one hand, Jesus took the coin, gave a slight bow, and thanked Marcus, then accepted a hug from Serah before the crowd pushed them apart.

Joseph took Jesus by the arm and tugged him toward the temple. Only the two of them would go, and Mary grasped James and watched them disappear through the crowd. "It was a wonderful speech," she said to Marcus.

"Yes, very short," James affirmed with a grin.

Marcus smiled and bowed. "I am glad to have pleased you both. Come, I told Joseph we would wait for them under Solomon's Porch, near the eastern gate." They started through the crowd, and Mary glanced over her shoulder. She could see Joseph and Jesus just mounting the steps that led through the gate and into the Court of the Women.

Jesus turned and scanned the crowd. Their eyes met, and his mother raised a hand and waved gently. He smiled, both arms cradling the lamb, then disappeared through the gate.

* * *

The gates that separated the Court of the Gentiles from the Court of the Women slid on their hinges and banged shut with a thunderous clap, the deep guttural sound of the shofar horns reverberating off the walls. The sacrifice was about to begin, and tens of thousands of people hushed one another until an uneasy silence fell across the complex. Men, women, and children shuffled here and there, coughed, whispered, and cried sporadically, but most simply listened for the sound of the Levites singing the Hallel. Then came the distant sound of lute and harp and finally the united voice of the choir. Mary stood and, along with all other women, covered her face as voices called everyone to prepare.

"Hallelujah," sang the choir.

"Hallelujah," the people repeated.

Mary felt the goose bumps on her flesh. So many voices all praising God! All of one mind, many of one heart! They had come to worship, and for the moment it did not matter who they were or where they were from, how much they knew or didn't know. They were here to remember what they could and to give thanks. Surely God must be pleased!

"Praise, O ye servants of Jehovah," came the melodic tones from inside the Court of the Women.

"Hallelujah," the people responded.

The words were comforting to Mary. By the time the ceremony was finished, all present would be reminded of the coming out of Egypt, the dividing of the sea, the giving of the law, the resurrection of the dead, and the role and mission of the Messiah.

The singers continued, and all present responded with different phrases as inside the Court of the Priests the sacrifices began. She watched, listened, and felt the reverence and sacred awe all around her. Even the thousands of lambs spread throughout the crowd and waiting their deaths seemed to be quieted by it all. There would be no pushing or shoving here, each waiting their turn, worshipping, doing their best to invite God into His house.

"Who is like unto Jehovah, who dwelleth on high?" sang the choir of Levites.

"Hallelujah," came the reply.

Mary listened to each word, sang, and waited, trying to picture what was happening inside. Surely Jesus had reached the place of slaughter by now. She lifted to the tips of her toes and tried to see. There seemed to be a steady stream of men coming out, moving through the crowd, but she did not see Jesus or Joseph. She let herself down on the flats of her sandals only to have James, who was now nearly six inches taller than she was, say they were coming. Another man brushed passed them, his sacrifice carried in cloth that was already saturated with blood.

"Ah," Marcus said, slapping Jesus on the shoulder. "You have completed your task. Congratulations."

Mary looked up at her son, who only nodded his head and tried to smile. He looked pale, and Joseph had that worried furrow to his brow but only shrugged when their eyes met.

James asked a half dozen questions in rapid succession, and Joseph put an arm around his shoulder and began moving him south along the eastern wall, answering the questions as they went. They would have to go the long way around to the west gate as the place was packed.

Mary put an arm through Jesus' and walked with him, Marcus and Serah just ahead of them. She felt the tension in Jesus' arm and rubbed it with her hand.

"Are you all right?" she asked.

He didn't answer for a moment, his eyes glued to the bloodstained rag in his hands. It was then that it dawned on Mary. He knew.

She felt her heart ache and pick up its beat all at the same time. She tried to shove the feeling aside, but it would not go. He knew, and it was ripping at his heart. She thought desperately of what to say, how to give comfort, but both eluded her. She felt panic, indecision, and pain all at once.

"Give the sacrifice to Marcus," she directed. The words were a shock even to her, and she wasn't sure if she had simply thought them or not, but when Jesus came to a standstill and stared at her, there was no longer a question.

"Give it to Marcus. Tell him you want to stay for a few minutes longer. Your father and I will stay with you."

He nodded and hurried to catch Marcus. She watched as Joseph and James stopped when they heard Jesus' request, and Joseph looked at Mary with some confusion. She gave him the signal to stay but let James go with Marcus and Serah, and a moment later the three of them were passing through the east gate and onto the bridge that spanned the Kidron Valley.

They walked slowly toward the Mount of Olives without speaking until Jesus finally broke down and cried. Joseph took him into his arms, and Mary wrapped hers around them both.

Yes, he knew.

* * *

Jesus had accepted her explanation of his birth without question, but he never did tell them exactly what had happened during his offering of the Passover sacrifice. Mary assumed he would someday, but it was not necessary. She understood better than anyone how sacred such an experience was. Some things were not meant to share with others, even those you loved most, and neither she nor Joseph felt in the least inclined to pry out of Jesus what had happened to him.

They had returned to Marcus's house and completed the Passover celebration. Jesus had been uneasy at first, his perspective apparently changed by whatever had happened. But God was with them more strongly that evening than Mary had ever remembered, and by its end, Jesus seemed marvelously comforted.

The rest of the week, Jesus spent most of his time at the temple. He attended the morning and evening sacrifice, then spent the rest of the day either listening to the sages or exploring the city streets with James, Joses, and Jude. They had even gone to the Mount of Olives to enjoy the marvelous view of the temple from its peak. The day before the feast was over, Jesus had said he was leaving for the day but would return in time for supper. They did not know until that night that he had visited Bethlehem.

It had not been the first time Jesus had expressed interest in the village of his birth, but in the past, they had said little of it. Joseph had told him about the cave and their new home, where they were located, and how much joy they had found there, but they had never told him about the visit of the shepherds or the wise men, or the reason for leaving. But when Jesus returned that night, he had questions, and they answered them while sitting under the stars some distance from the camp above the city.

He had found the house, and Mary and Joseph were happy to hear it was being used by a family related to the rabbi. Jesus told them his father had built it and asked if he could see the stable and cave below, and the woman had taken him down a set of stairs. His description of what he saw brought back pleasant memories to Joseph and Mary, and they relished it, but then the questions began.

"Why did we leave such a place?" he asked.

"Because your life was in danger," Joseph said. For nearly two hours, they talked quietly of Bethlehem, telling him of the vision of the shepherds, the visit of the wise men, the warning of the angel, and Herod's slaying of the children. Jesus listened, his face solemn, and Mary found it quite amazing that he did not question their answers.

But as she thought about it, she realized that it was simply a sign of the significance of what had happened to Jesus during the Passover sacrifice. There was no doubt in his mind as to who he was, and these stories simply added witness to what he already knew.

"Then the children died because Herod wanted to kill me," he uttered softly.

"Yes," was all Joseph said.

Jesus pondered for long minutes before he asked his next question. "What am I to do now?"

"Wait upon God," Joseph replied. "He has shown you who you are; He will show you the rest, you can be sure of it."

Jesus only nodded before retrieving his prayer shawl and standing. "I will see you in the morning." He disappeared into the darkness.

"He will have a thousand more questions," Mary asked.

"God has opened the door to where he will find the answers," Joseph stated. "His real schooling has begun. His Father will teach him now."

CHAPTER 36

The next day was the last day of the celebration and the day everything would be packed and the first part of the journey home completed. Everyone rose before dawn, ate, and began packing. The entire camp was in commotion as large segments of its population prepared to leave. The women, children, and a few men would leave early, with the rest of the men remaining behind for the last sacrifice, then hurrying along to be in camp for supper and bedtime.

The entire hillside was lit with lamps as everyone finished the last of their packing in the darkness that preceded dawn. James, Jesus, and Joseph finished loading the second mule just as the trumpets sounded for the beginning of the morning sacrifice. Joseph gave final instructions to the boys and hurried off with the rest of the men. Mary was struggling with Anna's loincloth as James and Jesus finished packing the donkeys. When she finished, she found that Jesus was gone.

"Where is Jesus?" she asked James as she put Anna in her perch atop Alexander.

"He went to the temple," James replied. "He'll probably come with Father."

Mary only nodded. One last visit to house of his true Father. She did not begrudge it. She picked up the lead rope of the donkey and instructed James to put Joses and Jude on the second donkey and follow her. They were falling behind the caravan and needed to catch up. Thieves watched for easy targets, and she did not wish to tempt them.

The day was hot, the journey tiring and lacking the exuberance of their arrival. The trip home was always harder—the celebration over, the excitement dulled with the thoughts of getting home as quickly as they could, with the many chores and the work that lay ahead.

They made camp at the base of the hills west of Jericho, and after Mary and James quickly set up the tent, she began preparing dinner. James and Joses finished unpacking their bedding, and Jude played with Anna. Mary was just finishing when she heard the men come into camp and saw Joseph approaching. She accepted his hug while looking over his shoulder for Jesus.

"Where is he?" she asked.

"Where is who?" Joseph responded.

"Jesus. He went to the temple after he finished packing."

Joseph felt his mouth go dry. "I never saw him."

Mary went pale. "Then he is still there?"

"No, no, he probably came earlier and is visiting with some of the others in the caravan. James and I will look for him."

He called to James, and they strode off in two different directions. Mary paced in front of the tent door, her arms folded across her chest until Anna cried, momentarily distracting her from her worry. Mary dished up some food, picked up her daughter, and fed her while waiting for what seemed like an eternity. When she saw James and Joseph coming back, her heart sank.

"No one has seen him," Joseph reported.

James looked as worried as she felt, and she glanced at Joses and Jude, whose eyes were wide with fear.

"We can't leave him, Mother," Jude entreated.

"No, no, of course we won't leave him," Mary replied, brushing back his hair. "He is probably on his way. Not everyone came at the same time, right, Father?" She looked at Joseph, who quickly nodded and ruffled Jude's hair.

"She is right. I'm hungry, how about you?" he asked Jude.

Jude nodded, and Mary hurried about to get them food. The younger children ate, but Mary and Joseph hardly touched their food. When supper was finished, the boys ran off to play, but Joseph held James back.

"If Jesus does not appear by morning, your mother and I must go back to Jerusalem and find him."

James nodded. "He will come tonight. Why would he stay longer?"

"I hope you are right, but if not, you will take your brothers and sister and go with the caravan. I will ask Micah to help. Can you do it?"

James nodded, a bit of doubt in his eyes. "With Micah's help, yes, but he will come. I know he will."

They all slept little that night, but James slept the least. As the sun poked through the clouds, he had the fire going and helped Mary prepare food.

"I think we should all go with you," James suggested.

Mary glanced at Joseph, who was already preparing for the journey. "I think he is right, husband."

Joseph hesitated only a moment, then nodded his head. "We will go to the house of Marcus and Serah first. He may be there, but if he is not, you will watch over the children while we search for him, James."

Relieved, James nodded quick agreement, stood, and went inside to wake his brothers and sister. An hour later, they were trudging back up the road to Jerusalem.

The road was packed with travelers in a hundred camps, and they searched each camp for some sign of Jesus but found none. Arriving late in Jerusalem, they went directly to the house of Marcus and Serah, who welcomed them with questioning looks but open arms.

"We will search the city," Marcus declared. "I know it like the back of my hand."

Torches in hand, he and Joseph spent half the night searching every inn, every corner, every camp, but found no sign of Jesus, and they returned home to find an anxious Mary waiting.

"That leaves only the temple," Mary responded.

"It is locked for the night. We will go as early as the doors open."

Exhausted, they fell into bed for several hours before rising and dressing.

"I thought of something else," Marcus said soberly. He glanced at Serah. "The Antonia."

Mary gasped. "But that would mean—"

"He would be a prisoner," Joseph finished. "We must check."

"I will go. I still have some influence there," Marcus insisted.

They set out in two separate directions, Mary and Joseph hurrying to the temple and Marcus going to the Antonia fortress. Serah stayed home to care for the children when they awoke.

Desperate with worry, Mary and Joseph walked through the western gate as it opened for the morning sacrifice, searching the porticoes of the Court of the Gentiles before entering the Court of the Women. It was then that they saw Jesus.

He was sitting among a group of sages, listening and speaking as if he had no concerns in all the world.

Mary and Joseph felt tremendous relief, and each took a deep breath and gave a quick prayer of thanks to God. With that, Mary's first emotion was quickly replaced with an even stronger one—anger.

"How could he do this?" she asked harshly.

Joseph gripped her arm gently. "Calm down, Mary, and look at what is happening."

Mary looked, but her angry heart was in no mood for riddles. "Joseph, I—"

Joseph put his arm around her. "Watch."

Mary took a deep breath, controlling her desire to grab her eldest son by the ear. After only a moment, she saw what Joseph meant.

"It is not Jesus who is asking the questions," she realized out loud.

"Even more stunning is that they are so interested in his answers. They're not only interested, they are very pleased. I have never seen such a thing before."

Mary only nodded. She was still upset and was grateful that Jesus saw them and excused himself. The sages stood and returned Jesus' bow as he walked through their midst and came over to his parents. Mary was the first to speak.

"Son, why have you dealt with us this way? Your father and I have sought you sorrowing." Her voice was tinged with more frustration than she felt, but they had feared and looked, and looked and feared for two days. She was tired and still afraid and frustrated with him.

Jesus sensed her unhappiness but only smiled, putting an arm around her shoulders and squeezing. "How is that you searched for me? Did you not know that I must be about my Father's business?"

Mary was startled at his answer, but Joseph was already moving them out of the temple and toward the east gate. Of course they would search for him. He was their son, under their care, and if he was to be about his Father's business he should have told them, not caused them this grief.

They walked from the temple grounds without speaking and were crossing the Kidron Valley before Jesus put his arm around her shoulder again.

"I am sorry, Mother. I should have let you know."

Mary put her arm around his waist but only nodded. She was feeling so many things and she just needed time to sort them out. What did this mean? Was it time? Was she to lose him now? She could bear that thought least of all.

He seemed to sense her concern and squeezed her shoulder again. "My learning has begun, Mother, that's all. Father taught me things back there I had never heard before. It was like water flowing through me!" He paused. "But there is much more. It will take time." He gave her another tender squeeze that brought such relief that tears filled her eyes. She tried to blink them away but to no avail. Only Joseph taking her hand seemed to curtail the flow.

* * *

Joseph, Mary, and Jesus were reunited with the rest of the family at Marcus's house, and a celebration ensued. James hugged his brother tightly then slugged him on the shoulder. "Never do this again, brother, or I will skin you alive."

Jesus smiled. "I think not. Mother will have it done before you ever get a chance."

Jesus went to bed exhausted. He had slept just outside the temple gates the last two nights, and without bedding, the chill had kept him from getting adequate rest.

Mary lay awake that night thinking, trying to fathom what really lay ahead, how much longer Jesus' preparation would really take.

"Are you awake?" Joseph wondered.

"What are you thinking?" she asked as he put an arm around her and she snuggled in close.

There was a brief pause before he answered. "I am in awe of him. Today, what I saw, no, what I felt . . . I . . . I can't find words for it. He changed, Mary. Right before my eyes, he changed. We brought our son to Jerusalem; he leaves belonging to someone else." He took a deep breath. "And I don't know what to feel, not exactly. He and I have been so close."

"That won't change, Joseph. He loves you deeply."

"And you, how do you feel?"

"Honestly, I was stunned by his answer at the temple. I didn't understand how debating with sages could possibly be more important than being with us. Surely even the Father would not wish him to be so insensitive. But now I know I was wrong. God rebuked me through Jesus today. God told me, as gently as He could, that His work comes first." She paused, rolling onto her back and staring up at the roof of the large room, dimly lit by streams of moonlight cascading through the windows. "Jesus is still our son, Joseph, but it will never be the same. Up to now, he relied on us for everything. Now God says it is His turn. What will happen from here, how he will be prepared, when he will leave us, how he will do his work, is no longer our concern. He will always care for us and probably live with us, but the rest is between Jesus and his Father."

She turned into him again. "You should be proud, Joseph. This day couldn't have come without your love of him, without your teaching and training. I know God must be very pleased with you."

He kissed her lightly on the forehead. "I might have taught him Torah and how to work wood, but he owes his faith to you, Mary. From the time he was small, you taught him that God was only a step away. That God could touch him so easily comes from this, nothing else."

There was a long silence between them before Mary finally spoke. "There are so many things in my heart, Joseph. So much of wonder at what has happened to us, and so much I still don't understand."

"In time, my love, in time," Joseph said.

Joseph held her close and they slowly drifted off to sleep.

When they arose the next morning, Mary watched Jesus as they rushed about packing, getting ready, saying good-bye to Marcus, Serah, and their children. Nothing seemed to have changed. He still teased his brothers and treated Anna like she was his angel. But inside, in her heart, Mary knew he was different, and she loved him even more.

"Ready?" Joseph asked her with a smile.

She nodded and helped Jesus finish tying Anna to the donkey's back. Their eyes met, and she whispered that she loved him. He smiled and told her he loved her too. As the donkey moved away, he put his arm around her and started walking. Though he was God's, he was still her son as well. That was all she needed.

PART FIVE
THE SEPARATION

CHAPTER 37

Mary looked at Joseph, choking back the flood of tears. His breathing was shallow, his skin waxen and pale. She was losing him and had never been so frightened.

"Has he come yet?" she asked softly. She reached out and touched Joseph's hand gently. It felt cold.

"No, Mother," came the soft answer.

Rebecca, Mary and Joseph's youngest daughter, stood behind her mother, her brother Simon near the door.

Jude, Joses, and Anna were sitting on chairs or the floor of the room. Only Jesus and James were not there. Jesus was working in Capernaum, and James had gone to bring him back.

Joseph had fallen from the scaffolding while he and Matthias were building a high wall on a house in Sepphoris. The scaffolding had been built quickly, but James, Joses, and Jude had made certain it was secure. It had been the rope that had done it. Weak, it had broken, dropping the heavy block of stone on the end of the top shelf of the scaffold, collapsing everything. Matthias had jumped and grabbed what was left of the rope, but Joseph had no place to go but down, his body crushed by falling stone. They had brought him to the house belonging to Seth and sent for Mary and the rest of the family.

Anna knelt down beside her mother and looked up at her worried, moist eyes. "He'll come, Mother. James and Seth will find him."

Mary smiled down at her eldest daughter. She was married now and lived in Nain with two children of her own. All of Mary's children had moved to other villages except Jude, Simon, and Rebecca.

Joseph moaned and stiffened, another wave of pain coursing through him. Mary knelt by his bed, caressing his hand, her heart aching until she thought it might break. Finally, the worst of it passed, and his body relaxed some. He had not regained consciousness since his fall, and his head was bandaged, fresh blood oozing through the white cloth. She stroked his hair and kissed his cheek. Oh, how she loved him.

Joses signaled to the other boys, who left the room. A moment later, Mary heard them praying, begging God for a favor. Joseph was everything to all of them. He had been a wonderful father, raising each as an individual, never holding one up to the other, never criticizing or demeaning. She heard them beg God to let him stay, but he was so broken—so many cuts, so many bumps and breaks! Their life together had truly been a wonderful gift. And now he . . . he was . . .

Her fingers stopped in midair, her tear-filled eyes on her husband's swollen face. No, she refused to think of it. It could not happen. God would not take her love. When Jesus came, it would be all right. "Joseph," she said, softly squeezing his hand, "you must hold on, my love. You must."

Mary heard the sound of voices in the entry of the large house, then Marcus and Serah appeared at the door, Matthias just behind them. All were dusty from their journey, but they quickly threw off their outer robes and came to Mary, who stood and melted into the arms of Serah. Matthias and Marcus bent over Joseph, their eyes searching for hope. Matthias could see he was getting worse.

Knowing Marcus and Serah were in Sebaste on business, Matthias had borrowed a horse from Seth to go search for them. He had ridden all night, and they had returned immediately.

Salome entered the room with water, her face furrowed with concern. She poured drinks for the three of them, then poured more into a bowl on a small washing table. Matthias drank and fell onto a large chair near the wall, exhausted.

"Is Jesus not here yet?" he asked softly.

"No," Salome said.

Marcus knelt down by Joseph's bed, Mary and Serah just behind him, the children gathering closer. Marcus had been a dear friend to all of them, the man with whom they stayed whenever in Jerusalem. He loved their father like a brother.

"Hello, my friend," he said softly, his hand gently rubbing Joseph's arm. "It is I, the Roman you made a Jew." He smiled briefly, then choked back the tears as Joseph stirred. Everyone tensed, and Mary's hand went to her mouth as Joseph's eyes fluttered open and a wan smile creased his lips.

Then the pain struck again, and Joseph's whole body jerked with it. Marcus felt helpless but tried to hold him, steady him, without adding to his discomfort. Finally, Joseph relaxed, but his eyes were closed, the grip gone out of his hand. Mary knelt down and put her hand near his mouth and nose, her shoulders sagging with relief when she still felt breath in them. Marcus's head went down, and he could contain his sobbing no longer; Serah slipped to his side, gently holding him.

Marcus sniffed away his sorrow to speak. "Physicians. Surely . . . surely they can give him help!"

"They cannot," Mary answered. "He is broken, Marcus. They say it is a miracle he is still alive." She stroked Joseph's face softly. "I only hope that he will be awake when . . ." she bit her lip, "when Jesus comes."

"And where is he?" Marcus asked.

"Seth and James took horses to Capernaum to see if he is there, but we are not sure . . . He may be gone already," Jude said.

"Joseph sent him to carve doors for the synagogue, then he was to go to Caesarea Philippi to work on some shutters for someone there. If he finished at Capernaum . . . and left for Philippi . . ." Matthias took a deep breath. "It is a great distance."

"He will come," Mary said. "God will make sure."

All of them looked at Joseph, who once more was trying to regain consciousness, his eyes thin slits in swollen and bruised flesh. Mary gripped his hand and leaned against the edge of his bed, her lip quivering. "Do you need something more for the pain, my love?" she asked.

He forced a smile. "Just . . . a little water," he whispered. Anna handed a filled cup to Mary, who dipped a cloth in it and gently pressed it against her husband's lips.

She noticed the whispers of relief, heard the sound of thankful greeting, as Jesus touched her shoulder and lifted her into his arms. She grasped him, fighting back sobs. Jesus stroked her hair and held her close, his eyes on his father, crushed and broken on the bed.

After a moment, he released Mary and knelt by Joseph, taking his swollen hand and pressing gently. Joseph's eyes opened to slits again, and he forced a smile.

"Jesus." He breathed slowly.

Jesus blinked back the tears, knowing his father was dying. God had spoken to him, sent him on the road to Sepphoris this morning. He had met Seth and James halfway. "Yes, Father, I am here."

"Alone," Joseph said. "You . . . and your mother . . ."

Jesus turned to James, but all of them understood and were already leaving the room. Jesus was the eldest and the one responsible for the family should their father die, the one who must take care of their mother and unmarried brother and sister.

"Only a few minutes," Jesus said softly.

James nodded, his eyes filled with sadness, then closed the door.

"Mary," Joseph mumbled weakly. "Come closer."

Mary knelt next to Jesus and felt her son's arm go around her shoulders as she laid her hand across both of theirs.

"I must leave," Joseph stated.

"No . . ." Mary anguished, her head shaking firmly. "No, Joseph, you can't leave us. Please, I couldn't bear it without you. I . . ." She couldn't go on, sobs filling her chest.

Joseph grimaced but held off the pain. "Shh. Shh, it is all right," he croaked in a weak voice. With effort, he took Mary's hand in his. He forced a smile, then looked into Jesus' eyes. "Our Messiah. Our Lord." The pain struck hard again, and Jesus touched his father's forehead and closed his eyes in prayer. The pain eased immediately, and Joseph smiled up at him. "Things are never quite what we want them to be, are they?"

"Joseph, please, you should rest," Mary said.

"I will, Mary, soon. I promise." He looked at Jesus. "You found John?"

"Yes, he is in Bethabara."

"Then you will begin soon."

Jesus only nodded.

Joseph smiled. "I will be waiting."

Jesus choked back his tears. "Father, God would heal you if I . . ."

"Yes, I know," Joseph interrupted, "but God has already spoken to me. I . . . I must go."

Mary thought her heart would break, and Joseph slowly lifted his arm and touched her soft hair, then looked up at his son. "Jesus, take care of her. You know she is everything to me."

Jesus could not control his own tears, and they rolled off his cheeks to land on Joseph's shoulder. "Yes, Father, I will."

"I love you," Joseph voiced quietly.

Jesus forced a smile and softly touched Joseph's cheek. "And I love you. God is pleased with you, Father. He loves you more than I can say."

Joseph nodded, but did not speak, his eyes searching those of his eldest child. "I am so grateful that He shared you with me." He took a bit of a breath. "Give your mother and me a moment will you?"

Jesus nodded and stood. He dried his eyes and turned to leave the room when Joseph called to him.

"Son," he said.

Jesus turned back. "Yes, Father."

"Your brothers will have a hard time at first. Be patient with them."

Jesus smiled. "In the end, they will make you proud." He turned and left the room, and Mary drew closer.

Joseph quietly thanked God for the lack of pain and the peace he felt, but he knew he didn't have long. "We have spent a good life together," he pointed out.

She nodded. "No two people have loved more."

"What Jesus has to do to bring us together again will not be easy. He will need you and our sons. It is one reason God sent them to us. When Jesus declares who he is, help them understand, help them see. It is you who can open their eyes, and when they do, Jesus is right—they will make us proud."

Mary nodded again. "You have seen it, haven't you?" she inquired.

"Most of it. God will be with him, but Jesus needs you as well. That is why you must stay."

Mary nodded again, a sweet, peaceful feeling cascading through her. "Another surprise." She forced a smile.

"There have been so many," he agreed. "Why should we wonder at one more?"

She chuckled lightly, took his hand and leaned forward, kissing him lightly on the lips. "I love you so much it hurts," she sighed.

"Pain is a good reminder," he said. "You won't forget me so easily."

He pulled her fingers to his lips and stroked them with a kiss, his eyes closed, his heart filled with love. When he opened them again, he felt the pain returning.

"I must go." He groaned.

Mary nodded, tears filling her eyes again as her husband gave her one last look before the breath left him and a peaceful, contented feeling set his features. After a few moments, she gently laid his hand to his side then lightly kissed him on the forehead. As she forced herself to her feet, she felt his spirit close by, knew he was watching her, reluctant to leave. She smiled and said she loved him, that she would be all right. Then a gentle warm breeze passed by and seemed to drift through the window. She thought she would feel lonely, but there was a warmth in her, an unsurpassable feeling of comfort she had never felt before.

"Mother."

Mary turned and let Jesus embrace her. She felt her son's tears fall onto her hair, felt the sobs in his chest, and held him close. The others encircled them, held them, cried with them. They would all miss him. But Mary knew she would see him again.

BIBLIOGRAPHY

Jerusalem, the Temple, and the Purification Laws

Although the temple and its ceremonies are still somewhat shrouded in mystery, we do have a good idea of what took place, what it looked like, and how important and wonderful it was for the people of Jesus' time. I found the following sources very helpful.

Edersheim, Alfred. *The Temple: Its Ministry and Services.* Peabody, MA: Hendrickson Publishers, 1994.

Holzapfel, Richard Neitzel. *My Father's House: Temple Worship and Symbolism in the New Testament.* Salt Lake City, UT: Bookcraft, 1994.

Jeremias, Joachim. *Jerusalem in the Time of Jesus: An Investigation into Economic and Social Conditions During the New Testament Period.* Philadelphia, PA: Fortress Press, 1969.

Milgrom, Jacob. *Leviticus 1–16: A New Translation with Introduction and Commentary.* Anchor Bible series. New York: Doubleday, 1991. (This source was particularly helpful on the purification laws.)

Sanders, E. P. *Jewish Law from Jesus to the Mishnah: Five Studies.* London: SCM Press, 1990.

Religion, History, and Culture

The sources in these areas are numerous, and some conflict with others, but the most recent and what I feel are the best are listed first. I should also state that some of those listed above were also helpful here.

Safrai, Shemuel. *The Jewish People in the First Century: Historical Geography, Political History, Social, Cultural and Religious Life and Institutions.* Compendia Rerum Iudaicarum ad Novum Testamentum. 2 vols. Asse, Netherlands: Van Gorcum, 1974.

Batey, Richard A. *Jesus and the Forgotten City: New Light on Sepphoris and the Urban World of Jesus.* Grand Rapids, MI: Baker Book House, 1991.

Hanson, K. C., and Douglas E. Oakman. *Palestine in the Time of Jesus: Social Structures and Social Conflicts.* Minneapolis, MN: Fortress Press, 1998.

Murphy, Frederick J. *The Religious World of Jesus: An Introduction to Second Temple Palestinian Judaism.* Nashville, TN: Abingdon Press, 1991.

Horsley, Richard A. *Archaeology, History, and Society in Galilee: the Social Context of Jesus and the Rabbis.* Valley Forge, PA: Trinity Press International, 1996.

Gaventa, Beverly Roberts. *Mary: Glimpses of the Mother of Jesus.* Minneapolis, MN: Fortress Press, 1999. (This source was helpful only so far as it helped me understand the traditions established about Mary long after her death. It has a fair discussion of the *Protoevangelium of James,* a much later, extremely apocryphal document that was used to establish Mary's perpetual virginity and raise her to a place next to her son in some Christian traditions.)

People, Places, and Terms

Arnold, Clinton E., ed. *Zondervan Illustrated Bible Backgrounds Commentary.* 4 vols. Grand Rapids, MI: Zondervan, 2002.

Brown, S. Kent. *Mary and Elisabeth: Noble Daughters of God.* American Fork, UT: Covenant Communications, 2002. (This was an excellent read and I recommend it for its historical perspective and insight.)

Moore, George Foot. *Judaism.* 3 vols. Peabody, MA: Hendrickson Publishers, 1997.

Painter, John. *Just James: The Brother of Jesus in History and Tradition.* Minneapolis, MN: Fortress Press, 1999.

Richardson, Peter. *Herod: King of the Jews, Friend of the Romans.* Minneapolis, MN: Fortress Press, 1999.

Sanders, E. P. *Judaism: Practice and Belief, 63 BCE–66 CE.* Valley Forge, PA: Trinity Press International, 1992.

Tenney, Merrill C., ed. *The Zondervan Pictorial Encyclopedia of the Bible.* 5 vols. Grand Rapids, MI: Zondervan, 1975.

The Wars and Rebellions under Herod the Great and His Sons

Horsley, Richard A., and John S. Hanson. *Bandits, Prophets, and Messiahs.* Harrisburg, PA: Trinity Press International, 1999.

Whiston, William. *The Works of Josephus, Complete and Unabridged.* Peabody, MA: Hendrickson Publishers, 1987.

Doctrinal Commentaries

Holzapfel, Richard Neitzel, and Thomas A. Wayment, eds. *From the Last Supper Through the Resurrection: The Savior's Final Hours.* Salt Lake City, UT: Deseret Book, 2003.

———. *The Life and Teachings of Jesus Christ: From Bethlehem through the Sermon on the Mount.* Salt Lake City, UT: Deseret Book, 2005. (This volume was particularly helpful, though my story does not always agree with the authors' opinions.)

McConkie, Bruce R. *Doctrinal New Testament Commentary: The Gospels.* Salt Lake City, UT: Bookcraft, 1976.

———. *The Mortal Messiah: From Bethlehem to Calvary.* Salt Lake City, UT: Deseret Book, 1981.

Talmage, James E. *Jesus the Christ.* Salt Lake City, UT: Deseret Book, 1982.